RIDE THE WILD RIVER

• • • • •

"Hold it right there!" Baker said. There was a strange glint in his eyes as he surveyed the crowd. "You got the drop on us, right enough, but there's this one thing." He stared at Reno, then lifted his guns toward Dooley and Lee. "You think I'm scared to die? Not likely! But let me tell you this—ain't nobody here can stop me from placin' at least two shots. And they'll be right in them two boys yonder, Reno!"

Reno moved to stand before Baker, and he saw at once that the nervy little gunman meant exactly what he said. Carefully he said, "Looks like it's your play, Baker. Make your deal."

Baker nodded, and a faint grin touched his lips. "Just you and me, Reno—that's the way. We'll shoot it out."

"Ready when you are, Baker."

GILBERT MORRIS
RIDE THE
WILD RIVER

Tyndale House Publishers, Inc.
Wheaton, Illinois

Library of Congress Cataloging-in-Publication Data
Morris, Gilbert.
  [Runaway]
  Ride the wild river / Gilbert Morris.
    p. cm. — (Jim Reno westerns series ; no. 3)
  Previously published as: The runaway.
  ISBN 0-8423-5795-5
  I. Title.   II. Series: Morris, Gilbert. Jim Reno westerns series;
no. 3.
PS3563.08742R8   1992
813' .54—dc20   92-9437

Printed in the United States of America

98 97 96 95 94 93 92
8   7   6   5   4   3   2   1

To Martin Jones,
* a man full of faith and*
* of the Holy Ghost*

ONE
Runaway

Julie Wade stared at herself in the mirror, scowling at her reflection. Most young women close to seventeen would not have glared so sourly at such an image. Glossy brown hair with reddish highlights fell in an abundant shower down her back, and the face gave promise of more beauty to come. Olive skin, smooth and clear, was set off by a wide mouth with a full lower lip and a dimple in her right cheek. She had a straight nose, even teeth, and good bone structure, but most striking of all were her eyes, which were almond-shaped, gray-green in color, and shaded by long lashes.

As she bit her lip and whirled from the mirror, there was a coltish grace in her movement. She was a tall girl, just short of five-foot-eight, and after being teased about it she had retreated into a boyish behavior. She was just emerging from the awkward stage of youth into rounded womanhood and was confused by the changes it brought. If her mother had lived, she would have made the transition smoothly, but she had died of cholera fifteen months earlier. Thus, Julie had been iso-lated on the farm at the most critical time of her life.

An understanding father would have made the difference, but her own father had died when she was thirteen, and Jake Skinner, her stepfather, brought nothing but fear and loathing to her.

Even now she hurried downstairs, hoping to get into the buggy without an encounter with him, but she stopped short at the foot of the stairs, her lips suddenly tight as she saw him standing in the door waiting for her.

Jake Skinner had been attractive enough to capture the heart of Helen Wade only six months after the death of Julie's father. There had been a flashiness in his swarthy features, and there had been a gallant quality in the way he courted the widow, who was twenty years his senior. He had plenty of money, or so it seemed, but it was the end of the world for Julie when he swept her mother off her feet.

"Well, aren't you the little beauty now!"

Skinner had put on weight, the easy life and rich food padding his waist. His neck had thickened, and his bold eyes were now fixed on Julie in a way that had begun to make her feel odd.

"I'll have me the prettiest girl at the ball," he said, and stepping forward he put his thick hand on her bare shoulder. "We'll have us a time, won't we, Julie?"

The weight of his hand on her flesh was revolting to her, and there was something in his loose-lipped expression and the hungry light in his eyes that made her pull away abruptly. "I'm ready to go," she said shortly. Skinner had never paid the slightest attention to her while her mother was alive, but for the last few months she had felt his eyes following her, and there was an attempt at intimacy in his speech. And the clumsy caresses he passed off as being fatherly affection had gone beyond that.

She tried to squeeze by him, but he moved so slightly from the opening that their bodies touched, and he quickly put his heavy arms around her. When she raised her head to protest, he suddenly kissed her, ignoring her efforts to pull free.

When she managed to free herself, her heart was beating furiously. Her voice quivered with rage and fear as she said, "Don't—don't do that!"

He laughed, throwing his head back, then taking her arm he said with a smirk on his full lips, "You'll get used to it, Julie. I been watching you." He kept a firm grip on her arm, and as he helped her into the buggy he added, "You're a woman now, not a kid. We'll talk about it."

The trip from the farm to Fort Smith took four hours, and although Julie pressed herself against the outer edge of the seat, Skinner sprawled loosely, letting his leg rest against hers. There was something so suggestive in his manner that it was with real relief that Julie got out of the buggy in front of the town hall in the center of Fort Smith. The town itself was a dusty jumble of unpaved streets and low wooden buildings. It was perched on the border of the Indian Nations. Some of the worst outlaws in the world used it as a convenient source of information and supplies, disappearing into the trackless plains and mountains of the Nations when the law breathed too heavily on them.

A new pavilion had been erected. Raw lumber reeking of pine sap formed the structure, and the elite of Fort Smith had come to celebrate with a ball. It was dark enough for the myriad lanterns to be lit as Julie saw her best friend, Lorene Dickerson. "I'll be around to get the first dance, Julie!" her stepfather said with a broad grin, then left to put up the buggy.

"Julie! You look so pretty!" Lorene said as she hurried up

to hug her. She was a short, plump girl, two years older than Julie. Her father was a local lawyer, and Lorene knew much more about Julie than most. "Did you make that dress?" Julie allowed herself to breathe freely. She was going to spend the night with Lorene, and she refused to think about the trip home.

The two girls went inside the large hall and spent an hour getting caught up on things. Julie kept glancing nervously toward the door, dreading to see her stepfather. "I don't want to dance, Lorene. I'm just going to watch."

"Why, you can't do that, Julie! There are so many new men here!"

When Julie remained steadfast, Lorene said, "Well, all right—oh, I almost forgot, Julie, there's someone here you must meet."

"I don't really want to, Lorene," Julie protested, but she was pulled into a large room containing a series of tables with bowls of punch and some fancy foods.

"Oh, Mr. Stevens, here she is!" Lorene said, and she pushed Julie in front of a tall man, adding, "I'm going to dance, Julie. Meet you there later."

Julie was nonplussed as the tall man smiled down at her. He had a sunburned face and mild blue eyes.

"You don't remember me, do you, Julie?"

"No, I—I don't think so," she faltered. He looked vaguely familiar, but she could not place him.

"Be strange if you did," he said. "Last time I saw you, you were two years old. I'm your cousin, Julie. You probably heard your mother mention me—Thad Stevens."

"Oh! Your picture is in the album," Julie said, and she smiled up at him.

"Stacy, come here a minute," Stevens called, and a pretty woman with blonde hair and gray eyes came to stand beside him. "This is my wife, and this is my cousin I told you about, Julie Wade."

"Hello, Julie," Mrs. Stevens said, and she put out her hand with an easy gesture. "I'm glad to meet some of Thad's family."

"Well, not much family left for you to meet," Thad said ruefully. "Julie's mother, my aunt, was about all the kin I had left. I didn't know she'd passed away until I got here, Julie."

He was not a handsome man, but there was a warmth in his manner, and he seemed genuinely interested in his cousin. His wife got them all seated and skillfully put the shy girl at ease.

Without realizing it, Julie let slip the misery of her circumstances, and she did not see the quick nods exchanged by the couple when she looked out at the crowd. It was obvious to them that the girl was lonely and afraid.

"We'll only be in Fort Smith for a couple of days," Stevens said, "but maybe we can have some good visits before we leave."

"That would be nice," Julie said, then she asked suddenly, "Mr. Stevens, your picture in the album . . ."

"Yes?"

"There's a man with you in it. Who is he?"

Stevens grinned and said, "Has to be Jim Reno, my half brother. We had it made in Texas and sent a copy of it to your mother." He laughed and added, "You ought to see that picture, Stacy! We were both young punks, but we thought we could whip the army! Got all dressed up as close as we could to what we thought Wild Bill Hickok might wear, two six-guns apiece, furry chaps, and a mean look." He laughed in delight at the thought. "We were really young and full of beans!"

"I thought you looked very nice," Julie protested.

"I'd like to see the picture, Julie," Stacy said.

"Don't you give it to her!" Thad said with a mock frown. "That son-of-a-gun Jim nearly stole her from me! I'm still jealous of that cuss!"

"Really?" Julie asked.

"He's quite an attractive man, Julie," Stacy said.

"Some would say he's better-looking than me," Thad said with a grin.

"Those with eyes," Stacy commented with a barbed wit.

"Where is he now?" Julie asked.

"Well, he was a peace officer in Kansas last year. Had some sort of personal trouble. Jim would never talk much about his troubles. But I got a letter from him just before we left—last week, wasn't it, Stacy? He said he was headed for California." He turned to his wife and snapped his fingers. "He said he'd be at Independence, Missouri, if I wanted to write him. I've got to do that tomorrow!"

He would have said more, but he broke off, for he had seen the girl stiffen and her face grow tense. A heavy man with a swarthy face came over and said, "Dancin' is about to commence, Julie. Come on."

"I don't want to," Julie began, but the big man took her firmly by the arm and pulled her off without a word to the Stevenses.

"That girl has problems, Thad," Stacy said quietly. "I was talking to Lorene earlier, and from what I understand, Julie's stepfather is lower than a snake. Took the mother for everything she had and broke her heart. Now he's got designs on the daughter."

"Why, that's—that's obscene!" Thad sputtered. "He can't get by with that!"

"Why not?" Stacy asked, and the fire in her eyes belied her even tone. "Lorene said that Skinner made Julie's mother sign all the property over to him, but Julie's name is still on the paper. Lorene thinks that he'll force her to sign the papers over to him—or he'll make her marry him to get control of the place."

Thad said at once, "I'll look into it."

"You know how these things are, Thad. You start interfering into family matters and you can get shot for it."

Stevens said grimly, "I *am* her family, Stacy. I'll see what can be done."

"We're leaving day after tomorrow. What can you do in two days?"

Frustration scored the cheeks of Stevens, and he shook his head. "I ought to do *something.*"

He did try, but when he and Stacy saw Julie the following day, there was nothing to say to her except good-bye. They left for home feeling that they had seen the beginning of a tragedy, but they were powerless to do anything.

Julie tried to get her stepfather to allow her to stay with Lorene for a longer visit, but he ignored her request, and on the second day after their return, what Julie feared most happened.

She was turning down the covers on her bed when a heavy knock sounded. Fear gripped her at once, and she said, "What is it?"

"Open the door!"

"I'm—I'm ready to go to bed," she faltered. Jake had been drinking steadily, and at the evening meal there had been a strange expression on his heavy face that frightened her.

He struck the door hard and said, "Open the door or I'll break it down! You hear me, Julie?"

She looked around for some escape, then, finding none, she turned the key and stepped back as he entered. His face was flushed, and he advanced toward her with burning eyes.

"Time we understood each other," he said thickly. She could smell the liquor on his breath, and she retreated until she felt the wall at her back. He laughed at her, a coarse sound that raked at her nerves. "I been purty patient with you, Julie, waitin' for you to grow up. But I'm tired of waitin'!"

"What—what do you mean?"

Skinner put his hands out, took her by the shoulders, and pulled her to him. He was a powerful brute, and she was as helpless in his grasp as a bird. "Aw, you ain't all *that* innocent," he said, grinning. "You've grown up to be a good-lookin' woman, Julie, and you need a man."

"No—please, let me go!" she pleaded, but he only pulled her closer.

"Shore, that's what you need—and I'm the man for you. Like I say, I've been patient for a long spell, but now it's time for a little action." He ran his eyes down her slim body encased in the light robe and licked his lips, adding, "Why, ain't no need to be trembling, girl! I'm talking marriage to you."

"Marriage!" She couldn't believe it! "But you're my stepfather!"

"No kin at all," he said. "I guess you don't maybe love me now, but I've got ways of making women care for me. I ain't had no complaints!"

With all her strength she jerked herself loose, and her eyes were wide with fear and anger as she said, "You get out of here! You leave me alone!"

He threw his head back and laughed. "Go on, I like a lot of spunk in a woman—more you fight, the better I like it!"

"I'll never marry you, Jake Skinner!" she cried out. "I'll run away!"

"Go on," he said, and his grin didn't change. "You're in my charge till you're eighteen. Reckon I can have you brought back just as often as you run off." Then he stopped laughing and said in a voice totally devoid of mercy, "I'll have you, Julie, get that straight. You can't leave this place, and I'm your pa in the sight of the law. You can't get away, and I'm tellin' you flat, you might as well get used to the idea of having me for a husband!"

Then he smiled again and said, "Oh, I won't bother you none tonight. But you better get your mind made up. We'll be married in a month."

He laughed at her pale face and left the room, slamming the door behind him.

Trembling and weak, Julie collapsed on the bed, biting her lip to keep back the tears. For over an hour she lay there, her mind fluttering like a wounded bird in a cage, but could think of no escape. She knew that Skinner would do as he said, and she realized as well that her chances of getting help, legally or otherwise, were nonexistent. Skinner was a violent man, generally feared for his fits of rage. She knew that wives—and daughters—had little recourse against the will of a husband.

She lay so long on the bed, her mind racked with confused thoughts, that the oil in her lamp burned down, and finally she got up to refill it. Then she sat down and her hand fell on the worn Bible that her mother had used for many years. Aimlessly she opened it. The pages were thin as tissue from endless reading, and when she let it drop open on her desk, she noticed a verse was underlined—by her mother, she knew at once. A thin, spidery line of black ink underlined these words:

"Get thee out of thy country, and from thy kindred, and from thy father's house, unto a land that I will show thee."

Julie had given little thought to religion and had read little of the Bible. As she sat there, however, in a silence so intense that the loudest sound was the guttering out of the lamp, she was filled with a sudden purpose. Her jaw set firmly, and she nodded to herself. Blowing out the lamp, she went to bed, but she did not sleep, for her mind was putting together a plan. Just as dawn cast a red glow through her window, she said softly, "God, I don't know how to pray like Mama did. I've never paid you much attention. All I can do now is ask you— get me out of this mess I'm in!"

She let her stepfather get out of the house before she went downstairs, then she saddled her mare and rode across the freshly plowed fields, taking a winding course toward the north. In less than an hour she dismounted in front of a two-room log cabin and called out, "Jackson! Leah! You up yet?"

The door opened and a small black man came out with a wide grin on his thin face. "Miz Julie! Whut in de world you doin' here so early?" He came over and took the reins from her hands, and after tying the horse to a post of the porch he said, "Come on in. Leah fixin' breakfast."

He was very thin and stooped, but he hopped about like a cricket as he hustled before her, speaking to the large woman cooking at a stone hearth. "Leah, here's Miz Julie. Put some mo' aigs in dat pan!"

Leah was clearly a mulatto, her yellow skin much lighter

than Jackson's. She was larger than the man as well, and she looked sharply at the girl who sat down in one of the two cane-bottomed chairs in the cabin. "Whut's the matter, honey?" she asked at once. She pulled the frying pan out of the glowing coals and came to take Julie's chin in one hand, forcing the girl to lift her head.

Jackson and Leah had been slaves of Julie's father. After the war, he had given them land, and they had worked it, but had also done much of the work around the home place. Their loyalty to the family had been deep, and it had been a source of deep grief to them both when Julie's mother had married Skinner.

They had practically raised Julie, and now they exchanged troubled glances over the girl's head, and Leah asked again, "Whut's the trouble, Julie?"

Slowly Julie looked up at Leah, then at Jackson, and she said slowly, "I've got to run away."

"Run away!" Jackson said in stunned wonder. "Whut fo' you hafter do a thing like dat?"

"Skinner is after me." She saw Leah nod, and her mouth went tight.

"I seed it comin'," Leah said heavily. "He a bad man."

Jackson looked at Julie, then at Leah. His voice trembled when he finally spoke. "White trash! I cut his gizzard out!"

"Hesh up, Jackson," Leah said. "You ain't gonna do no sech fool thing."

"Will you help me?" Julie asked. "I can't trust anybody else."

"How you gonna do it?" Leah asked. "He gonna find you if you run off."

"I'll have to fool him, Leah. There's one thing he doesn't

11

know—I've got some money." She took a heavy bag out of her pocket and held it up. "It's gold pieces my daddy saved. Mama kept them and gave them to me before she died. She told me not to let Jake know about it."

"Pore leetle thing!" Leah clucked mournfully. "She grieved herself to death 'cause she married that man. And she seen whut he wuz afore they'd been married a week!"

"How you gonna get away, Miz Julie?" Jackson asked.

"I've got to get a long way off," Julie said. "If I just go east to the next state, he'll find me. I've got to go west." She held up the bag and said, "This is enough to get to California—and that's where I'm going!"

"Lawd!" Jackson breathed quietly. "You can't go way out to dat place!"

"Be hard, child," Leah said with a nod.

"I know it will, but I'm going. Will you help me?"

Leah and Jackson exchanged glances and they seemed to read one another's mind. "You don't think I'se gwine to let my baby go all dat way without me, does you?"

"But—"

Jackson patted her head. "We done already decided to leave dis place, Miz Julie. It ain't lak it used to be when yo' daddy was here."

"We wuz goin' to Louisiana," Leah added. "But now we gwine to California!"

Julie tried to protest, but not very hard. The thought of making her way to the coast alone had frightened her, but with Jackson and Leah it seemed possible.

Finally they convinced her that they actually wanted to go, mostly by saying that they'd heard that the color of a person's skin didn't matter so much out there. Then she said eagerly, "All right, here's what we'll do. You sell this place as soon as you can, and let it out that you're going to move to Louisiana. Then you leave—but you go to Fayetteville."

"Why we go there?" Jackson asked.

"Because I've got a friend there, and I'm going to pretend to go see her. When I get there, you be ready. You get on that coach and we just keep right on going all the way."

"All the way to California?" Leah asked doubtfully.

"No—but all the way to Independence, Missouri. That's where all the wagon trains going to California leave from. We'll buy a wagon and join a wagon train."

By the time Julie had left the cabin and ridden back to the home place, she knew exactly what she must do.

The most difficult thing was waiting for Jackson and Leah to sell their place and leave, but that went faster than any of them had expected. Skinner was always anxious to buy land adjoining the plantation, and he jumped at the chance, giving cash money to be sure the old people didn't back out.

He gloated to Julie after the papers were signed, "I been waitin' for a chance to get that property for a long time! Now I got it!"

"You did real fine, Jake," Julie said. She had forced herself to endure his heavy-handed caresses, even to appear to welcome them. A less callous man would have seen through her in an instant, but the colossal vanity of Skinner blinded him.

Now that Jackson and Leah were on their way, Julie drew her breath and said, "I—I've been thinking about what you said, Jake—about getting married."

"Yeah?"

"Well, I was a little bit scared when you first came at me."

"Sure," he said soothingly. "Natural thing for a girl. But you feel different now, don't you?"

"I—I *think* so Jake." Julie tried to look shy and added, "I'm almost sure about it. The only thing is . . ."

"Yeah?"

"Well, I'd really like to talk to my friend, Martha Dutton, you know, the girl from Fayetteville who visited here last summer. We were best friends until her family moved away. I'd like to go see her and talk, you know? A girl needs to find out some things about marriage."

"Reckon I can teach you all you need to know." He grinned, and she forced herself to endure a kiss.

"Yes, but I'll need help with my dress and my clothes and all. Please, Jake," she said softly, and moved closer to him. "Just this one little thing—please!"

He stood there, plainly torn by the need for a decision, then finally he asked, "How long you plan to stay?"

Julie's heart lurched, and she said with a smile, "Oh, just a little while, whatever you say, Jake."

"A week be enough?"

"Oh, that's fine!"

"All right, I'll get you a ticket on Tuesday's stage."

Time crawled by for Julie, and she expected Skinner to call the trip off at any minute, but finally she was in the stage, looking down at him as he stood in the street.

"You got your return ticket, Julie?" he asked.

"Right here. I'll be back next Friday." She made herself smile and throw him a kiss. "It won't be too long—and then we'll be together!"

The stage lurched at the command of the driver, and she fell back against the seat, weak with tension.

The trip to Fayetteville took two days. The coach stopped at one roach-infested station for the night, but the next day she sighed with relief as Leah and Jackson appeared in the crowd at the stage station in Fayetteville.

As the stage rolled on northward toward Missouri, Leah leaned forward and said "Chile, we's got a long ways to go. I hope you is prayed up!"

Julie laughed, but there was a thread of seriousness in her voice as she answered, "I hope so too, Leah. I have the feeling we're going to need all the help we can get!"

Two
A Man Can Change

"It ain't gwine to be no trouble at all fo' that Skinner man to foller you, chile," Leah had said on the fourth day out of Fayetteville. "All he got to do is ask, 'Who done seen a pretty little gal with big eyes and two niggers?'"

Julie mopped at her brow, leaving a path in the fine dust that boiled into the coach. She leaned her head back wearily on the leather seat and murmured, "I know it, Leah. A blind man could follow the trail we've made. And if you want something to *really* worry about, just as we were leaving Fayetteville, the station agent saw me. His name is Moore, and he's close to the family I'm supposed to be visiting. He looked real strange when I stayed on the coach. I think he'll start asking questions. And somebody's going to get in touch with Jake."

Jackson's eyes closed and he said, "Lawd, Miz Julie! He be on our track like a duck on a june bug!"

"I know it, Jackson, but there's nothing else to do!"

They were alone in the coach except for a middle-aged couple who spoke little English and were nodding as the coach rolled and swayed along the rutted road. The privacy was a relief, for there had been trouble over Jackson and Leah several times. Once Jackson had been forced to get out and ride with the driver when a belligerent man cursed and threatened to throw him out. In addition to this, the bulk of passengers had been male, and Julie had been the object of their attention. An attractive young woman, especially one who was alone, was looked upon as fair game, and one flashily dressed man with sharp features made her life miserable for twenty-four hours until he got off the stage.

Even those who did not molest Julie constantly eyed her, and the strain had worn her down. She had slept little at the overnight stops, and her eyes were red with strain, scored underneath by dark smudges. She forced herself to sit up and said in an angry tone, "We're getting off this stage at the next stop!"

"Gettin' off? Why we do that?" Jackson asked. "We still a fur piece from where we gwine."

"We've *got* to do something to cover our tracks," Julie said. "I've been thinking of something—what if we get off the stage at the next fair-sized town we come to? We'll buy a wagon and team, and we'll drive it to Independence ourselves!"

"I think dat'll answer," Leah nodded. "Be a heap harder for anybody to foller a wagon than this here stage. Everybody knows what roads them stages travels."

"An' I reckons a team and wagon be got a heap cheaper here, Miz Julie." Jackson nodded. "Dey's bound to be heaps of folks tryin' to get fixed up at dat place we headed fer."

"I hadn't thought of that, Jackson," Julie said. "We're going to have to buy a wagon anyway, and if we get it now it'll save time when we get there."

The daring of the idea refreshed her, and when they came

to a town with a wide main street and a sizable collection of houses, they left the stage and watched it leave without regrets.

"I saw a stable with some wagons in front of it back up this street," Julie said. "Let's go see about buying one of them."

"Now, you better do the talkin', chile," Leah said, "but afore you agree to anything, you look to Jackson. He knows a little sumpin' 'bout mules."

The stable was at the edge of town, and they were met at once by a fat, balding man with a heavy coating of amber snuff on his lips. "Help you, miss?" he asked, sizing up the trio with a practiced skill in his small black eyes. "Lookin' for a ridin' horse, mebby?"

"No, I'm interested in a good wagon and a team."

"Sho!" A gleam of interest crossed the man's round face, and he asked, "You want a buggy, is that it, missy?"

"Oh, no," Julie said. She hesitated, then invented a lie. "Actually, it's for my brother—he'll be in later in the week, you see? But he asked me to find him a stout wagon—real stout, he said, and the best team I could find to pull it."

"You know about wagons and teams, Missy?"

"Well, no . . ." Julie felt a trap in the question, and she waved at Jackson, saying, "This nigger has been an overseer for my brother for a long time. He'll help me choose the team and the wagon."

"Well, guess I can find you a good rig. My name's Si Hoskins." He began a little patter, taking them around to look at a lightweight farm wagon, but Jackson shook his head at once. "Won't do? Well, come on around in back. Got something there you'll appreciate."

He led them through the stable to a large lot full of mules and horses, and beside the back wall stood what looked like a practically new heavy-duty wagon. It looked like the ones in the pictures Julie had seen of pioneers making the trip to California, and her eyes lit up.

Hoskins didn't miss that, and he waxed eloquent over the wagon. "Now, this here wagon, why, no matter *what* your brother has in mind, why this will do 'er! Hold up to twenty-five hundred pounds, but made mostly out of hickory so it won't kill a team to pull it. Got iron on the wheels, axles, and hounds." Hoskins saw a blank look on the girl's face and added quickly, "The hounds is these here bars that connect the undercarriage. And you got a nice jockey box here in front to hold tools, you got a almost new canvas with drawstrings to close it up. Why, this rig has got it all, even a grease bucket here plumb full of tallow!"

Julie tried to look unimpressed, but didn't do a very good job. It seemed like the very thing they would need, and she said, "Well, I don't know. How much is it?"

"Well, I guess I could let it go for two hundred," Hoskins said in a pained voice.

Jackson laughed, his black eyes shining. "Guess you *would,* boss!" he said slyly with a wink at Julie.

Julie said, "That's way too much. We'll have to look around, Mr. Hoskins."

"Wait now!" the fat man said, and his grin slipped as he stared at Jackson. "Mebby I can shave that a mite."

Julie had been around horse traders all her life, and for the next hour she did little but shake her head and try to look bored. Hoskins threw himself into the work of selling, but it turned out that the slim young woman and the black man could not be stampeded. By the time he had battled with them for an hour and they had agreed on a price of $185 for the wagon and a fine-looking team of two-year-old mules, he was wringing wet and not at all happy over his failure to cash in on what had seemed to be an easy mark.

"All right, you got a bargain for your brother," he grumbled at last. "When you say he'll be here to pick up the rig?"

Julie smiled and pulled a small sack of gold coins from her purse. "Oh, we'll take it with us, Mr. Hoskins. Just make out a bill of sale."

Hoskins made out the bill of sale while Jackson and Leah hitched the team. "Which way you headed, missy?" he asked as he took the cash and handed her the receipt.

"Going to St. Louis, then down to Nashville," Julie lied, and then she was gone, leaving Hoskins to watch her climb aboard. As the wagon left the yard and headed down the broad main street, he said with displeasure, "More to that than meets the eye!"

"I want to get away quick as we can," Julie said. "Let's pick up some food and bedding and get as far as we can before dark."

They stopped at a general store, and while Leah got the food supplies, Julie picked out blankets and cookware. She also bought a Henry .44 rifle, a Remington ten-gauge shotgun with twenty-eight-inch double barrels, a Smith and Wesson pocket .32, and ammunition for all of them. As a clerk loaded the supplies into the wagon, Julie paid the bill, and she left town at a sprightly gait.

Two hours of daylight remained, and Julie enjoyed driving the team. She had never driven mules before, but the team was well-trained, and Jackson gave her the instructions she needed. At dusk they crossed a small creek, and Leah said, "Water here. We might ought to camp here about."

They found a spot by the stream in a clump of tall pines, and Julie got her first lesson in making camp. They staked out the animals, gathered wood, made a fire, and cooked in a short time. As they sat around the campfire, listening to the rippling of the creek and the breeze in the pines, Julie said, "I really think it's going to work. I really do!"

"Long way to go." Leah began to collect the tin plates, and she added as she left to go to the creek, "We got to make some good time. And we got to cover our tracks."

"I know, Leah," Julie said. She went to her bed inside the wagon, and listened while Leah and Jackson settled down beneath in their blankets. She was so tired from the long trip and so tense from the strain that she lay there for a long time, listening to the night birds and watching the stars pass across the open end of the wagon. She thought of the hundreds of miles that lay between her and safety, and when fear tinged her thoughts, she prayed a prayer she had not prayed for years, a child's prayer that her mother had taught her. It was a potent prayer, evidently, for before she had finished, she was sound asleep.

The next three days went smoothly insofar as travel went. Routines were quickly established, the three of them falling into habits of the trail easily, and they had little trouble adjusting to the problems that arose.

Julie had expected trouble, but it came in a form that caught her off guard. The main road to Independence lay close to Indian territory, which meant that it was heavily traveled by many who did not choose to risk the dangers of that area. The bulk of travelers were male, and most of the other folks headed north were the land-seekers who were going toward a jumping-off place into the new land. Some of them were families, some with large bands of children, but single men and small groups of men banded together for safety outnumbered these groups.

As Julie had found on the stage, a single woman was a magnet, drawing male attention constantly. If her wagon passed a rider, almost inevitably the man would increase his pace and attempt to strike up a meeting with her.

"They're worse than flies at a picnic, Leah!" Julie cried in exasperation as they sat around the campfire on the fourth night of their travel. "Why can't they leave me alone?"

"Nobody can answer that, chile," Leah answered. She poked at the fire with a stick, shook her head, and said gloomily, "Women in this country is scarce as hen's teeth, and the men folks jes' has to see one, and he has to stalk her like she was some kind of game."

"I'll just stay in the wagon," Julie said angrily.

"Be a long time to stay in—all de way to California," Jackson remarked mildly.

"I'd like to take a gun to them!" Julie snapped.

"Can't do that, nuther," Leah said practically. "If we had a man with us, it'd be different. And the wust thing is, we is about as noticeable as we wuz on that stage. Ain't gwine to be hard to foller us, if anybody minds to try."

They sat around the fire, and Julie's face was flushed with anger and tense with apprehension. Lately her sleep had been broken by bad dreams—dreams of someone dragging her back to Arkansas and the arms of Jake Skinner. The successful break from her home had brought hope, but every day it seemed inevitable that sooner or later they would meet disaster. Either they would be found by pursuers, or possibly would encounter a man so lawless that he would force himself on her. She kept her pistol close, but she was no match for the roughs that inhabited the territory, nor could Jackson and Leah offer much protection.

The stars laced the skies with a delicate pattern of icy-blue points that glittered coldly in the summer sky, and there was a stillness in the night as the trio sat there thinking of the days and the problems that lay ahead of them. The fire snapped, and Julie extinguished a spark that sailed out of the glowing coals to light on her sleeve. Then she said, "We're not going to be caught! Tomorrow it'll be different!"

She got up abruptly and went to the wagon. Jackson stared at Leah. "Whut does *dat* mean?"

Leah shook her head, an ancient wisdom lurking in her deep-set eyes. "I speck it jes' means dat chile is scared to death. Doan see no way we is gwine to keep men away from her."

The next day was much the same as the one before it, except that as the trio passed through a small town, Julie made a stop at a supply store. She returned carrying a bundle wrapped in brown paper, and she was so noncommittal about the whole matter that neither Leah nor Jackson made any inquiry.

That night Leah and Jackson went to their blankets after supper, and Leah kept Jackson awake for a long time tossing and turning. They felt the wagon move above them, for Julie was moving about also.

At first light Jackson got up first and built the fire, then Leah rose and put bacon in the skillet, following their custom. When the meat was done, Leah raised her voice, "Chile, you get yo'self up. Breakfus' 'bout ready."

Her eyes were on the skillet as she cracked an egg and dumped it in the bubbling bacon fat, but she heard the creak of the wagon as Julie dismounted. She heard Jackson draw his breath sharply and whisper, "My Lawd! Whut is you done to youself, Miz Julie?"

Turning quickly, Leah looked at Julie and dropped the next egg in the dirt. "Lawd have mercy!" she said quietly, then she said evenly, "You done it now, chile."

Julie stood there, her face burning.

What they saw was not the beautiful young woman with long wavy hair. They saw a young man with short-cropped hair sticking out from under a floppy black hat. The girlish figure was lost in the shapeless waist overalls, the slender feet concealed in a pair of thick-soled work boots, blunt-toed and ugly. The roundness of her upper body was enveloped and disguised by a bulky denim jacket, and the feminine contours of her face were somehow turned angular by the crude haircut and by the removal of all feminine adornment. She had, Leah saw, even trimmed the long, thick eyelashes. Now Leah and Jackson knew what she had bought at the store.

"Well, let's git this here rig on the road!" Both of the spectators started, for it was a new voice. Julie had always hated her voice, thinking it far too deep for a girl, and even though it meant she could sing a lovely contralto solo at church she had spent much time training herself to speak in a high pitch. Now she deliberately made it deeper than it was, and added a gravelly sound which was nothing at all like a girl's voice.

Leah stared at the figure, then turned to fry another egg. Slowly a smile crept across her lips, and she said finally, "Doan reckon you gonna have a heap of men tryin' to git up on the seat wif you today."

25

Julie smiled and immediately straightened her face, know-ing well that the dimple on her right cheek did nothing to add to her disguise. "I thought of it last night," she said. "All I have to do is be as unfriendly as possible, and we'll be just another wagon headed north."

"You better learn to cuss a little, Miz Julie," Jackson said, grinning. "And I 'spect you better have a plug of 'bakky, mebby, or learn to roll one of them cigarettes like most young bucks do."

"Don't call me *Julie*," she said instantly. "You remember what you used to call me when I was little, Leah?"

"Sho does! Called you *Dooley,* coz dat wuz de way you named youself."

"I want you both to call me that from now on. I'll be Dooley Judd, at least until we get away for good."

The new member of the group stared at them, then said in the rough voice that they still found hard to believe, "Come on! Git movin'!"

As she walked to catch up one of the mules, Leah laughed and said, "You doin' putty good wif de voice, Dooley, but I reckon you can stand a little practice on that there walk! Ain't nobody gonna believe you is a man when you walks like *dat!*"

Dooley halted at once. "Right. How's this?" With an exag-gerated swagger she ambled over to the mule, kicked the sur-prised animal in the belly, then turned back to sneer at them.

"Hoo! Real fine!" Jackson shouted. "Now, boss, you jes' learn to mebby spit a little and you is all set!"

Julie had always had a flair for dramatics. For the next week she threw herself into her role with enthusiasm, and by the time their wagon reached the outskirts of Independence, she had come as close to portraying a rough, surly young man as any girl was likely to.

The rough voice had become automatic for her, the swagger, the habit of wiping her lips with the back of her hand—
she had them all down and even learned to roll a cigarette
from the thin papers she'd bought at a store. She never
inhaled; the taste of it made her slightly ill. But the action lent
an air of authenticity to her performance.

She had been nervous the first time she'd met a stranger,
a man named Martindale who'd ridden by on a fine bay stallion. She'd hailed him, talked to him about the horse, and
when he'd ridden off without a backward glance, she'd
laughed delightedly and cried out, "Leah! I'm a man!"

They'd stopped several times to buy supplies and often
exchanged a few words with fellow travelers, and day by day
they felt that for any pursuer to follow them, he'd have to have
second sight.

Independence had been the jumping-off point for wagon trains
for several years, and it had grown considerably despite the
fact that most people came simply to leave. The main street
was wide, with a steepled brick courthouse dominating the
south end. There were many stores catering to the migrants
who wanted to lay in last-minute supplies.

The streets were not as crowded as Dooley expected, however, and there was little sign of wagon trains. "Guess I'll go in
and find out where the trains are located," she said. "We better
stock up, too. We'll need lots of stuff for the trip."

Walter's General Mercantile Company was a jumble of
every sort of thing one could imagine. Picks and shovels were
leaned against sacks of potatoes; racks of guns were almost hidden by long bolts of cloth and rolls of canvas. Tinned goods of
all sizes filled the shelves, and Dooley stood there bewildered
at first by the abundance of goods.

"Help you?" A young man in a white shirt and string tie came over to stand before her, and she said in her roughest male voice, "Got a long trip ahead. I'll need heaps of gear, but first, I gotta hook up with a train. Whereabouts you say I can find me a good one?"

The young man said, "You're too late. The last train left over a week ago—and it was a week overdue."

Dooley stood there in shock. Never had it crossed her mind that there was a fixed deadline on the trip. "You mean there's not *one* train left?"

The clerk hesitated, then grinned and said, "There is *one* train left, but, well, it's going pretty far to call it a 'train.' If you want to find it, I can tell you where it is. But if I was you, I'd steer clear."

"What's wrong with it?"

"Well, in the first place, you gotta leave in April or May. If you start too early, there ain't enough grass for your livestock. If you start too late, you get fouled water holes and maybe you catch a winter blizzard in the mountains. In the second place, they ain't got but 'bout twelve wagons, and that ain't enough to discourage the Injuns."

Dooley listened as the moon-faced clerk recited his facts, then asked, "Where can I find this bunch?"

"Go west of town past the big windmill. You'll see it, all right. It's the only one there."

Dooley left at once and piled in the wagon, explaining the crisis to Jackson and Leah. "We *have* to get in with that train! We'll be stuck here all winter if we don't!"

They found the train easily enough, nine wagons drawn up in a circle just outside of town. Dooley halted the team, jumped down, and said, "I'll see who's in charge."

A tall man in a high-peaked hat was leaning against a wagon, watching her approach, and Dooley said, "Howdy. Who might be in charge here?"

The tall man looked Dooley over carefully. He had craggy features and cold pale eyes. There was no warmth in his voice as he said, "I'm Daniel Slade—captain of this train. What's your business?"

"Why, I'd like to join your train."

Slade looked carefully at Dooley, then said, "You got any men in your party? I only see two niggers."

"There's just the three of us."

"You ain't over fifteen," Slade said. He shook his head. "Can't allow it, boy. You're just too young, and you'd be a hindrance to us."

"Wait a minute, Mister Slade," Dooley said anxiously. "I don't aim to be a hindrance. I can shoot, and them two there can cook or do any other kind of work."

Slade stared at Dooley, and there was a long silence as she held her breath. Then the man said, "Nope, can't do it. Tell you what, though. You can hire you a man in town and that'll be all right. I know there's several who'd like to get to Oregon. Go take one of 'em on. You got any money?"

Dooley at once grew cautious. "What you want to know for?"

"We got a rule that every wagon got to have certain supplies. Takes money to buy supplies."

"I've got the money, but . . ."

"You best git on into town," Slade said. He got up and turned away adding, "We're headed out maybe tomorrow, day after at the latest."

Dooley opened her mouth to argue, but Slade disappeared into the ring of wagons, so she turned and plodded back to the wagon.

"Said I was too young," she explained to Leah and Jackson. "But if we can hire a man, they'll take us on. Let's head back to town. Got to be at least *one* man who wants to go to Oregon."

"Oregon?" Leah asked sharply. "I thought we wuz gwine to California."

"That's the only train—and it's going to Oregon," Dooley said. She clamped her jaws shut, and said between clenched teeth, "Leah, I'd join it if they were headed to Africa!"

Finding a man may have sounded like an easy matter, but after searching all day, going from business to business up and down the street, Dooley plodded wearily back to the wagon with no takers.

"They all say it's suicide to leave this late. Nobody would even talk to me—except one man in a saloon, and he was too drunk to stand up."

"Maybe they right, Dooley," Jackson suggested. "Maybe we better not even try to go wif dem."

"We *have* to, Jackson!" Dooley said. "Jake's going to have somebody on our trail."

"Well, I guess you is right 'bout dat," Jackson said. With a grimace he reached into his shirt pocket and handed Dooley a folded paper. "Me and Leah wuz hopin' we'd git gone from dis place quick so's we wouldn't have to tell you 'bout it."

Dooley unfolded the paper and stared at the large broadside. In heavy type she read the words REWARD—FIVE HUNDRED DOLLARS, and in finer print that seemed to jump out at her she read a description of herself and a notice that the reward would be paid when Julie Wade was in the custody of the local police or returned to her guardian.

"Why, this makes it look like I'm a criminal!" she exclaimed. "But nobody will think of me as a girl now that I'm in this rig."

Leah said at once, "Better read all that paper. It says as how she's probably travelin' with a couple of ex-slaves named Jackson and Leah, and it ain't gwine to be too hard for a real sharp man to see through dat garb of yours."

Dooley read through the notice then exclaimed,

"Why, this says that a man named L.D. Hardin is here in Independence! How'd he get here so fast?"

"I found out 'bout dat," Jackson said. "When I seen de notice, I pulled it down, but dey's scattered all over town. So I float around and find a nigger from Louisiana and I pump him till I find out dat dis here Hardin man is a policeman what lives heah."

"Jake must have sent a telegram," Dooley moaned. "He found out that we headed north toward Independence. And he'll probably keep a close eye on wagon trains, because they mostly leave from here. Oh, what can we do?"

"We better git out of dis place quick!" Jackson said.

"But we'd be caught sure if we stayed on the road!" Dooley exclaimed. "I'll bet there's reward notices all along the way."

"We is jest *got* to get on that train," Leah insisted. "Ain't no law gonna traipse all the way to Oregon to ketch us!"

"But I can't find a man—" Suddenly she slapped her hands together and said, "Wait a minute! I think I've got it!" Her eyes sparkled and she spoke rapidly. "I told you about my cousin, Thad Stevens?"

"I remembers him, Dooley." Leah nodded. He come to see Miz Helen once way back."

"Well, he told me at that party that his half brother was headed for the coast, and that he'd be in Independence." Dooley whirled and said, "I've got to find him! You wait here!"

It took only one stop to discover her man.

"Reno?" the bartender at the Eagle asked. "Sure, I know him. He's been in here enough. Don't know where he lives, though." He lifted his voice and called to a man sitting at a table alone with a bottle, "Hey, Calvin, you know where that guy Reno holes up?"

"I heard he had a room at Mort's place," the man said. "But he may have got throwed out of there by now."

"What you want with this guy?" the bartender asked curiously.

"Oh, I've got a message for him. Where's this place he's supposed to be?"

"Go down this street to the next corner—that's Elm. Take a right and go to the end of it, then go right. There's an old two-story building there. Guy name Mort runs it, but he's likely not there. Just go in and holler for the guy."

"Thanks!"

"Watch out for this bird," the bartender called out as Dooley left. "He's rough when he's drinking!"

Dooley found the place with no difficulty. When nobody answered her knock, she stepped inside and found a long hall with doors on each side. She went down the hall calling out, "Reno! Jim Reno!"

At the end of the hall a door opened, and a young boy stepped outside. He was not over twelve, a thin boy with fair hair and the bluest eyes she'd ever seen. He stood there watchfully, and she asked, "You know a man named Reno?"

He looked at her steadily, then asked, "Why you askin'?"

"Got some business to do with him, son. He around?"

The boy regarded her and asked in a hard voice, "You come to get money, you might as well forget it."

"Didn't come for that."

They stared at each other, and finally the boy said, "Jim ain't here. He's been in jail for the last four days."

Dooley was taken aback; the man would do her no good if he was not available to join them. "What's he in jail for?"

"Gettin' drunk and raisin' cain."

Dooley stared at the boy carefully. He appeared at first glance to be hard, but there was a vulnerability in his face that the assumed toughness could not cover. "Is he your pa?"

"Ain't got no folks," he said sharply in a tone that shut the door to further questions. "Me and Jim run together. What you want with him?"

Dooley stood there, trying to think of something. Her impulse was to leave, but to what? Finally she decided to make a last attempt. "I need a man. I got me a wagon and everything and there's a train leaving for Oregon right off—but I got to have some help. I heard that Reno was on his way there."

The boy stared at her, and there was such a careful look in his bright blue eyes that Dooley felt her story was pretty thin. But he finally shrugged and said, "You kin get him out if you got the money for his fine. Don't know if he'll work for you."

Dooley took a deep breath and said, "Where's the jail?"

"I'll show you." The boy led her out to the street, turned toward town, and said, "My name's Lee Morgan." He nodded when Dooley identified herself and said little until they got to a squat building with a flat roof. "There's the jail," he said, then after a moment's hesitation he added in a halting voice,

"Dooley, I better tell you that Jim won't look too good. He's—
well, he's had a pretty tough knock, not too long ago, and he
just ain't had time to get over it."

"What happened?"

"Guess he'll tell you—if he wants to," Lee said, "but don't
judge him by what you see right now." He clamped his lips
together and led the way into the jail.

A fat man with his feet propped up on a battered desk
looked up and said, "Hello, boy. You wanna see Reno?"

"Sure. And this here feller needs to see him, too. Name's
Dooley Judd. This is Sheriff Bentley, Dooley."

"Leave your gun here, Judd." Bentley heaved himself up
and took the weapon from Dooley, then led the way to a row of
four dark cells in the rear of the building.

"He's drunk again. If I catch you givin' any more whiskey,
Lee, I'll throw you in with him."

"You ain't caught me, Sheriff."

The sheriff snorted and said as he left, "Holler when you
want out."

As soon as he left, Lee walked over to the man asleep on
the narrow bed, his face turned to the wall. "Jim, wake up."

The man gave a sigh, mumbled something thickly, then
rolled over. "What's it you say?"

He pulled himself into a sitting position, and Dooley saw
that he was bleary-eyed, unshaved, and practically in a stupor.
He was dressed in a tattered shirt that had once been white,
but was dirty and wrinkled. The wedge-shaped face topped by
a broad forehead was crowned by a mat of tangled hair, black
as a crow's wing, and the bleary eyes that peered out at her
from under heavy brows were angry and suspicious.

"Whosis?" he mumbled thickly, and he began to weave in
the bed as if he were about to fall backward.

"Better have some water, Jim," the boy said, and he poured from a pitcher into the single glass on the table.

"Yeah—need—a drink!" the man said and drained the glass. "Thanks, Lee." He stared at Dooley and asked, "What you want with me?"

"My name's Dooley Judd." There was no recognition in the dark eyes, and Dooley said, "I—I think we're sort of kinfolks."

This brought a response, for the man's gaze which had been wandering across the room swept back to her face and he said, "I got no kin."

"Thad Stevens, he's your brother, right?"

Reno batted his eyes, and ran his tongue across his lips. "Thad? Sure—well, half brother."

"I'm his cousin," Dooley said. She had little hope, for the man was a drunk, but she added, "You must have known my ma—Helen Wade?"

Reno seemed to have trouble with his thoughts. His brow knotted and he swayed slightly in the bed. Finally he mumbled, "Sure—knew her a long time ago."

"Well, I'm going to Oregon, Reno, and I need a man. I heard you were on your way to the coast, and—well, I thought I'd see if you wanted to make the trip with me."

"Coast? No trains goin' this late," he said.

"Daniel Slade's train is leaving tomorrow."

"Slade?" Reno swung his legs over the bed, braced himself, and stood up. He was so dizzy the boy made a grab for him as he swayed back and forth.

"You going with Slade?" Reno took the glass from Lee, filled it, and drank it thirstily. Then he stared at her and shook his head. "You better stay away from that bunch, kid. What's your name again?"

"Dooley."

"I wouldn't go with that bunch to the general store. And anyway, they're headed for Oregon, not California."

Dooley's shoulders dropped, and she wanted to cry. This man was her only hope, and he was turning her down. Then she was filled with sudden anger—she had come so close, and now this drunk stood between her and freedom.

There was a mindless quality in her anger as she struck out at him, "You're just a drunk, Reno! All the things Thad Stevens said about you, they're all lies! You're no good!"

With a sudden catlike motion Reno struck, and, drunk as he was, the crack of his hand across her face drove her back against the wall with a crash. The power of the blow brought bright lights to her eyes and a roaring in her ears.

"Hey, Jim!" Lee said, and he thrust his slender body in front of Reno. "You ain't actin' right!"

"I didn't send for him," Reno said, then he sat down on the bunk. "Better get out, kid." He lay back and closed his eyes as if he were tired of the scene.

"Jim, we got to get out of this place," Lee said. He reached down and pulled at Reno's arm, a plea in his high voice. "We ain't got any money. I gotta get out of the room today."

The man opened his eyes with an effort and stared at the boy. There was a long silence, and then he pulled himself up again, getting to his feet. He swayed and grabbed his head. Then he stared at the boy and said, "Been pretty tough on you, Lee, hasn't it?" Then he turned to face Dooley. "You got the money to get me out of here?"

"Yes," Dooley was uncertain about how dependable Reno was, but she knew that she had no choice. It was him or no one.

He seemed to know it, too, for he nodded and said, "Well, you'll have to buy two horses." He saw the uncertainty in her eyes, and a small grin touched the corners of his broad mouth. "You don't have to worry, Dooley. I'll be sober as is necessary to get you to the coast." Dooley nodded, but she was still smarting from the blow he had given her. "Well, they said I had to have a man before they'd let me make the trip. Guess you're as close as I'm going to get. *Real* men aren't so easy to get."

She expected him to flare up at that, but to her surprise he smiled broadly, and a chuckle sounded deep in his chest. "You know who you sound like? You sound like a kid trying to be tough." Then he cocked his head and looked at her with a peculiar look in his dark eyes. "I'm just startin' to get things straight. Your mother—she was Lige Stevens's sister?"

"That's right. What about it?"

Reno took his eyes off her and stared out the cell window. He was still for so long that she thought he'd forgotten her, but finally he brought his glance around, and there was a steadiness on the angular planes of his ravaged face.

"I owe Lige something. He died on me before I could pay it back. Guess maybe the best I'll ever do is to pay his kinfolks."

"You just stay sober!" she said quickly. "I'll check your stuff to see you don't take any whiskey. What I don't need is a drunk to nurse along for two thousand miles!"

In an even tone and with a humorous light in his eyes, Reno said, "I'll appreciate any help you can give me, Dooley." Then a sober light flashed across his face, and he looked older and very tired as he murmured gently, "If you can, it'll be more than anybody else has done."

THREE
To a Promised Land

By the time Dooley drove the wagon around the western edge of town and pulled up a few yards from the train, the July sun had heated the parched ground. An ineffectual breeze occasionally whipped up a thermal that sent small dust devils scampering across the open space. By noon the heat would transform straight lines of trees or buildings in the distance into quivering, distorted shapes.

Dooley had been proud of the way she handled the team. Her hands had toughened on the trip, and she had cast several guarded glances to see if the two new members of the group appreciated her skill. Reno and the boy had fallen behind, however, and when she said, "Whoa!" and threw the reins to Jackson who was sitting, along with Leah, beside her, Reno and Lee were still a hundred yards away.

Careful to maintain a swagger, she made her way along the line of wagons to a gap, then stepped inside the circle. It was an active place—children of all ages playing games, women washing and tending blackened pots over small fires, men engaged in myriad details of work—but there seemed to be no urgency such as she had expected. It would not have surprised her to have found the train pulling out or already gone.

"Lookin' for somethin'?" Dooley turned to meet the direct gaze of a young woman about her own age. She had pretty features, but her face had a kind of bold insolence. "You joinin' up with the train?"

Dooley nodded. "That's right. Mr. Slade around?"

"Over there—the big wagon." She moved closer to Dooley and there was a direct boldness in her glance. "I'm Ellie Satterfield."

"My name's Dooley Judd." Her stare made Dooley uncomfortable for some reason, and she said, "Guess I'll be seeing you, Ellie."

She turned her head to one side as if filing some information about what she saw, and said with a curious smile, "I'll look for you."

Dooley walked away quickly, not realizing until she approached the three men standing beside the large wagon that Ellie had been sizing her up for a future conquest. She almost smiled at the situation, then sobered at once. *Just what I don't need,* she thought grimly. Then she stopped and nodded to Slade, who had been watching her approach. "Got me some help," she said in her husky man's voice. Pulling a tobacco sack from her shirt pocket, she built a cigarette expertly and lit it. "He ain't much, maybe, but he's all I could get."

"Let's have a look at him," Daniel Slade said. "These are my boys, Carl and Beau. That's my woman."

Neither of the men offered to shake hands, but both of them looked her over carefully. Dooley drew on the cigarette, trying not to let any of the smoke trickle down her throat.

Carl Slade said, "How old are you, kid?" He was a massive

man, six-foot-three at least, with a thick neck supporting a massive head. His shoulders and chest were so bulky that his lower body looked small. Short curly hair made a crown over his square face, and there was a brutal quality in his wide, thick lips.

"Old enough to hold up my end," Dooley said with a shrug.

"I'd say maybe fifteen tryin' to look a lot older," Beau Slade said, grinning. He was dressed in a formfitting cotton shirt with fancy embroidery on the collar and pockets, and the tailored trousers tucked into the finely tooled high-heeled boots were somewhat incongruous in the setting. He was a dandy, Dooley saw, but there was a quick competence in his air, and he was the best-looking man she had ever seen. He had chiseled features, proportioned to perfection—wide eyes, deep-set and bold, dominated his face, and the curve of his lips would have been effeminate if they had not been strong and blended with his raw masculinity. He moved away from the wagon, saying, "Let's take a look at your folks, Judd."

Dooley was weak in the knees as she led the trio outside the circle and to the wagon where Reno and Lee had arrived and dismounted. She had passed the test so far as her disguise was concerned, but she was still apprehensive about the whole thing.

"That's Jackson and Leah," she said, waving toward the couple on the wagon seat. "Used to belong to my folks—goin' to work for me when we get a place."

"Well, well!" Beau said, and there was a broad smile on his lips. He was staring at the man and the boy who had dismounted and were standing a few feet from the wagon. Didn't hardly recognize you standing up, Reno."

"What's that?" Daniel asked quickly, his brow contracted to a frown.

"This is the town drunk," Beau answered. "He slept in the jail until the sheriff got tired of boarding him free. After that he usually slept in the mud or wherever he fell."

"Yeah, Pa, that's right," Carl said. "Way I heard it, he ain't been sober a day since he hit town."

Daniel Slade's thin lips contracted to a slit, and he shook his head saying roughly, "Won't do. We don't need no drunks to nurse along to Oregon."

Dooley shot a glance at Reno, but he was staring out across the flat plain, his eyes hooded by heavy lids and apparently paying no attention to the talk. In desperation she said, "Oh, we got that all settled, Mr. Slade. He's promised to stay sober all the way."

Beau laughed and slapped his thigh. "You know how long that will last, Dooley? Until he gets a chance at a bottle!"

Dooley said, "I told him he'd get a whippin' if he fell off the wagon."

It brought a delighted laugh from Beau, and even the heavy face of Carl revealed a smile. "Let's take 'em on, Pa," Beau said. "I reckon Dooley here is a mite young to take on even a drunk like Reno—but I'll promise to administer a spankin' the first time he gets drunk."

"We can take turns, Beau," Carl said with a contemptuous glance at Reno.

"Well, you see to it," Daniel said. "Now, we're leaving at daybreak. I'll give you a list of provisions every wagon's got to have." He pulled a piece of paper from his pocket and handed it to Dooley. "We'll check this when you get back from town, and you'll have to have more animals."

"Nothing wrong with this team," Dooley said.

"Got to have spares—we're bound to lose some. Every wagon's got to have an extra team—and a team is four animals, not two. You go get more mules and I'll check them over when you get back."

He was a stern man, hard in voice and demeanor. Dooley saw at once that his word was law, so she said with a shrug, "All right."

"I'm goin' in for a last fling, Dooley," Beau said. "I'll show you the most likely mules for sale. Then maybe we can have a drink together." He gave her a playful blow on the shoulder, adding with a wide grin, "And I'll even introduce you to a little gal who'll take to you. Likes 'em young and tender. Good-looking young feller like you probably got to fight the women off with a club!"

Dooley felt her neck beginning to burn, and before the flush reached her cheeks she said, "Reno, you come along, and you, too, Jackson. Leah, you make a fire and get some grub cooked for supper."

Beau mounted a sorrel gelding and rode along beside the wagon. Reno and Lee trailed in the rear, and they pulled up at a corral attached to a large stable.

The mule trader was a scrawny man with a long neck and a bobbing Adam's apple. "Need some mules?"

"Yeah," Dooley said, climbing down to look at the mules the dealer pointed out. Reno and Lee dismounted and leaned against the rail fence.

"Treat 'em right, Slim," Beau said. "They got a long way to go."

"Shore. Now you take that big sucker there. He'll take you there and git you back in one piece. Broke to drive and to saddle, too. Fine animal. If I was on my way to Oregon, I wouldn't have nothin' but a mule pullin' my wagon."

"Lots of people seem to favor oxen," Dooley said.

"Mule's faster, smarter, quicker handled," Slim said. "Now you take an ox, get him down, and it'd take an act of Congress to get him up."

"How much?" Dooley asked.

"Forty dollars each, two for seventy-five, and take your pick. That's dirt cheap!"

"Where you come from that dirt's so expensive?" Reno had not moved, but he was looking at the trader with a bored look on his face.

The man ignored him and said, "Now oxen is cheaper, but you can't ride one and you can't pack with one. If you want to circle up against Indians, where'd you be with an ox?"

"Ask him how Indians like mules, Dooley," Reno said mildly, as if he were not very interested.

"Why, they like 'em, just like everybody else!" the dealer said quickly.

"Reckon you told the truth that time," Reno agreed.

"What you talking about, Reno?" Beau asked shortly.

"Never heard of an Indian stealing an ox," Reno said with a shrug.

"You got a long nose, mister," the mule dealer said angrily.

"Yeah, who made you an expert, drunk?" Beau snapped. "We're using mules for our own wagons—and we'll have to wait no telling how long on those usin' oxen!"

"Maybe I talk too much," Reno murmured.

Dooley stared at Reno, then at Beau. She had already sensed the Slades could not brook opposition, and if she took Reno's advice, it would be a challenge to Beau that he would

44

take personally. They were probably a solid family, and anyone who incurred the enmity of one member could probably count on taking on the whole family.

To gain time she said, "Let's go get the supplies first—we can look around at the other animals for sale."

Beau's handsome face broke into a scowl, and he said, "I got no time to waste, Dooley. You'll be making a mistake if you buy oxen, I'll tell you that." He rode off at a breakneck pace, spurring the gelding mercilessly.

"You ain't gonna find no better mules than these," Slim said sullenly.

"We'll take a look," Dooley said. She got back on the wagon, and as they headed for the store, Jackson said, "Whut you think?"

"I don't know, Jackson," she answered. "I don't have much money, and oxen are cheaper."

She wrestled with the problem, and as they piled the wagon with supplies she turned to Reno, who was tossing a sack of flour to Jackson, and said, "Do you know a good ox when you see one?"

"Sure." He dusted his hands off, then gave her a sudden grin that made him look younger. "You sure you want to take the word of a drunk instead of an upstandin' citizen like Beau Slade?"

"We've got to do it. I'm just about broke. Rules say we've got to have two teams. I don't know if we can do it, even by selling the team we've got."

Reno nodded. "Figured that. Want me to look around?"

Dooley stared at him, and she was still angry over the blow he had given her at the jail. He was not what she had hoped for, and if there were any other way, she would have taken it, but as it was she could only say, "I guess so." Then she snapped at him, "Think you can stay sober long enough, Reno?"

"Won't know till I try it. Up to you, Dooley." He stood there, an idle shape in the hot afternoon sun, his face shaded by a low-crowned hat. A tiny break on the bridge of his straight nose and a small scar on the right temple spoke of past battles.

Finally she said, "We've got to do it. Let's get going."

All afternoon she followed him around, and most of his actions seemed pointless to her. He wandered up to those with oxen for sale and appeared to be uninterested. After seeing every animal in town, he went through a similar process with the mules, finally trading them for four oxen and a little boot. He found two more oxen and managed to trade the harness and a surprisingly small amount of cash for the two animals. Reno climbed up to sit with Dooley, giving her a few instructions on the art of driving oxen. "Sore feet," he said to Dooley as they headed back to camp with the animals. "Only real problem with oxen—those cloven hoofs get splintered to the quick if you don't take care of 'em."

"They're so slow!" Dooley said. "They don't walk—they just *plod!*"

"Yep. Nature of the beast." Reno shrugged and added, "But they'll be plodding when mules and horses are meat for buzzards. Besides, I've always liked to eat ox better than mule. Man who likes mule meat ain't normal, Dooley!"

"*Eat* them!"

"Might come to that."

When they reached the train and made their way inside, some sort of meeting was underway. A crowd was gathered in a loose semicircle, with Daniel Slade in the center. Facing him was a tall man wearing clothes so tattered they seemed to hang on by chance. He was nearly six feet, but skinny as a snake, his face sunk to the bone, cavernous and hollow. His age was impossible to guess, somewhere between thirty and fifty. There was a stolid patience in the way he stood, his thin body in stark contrast to the solid bulk of Daniel Slade.

Slade looked up and said, "Get the animals and supplies?"

"Yes."

"I'll check them now." He turned to the thin man and shook his head ponderously. "No, Brother Finney, I can't permit you to join us. I've explained to you about what every man's got to have in the way of food and supplies, and you come up short."

"Short?" Carl laughed. "He ain't got a pot to spit in!"

"The Lord will provide." The man called Finney spoke slowly, and there was a monumental patience in him as he waited for Slade's answer.

"We've got our rules."

"I'm asking you to bend them, Mr. Slade."

Slade looked around the circle and spoke to Finney as if he were a child. "We can't allow you to go, because you'd be a burden on the entire train. Can't you see that, Brother Finney?"

Slade was forcing himself to be genial, which was not his nature, but Finney said, "The Lord will provide. I have heard the Lord calling me to minister to the heathen, and I've got to go!"

"We'd have to feed you, can't you see that? We'd have to divide with you, no matter how little we had."

"I'm asking you to take me." There was a simple look on Finney's face, and Dooley realized suddenly that if he were denied a place on the train, he would probably start walking across the continent alone.

Finney began to speak, not begging but just stating his case, and Dooley wanted to help him. Once she opened her mouth to agree to share her stores, but fear of running short kept her quiet.

"I'll stand for him, Slade." It was Reno who spoke.

Dooley started, for Reno had been standing close to her side. She turned to stare at him, and Slade said in surprise, *"You'll* take him on? Why, you ain't got nothing either!"

"You won't have to worry," Reno said. He looked around the circle and saw several members of the train nodding in agreement. "Be hard for a man to starve with all the buffer we'll hit after we cross the Platte."

"You've made this trip?" A young man of about twenty-five, built along the lines of a draft horse, stepped forward and stared at Reno. He was massively built, with placid blue eyes, and he spoke very slowly.

Reno shrugged and said, "Been as far as the Sublette Cut-off. Went on to California from there."

"Well, that's good news!" the young man said. "Ain't a one of us ever been even that far."

"Got any proof of all this here travelin' you've done, drunk?" Carl asked. He had an angry flush on his face, and Reno realized that he saw himself as the leader of the train, along with his father, and now he shook his massive head and added, "I don't reckon we can put much stock in his talk."

Dooley spoke up without thinking, "We'll stand for Brother Finney. Got more than enough for another man."

"Bless you, brother!" the preacher said, and stepped forward to offer a skinny paw which swallowed Dooley's hand. "The Lord reward you a hundredfold!"

The Slades argued and swelled up, but there was little

they could do. Finally Daniel said, "You're responsible, Dooley. Don't come crying to me when you run short!" He led the way to the wagon, walking with angry strides. When he saw the oxen he said accusingly, "Where's your mules?"

"Decided on oxen," Dooley said.

"You're a fool! Just like the rest of them!"

As he was checking the supplies, a tall man with white hair came to stand by her. He was straight as an arrow, and there was a natural courtesy in his thin voice as he said, "My name is Vinson Grant." He waved a hand toward a man and woman who had come with him. "This is my brother, R.G., and my sister, Addie."

The brother was a shock. He had a scar on his face so terrible that it seemed impossible that any man could have endured such a wound. He had a sunken section over his left eyebrow, and he wore a black patch over his right eye. His voice was gentle, as was the remaining eye. "Glad to have you folks," he said to Dooley.

"It was generous of you to take Brother Finney on," the woman said. She had the same straight form and direct gaze of her brothers, but she was much younger. The lock of hair that escaped the bonnet was a rich chestnut, and her brown eyes were wide and beautiful. She had been marked by smallpox, but even this did not obscure the beauty of her face. She was, as far as Dooley could judge, about thirty-five. "I wanted so much to agree to take him," she added.

"You did?" Vinson said in surprise. "Why didn't you say so, Addie?"

"Oh, I didn't know if we had enough."

"Should have spoke up," R.G. said with a fond look at his sister.

She colored and gave a small laugh. "It worked out anyway, didn't it? God will bless you, Dooley." Then she said tentatively, "You're so young! Don't you have a family?"

"No, ma'am," Dooley said quickly. "Lost my folks a few years ago."

"You're a good-hearted young man," Addie said, giving Dooley a warm glance, and looking at Reno she said, "And you too, Mr. Reno."

Reno seemed uncomfortable, and he shrugged, saying only, "How much can one skinny preacher eat?"

Later when they were sitting around the campfire, Dooley asked, "Why'd you speak up for Brother Finney, Reno? You got a fondness for preachers?"

The firelight flickered over his face as he glanced at her and said, "You ever see your uncle?"

"Lige Stevens? No, I never did. He wrote to Mother once or twice, and they wanted to see each other, but it never worked out. Why?"

Reno picked up a stick and probed the fire, his face sober in the firelight. Then he looked at her and said, "He looked a whole lot like Preacher Finney. Not as skinny, but the same craggy sort of face." He started to say something else, then suddenly his face hardened and he got up, walking out into the darkness without another word.

Jackson was asleep, but Leah's voice floated across to her clearly: "Dat man is shore got miseries! Blame if he don't!"

Dooley picked up the stick that Reno had dropped, poked the glowing coals, and watched the sparks swarm into the sky. Finally she sat there hugging her knees until the fire died down, then went to bed. Her last thought before she dropped off to sleep was of Reno's face as he had disappeared in the night.

A week on the trail had shaken the train into order. A shot fired by one of the guards at six signaled that the hours of sleep were over. Every wagon and tent poured forth its tenants, and slow-kindling smokes began to rise. From six to seven breakfast was eaten, tents struck, wagons loaded, and teams yoked and harnessed. The wagons pointed the way, followed by the riding stock and trailed by the large herd of cattle bringing up the rear.

The march continued until the nooning place, where the teams were not unyoked but simply turned loose from the wagons to graze. From late afternoon on, boredom fell, and teamsters sometimes fell asleep behind the plodding oxen.

At a signal from Daniel Slade, the wagons pulled into a circle, and by the end of the first week it was simple for the hindmost wagon to fall into a position with the first one that closed the gateway, forming a barricade.

Fires sprang up, made of small sticks and branches picked up on the march, but these were scarce, the ground having been picked clean by previous trains.

"Kind of like a picnic, ain't it Jim?" Lee said to Reno. They had taken care of the stock and were standing idly by waiting for the supper call. A yearling calf belonging to a Barney Moore had broken its leg, and Moore had invited the train to a celebration of their first week on the trail.

Reno took in the busy scene: women laughing and setting out the food on tables rigged out of planks, small children playing their games under their feet, the men pulled into small groups smoking and talking. "Sure does, Lee."

He stood slightly apart from the rest, a solitary figure, and it was typical of the way he had kept on the outside of things all that first week. The intimacy of life on the trail had knitted the families together quickly, but Reno kept to himself, doing his work efficiently but speaking seldom, even to Lee. He had been approached by several of the men, but though he was never surly, there was a wall that none of them could penetrate.

Now as Barney Moore lifted up his voice, crying out, "Come and git it!" there was a surge toward the food, but Reno simply stood there watching.

Barney Moore was a tall, gangling man of thirty-five. He had lost his teeth, which gave his face a pinched look, but his grin was engaging, and he had proved himself to be one of the most optimistic members of the train. His wife, Mary, was no less cheerful. She was thirty, short and plump, with a red face. She was the daughter of a naval officer and had made long voyages as a girl, and she was musical. The sound of her dulcimer floated over the still night air, and she could whistle in a marvelous fashion, so that if you had not seen her you would have thought several people were whistling.

Nelson Moore, age thirteen, was a caricature of his father, gangling and cheerful. Robin Moore, age twelve, was small and plump like her mother and could play a guitar well.

"Brother Finney, would you express our thanks?" Barney said, nodding to the thin preacher.

Jude Finney looked like a ragpicker, but he had a high clear voice, and when he prayed, it was with utter simplicity and confidence that he had the ear of God.

"Our Father, we are the sheep of your pasture. You have kept us as the apple of your eye, and this food is your gift to us.

Bless the Moores for their generosity, and restore this critter to them a hundredfold. We thank you in Jesus' name."

The food was shoveled onto tin plates, and everyone had pooled the remnants of vegetables to supplement the meat. They sat down before steaks pounded and floured and fried and drenched in gravy, red beans laced with onions and green peppers, hot enough to scald the throat, potatoes boiled until their fluffy interiors burst out of their jackets, hot apple pie gently steaming through its openwork crust, sliced cucumbers soaked in vinegar and cream, spongy-fresh bread with a thick golden crust, butter that had been churned in buckets swung beneath the wagons, and topped off with corn relish, pickled beets, huckleberry jam, and draughts of steaming black coffee.

Dooley found herself sitting with a group composed of the Henrys, the Prathers, the Burnses, and the Edwardses.

"This is so nice!" Jane Ann Burns said, looking around with a smile. "I hated the idea of leaving the city—but this *is* romantic!" She was an attractive girl, no more than twenty, with a trim figure and a fragile bone structure that seemed out of place on the trail. Her blonde hair was carefully brushed and her clear blue eyes moved restlessly over the enclosure, settling on the Slades who were opposite. "I'd be *petrified* if we didn't have such wonderful leaders!"

Her husband glanced at her, and Dooley noticed a guarded look on his face. He was a small man of thirty, a Scot with sandy hair and fair skin that never tanned. He was colorless next to the striking beauty of his wife, and it was apparent that his love for her was total. That she was not so dedicated to him was also evident. She was a flirt, and although it was more of a social habit than something more serious, the gray eyes of Robert Burns filled with pain as she laughed and said, "That Beau Slade—now if *he* isn't a handsome thing, Lena!"

Lena Prather was only three years older than Jane Ann, but she did not even glance at Beau Slade. She was the wife of Pete Prather, a wiry man of sixty-three, who said, "He's purty enough, all right. We'll see how he looks when we hit the Columbia. Reckon he'll git his frilly shirt messed up a leetle then!"

Prather had picked at his food, and a look of pain passed across his face. He rubbed his stomach in a motion that had become habitual.

Lena caught the look and said, "Can't you eat anything else? You ain't had hardly a bite." She was holding Esther, a child of two, on her lap, but she reached out and patted her husband's thin shoulder with her free hand. Esther was her own child, but the three younger Prathers in the group were children born to Pete's two previous wives. Marie, a pretty girl of sixteen, and Harry, age fifteen, sat to her left. Molly, a red-haired girl of seven, sat close to her. Pete also had a set of twin boys, Leon and Clyde, who had their own wagon in the train.

Dooley thought suddenly that there was a strength in Lena Prather that bound the family together, and she saw a loyalty between the aging Pete and his young wife that was lacking between the Burnses.

Buck Henry was the largest man in the train, but there was something almost childish in his broad face, a vulnerability visible to everyone as he looked across at Beau Slade. Ellie Satterfield had drawn close to Beau. She was reaching out to touch his arm, her head thrown back as she laughed loudly at something he had leaned over and whispered in her ear. There was a boldness in her manner that pained Buck. That he was hopelessly infatuated with Ellie was obvious to everyone, not least to the girl herself, for she teased him shamelessly.

Buck's parents, Josh and Alice, exchanged glances, and Alice shook her head in a guarded fashion. Mrs. Henry was in her late forties, a larger woman than her husband, with Swedish blue eyes and blonde hair. Josh was a thin six-footer with mild brown eyes. Buck's feeling for the Satterfield girl pained them both, but they had not spoken to him about it.

Even as they watched, Ellie pulled away from Beau and left him to walk across the enclosure. She let her eyes fall on every man under sixty, and Robert Burns said, "That girl needs a strong hand. She's a tease."

"Oh, she's just young and full of fun," Jane Ann said at once. "You've forgotten what it's like to be young!"

The cut embarrassed most of those who heard it, and there was a feeling of sympathy for Burns, who lowered his eyes and picked at his food.

"She won't do no good with that one!" Pete Prather said as they all watched Ellie make her way to where Jim Reno was standing in the shadows, drawn back from the crowd. "He ain't nothin' but a hermit!"

Josh Henry took in the full-bodied beauty of the girl and remarked wryly, "Even a hermit would have a tough time ignoring that one!"

Ellie could feel Beau's eyes on her as she went to Reno, and she deliberately took his arm and pressed her body close to his side, knowing that Beau Slade was a man who would be stirred to action by the quick possessive streak that ran through him.

Reno noted the action, and a smile touched his lips as he took in Ellie's expression with a swift glance—noting the round face and broad mouth—an erect and rather taut upper lip lying against the lower lip's pronounced roll, and her lids heavy over brown eyes.

"Jim, you better get something to eat. Come on, I'll wait on you."

He was amused at the way she was using him to stir up Beau's anger, but sobered when he realized that Beau was glaring across the opening, clearly angry.

"Not hungry, Ellie," he said.

"Aw, Jim," she gave his arm a tighter squeeze and her breath was sweet as she said, "Man's got to eat—got to do other things, too!"

Reno knew that she would be an explosive danger on the trip, setting man against man. Even now he noted that Carl had said something to Beau, and the younger man had responded by grabbing a bottle and making his way across the enclosure. He was aware that the party had seen the drama, and as he came to stand before Reno and Ellie there was a sly light in his eyes.

"Been meanin' to tell you somethin', Reno. You sure have been a good boy this week! Haven't been drunk a time."

"Did my best to make you happy, Beau."

"Well, you done good, and I didn't have to give you a spankin'—in fact, you deserve a little reward." He held out the bottle of whiskey that he had snatched from the table, and said, "Drink up."

"Hate to spoil my record."

"You refusin' to drink with me, drunk?" Beau's lips turned cruel, and he moved his shoulders aggressively, feeling the silence of the crowd and said in a louder tone, "I'm gonna have to take this personal."

The man was determined to fight, Reno realized, and he shrugged and said, "I guess one won't hurt, Beau." He reached out, taking the bottle and lifting it to his lips. He took a large swallow. "Much obliged."

Slade had prepared himself for a fight, and the easy submission of Reno took him off guard. He finally nodded and said angrily, "Keep the bottle, drunk. I'd like an excuse to give you that spankin' you got comin' sooner or later."

A cry had leapt to Lee's lips as Reno took the bottle, and he noted that Dooley had made a sudden noise that she quickly cut off. But it was done, and now they watched as Beau took Ellie by the arm and drew her back to the table where the rest of the Slades watched with broad grins.

Reno looked at the bottle, then straight across the crowd at Lee, and he saw the fear in the boy's eyes. He thought of how the boy had stuck with him, even when he was wallowing in the mire at Independence. Lee had gotten him off the street with whatever help he could muster, put him to bed, and made him eat after one of his binges. *Sure have hurt that boy,* he thought, then he saw that Dooley was staring at him. He knew Dooley didn't trust him and was afraid that he'd fall back into his old ways. *Boy's got a right to feel that way, I reckon,* he mused, then straightened up and made his way to the party. He stood before Lee, considering the steady eyes in the thin face, then he smiled and said, "Better keep this in a safe place, Lee. Somebody might get snakebit."

"Yeah, sure, Jim!" A warmth replaced the apprehension in Lee's face, and he shot a glance at Dooley, who was looking vastly relieved.

The tension that had fallen on the group lightened, and Barney Moore called out, "Let's have us a play party!"

Soon the sound of Mary Moore's dulcimer, joined by Robin's guitar and a banjo plucked with more enthusiasm than skill by Jackson, filled the evening with melody. A square dance was organized, and Barney called out the sets while couples made the rounds.

Dooley was standing beside Leah, clapping her hands and watching the dancers happily, when Marie Prather came up and caught her by the arm.

"Come on, Dooley," she said with a smile on her face. "There's not enough men. Dance with me!"

Dooley heard Leah break into a cackle of laughter, but then she was drawn into the dance, protesting all the time of her inability to dance.

"I'll teach you, Dooley," Marie said firmly, and Dooley had no choice. She was a good dancer, but was accustomed only to following the lead of a man, and she had to be pushed and shoved into place by Marie as she held back, feeling awkward and out of place.

"You're such a nice-looking boy, Dooley," Marie said as they rested between sets, drinking punch made with lemons, water, and a touch of something so strong that it took her breath. "I'll bet you've had lots of girls after you."

Dooley nearly choked over a swallow of the punch, and said, "To tell you the truth, Marie, not a one."

"Oh, I know better than that! You men are all alike!"

"Well, no, we're not *all* alike!"

It tickled Dooley that she had fooled Marie, and she was congratulating herself when suddenly a shout sounded over the music that brought a stop to the laughter.

"Indians!"

Instantly men were grabbing for guns, and women were frantically pulling children to safety.

"Where are they?" Daniel Slade yelled to the guard.

"Over here!" came an answering yell, and a dozen guns were trained at once on the gap between the first and last wagon.

Ty Edwards, a skinny towheaded man of forty-five, came rushing through the gap. "We got 'em, Slade—we got the varmints!"

"What?"

Daniel stepped forward, his rifle lowered, and there was a silence as two Indians came through the gap, prodded from behind by Luke Edwards, Ty's seventeen-year-old boy, and Will Satterfield.

They were miserable specimens, resembling not in any fashion the expectations of the train. Undersized, skinny to emaciation, and dressed in rags made from the cast-off clothes of whites, they were empty-handed and looked like frightened birds as they were prodded forward by the guns of the guards.

"Any more of 'em?" Daniel asked.

"Don't think so," Satterfield answered. "They just came walking up, didn't have no guns or bows."

Daniel lowered his rifle and came to stand before the two Indians. He had a theatrical touch in his pose and his voice was too loud as he asked, "What you want? You come to fight with white men?"

The Indians stared around at the circle, and one of them stuck his hand out, saying in a guttural voice, "Want to eat."

There was nothing threatening in the two, but Slade decided that it was the time to establish the train's policy on Indians.

He began a long speech, waving his rifle in the general direction of the pair, threatening them with total destruction if they ever showed their faces around the train.

When he ended, Carl Slade grabbed the two, one in each of his hamlike hands, and brought their heads together with a sound that brought a wince to the faces of many. He towed them to the edge of the camp and sent them out into the darkness, throwing them like children.

As they painfully got to their feet and limped off into the darkness without a word, Carl grinned and said, "Reckon I'm an Indian fighter now."

Reno had moved quietly along the table, picking up some food, thrusting it into a cotton sack, and Carl saw him moving toward the spot where the Indians had disappeared.

"You an Injun lover as well as a drunk?" he asked with a harsh laugh. "Ain't no sense wastin' good food on them. You seen how easy I handled them two!"

Reno turned, and the firelight cast a flicker on his even features. His eyes were pools of darkness in the night as he said in a voice that was deceptively gentle, "You did that real easy, Slade." He gave a strange smile then, and just before he wheeled and disappeared into the darkness, he added, "I'd like to see you do it to a couple of Sioux or a Comanche war chief!"

FOUR

Sparks Fly Upward

By the time the shadows of the horses were directly under-
foot, Buck Henry was red-faced and dry-mouthed with the
scorching July heat. He glanced at his two companions, noting
that even though Dooley wore a long-sleeved cotton jacket
there was only a fine sheen of perspiration on his tanned face.
The month on the trail had burned the face of Reno to a deep
mahogany brown, and he appeared almost cool despite the blis-
tering heat.

Buck longed to drain the canteen on his saddle, but was
ashamed to display weakness before the two. Instead he stood
in his stirrups to ease his aching hind-quarters and said,
"Wish I wasn't so blasted *big!*" He eased himself down and cast
a rueful glance down at the heavy buckskin that carried his
weight. "You little fellows can get by with good horses, but I
got to ride a draft animal."

Reno smiled, the white teeth making a slash in his dust-
caked face. "Must be nice to know you can whip anybody,
Buck. Big as you are, all you'd have to do is just fall down on a
man."

"Well, it don't work that way, Jim." The huge man bit his lip and added, "I'm too big to fight anybody. You boys don't know what that means. I got to be good-natured. Got to be careful who I step on, like an elephant."

"Must save a lot of trouble," Reno observed. "Never have to wonder whether or not you can whip anybody."

"I do, though. I look at some little fellow and ask myself, 'Wonder if I can lick him? Wonder if I've got as much brass as him?' But I can't fight him and find out. I'm too big. Now you know what you can do, both of you, 'cause you've been in some fights, but I—I just ain't sure what I'd do if it came to a real eye-gouger! What you think—"

Kapong! Kapong!

Buck was cut off as Reno drew his Colt and got off two shots so close together they sounded like one rolling explosion. All three horses shied at the sudden sound, and Buck nearly fell off. "What was *that* for?" he gasped, regaining his seat. Reno spurred forward, his gun seeming to slide back into his holster of its own accord. With a grace that made the act seem easy, he bent down out of the saddle and picked up two bloody bundles of feathers—two prairie chickens—and held them up. "Supper!" he said with satisfaction.

Dooley had been watching Reno as he drew and shot, and she could not believe what she had seen. The hand had blurred and there was no hesitation between the draw and the explosion. She bit her lip and said nothing, but it was something to remember.

"You've kept the pot full, Jim," she said finally. "We haven't had to use much store-bought grub."

"Try to please the boss," Reno said with a straight face. Then he added, "When we get to buffer country, you'll really see some eating."

"How long you figure, Jim?" Buck asked.

Reno waved his hand toward the horizon. "Could see some stragglers anytime—maybe today."

The Platte valley was a plain, bare of trees, the land rising in sandstone cliffs to the north, higher and more broken each day. They had passed through prairie-dog villages covering five hundred acres, and the plain abounded with wildlife—antelope and coyotes, grizzlies and black bears.

Reno, Dooley, and Buck had left the train early to hunt for game, but also to try to discover how far they were from the Platte River. Only a little over an hour after Reno had shot the prairie chickens, they crested a rise and Reno said, "There she is, boys."

Buck had heard about the Platte and thought he had it pictured in his mind, but what he saw when his horse stood on the summit was beyond belief. He had been brought up in mountain country, and now the earth before him was so flat the distance ran off past his line of vision. The sky seemed to tilt crazily to meet the flattened ground. He had never known *distance* before. He had lived shut off by trees and hills. The world was a play world for dolls, and distance was a quarter of a mile to the next rise.

"Look at it, Jim! Look at it!"

The three of them stared across the vast plain, and Dooley whispered, "I never knew anything was like this!"

"Makes a man feel a mite small, for a fact," Reno said softly. Then he nodded toward the west, where a river sluiced across the plain, punctuated by a line of cottonwoods and willows. "Let's water the horses and get back."

The horses drank thirstily, and the three men had a drink. The water tasted brackish, but it was fairly cool under the shade of the stunted cottonwoods. Reno said, "Know what, boys? I got a notion to sluice away about fifty pounds of dust. I ain't had a bath since we left Missouri."

Buck nodded and said, "Sounds good, Jim," and began pulling his shirt off.

Dooley stood there paralyzed as the two men removed their shirts, then she gasped and made a run at her horse. She grabbed the reins and was ready to swing into the saddle, when a pair of strong hands caught her and pulled her around.

"Where you headed, Dooley?" Reno asked. There was a bright amusement in his dark eyes as he held her easily. "You got to learn to have some respect for your fellowman. Here, I'll be all nice and smelling sweet and you'll still smell like a buffalo hunter."

He pulled her toward the stream with one hand, with the other plucking at the cotton jacket she wore. "You dirty boy! Don't you ever bathe?"

Buck was doubled up with laughter as Reno ignored Dooley's frantic struggle, calling out, "That's right, Jim! Give the baby a bath!"

Dooley was screaming, "You turn me loose!" but her frantic struggles were useless against the iron strength of Reno. She felt the jacket slip off, and as a steely-fingered grip grasped the front of her thin shirt she drew back a sharp-toed boot and drove it against Reno's leg with all the force she had.

"Ow!" Reno squalled. He hopped about on one foot, his face contorted with pain. "You crazy kid! You broke my leg!"

Dooley made a wild dash for her horse, mounted, and without a backward look headed back toward the train. Her face was flaming and she knew that the thin shirt revealed her figure, so she did not turn but galloped out of sight over the rise as Reno hollered, "Dooley! Wait a minute! You can get lost out there!"

"Haw! Haw! I guess you'll let the boss tend to his own bathing next time!" Buck laughed.

"Fool kid!" Reno said, testing his leg carefully. "I'll have to give him a paddling sooner or later." He slipped out of the rest of his clothes, and he and Buck splashed and enjoyed the water for half an hour, then dressed and headed back in the direction of the train.

Buck Henry cast several looks at Reno, and finally said awkwardly, "Jim, I been meaning to talk to you about something."

"Shoot, Buck."

"Well, it's about—" Buck stopped abruptly. "Well, we're going to have trouble sooner or later."

"What kind of trouble, Buck?"

Again there was a noticeable pause in the big man's speech. "What I mean is, we're all cooped up together like, and I been noticin' Miz Burns has been carryin' on with Beau."

Reno said lazily, "Noticed that."

"Sure, everybody has," Buck went ahead eagerly, adding quickly, "Course, I don't think she's a *bad* woman—just a flirt."

Reno did not look at Buck. He kept his eyes fixed on a herd of antelope that swept across the plain in the distance. His voice was gentle and he said, "Well, Buck, I guess you'd be right in that. And maybe you've noticed that Ellie has been keeping the young bucks stirred up, too."

If Reno had struck him in the stomach the big man could not have been more speechless. His mouth dropped open and his face worked nervously. For all his massive form and terrible strength, he was basically a simple fellow. He mustered a weak grin and said breathlessly, "I—I guess you read me pretty good, Jim."

Reno swept his gaze around, and there was a steady ease in his dark eyes that was, somehow, a comfort to Buck. "Ellie's not a bad girl, Buck. Just needs a good man."

"Yeah, I know, but I'm not exactly what she's looking for."

"Take a try, Buck. She'll be handful, I'll admit."

Buck nodded glumly, and there was a sadness in his voice. "She likes 'em flashy, Jim. Ain't got much flash myself."

"Life is tough, Buck," Reno said. He looked off toward the sandstone rise to his left. "'Man is born to trouble as the sparks fly upward,' the Book says."

Buck did not miss the twist of Reno's lip, a look of pain that broke through his calm expression. "Guess you've had your share, Jim. Didn't mean to cry on your shoulder."

"Buck, I reckon a bunch of folks are going to be cryin' before we hit Oregon. This is a tough trip—nobody seems to think so, but I'm tellin' you there'll be some markers set up between here and the coast." A grim sobriety passed across his dark features, and Buck saw for the first time beneath the iron control of the man, and it shook him.

They said little until they pulled up to Slade's wagon a little past noon. Something was wrong, they both saw at once. The small fires built at noon were lit, but small groups were drawn together, and there was an angry light on Daniel Slade's face.

Reno and Henry were met by Barney Moore and Vinson Grant. Both of them looked angry and Buck asked, "What's wrong, Vinson?"

"We got a sick man."

"Who?"

"Pete Prather."

"What's his trouble?"

"Dunno," Vinson said, "but he ain't good."

"We'll move on!" Daniel Slade nodded shortly, an impetuous arrogance in his face. "We can't hold up for one man."

"We ain't decided that, Slade," Vinson said sharply.

"I'm wagon master—and I'll say when we move on."

"Hold on, now," Barney Moore said. He stood there, a tall, gangling shape in the hot sun, his face pinched around his toothless mouth. "Maybe we can work out something."

"Your ma is with him, Buck." Vinson ignored Barney and stared at Slade with a cold dislike in his sharp face. "We ain't gonna kill a man just to make a few miles."

He whirled and walked away, and the rest of them followed to the Prather's wagon.

Pete Prather lay under the wagon, his face flushed and his eyes closed. He was breathing rapidly, and Lena bathed his forehead with a damp rag.

"How are you, Pete?" Buck asked. He placed his hand on the old man's shoulder in a gesture that was unusual in such a big man.

Pete opened his eyes but seemed not to recognize anyone. He licked his lips and closed his eyes.

"You can't be that sick, man," Slade said.

Buck looked across at Slade and said in a rougher voice than anyone had heard him use, "Slade, he's too sick to move. Pull the wagons in a circle."

The order struck against Daniel Slade like a whip, and he rose at once saying, "If I say we move out, we move out."

Then Buck stepped close to Slade. His massive form made the other man look like a child, and he looked down with

an anger on his round face that caused the wagon master to
step back with a sudden movement. He opened his mouth, but
Buck suddenly reached out, and his massive hand closed on
Slade's shoulder like a trap. He gave what was meant to be a
gentle shake, and the tall figure of Slade was swept like he was
weightless. "Mister Slade, you're wagon master, but you can't
move this man. Now draw the wagons around!"

Slade fell back as Buck released him. He was breathing
hard, and his hand dropped to the gun on his side, but when
Vinson Grant touched his own Colt, Slade said, "Well, see to
him! But we move tomorrow morning for sure!"

As he left, Lena looked up, a light of gratitude on her plain
face. "Thanks, Mr. Henry."

Reno stared at the round face of the young man and gave
him a sudden punch on the massive arm. "You done the necessary, Buck."

Buck flushed at the word of approval and turned to his
mother. "What is it, Ma?"

"I don't rightly know, Buck," Alice Henry said. "I hope it
ain't cholera."

The word sent a chill through everyone there. All knew
that along some stretches of the Oregon Trail graves were so
numerous that the trail developed a saw-toothed edge—a border of footpaths worn by the curious going off to the side to
read the wooden grave markers. Most of them read "Died of
Cholera." The virulent Asiatic plague had moved up the Missis-
sippi valley from New Orleans. It spread its horror of vomiting,
diarrhea, fever, convulsions, and death along the roads from
Independence out into the Platte valley. At some of the larger
campsites an entire cemetery was required for its victims.
Reno knew that only the higher elevation of the Rocky Mountains could stop it.

Reno squatted down and looked carefully into Prather's face. "Could be camp fever."

"What's that?" Lena asked quickly, hope in her face.

"Camp fever. No other name to it."

"Is it catchin'?" Mrs. Henry asked.

"No."

Reno got to his feet, and there was a scurry as the women began to fix a better bed for Prather, talking themselves into believing that calomel was the best thing for the sick man, rather than Sarsaparilla Blood Pills, Balsam of Life, or bloodletting.

All afternoon the camp was busy, women using water from a nearby stream to catch up on their washing, men busy with patching up wagons and a dozen other chores that had been put off. Dooley, who had run from Reno and Buck when they bathed in the Platte, took advantage of the clear water and had a much-needed sponge bath in the privacy of the wagon. With herself and her clothing all cleaned, she hoped the incident by the Platte would not be repeated.

Slade stayed close to his wagon, a cloud on his face. "Ought to be moving," he complained to Beau and Carl. "System is the thing. A time to get up, a time to travel, a time to bed down. Only way we'll get to Oregon. Got to have discipline."

"You shouldn't have let Henry push you into stayin' here, Pa," Carl said. "He might get some kind of fool idea that he can make decisions for us."

"Needs a little lesson, Carl," Beau said with a nod, and the two exchanged a look and nodded as if agreed.

Night had fallen, and from the firelights of a dozen campfires, sparks swirled into the sky in a lazy dance.

Jackson and Leah had put away the pots and pans, coming back to join the others seated around the fire. Dooley had ignored Reno, who sat gazing out into the moonlit plain, and Jude Finney broke the silence.

"Mighty good cookin', Leah." He looked over across at the Prather's wagon and said, "I think I better go over and pray for Brother Prather." Then he looked at Reno and said softly, "Guess you don't see much use in that, do you, Jim?"

Reno shrugged. "You better do it if you think it's right, Jude."

The lanky preacher sat there, gazing across the fire at Reno, then asked, "Don't believe in much, do you, Jim?"

"Not too much."

"Shame. You're too hard." He got up and ambled across the circle in his loose-jointed fashion. A small group was gathering around a fire close to the Prather wagon, including Addie Grant and both her brothers. Jude had gotten to know the trio very well, and he paused beside Addie to ask, "He any better?"

"I don't think so, Reverend." Some of the settlers called Jude that in sport, but there was no mockery in Addie Grant's face as she stood beside him. In the darkness the smallpox scars were invisible, and there was a beauty in her face that made Jude feel awkward.

"I thought I'd pray for him."

"Yes. You should do that." She turned and the two of them went to where Lena and Marie were sitting beside Pete. Clyde and Leon, Pete's twin boys, watched carefully as Jude approached with Addie. "Brother Finney wants to have prayer with Pete, Lena."

"Oh, I—I think that would be fine," Lena said. She touched the face of her husband tenderly, and there was something in the act that wrenched at the soul of Finney. The youth of the wife, her innocence and devotion to the time-blasted figure of Pete Prather, moved him. When he prayed there was a strain of compassion that went beyond his usual concern.

He said, "Lord, I call your attention to your servant, Pete." The low mumble of talk around the wagon fell silent, and the simple words of the tall, gangling man carried on the air clearly. The twins looked surprised, then Clyde shrugged, and both of them looked down at the ground.

"You've brought us on this journey, Lord God," Finney said in a conversational tone, "and we've trusted you from the start. Pete is a good man, and he has a wife and a family. Lord, will you spare him? Not because he deserves it, for he is a weak man, as we all are. But spare him because you are a God who delights in mercy. Let your mighty hand light on Pete and restore his strength."

He paused and said, "I ask you to do this in the name of Jesus Christ."

The brevity of the prayer caught most of those who listened off guard, being accustomed to prayers that ran up to thirty minutes or more from the frontier preachers.

Jude touched Lena on the shoulder and said, "Sister, I have a hope that your husband will be made whole. Will you believe with me on that?"

Tears glistened like diamonds in Lena Prather's large eyes, caught by the light of the flickering fire, and she whispered, "Yes. Thank you, Brother Finney!"

He nodded his head awkwardly and moved away from the wagon. Addie walked with him across the open space and she said, "That was good, Reverend."

"I ain't no Reverend, Addie," he said quickly. "I got no education. Just a call from the Lord to spread his Word."

She paused and he stopped with her. She leaned against the side of a wagon and asked, "What will you do in Oregon?"

He struggled as if there were something keeping him from speaking freely, then said with a halting voice, "Well, Addie, I—I guess it sounds crazy—at least it did to everyone back home. But what I got to do is preach the gospel to the Indians."

"Why, Jude, that's not crazy," Addie said quickly, and her smile in the moonlight was gentle. "I think that's wonderful!"

He laughed and slapped his leg suddenly. "That's not what folks said back in Virginia. They said I was out of my mind. Guess they had reason. There I was, a plain blacksmith, not even a good church member. All of a sudden I was going across the whole country to preach."

She gave him a warm smile, saying, "It must have taken great courage, Jude."

Her use of his first name sent a warmth through Jude, but he shook his head and remained silent so long that she asked quietly, "What's the matter?"

"I—I ain't told you all of it," he said. Then he looked directly into her eyes and said, "I—I can't read, Addie. Not a word. Can't write my own name." He tried to keep his voice steady, but suddenly there was raw desperation in his tone as he cried out, "How can I do it? How can a man preach if he can't read the Word of God?"

He ducked his head, ashamed at his outburst. He gritted his teeth and turned to go.

"Jude." She put her hand on his arm, and when he turned to face her, shame in his homely face, she said quietly, "I'll teach you to read."

He stood there, head bowed, and there was a swimming

in his mind and a moistness in his eyes. He had endured the taunts of many, and her kindness left him vulnerable.

"You can learn," she urged. "I—I'd like to do it, Jude. If you would let me."

He stood there for so long she thought she had offended him. But then he said, "It would be a wonderful thing to be able to read, Addie. I—I'd like it more than anything."

She saw how moved he was, and she said quickly, "Let's begin now, Jude. I've got some paper. And I'll get my Bible." She led him to her wagon and soon he was staring at the open Bible, watching as her finger traced the words.

Over near her wagon, Dooley was staring into the fire, thinking of the journey to come, when Reno's voice broke the silence.

"Leah," he said lazily, "you have anything to do with raising this boy?"

"Sho!" Leah said instantly. "Why you ask?"

"Well, I got to tell you, Leah, you didn't do a very good job."

"How is dat?"

"Why, he won't take a bath." Dooley's face flamed at the memory, and she wanted to fling the stick in her hand at his face as he went on, "We had a nice bath this afternoon, me and Buck, and Dooley wouldn't even come close."

"Is dat a fack?" Both Leah and Jackson burst out laughing, and Leah said, "Well, he ain't real partial to soap, fo' a truf!"

"Found that out," Reno said, turning to smile at Dooley, who stared at him with hatred. "Why, I even tried to help him, and the fool boy acted like I was going to scalp him. Dooley, you maybe haven't had a bath because you think it's unhealthy or something. Now the next time we get close to a creek, I'm going to prove to you bathin' ain't dangerous to your health. Yep, I'm gonna' scrub you down good."

"You put a hand on me and I'll shoot you, Reno! I had a bath not two hours ago. I don't need any help from you at—at bathin' or anything else—and you two shut your fool mouths!" she yelled at Leah and Jackson, who were doubled over with laughter.

Reno was laughing as well, but he stopped suddenly and got to his feet. He listened intently, then stepped out into the night.

Dooley and Lee got up at once and followed him. The sound of angry voices carried on the night air, and they made their way to where a group made a circle around several figures.

Reno stayed slightly outside, pulling Dooley back when she tried to crowd in. "Stay here," he said quietly. "May be trouble."

"Who is it?" she whispered.

"Looks like Burns and Beau."

"Oh." Dooley stood on tiptoe, and she saw the small figure of Robert Burns standing tensely in front of Beau Slade.

"Burns, you got it all wrong," Beau was saying. He was smiling and there was a jeer in his tone as he stared down at the small figure in front of him. "You ought not to say things like that in public. Don't you trust your wife?"

Jane Ann Burns stood at the edge of the crowd, her hands twitching nervously, but there was a light in her eyes that revealed that the sight of two men arguing over her was not unpleasant.

Burns was a small man, colorless in contrast to the florid masculinity of Beau Slade. Stubbornly he stood there, arms rigidly at his sides and his words coming in a rush, in a breathless tone as if he were afraid they would not be said. That he was afraid of Slade was obvious, but he stood his ground.

"You're a dog, Slade. You've been after every woman on this train, and I'm telling you to stay away from me and stay away from my wife."

"Well, now, that's fightin' talk, Burns," Beau said, and his teeth flashed in the firelight. He was a fighting man, and the wildness in him demanded release. He moved closer to Burns and said, "I don't take that talk from any man, Burns. You'll have to back it up."

Burns stood there before him, and for one moment, Dooley thought he meant to launch himself at Slade. It would have been futile, for in any sort of fight the slim Scot would be no match for Beau Slade.

Then he said in a shaky voice, "I—I'm not a fighting man, Slade."

Beau laughed harshly and said with contempt, "Well, you better take lessons then, Burns, because if you ever open your mouth to me again about your wife . . ." He grinned at Jane Ann swiftly, and seemed to enjoy the moment. "I'll put you down for keeps."

Dooley saw the restless movement go through the crowd, and she said so quietly that only Reno heard her, "It's not fair!"

"Hush!" he said, and they were both turning to go, not willing to watch the way that Beau turned to claim Jane Ann's attention. She was staring at her husband with contempt, and she shook her hair and gave Beau a smile as he came to stand beside her.

"Mrs. Burns, you shouldn't treat your husband like that."

The huge figure of Buck Henry loomed in front of Jane

Ann, and she flushed as he stood over her, looking at her with concern in his round face.

"Henry, you can butt out right now!" Beau said. He was still smiling, but there was a threat in the way he stood there watching Buck. A feline sort of cruelty in his handsome face showed that he was ready to fight. "You want some trouble, Buck?"

"Wait a minute, Beau," a voice said, and Carl Slade stepped into the circle. He was holding the arm of Ellie Satterfield, and there was a glitter in the girl's bold eyes as she became the center of attraction.

"You're real concerned about other men's wives, ain't you, Henry?" Carl said with a wicked grin. He nodded toward Ellie and said, "Everybody knows how you been following Ellie around like a sick puppy."

A sudden, dizzying rush of blood came over Buck. "I—I—don't know what you mean, Carl."

"I mean Ellie's my girl, and I don't want you even *lookin'* at her as long as we're on this trip. You hear me?"

Buck looked down at the ground, and there was a roaring in his ears. He had never said one word of affection to Ellie, but she had not been ignorant of his interest. Now he glanced up and saw that she was watching him, curious and alert for his response. Even as he looked she gave him a full smile, and he could not help himself from doing what he knew was a foolish thing.

"I won't promise that, Slade. It's up to her."

"No, it ain't! It's up to me!" Carl moved very quickly for a large man. He was six inches shorter and fifty pounds lighter than Buck, but he was a bruising bully of a man, a barroom brawler who knew every trick in the book. With one smooth motion he whipped his arm back and drove his fist into Buck's face.

The blow made a meaty sound and drove Buck backward a step, but no more. It would have knocked an average man unconscious, and there was a gasp when he did not fall. Carl Slade gaped at him, but there was no fear in the man, and he moved forward driving Buck backward with looping blows that landed with terrible power.

A suppressed cry went up from the crowd as Slade drove Buck toward the center of the camp, sledging blow after blow into the face and body. "Wear him down, Carl! He's nothing but a lump of butter!" Beau yelled.

Buck stumbled backward, trying to stop the torrent of blows. He had never had a fight in his life, and the strength that enabled him to lift the rear of a wagon single-handed was useless to him. The hard fists of Slade cut his face, mashing his lips to shreds against his teeth, and his eyes were both swollen and filled with blood as hard knuckles split his eyebrows. He fell backward, and even as he got to his feet a terrible kick from Slade's boot caught him in the kidney, sending unbelievable pain through his body. He tried to strike out, to catch hold of Carl, but he was blinded by the blood in his eyes, and terror seized him. He had never felt helpless in his life, but the awful blows drumming into his face and tearing into his midsection destroyed something in him.

With a small cry, he fell to the ground and drew himself into a ball.

Carl drew back his foot to kick the helpless man, but Vinson Grant stepped forward saying, "That's enough, Slade."

"You want trouble, Grandpa?" Carl snarled. He stood there, his huge arms dangling, and he was weaving like an animal.

Vinson Grant was a small man. There was nothing in his appearance that could have been a threat to the huge man in front of him. But he said in a clear voice, "You're scum, Carl—you too, Beau." And when Carl moved forward lifting his arms to crush the older man, Vinson Grant pulled a Navy Colt and leveled it toward the eyes of the charging man. "Come on, scum," he said softly. "I'd like to do it. You too, Beau," he said, shifting the heavy weapon to cover Beau who was reaching for his gun.

Beau stopped abruptly and said quickly, "Come on, Carl. He's whipped."

Carl looked around at the group, pleased with himself. He avoided meeting the eyes of Vinson Grant, and took Ellie by the arm. "Come on, let's have a drink, Ellie!" he said, and the pair moved off, followed by Beau.

There was a strange quiet, and Jane Ann Burns felt very much alone. Beau had not glanced at her, and she could not meet the eyes of any of those in the circle as she slipped away into the darkness.

Others turned quickly away, embarrassed now that it was over.

Reno waited until the others had gone, Dooley at his side. Buck slowly uncurled, got painfully to his feet, and turned his back on the pair.

"Buck," Reno said, and his voice was almost a whisper. "Everybody gets licked."

The big man did not turn, and Dooley wanted to run to him, but she realized that nobody could help him with this.

"Know what hurts the most?" Reno went on, and although Buck did not turn, he waited, listening to the voice. "You got some lumps that ache a little—but that's not the worst. The

bad thing is that you got whipped in front of folks." Buck
started as if caught in a guilty secret, but Reno went on, a sadness in his tone that held the big man. "Man never gets used
to that, Buck, getting whipped to the ground. I felt it when I
stacked my gun at Appomattox, and I've been beat so bad I
thought the sun wouldn't come up—and I hoped it wouldn't."
Then he said. "You got to whip that man, Buck. You got to!"

Buck stood stock-still, then shook his head and stumbled
toward his wagon without a word.

Dooley felt like crying. "What will happen to him, Jim?

Reno stared down at Dooley and said, "He'll either grow
up—or he'll die, I reckon. That's about the only two choices a
man's got in this world, son."

FIVE
Incident at Laramie

Late August bore down like a weight on the train as it crawled laboriously along, clinging to the meandering bank of the Platte. What thin grass remained was full of stickers and burrs, and the land was so rocky and coarse nobody could walk on the trail without boots. Dead animals—mostly mules, but oxen, too—littered the sides of the rough trail, and the sand was loose and blazing hot, causing the wagons to sink eighteen inches in the worst spots. Many of the animals developed ulcers in their noses, and if Vinson Grant had not known to treat them with a weak solution of alum, they might have turned into full-fledged cases of glanders.

Many of the wagons were in bad shape, and it was clear that some would not last the journey. The wheels, being constantly immersed in hot sand, took punishment of the most damaging kind. The felloes and naves shrunk, the tires loosened, and the spokes rattled like bags of bones. Several times they were wedged and submerged in water, but this was only a stop-gap remedy.

The train crossed the South Platte, with every wagon double-yoked and with ropes strung between some. The picnic spirit so evident the first few weeks had been ground down by the heat and heavy labor of walking through the sand. Nobody rode except the drivers and the very old and children. The rest walked to the sides of the wagons, far enough to avoid the clouds of choking dust raised by the wagon wheels. Everyone kept an eye out for firewood, and every branch was a treasure that had to be carried to the wagon and kept for the small cooking fires. For the most part, sagebrush had to be used, though Reno told Dooley that when they hit buffalo, fires would be no problem. The flat, dried chips, which he had called "pasture pancakes," made hot fires.

After Ash Flat, a fine campsite with several cold springs and many scattered groves of ash, the trail followed the banks of the North Platte for about fifty miles. The heat seemed worse after the cold springs, and Dooley scuffed along looking for firewood, feeling filthy to the bone.

"How much farther is it, Dooley—to Fort Laramie?" Marie Prather moved into step with Dooley and smiled as she waited for an answer. Dooley had been amused when the girl had begun hanging around, but the crush had become an annoyance.

"You better git shed of dat leetle ol' gal, Dooley," Jackson had said with a wide grin. "She gonna die wif grief when she finds out you ain't no young buck!"

Dooley had tried being abrupt and gruff, but Marie apparently liked whatever attitude she adopted. Even now Marie grabbed at her arm, as she took every opportunity to do, and said, "When we get to Laramie, maybe we can go looking at the stores together, Dooley."

"Don't guess we'll be there long," Dooley grunted. To her relief, Ellie Satterfield came up from behind and joined them.

"Where's Jim, Dooley?" she asked.

"Riding drag."

"Oh." Ellie glanced back toward the cloud of dust in the rear that marked the progress of the herd, then swept the horizon. "Lookee there—that's Chimney Rock." She pointed to a sharp point of rock rising from the flat plain. "Jim said when we got past that, we'd only be two or three days out of Laramie."

"He's just guessing," Dooley said shortly.

Ellie smiled and there was a sensual tone in her voice as she shook her head, "No, Jim ain't a man to do much guessing." She took Dooley by the arm and laughed. "I guess it takes a woman to see what Jim Reno is, Dooley."

Pulling away from the girl's strong grasp, Dooley snapped, "You linin' up all the men on the train, Ellie? Looks like the Slades would keep you busy."

"Why, Dooley, I swear!" Ellie laughed with delight and moved close to give Dooley a sudden hug. "I believe you're *jealous!* And if I was a mind to do me a little cradle-robbin', why, I'd set my cap for you. You are a good-lookin' boy!"

Ellie's grip was so strong that Dooley could not pull away for a moment, and Marie said shortly, "You're going to have them fighting over you if you don't quit stirring them up!"

"Why, what's wrong with that, Marie? That's what men are supposed to do over a pretty girl."

"Well, I think it's just awful!" Marie said, her face flushed. "I mean, about the way Buck has been since he got whipped!"

Ellie frowned for a moment. "I like Buck, but he's got to grow up."

"What about Mr. Burns?" Dooley asked. "He hasn't said ten words since his wife made a fool out of him."

"He ought to fight for her, Dooley," Ellie said. "If he can't take care of a women, he don't need one."

"You know he's not a fighting man," Marie said. "And anyway, I doubt if there's any of the men could stand up to them Slades."

"Oh, I guess there may be one," Ellie said with a strange smile.

"There's some brush," Dooley said, and left abruptly, making for a gully a hundred yards to the south. She waited until she was out of earshot, then muttered, "She'd like nothin' better than to see two men cutting each other to pieces over her!" Reaching the small dead branch, she yanked at it angrily. "She'd better leave Jim alone. I won't—" Then, standing still for a moment, she broke off and stared at the cloud of dust at the rear of the train. Vexed with herself for some reason she could not understand, she said, "What do *I* care what she does?"

Reno and Lee came back to the wagon at noon. The train halted and new men went to take the dirty job of riding drag. Reno and Lee were coated with fine dust. Dooley watched while they washed up in the river. Both of them had removed their shirts, and she could not help the reluctant admiration that passed through her as Reno splashed in the tepid water. He had broad shoulders capped by thick pads of muscles, and there was an economy in his trim waist. His stomach was flat with small squares of muscle beneath a swelling chest, and he had so little fat that every move he made sent cables of muscle into movement.

He stuck his head into the water, and remarked while drying his black hair with his shirt, "Dernedest river in the world, the Platte. Too dirty to bathe in and too thick to drink."

Lee grinned at him and said, "It's about an inch deep and a mile wide, ain't it, Jim?"

"Just about, Lee."

"Carl saw buffalo today," Dooley said. "He went out to shoot some, but didn't get one."

Reno nodded and slipped into his shirt, "Seen 'em over to the west. Want to go for one, Lee?"

"Yeah!" Lee said with his eyes glowing. "Can I take a shot, Jim?"

"Sure."

"I'm going," Dooley said.

"All right."

Reno borrowed a Sharps from Pete Prather, who had recovered somewhat from his fever. Dooley picked up her .44 Henry. "We won't need the horses," he said, and led them across the plain toward the west.

"Carl said he hit several but couldn't kill them."

"Hard to bring down a buffer," Reno said. They had been walking for nearly an hour, and suddenly he stopped and pointed. "There they are."

He started walking forward and soon Dooley saw a small herd of wooly humps. "Shouldn't we sneak up on them—crawl or something?"

Reno laughed. "No need. They ain't spooked by a man on foot."

He led them to within a hundred yards of the animals and said, "Close enough. Plop down there and shoot that big bull, Dooley. Use the Sharps."

She lay down and put the sight of the big weapon on the big head.

"Hit him right behind the shoulder," Reno said.

She pulled the trigger and the recoil from the Sharps hurt her shoulder.

"You got him!" Reno said. "I seen the dust fly right on target!"

Dooley looked up and said, "Why doesn't he fall?"

"He will." Reno seemed confident enough, and as they watched, the massive beast took two steps, swung his head from side to side, then lay over heavily. He kicked a time or two, then sank slowly into death.

"Get the cow beside him," Reno said.

"I don't want to," Dooley said. She got up and handed the rifle to Reno. "Let Lee have a shot."

Reno looked at her and saw that the killing of the bull had disturbed her. He didn't comment but handed the rifle to Lee. "Take the cow, boy."

Lee grabbed the gun and missed with the first shot, but put the animal down with the second. "I got her, Jim! I got her!"

Dooley was watching Reno. There was a small smile on his broad lips, and he nodded as if agreeing with something. "First buffer—something you'll tell your grandkids about, Lee."

"Can I get another one?"

"One more. That'll be meat enough for the whole train."

Lee knocked the third animal down with one shot, and they advanced to look at the kill. The rest of the herd moved away leisurely.

"They're not afraid," Dooley marveled.

"Nope. And that'll be the end of them," Reno said. "Won't be any herds left in twenty years or less."

"Oh, that's sad!"

A dark shadow passed across the man's face. There was a solidness about him, yet beneath the tough surface lay a streak of fatality, and Dooley hated to see it.

They made their way back to the train, and when they walked into the circle they were surrounded. Lee said at once, "We got three—Dooley got one and I got two all by myself."

The Slades had come close, and there was a flush on Carl's face as he heard the boy. He growled loudly, "Beginner's luck. Well, let's go git the meat."

He half-turned, but Reno's voice, soft as a summer breeze, stopped him.

"You ain't said 'Please' yet, Slade."

The burly figure of Carl Slade whipped around and there was raw anger on his broad face. "What's that you say, drunk?"

The violence that flared out of the man slashed across the quietness of the afternoon air. Dooley found it hard to swallow, her throat suddenly constricted. Reno looked almost slight as he stood easily in front of Carl, and she thought of how Buck Henry had been destroyed by those hammer-hard fists.

Ellie Satterfield moved closer, watching Reno the way a woman will watch a man. He made a vivid image before her— so solid and alert, so thoroughly masculine. The small smile, she thought, was a sign of his character. It showed the world a serene indifference, yet in it too was a sadness that seemed to imply that he had lost contact with the world and could depend on nobody but himself. It was as if he had fought too much and had played his chances out to the thin end.

The silence ran on, then Reno said, "Slade, if you're going to tree your coon, why, you just fly right at it."

The words, soft and almost offhanded, caused Carl to draw himself into a hunched shape, and there was a wildness in his face that warned everyone who saw it that he was ready to launch himself at Reno.

"Carl!" Daniel Slade pushed himself forward, stepping

between his son and Reno. His craggy face was angry, but he said, "I guess they're your buffer, Reno. I had hoped we could have a little cooperation on this train."

Reno shrugged and said, "There's plenty for everybody. Your son is too brash."

Carl jerked away from his father's restraining hand, casting a poisonous look at the smaller man, and walked toward his own wagon.

"He'll have a try at you sooner or later, Jim," Vinson Grant murmured as the crowd broke up. "Should have killed him."

"Not a killing matter, Vinson."

The old man snorted, the fire of battle in his eyes. "That Slade is a dog!"

"In that, you are right," Reno agreed. "But I guess he'll have to give me a better excuse to pull a gun on him."

Vinson stared at him, then shook his head. He went back to his wagon where Addie and R.G. were waiting. "I'll go help cut up the meat. You want to come, R.G.?"

"Sure do." The maimed face of the younger Vinson lit up, and he hurried away to get their horses.

"It was almost bad, wasn't it?" Addie said. She shook her head and there was trouble in her fine eyes. "I'd hate to see that Carl Slade ruin Jim like he did that Henry boy."

"He won't do that, Addie. Reno ain't like Buck. I seen too many like him in the war. He moves around slick as silk, and he talks soft. But let me tell you, if Carl Slade ever bucks up against Jim Reno, he'll think he's bumped into a buzz saw." He looked over suddenly at Addie and said, "How you doin' with the preacher—the readin' lessons?"

She met his gaze with a slight tinge of red in her cheeks.

"He's real quick, Vinson. It's—it's little enough to do for a servant of the Lord."

He held her eyes, and there was humor in his face. He put his hand on her shoulder and said, "Watch out for him, Addie. You know how these preachers are."

"Why, Vinson Grant!" she said smiling, putting up a hand to cover her burning cheek. "How can you think of such a thing!"

"You should have married, Addie," Vinson said, and there was a heaviness in his face. He shook his head and added, "You gave up a home to take care of all of us."

"No. Who'd want a woman scarred like this?" She touched her pitted face and saw that he was sad. "I've been happy, Vinson. Don't grieve over me."

"Men are fools!" he said, then turned to mount the horse that R.G. brought to him.

Fort Laramie had been the goal for so long that when the train finally reached there, most of the settlers were disappointed.

The fort itself was made out of the meanest kind of adobe, undecorated, formed in a military quadrangle. The walls had watchtowers on the corners, and the gate was protected by two brass swivel cannons. Along one side of the court, built into walls, were offices and storerooms and mechanical shops, like a smithy, and against the opposite wall was the main building. The whole enclosure took up about three-quarters of an acre. A few raggedy soldiers lounged here and there, along with Mexicans, Indians, traders, and trappers, the remnants of wagon trains that hadn't made it.

Slade drew the wagons around in a circle two hundred yards from the fort, and as they were making camp a tall officer rode up and dismounted. He was a tall, gray-eyed man, and although he spoke quietly, there was no doubt that he was a leader.

"Captain Colter. Who is wagon master?" he asked.

"I am. Daniel Slade."

"You're very late, Mr. Slade."

Slade was not a man to take advice or criticism. He threw his head back and said, "We'll do a little trading, and we'll be on our way in a day or two."

Colter stared at Slade, then said evenly, "I wouldn't advise it, Mr. Slade. There's a band of Sioux on the rampage. I'm waiting for reinforcements so I may take the field to round them up."

"Reckon we can take care of a few Injuns," Slade said contemptuously. "We ain't exactly babies."

Captain Colter gave him a level look, then said in a dry tone, "Your choice. If you need my help while you're here, just ask."

He turned, mounted his horse, then paused and looked across at Reno who was standing thirty feet away, his back against a wagon. He stared carefully for a long moment, then rode back to the fort.

Everybody who could be spared went into the fort, but Reno remained while Dooley and the others left. He was on his back in the shade of a wagon when a man walked into the circle, spotted him, and came over.

"Hidee," he said. "Yore name Reno?"

"That's right." Reno got to his feet and took in the visitor. He was very small, not over five-foot-six, and thin as a rail. Shaggy locks of tow-colored hair stuck out from under a dusty, worn Stetson, and he had a pair of light blue eyes, bright and quick, darting like a bird's. A large prow of a nose, a wide mouth, and a set of ears that stuck out like fans made up a homely face. He had the fair skin that never tanned, burning and peeling constantly. His neck was so long and skinny that he seemed to balance his rather large head with a bobbing motion. He wore a yellow shirt and a cowhide vest, and his skinny legs were cased in waist overalls shoved down into a pair of boots with the highest heels and the sharpest toes Reno had ever seen.

"Easy Jones—thet's me." He had a sharp grin, and his light blue eyes were intelligent as he sized up Reno. He seemed to approve of what he saw, for he bobbed his head, adding, "Hot as a June bride in a feather bed, ain't it now?"

"Sure is," Reno said with a grin.

"I met up with that wagon master you got. Stubborn as a blue-nosed mule, ain't he?"

"Pretty much."

"Jest my luck to git hooked up with a gent that looks like he et green persimmons three times a day!"

"You aim to join the train, Easy?"

"Yeah. I'm hired out to nursemaid a crazy man and his woman plumb to the coast." Jones spat a stream of amber juice, and shook his head mournfully. "Don't that take the rag off the bush, Reno?"

"Sounds interesting."

"Yeah, I reckon. Jasper's name is Algernon St. John. Comes from over the water and jest a fool to see Oregon. I was flat busted, and he waved more money in my face than I'd et punchin' cows in a year—so here I am."

"You came this far in a train?"

"Oh, yeah, but His Highness took a notion to rest up or

somethin'.'" The small cowboy winked and said, "Wait'll you see the heifer that keeps him company! Took her out of a saloon in Dodge City, and she's enough to make yore eyeballs pop!"

"You come to tell me that?"

"Aw, I come to tell you Cap'n Colter wants you to have supper with him. Come about six, he told me to say. His Highness will be there—and his lady friend." Jones stared at Reno and asked, "You must of knowed the cap'n afore, I reckon?"

Reno smiled and nodded. "A long time ago. I'm surprised he remembered."

"Seemed real anxious to see you. Said you could bring anybody you wanted with you." The bandylegged cowboy grinned and said, "You from the South, ain'cha, Jim? Well, you won't get no sawmill gravy and grits from that Yankee officer. But I will admit he don't leave much of the tablecloth showin'! I'll tell him you're comin'.'"

"Get your best duds on, you two," Reno said to Lee and Dooley when they got back from the fort. "We're eatin' high on the hog tonight."

"Who with?" Dooley asked.

"Captain Colter."

"How come he asked us, Jim?" Lee wanted to know.

Reno grinned and said only, "You two just don't know what a high-class gent you're runnin' with. Now get duded up."

Getting duded up wasn't easy for either Lee or Dooley. Leah had carefully washed out their clothes after they arrived at Laramie and had even helped Dooley trim back the thick, glossy hair and the lashes. Dooley had to keep looking as unfeminine as possible, but she wanted to look presentable for the evening's meal. She was able, while Reno and Lee were away from the wagon, to take a much-needed sponge bath.

The three of them found the way to Captain Colter's house—a low, adobe affair with a front porch running the length—and knocked on the door a little before six. A Mexican woman opened the door, nodded, and led them into a long room with a heavy wooden table in the middle. The two men at the table got up, and Captain Colter came forward putting out his hand. "Glad to see you, Reno. I thought I recognized you this afternoon. Had to ask around to be certain it was really you. You look a little different from the last time we met."

"Had a full beard. And I was pretty young, too." Reno paused and said, "Didn't think you'd remember me, Captain."

The gray eyes of the officer were warm as he shook his head. "Not likely to forget a man who saves your life, are you now?"

"Don't think it would have come to that," Reno protested. Then he turned and said, "This is Dooley Judd. And this is Lee Morgan."

"Glad to meet you." Colter turned and nodded to the other man in the room. "This is Mr. St. John."

"How do?" the man said, extending his hand. He was a very tall man and was wearing an expensive-looking suit, complete with cuff links and cravat. He looked lazy, but Reno noted that the mild blue eyes had a sharpness not seen in lazy men, and there was a hint of subtle humor on his broad lips.

"Sit down, all of you," the officer said, and soon the Mexican woman was bringing in a series of hot dishes—mostly Mexican, but with some fine potatoes tasting fresh in their jackets. "Mary raises a fine garden," Colter said as he urged them to try the fresh vegetables. "An old bachelor like me is lucky to have a cook like her."

"Mighty good after camp grub," Reno said. He smiled at Colter and said, "So you decided to stay in after the war?"

"Oh, yes," Colter said, nodding. "A family thing." He smiled and added, "I insist that I might not be here if you hadn't taken a hand in my problem."

"What happened, Captain?" Dooley asked.

"Oh, I'd been captured after Chickamauga by some marauders much like Quantrell's bunch. They didn't believe in taking prisoners much, and I was wounded, which made me more of a liability. They were about ready to finish me off when Sergeant Reno shows up with a squad and rescues me."

"Don't think they would have done it, Captain," Reno protested. "And you had to spend some hard time at Belle Island. I heard about that place!"

"It was bad enough—but not as bad as being shot down by that bunch of pirates. And they *would* have done it, Reno!" he added vigorously. "It wouldn't have been the first time soldiers were butchered by scum like that." His face lit up, and he laughed aloud. "I remember so well how you 'persuaded' their leader to let me go with you!"

"What did he do?" St. John asked, his eyes fixed on Reno.

"Man's name was Jakes—called himself Colonel Jakes. He started cursing and held a gun up to my head, so Sergeant Reno pulled a Colt out of his belt and blew the scoundrel's brains out—offered to do the same for any of his men who objected."

"I say, that must have been a relief!" St. John exclaimed.

"Yes," Colter said dryly. "I had given up on the thing already. I tried to write to you once, but the letter came back. So, here's my thanks to you, Sergeant Reno. Never thought I'd see you again."

Reno shifted in his chair and looked embarrassed. He shook his head and protested, "Should never have happened, Captain. Buzzards like that bunch were on nobody's side except their own."

They heard the door open and a woman stepped inside. They all rose, and St. John said, "This is Miss Jean Lamarr." He introduced the men, and Dooley took in the woman, who sat down next to St. John.

She was very beautiful in a bold, flashy way: high color in her cheeks, large greenish eyes with heavy lashes. Her hair was rich auburn, tinted with gold in the lamplight and falling over her creamy shoulders. She was a full-figured woman, and she probably knew as much of the world as any of the men there, Dooley decided. There was a boldness in her manner which showed she was accustomed to being in the company of men.

"Sorry to be late," she said in a husky voice.

"Better get your packing done, Jean," the Englishman said. "I understand we'll be pulling out tomorrow or the day after. Is that correct, Reno?"

"Probably."

There was a strange note in Reno's voice which drew Dooley's gaze from the woman. He was, she saw, staring at Jean Lamarr with something like shock in his dark eyes. His bronzed skin seemed to have gone pale, and she saw that his hands on the table were twitching nervously. She glanced at Lee and saw that the boy was staring at the woman also, and as she watched he bit his lip and shot a worried look at Reno.

As the meal went on, most of the talk was by St. John and Captain Colter, with Jean Lamarr commenting from time to time. Reno spoke only in monosyllables when spoken to, and as soon as the meal was over, he rose and said, "I hate to eat and run, Captain, but I've got a few chores that won't wait."

Colter was surprised. "Why, I thought we might have a little talk, Reno."

"Maybe we can a little later." Reno nodded to St. John, and then to the woman. "Excuse me," he said and left the room.

Dooley and Lee sat there, and for the next thirty minutes tried to think of a way to leave gracefully. Finally Dooley said, "Thanks for the meal, Captain. It was wonderful."

"We'll be seeing you on the train, Dooley," St. John said, waving a hand languidly as they left.

Dooley did not mention Reno's strange behavior, for she saw that Lee was troubled. When they got back to the camp, she asked Leah, "Jim get back?"

"Ain't seen him, Dooley."

Lee sat down with his back to a wagon wheel, and Dooley finally went inside the wagon. It was after midnight before she went to sleep, but she knew that Reno had not come back to the camp.

The next morning, she saw that Lee had not been to bed at all. He was standing before the dead fire, talking to a small cowboy. Dooley crawled out and asked, "What's wrong?"

"Jim—Jim is locked up in the stockade, Dooley," Lee said. "He got drunk after he left us and then got in a fight with some soldiers."

"He shore did explode!" the cowboy said, with a light of admiration in his eyes. "He took on about half of F Troop, and done right noble."

"We've got to get him out, Lee," Dooley said instantly.

"Wal, that won't be too hard. Hey, my name's Easy Jones. I'll be with you on this here trip—anyway, my boss says that

Cap'n Colter thinks a heap of Reno. He ain't got up yet, but I reckon if you'd go ast him, why, he'd do the right thing."

"Come on, Lee!" Dooley started for the fort at a fast walk with Lee at her side. They were almost there when he said, "Dooley, don't be mad at Jim."

"Why in the world did he do a thing like that?" she said angrily. She was afraid that they would not be able to get him out, and she realized at that moment just how heavily she had come to rely on him, but she showed none of this to the boy.

"Dooley, lemme tell you about what's the matter with Jim," Lee said. He pulled her to a halt, and there was a hint of sadness in his eyes as he said, "Jim ain't really a drinkin' man. You see, about a year ago Jim was a marshall in this town in Kansas where I lived. There was this woman, her name was Lola, and she was my best friend. She worked in a saloon, but I—I didn't have no folks, and she was good to me, you see?"

Dooley was looking at the boy, noting the way his hands twisted the material of his shirt, tension contorting his thin face. "Sure, I understand."

"You do? Well her and Jim fell in love." Lee smiled sadly and went on, "They were gonna get married, and I was—was gonna be their boy, see? But—"

He stopped abruptly and bit his lip, and his voice was unsteady. "What happened?" Dooley asked quietly, though she could guess.

"There was a bad fight, a gunfight, Dooley. And Jim come out of it safe—only—there was this one man in an upstairs room—and he—and he—"

The boy was trembling, and Dooley fought back the maternal instinct to put her arms around him. "She was killed, wasn't she, Lee?"

His thin shoulders shook. "She—seen the man aiming at Jim and she jumped in and took the bullet. Jim got the man—but it was too late."

Dooley could not help putting her arm around Lee. "But why did he wait until tonight to get drunk?"

Lee looked at her and said in a whisper, "That Lamarr woman—she's the picture image of Lola, Dooley!"

"That's why he looked like he was shot when he saw her!" Dooley whispered.

"Yeah, and now I'm scared he's gonna go back to drinkin'."

"We won't let him, Lee!" Dooley said with a quiet intensity. "We've got to get him away from here!"

"But that woman is going with the train!" Lee said, looking at her with troubled eyes. "Jim won't be able to handle it!"

"He'll just *have* to, Lee!" Dooley said. "Come on. Let's get him out of jail."

Getting him out was easier than she had feared. Captain Colter was disappointed, but he agreed at once to have Reno released. Lee and Dooley had gone with a corporal, and they had found Reno sitting on his bunk, hollow-eyed and morose.

"Jim, Captain Colter says he won't keep you here," Lee said. "Come on—I think the train's gonna pull out today."

"Not going." Reno got up and moved to the door, but there was a stubborn look on his wedge-shaped face. "I'm going to get my gear from the wagon, but I'm staying here."

"Lee, you go on," Dooley said. "I want to talk to Jim alone."

Lee gave her a startled look, then said, "All right, Dooley."

As soon as the boy left, Dooley said, "Jim, you can go to the devil if that's what you want to—"

"Just about what I'll do, I reckon!"

"—but don't take that boy down with you!"

Reno had started for the door, a hard light in his black eyes, but Dooley's words brought him up short. He whirled and said in a tight voice, "Dooley, it's no good! I'm no good for the boy!"

"You're all he has, Jim!"

He stared at her, pain in the lines of his face, and she did not argue, knowing it would do no good. Finally he groaned and slapped his hands against his thighs. "All right, Dooley. But I can't make any promises."

"Let's go, Jim," Dooley said quickly, knowing she had to get him into action. They left the jail and she walked quickly, not giving him time to think.

As they got to the wagon, Lee was waiting—and so was Carl Slade. There was a grin on his brutal lips and he said at once, "Well, you got the drunk out, I see. Hope you laid in a supply of whiskey to take care of him till we get to the next bar, Dooley."

Dooley looked quickly at Reno, expecting him to react to the comment, but he merely shook his head and turned to walk away, Lee following him closely. There was a sag to his shoulders. Slade laughed loudly, saying to Dooley, "Better get yourself another man, Dooley. That one ain't gonna make this trip."

"Don't bet on it, Carl," Dooley said quickly, but as she went about her chores that morning, there was a weight on her spirit. She kept seeing the despair in Reno's eyes. And she kept wondering about the woman who had died in his place. The one thought that kept coming back was: *That Jean Lamarr—she's not one to die for a man—not likely!*

SIX
Death in the Desert

"I been to three county fairs, two snake stompin's, and a passel of camp meetin's. But I ain't never seen nothin' like this!"

Easy Jones stood back, admiration gleaming in his bright blue eyes. He waved a hand toward the beautifully built wagon of his employer, then added to the small group of youngsters who had collected to watch him hitch up the splendid set of four matched pearl-gray mules: "Looky at how she's built, you tads—ain't she a sockdolager?"

The luxurious wagon of Easy's employer, Algernon St. John, made a striking contrast to the other vehicles of the train, most of which had been worn to the bare essentials by the rigor of the trail. Most of them were prairie schooners, built to carry as much as twenty-five hundred pounds across rough trails for two thousand miles or more. They were built of maple, hickory, or oak, iron being used only where the greatest pounding took place—tires, axles, and hounds, those bars that connected the undercarriage. The sole concession to passenger comfort was the cloth cover, which cut out some of the rain and dust. None of them had springs, and they were packed so full that only the hard seat was available for riders. A rough sort of bed could be made on top of the piles of weapons, tools, food, and clothing, but most of the settlers slept under the wagons or in small tents.

St. John's wagon was far larger than any of the others in the train, and the exterior was of walnut, highly polished, smooth, and cushioned by heavy springs. Easy climbed up on the seat, which sat higher than most and was covered by a canvas canopy that shielded the driver from the elements.

"Clamber up and have a look, you younkers!" Easy said. He reached down and yanked Lee up to the high seat with a mighty heave, and he was followed by a swarm of others, including Marie Prather, Nelson Moore, and twelve-year-old Becky Edwards, who Lee and Nelson both fancied themselves sweet on.

"Gosh!" Becky said in a whisper. "He must be rich!"

They stared at the interior, which was like a small room: a built-in mahogany desk with small drawers, a couch with a brilliant silk coverlet, a shining brass lamp bolted over the desk, a large leather case with brass fittings for water, and three windows with curtains drawn back to allow light and air. Overhead was a gleaming white cover of silk, sewn to the underside of the canvas top.

"He must be rich!" Nelson Moore said. He was thirteen, the same age as Lee—a tall, lanky, strong boy with his father's face. He and Lee had become fast friends, and except for the fact that both of them fancied themselves in love with Becky, they got on very well.

Easy let them look for a while, then said, "Better scatter now. The boss might git back from his huntin' pretty soon." He winked at Lee and added, "He shore is a caution! He done been to places and et in hotels, I tell you!"

"What's he goin' to Oregon for, Easy?" Lee asked.

"Aw, he done been every place else, I speck. He's whut they name a remittance man."

"What's that?" Lee asked.

"Feller who's such a no-account varmint his folks pay him to stay away from home." Easy shrugged and added, "I reckon it's better to be rich, healthy, and good-lookin' than it is to be poor, sick, and ugly! Last jasper I worked for was so ugly when he was a baby they had to tie a pork chop around his neck 'fore the dog would play with him! And plumb stingy, too. He wuz so tight his pancakes only had one side to 'em!"

Dooley had been drawn to the crowd of youngsters. She asked curiously, "What's he really like, Easy? I never saw any-body like him."

"Aw, sometimes I don't think he's got any more sense than last year's bird nest, Dooley!" Easy pulled off his hat and roughed up his tow-colored hair fiercely, then pulled it back down over his fan-shaped ears. "Then again, I get the idee he's playin' some kinder big joke on all of us. The sucker shore knows horses!"

"Sure would like to spend a night in that feather bed!" Lee sighed.

"Reckon that man's got someone purtier than you to sleep with!" Nelson Moore said. "That is some fancy woman he keeps."

"Shut your mouth!" Lee said, his face turning red. "That ain't a fit thing to talk about around girls."

Nelson grinned, threw a wink at Easy, and said, "Guess we better take ol' Lee off to one side and tell him all about the difference between boys and girls, Easy." He laughed at the blush on Lee's face, and added, "You don't think he's hauling her along to play cards with, do you, Lee?"

"I'm telling you to shut up, Nels!" Lee stepped closer to the larger boy and added, "If you can't act decent when girls are around, I'll just make you!"

Nelson was surprised at the attack. He was only slightly taller than Lee, but his muscles were already filling out, and he made the other boy's thin frame look frail. He stopped smiling and said, "I reckon I got as much manners as you. All you're doin' is showin' off in front of Becky—"

Lee cut him off with a sudden blow that caught Nelson unprepared. He was driven back, and Lee followed, swinging wildly. Most of his blows missed or caught the boy only on the arms and shoulders. Nelson got his balance and waded in flailing.

Both of them had more energy than skill, and as Dooley started toward them to break up the fight, Easy pulled her back, saying with a grin, "Let 'em go at it, Dooley. It's good fer a young feller to get in a leetle practice now and again."

As the two pummeled each other fervently, rolling in the dust at intervals, then rising again, a crowd gathered to watch and give advice.

"Lay it on, Lee!" "Punch his ol' head, Nels!" You boys stop that!" It was the noon hour, and the rigid monotony of the past week of hard trailing made the diversion a welcome relief. The train had left Laramie in fairly good condition, but the heat had soared, baking the earth and draining energy from man and beast. The meat was gone and game was scarce. The grinding travel and poor food were wearing them down.

Dooley saw Reno pass by on his way to the river. He stopped, stared at the boys, then moved away without a word. He had been, Dooley thought, like a sick man ever since Laramie. He was not drinking, or so she thought, but he kept away from the train all day, choosing the unwelcome job of tailing the herd. When he did come to the fire at night, he ate sparingly and sat off to himself, speaking little, and rolling in his blankets without saying a word. Dooley had hoped that the fight might stir some interest in his moody dark eyes, but he did not pause except for a cursory glance.

She shook her head, then turned her attention to the boys, who had reached the point of exhaustion. Both of them were bleeding around the mouth, and they were reduced to hanging on and pawing feebly at each other.

"Reckon thet's all she wrote," Easy said. He stepped forward and pulled the two apart. "You done right good, both of you," he said, grinning. "Now jes' shake and git right till the next time."

Lee and Nelson glared at each other, and Nelson finally managed a small grin and stuck his hand out. "I'm willin'," he said.

Becky stepped forward and put her hand on Nelson's arm, saying anxiously, "That's good, Nels."

Lee took that in and an angry look crossed his face. He shook his head and there was a bitter light in his eyes. "I ain't shakin' with no dirty-mouth like you!" he declared, and ignoring the other he wheeled and stalked off, his shoulders high and tense.

As the crowd dispersed, Easy remarked, "Boy's got a heap to learn about women, ain't he, Dooley?" He stopped smiling and added, "Thing is, Nelson is right about that woman of St. John's." Then Easy let flow a long descriptive utterance on the nature of men and women so raw that Dooley's jaw dropped. The blood rushed to her cheeks, and she whirled to keep Easy from seeing her blush.

He stopped abruptly and called after her: "Aw, pardon me fer chewin' tobacco in your presence! Didn't know I was addressin' such a delly-cut congregation!"

Dooley hurried to catch up with Lee, who was walking blindly away from the train. She caught at his arm, saying, "Lee, you better wash your face. Come over to the wagon."

He halted, and for a moment she thought he intended to pull away, but he turned to face her. "Dooley, what's the matter with girls, anyway? Becky's been shinin' up to me for a week, and now she just sides up to Nelson Moore like he was *somethin'!* I hate both of 'em!"

Dooley maneuvered him to the wagon and got some water from the canvas water bag hanging on the rear. While she mopped away at his face she tried to calm him down. "You're just mad, Lee. What Nelson said wasn't so bad. Don't guess it was anything Becky hadn't heard before."

"You're on his side!"

"No, I'm not," Dooley argued as she dabbed at the boy's mouth. "But you and Nelson are good friends, aren't you?"

"Well, we *used* to be."

"And now you're not? You don't think much of your friends, Lee—not if you can shuck them off so easy."

Her face was a little grim, and Lee said at once, with just a touch of shame in his voice, "Aw, I still like Nels, Dooley. But, shoot, every time a *girl* gets into stuff it all goes bad!"

"It wasn't Becky rolling around in the dirt, Lee!"

He had a sudden thought, and looked at her with a shrewd glance. "Dooley?"

"Yes?"

"Tell me about girls."

She stared at him in surprise and he rushed on, "I mean, you're older than I am, Dooley. You've been around, ain't you?"

She knew at once what he meant, and she felt her cheeks beginning to glow. "Why, I don't think . . ."

"Oh, come on, Dooley," Lee urged. "How's a fellow supposed to find out about how to act with women if somebody don't tell him?"

"Ask Jim," she said quickly.

"He's older, Dooley, and sort of like a dad, you know? I'd be ashamed to ask him. But you ain't too much older than me, and it won't bother me to find out about things from you."

Dooley longed to drop the cloth and run. She stammered, "Why, Lee, I don't think I could tell . . ."

"Well, shoot, Dooley!" Lee was staring at her with resentment, and he demanded, "Ain't you never messed around with a girl?"

"No! I—I never have, Lee, and that's the truth!"

He stared at her for a long moment, then got up. "Well, you ain't goin' to do me no good then."

As he walked off, Dooley felt so weak that she leaned against the wagon breathing shortly.

"Whyn't you tell the youngun, Dooley—all 'bout kissin' on the girls?"

Dooley leaped away from the wagon, and whirled to see Leah peering around the canvas top, her face wrinkled with a grin. "If you gonna keep up that playactin' at bein' a man, you bettuh study up on how to handle dis heah kinda thing!"

"You—you shut up!" Dooley screamed.

"Dooley, you jes' ain't gonna be able to keep dis up," Leah said. She came to stand beside the girl, put a hand on her shoulder, and looked at her with compassion in her eyes. "Why, it's de Lawd's own mercy you ain't been found out already! I doan care if you cut your hair and put on a man's garb. Why, who ever seed a man with such a skin, smooth as a peach? And you gets all red jes' like a young girl blushin' ever time you hears som'en a mite unladylike!"

"Leah! I've got to keep people from finding me out!"

"How you gonna do dat, chile?" The face of Leah was filled with wisdom, and she went on relentlessly. "You might as well git ready, 'cause sooner or later you gonna get found out. You don't hang out with the young men, you don't mess with de gals, and all you gotta do is jes' forget and leave off dat coat one time an' dat girl figure gonna give you 'way! Why, Jim Reno woulda found you out long ago iffen he wasn't jes' a boy hisself in some ways."

"Just till we get to Oregon, Leah," Dooley pleaded, as if the black woman held her fate. "If we can just get there, why, there's a thousand places we can hide from Jake!"

Leah put her arm around Dooley and said gently, "It's all in de good Lawd's hands, honey. He ain't gwine to let us down!" She patted Dooley's shoulder and said, "Now, you jes' put some bacon in de pan fo' Leah." She watched as Dooley moved toward the campfire, and there was infinite pity in her brooding eyes as she shook her head and turned to her work with a heavy sigh.

By the second week out of Laramie, the lack of fresh meat had become serious. Most people had salt meat or cured bacon, but it didn't satisfy. The buffalo were not in evidence, and neither Carl Slade, who went out every day looking for game, nor any of the others had any luck.

Water also became a serious problem. After leaving the Platte there were only scattered waterholes, most of which were dried up, caked, and broken into large chunks of stone-hard earth.

The stock began to break under the terrible heat, and all the people were forced to lighten their wagons. Alice Henry, Buck's mother, wept as her son took a walnut chest that had been her grandmother's in England and put it beside the deep ruts of the trail. Every wagon, except that of St. John's, had to be stripped. The Englishman had two wagons, one for his bedroom, driven by Easy, and another filled with supplies, driven by a Mexican named Juan. The first-class stock was rested, so he appeared oblivious of the suffering of the rest of the train.

By Saturday of the second week they had to delay, despite objections by Daniel Slade. He said to the crowd that had collected around his wagon, "We can't spare the time! Winter is going to catch us if we don't make good time."

"Easy for you to say, Daniel," Will Satterfield muttered, resentment on his long face. He was a short man with thinning hair and a worried frown built on his face. "You got plenty of pullin' stock. You kin give your critters a rest, which the rest of us can't."

"Not my fault if you ain't got enough stock!"

Slade had brought along his cattle, which he planned to use as the basis of a cattle operation in Oregon, and the others resented having to spend so much labor on the herd when most of the cattle were his.

Jude Finney had been standing by quietly, as was his custom. "Folks are pretty worn down, Slade. And they're pretty hungry. You can't make time on hoecakes and salt pork."

"Wouldn't hurt you to kill a beef," Pete Prather said. He was still weak from whatever sickness had laid him low. He moved painfully, and there was an unhealthy pallor to his face. The flesh was dropping off so fast that his clothing draped over his bones in a scarecrow fashion. "Little fresh meat might make things go faster."

"I'm supposed to feed you all, am I now?" Slade asked sarcastically. "You're mighty free with my stock, Prather!"

Easy muttered to Buck Henry, "That man's so tight I bet his toes curl up every time he blinks!"

Slade looked around the crowd and the sullen resentment in every face gave him pause. He valued his place as wagon master; it fed the ego that was in him. Finally he said with obvious reluctance, "Well, all right. Just this *one* time. Carl, take that yearlin' that's got a limp and butcher him."

"You don't have to knuckle under to 'em, Pa," the hulking Carl said, sweeping his eyes around the circle. "They ain't none of our raisin'."

"No, but I'm in charge, and I'll get this train to Oregon no matter how much trouble they are!"

The yearling was slaughtered and after the Slades took the best cuts, it was parceled out to the others. "I hate to take anything from that man," Dooley muttered, "but I'm not going to cut my nose off to spite my face."

The thought of fresh meat broke the gloom, and the sound of laughter mingled with the rattle of pans as cooking fires broke out inside the circle.

"You know, Jim, this is kinda like a family, ain't it?" Lee asked. He was sitting beside Reno, who for once had joined the little group. "I mean, when the wagons are in a circle, everything is outside and we're safe. And we're all in little groups, all cookin' and eatin' together. It's not so bad."

Dooley paused. Reno, she saw, was thinner than he had been, as they all were. But there was a remoteness to him, and he merely nodded at Lee.

Pete Prather wandered over, accompanied by fifteen-year-old Harry. "Need that Sharps gun, Jim."

Reno got up and pulled the weapon out of the jockey box at the rear of the wagon. Handing it over, he said, "Meant to get it back to you before this, Pete. Sorry."

"Aw, it don't matter, Jim." A spasm of pain took the older man, and he clutched his stomach suddenly. "Thought I'd meander out whilst supper's on. Me and Harry might get a shot at something.

Reno shook his head. "Don't believe I'd do that, Pete."

"Why not?"

"Injuns."

Prather stared at Reno. "Injuns? You seen any?"

"No. But that doesn't mean a thing, Pete."

"Aw, that's just scare talk, what that soldier said, Jim." Pete shrugged his thin shoulders. "Anyways, me and Harry ain't goin' but a little ways—and we can shoot!"

As the pair walked away toward a steep arroyo, Dooley bit her lip and said, "If you think there's danger, you shouldn't have let them go, Jim."

"I made me a rule once. If a man wants to do something, I let him do it."

Dooley hated that manner of his. He had the ability to drop behind a wall, hiding his thoughts and sealing off anyone who came close.

"Aw, Jim, that ain't right," Lee said, looking at Reno with disappointment.

"Nothing much is," Reno said, then got up and walked away from the cooking fire.

"He is one sour man!" Leah said grimly. "Ain't no sweetness in him."

Dooley stared at Reno, and said only, "I guess all of us are that way sometimes."

Reno came back three-quarters of an hour later when Lee called, "Supper, Jim." They had sat down to the meal with real enjoyment, not only the fresh steaks, but the white gravy and grits that Leah had fixed, together with candied yams. Even Reno brightened a little, pleased at having real meat on the plate.

When they were almost finished, Lena Prather came from across the circle, carrying Esther. There was a puzzled look on her face as she asked, "Did Pete tell you when he'd be back?"

"Why, no, he didn't, Lena," Dooley said.

"He said he'd be back for supper. I—I'm a little worried." She looked very young standing there, her gaze sweeping the horizon in the falling light. "Maybe I'd better ask Leon or Clyde to look for him."

"Oh, I'll fetch him up," Dooley said cheerfully. "He's probably lost track of the time."

She started off in the direction the Prathers had taken, but Reno's voice caught her. "You'll need a gun." He pulled the Henry out of the wagon and tossed it to her. "I'll tag along."

"Me, too, Jim," Lee said, and the three of them walked quickly toward the arroyo.

When they were a hundred yards away, Reno said, "You two hold back. Stay behind me." He pulled his Colt from the holster and checked the loads, then led the way, his eyes restlessly searching the ground.

Dooley followed twenty feet behind with Lee beside her. Her heart began beating very fast as Reno reached the lip of the small gulch, and she said, "Jim—"

"Quiet!" he snapped, then he dropped down and began to move slowly toward their left.

Feeling suddenly vulnerable without his presence, Dooley said nervously, "Come on, Lee!" and the two of them followed Reno into the gathering darkness.

It was very quiet, and the wagon train seemed far away now that it was out of the line of vision. An owl's faint cry sounded thin and clear, and the sound sent tingles along Dooley's nerves. She moved faster, anxious to catch sight of Reno, and the scuffing of her boots across the rocky ground seemed very loud.

"I can't see him!" Lee said nervously. "Do you see him, Dooley?"

"No! I think—"

Then a movement to her left caught her eye and suddenly what she had thought to be a bush or small rock turned into a dark body that exploded in her direction! She had no time to yell, but the gleam of a knife seemed to flash in the twilight, and she was aware of a fierce face rushing at her. She even saw the black and yellow stripes of paint along the cheeks and the flash of white teeth.

Blam!

She did yell then, for the Indian was driven sideways by the explosion of Reno's shot. She dropped the rifle as he fell, then looked with horror as he pushed himself up with blood pouring out of his throat where the shot had taken him. With a terrible cry he clutched his throat and tried to hold the blood back. Reno appeared at her side, snatched the Henry up, and swept the horizon with bleak eyes as the man went slack, his arms falling loosely beside him.

"J-Jim!" Lee stuttered. "Are there more?"

Reno holstered his Colt, but held the rifle on ready, his eyes moving constantly. "I reckon so."

Dooley felt light-headed. "What about—what about the Prathers?"

Reno turned to look at her, and there was a look in his face that told her before he said, "Over there—both dead." She moved to look and he said, "Don't look, Dooley. It ain't pretty."

"Are they—scalped, Jim?" Lee whispered hoarsely.

"That and worse." He pulled Dooley around, saying urgently, "You got to go tell Lena. Go quick. They must have heard the shot."

"I can't do it!" she said with a constriction in her throat.

"You want her to come out here and see 'em?" His voice struck her like a whip then. "Boy, you ain't gonna dodge this chore! Now you get it done or I'll tear you apart!"

Dooley stumbled blindly away, the horror of the thing tying her stomach into knots. She clawed her way out of the depression, falling more than once, then broke out into a run toward the train, trying to hold back the tears.

She was met by Leon Prather, who took one look at her and asked in a tight voice, "Pa? Is it Pa, Dooley?"

She stared at him and nodded mutely, unable to bear the look on his face. She turned away and saw Lena running toward her, the baby bouncing as she ran.

"Pete!" she was crying, and as Dooley grabbed her, she struggled to get away, "Pete! Oh, my God! They've killed him!"

Then there were others, and the women took Lena away, her voice keening across the falling darkness like a wild thing: "They've killed him! Oh, they've killed him!"

Easy came to stand beside her, asking in a tight voice, "Both of 'em?"

She stared at him, nodded, and said with a strangle, "Both of them!"

114

Easy nodded, and then he cursed and threw his hat at the ground. The sound of his voice seemed to come from far away, and Dooley, when she turned shakily toward the camp, was conscious of a swimming in her head, and she never knew when she simply collapsed limply on the hard-packed soil.

SEVEN
By the Sweetwater

Reno had worked on the grave along with Buck Henry and Barney Moore. It was a raw day, the dirty-looking clouds scudding across the gray morning skies. Even though the sun was no more than a hand above the eastern skyline, he felt the touch of it on his back, knowing that later it would burn and hurt the eye.

He stood with the rest, waiting for the preacher to start. Jude had on a tie and had his Bible under his arm. He stood beside the pile of sand and rocks the men had pried so laboriously, and beside it were the wooden coffins that held Pete and Harry Prather. They had been built from boards taken from a spare wagon belonging to towheaded Ty Edwards. He had a wife and several children, and he was a shiftless man, aptly described by Easy: "Ty Edwards? Ain't got the spirit to lift a louse off a hot griddle. Ain't worth a milk bucket under a bull!"

When Jude had inquired about using the wagon material for coffins, Edwards had slowly cut a piece of tobacco, examined it carefully, then said, "Wal, now, reckon that's purty good lumber. Ort to be worth somethin'."

Dooley had paid him two dollars for it, and Edwards had stuck it in his shirt pocket, saying, "Sho, now, a man's got to do his Christian dooty, ain't that a fact?"

Luke Edwards, his oldest boy at seventeen, had ducked his head in shame while his father said this. Then Luke said, "I've done lots of carpenterin'. I'll make the coffins."

He took after his mother, a woman of forty who had had a baby a year for ten years. She was worn to a shadow, but there was something of quality in her, as there was in all the children. Sally, a plain-looking girl of sixteen, said, "I'll help you, Luke." The baby, Missy, was seven, and Hiram, an undersized boy into everything, was ten. They had worked on the coffins all night, and Dooley had helped, learning to like the younger Edwards as much as she disliked the father. Twelve-year-old Becky Edwards was grieved over the death of Harry, for she had had quite a crush on the boy.

The train was ready to pull out as soon as the grave was filled in. Addie Grant had told Vinson that it would be easier on the Prathers if they didn't have to stay around, and Daniel Slade had agreed, always ready to drive ahead.

Jude stepped forward and without opening the Bible under his arm, lifted up his voice: "The Lord is my shepherd, I shall not want. . . ." Poorly dressed as he was, homely in face and awkward in form, there was a dignity in him that held them all. He had been a figure of fun to most of them, but standing there, his thick brown hair blowing in the morning breeze with his bony features cast into sharp planes by the dawn's light, they all held themselves still as he finished the psalm, then turned to face Lena.

"Pete Prather was just a man. So was his son." Then he swept his hand across the horizon. "They looked mighty small out here in all this big country. We all do. But they were *men*. And that means, Lena, that when all this is gone—all this plain, all the stars, and every bit of stone and every tree and every bit of dirt—when it's all gone—" Jude dropped his voice to a lower pitch and there was an iron certainty in his tone as he went on, "—when it's all gone, Pete and Harry will still be!"

As Jude went on speaking, Reno searched the eyes of the listeners, noting the comfort Lena was receiving from the words, the indifference in all three of the Slades, the inquisitive light in the British eyes of Algernon St. John, and the boredom in Jean Lamarr's face.

Jude went from verse to verse, never opening the Bible, but stacking up promise after promise that this pitiful thing called man was different from anything else in the universe.

Finally he said a short prayer, ending with the words: "Lord, you won't be hard on these men, for they loved you, and you ain't gonna forget that. You got to take care of Pete's family now, for you done said you are a father to the fatherless. We're thanking you for Pete's life, and we're thanking you that you seen fit to take him away from the pain that laid in his path. In Jesus' name."

They moved away from the grave as Lena turned and murmured, "I'll never know where their grave is."

Reno paused, and there was a light of pity in his dark eyes. He stepped close to the grieving woman holding the child.

"I can find it for you, Lena, anytime."

He helped her mount to the wagon driven by Clyde. As he turned to go to his horse, Carl Slade said loud enough almost to be heard by the woman, "Purty woman like that, she won't sleep alone long."

Dooley heard this and could feel tears of anger welling in her eyes. She was not three feet from Carl when she whirled and said without thought, "Carl, you're lower than a yellow dog!"

Carl's face darkened and his huge hand shot out to grab Dooley's arm. She cried out with pain as the iron grip caught her, the blood draining from her face.

"You can get hurt, Dooley, if you don't watch your mouth, even if you are just a punk kid." He looked up to see Reno watching the scene, and he shoved Dooley in his direction. "You wanna take it up, drunk?"

Reno stood there, and Lee expected to see him take up Slade's challenge, but Reno merely shook his head. "None of my fight."

"I didn't reckon you'd think so." Carl grinned and winked at Beau, who was taking it all in with a smile. Then he looked at Buck Henry and asked, "How about you, Buck? You about ready for another lesson from Poppa?"

Buck stood there, his face pale and sweat on his upper lip. He shook his head and wheeled to go to his wagon.

"Ain't a fight in the whole bunch, Carl," Beau said. "Sure hope we don't have any trouble with Injuns. You and me would have to do all the fighting!"

All day the train crawled slowly across the plain like a crippled centipede, stopping only briefly at noon before pushing on. Reno was walking along a few yards out from the wagon, sweeping the horizon constantly. When he heard a cry from the rear, he turned at once and went back to where Will Satterfield's wagon was leaning over crazily, one of the wheels lying in pieces on the ground.

Satterfield reached down and picked up a piece of a spoke which was shattered. "Too much for wheels, this country!"

"You got a spare?" Reno asked. Robert Burns's wagon was right behind and he came up to see the problem. Ellie came close to Reno, her eyes heavy-lidded and her face puffy from the heat.

"No, I ain't," Satterfield said.

"I've got one," Burns said at once, turning to go back to his wagon.

The whole train had stopped, and Daniel rode back at once to see what was causing the delay. Carl was with him, and they both got down to stare at the wheel. "Get this fixed, Satterfield," the older man said. "We got to make up for that day we lost."

Will said shortly, "Doing the best we can, Daniel."

Ellie let her eyes fall on Carl's broad chest and thick arms, and his eyes caught at her. He grinned broadly. Suddenly Buck appeared and said, "I'll help Burns with the wheel."

"See any more of your Injun friends, Reno?" Carl asked with a sneer. Reno had taken a shovel and buried the Indian he had killed, an act which puzzled everyone, but he had simply done it and made no defense.

Daniel could not let the issue drop. He stared at Reno with obvious hostility, and there was contempt in his voice as he said, "Still don't see why you buried that Sioux, Reno."

Reno let the silence run on, then said, "Wasn't a Sioux, Slade. A Crow."

"Ain't no difference," Carl snapped.

Reno almost grinned, and there was a light in his eyes as he said, "If those were Sioux, some of us would be feeding the buzzards right now."

"Are they so bad, Jim?" Ellie asked.

"They're tough as anything a man's apt to meet on this earth."

Carl snorted with disgust, but just then Buck came rolling a new wheel back. He rested it beside the down end of the rear axle.

"Got to rig a lever," Burns said. "That wagon's got to weigh near to three thousand pounds." He did not look at the Slades, and there was a beaten look in his eyes.

"We got hands enough to pick it up," Carl said. "Hold that wheel, Buck. Come on, let's get it did."

Reno joined the two Slades, Burns, and Satterfield, and when Carl yelled, "All right—now *lift!*" they all heaved. The axle cleared the ground a few inches, then slammed back down hard as the weight lurched back.

"Like a bunch of women!" Carl snapped, his face flushed with effort. "All right, get the pole for a lever."

Buck was standing there, a strange light in his light blue eyes. He looked at the wagon, then at Carl Slade. Then he said quietly, "Don't need no pole. Hold the wheel, Jim."

A sudden quiet fell across the group then, as Buck handed the wheel to Reno and walked to the back of the wagon. Others came to watch, but he ignored them all. Turning his back, he squatted on his heels and forced his huge shoulders back under the weight of the wagon. He placed his hands on his thighs, and there was a look of powerful concentration on his round face.

"He'll bust his gut!" Carl said loudly. "Ain't no man can lift three thousand pounds!"

If Buck heard, he gave no sign. He stooped there, pushing his shoulders against the bed, feeling with his feet for firm ground to grip, his eyes distant and staring at nothing.

There was a creak of wood, and Buck released his breath in a snort. Reno saw his fingers splay and grow white as he pushed against the swelling muscles of his thighs, and the weight of the wagon dug into the thick cords of muscle that padded his massive shoulders.

There was no jerking, just a slow steady motion as he straightened his legs. The heavy wagon slowly rose until he was standing there holding the entire weight.

"He done it!" Satterfield yelled. Reno slipped the wheel on quickly and said, "Good, Buck!" and the big fellow bent his legs until the wheel touched the earth.

He stepped out from the wagon, straightened up, and took a deep breath. His face was red, and they could see the blood pounding in the veins on his neck. The effort had ripped his shirt, and the rolling mounds of muscle that showed as he lifted his arms for relief were fearful.

Ellie was staring at him, her lips parted in admiration. She stepped close and said, "I never saw anything like that, Buck! Ain't no other man in the world who could lift that thing."

A chorus of assent went around the group, but Buck seemed to be aware only of Ellie. He took another deep breath, swelling the great muscles of his chest, and a trace of a smile touched his lips.

"Let's get moving!" Carl yelled, and there was a sullen look on his broad face as he wheeled his horse and drove out of the camp, spurring the animal cruelly.

The train started up, and Burns caught up with Reno and Buck as they walked alongside the train later in the day. There was something bothering the little Scot. His thin face was tense, and he looked down at the ground for a long time, listening as Buck and Reno talked about the trail ahead of them.

Finally he threw away the stick he had been swinging aimlessly, and broke out in a high-pitched voice, "If I only had your strength, Henry, I would kill Beau Slade!"

Buck broke off what he was saying to stare at the small man, but it was Reno who said, "Only thing that's going to stop Beau is a bullet in the head."

Burns stared at him with burning eyes and said, "Will you teach me to handle a gun, Reno?" When Reno hesitated he said bitterly, "You think I don't know what everybody is saying? That I'm a coward, that I can't hold on to my wife. You think I don't know about that?"

Reno shook his head. "You wouldn't have a chance, Burns. I've seen Beau practice a few times. He's quick and a good shot." He paused and added in a kindly tone, "You'd best forget it, Bob. When this trip is over you won't have to put up with him."

"What about my wife? You think she's going to forget?"

Reno shrugged, knowing there was no answer to that one. "I can show you how to pull a gun. In most gunfights you don't have to be all that good a marksman. Get five feet from a man, blaze away until you get him, or he gets you.

"Well, will you do it, Jim?"

Reno still hesitated. "There's a little more to it, Bob. I think Beau can put a bullet in a man. Not so sure about you."

"I'd like to kill him!" Burns said in a voice that trembled with emotion.

"You think so now, but when your gun's aimed at his heart and you're sending him to hell—well, most men can't do that."

"Can you, Jim?" Burns asked instantly.

Reno looked across the plain toward the low hills up ahead, and then he swung a pair of smoky eyes to Burns.

"Yes—God help me!"

Robert Burns was about as civilized a man as Reno had met, but there was a savage wildness in his dark brown eyes as he said, "Teach me!"

Reno stared at him, a grim smile on his broad lips. He glanced at Buck, who was taking all this in with astonishment on his face, and he let his breath go with a sigh. "All right, but it's a lesson you won't be able to get away from." He shrugged and said in a heavy tone, "I ought to know about that!"

They hit the Sweetwater two days later, and the land began to lift. The fresh waters were a relief after the bitter springs of the plains. By the time they got to Independence Rock the stock was so exhausted they had to rest up for a couple of days.

The people had not had fresh meat for weeks, and no one could spare a cow except Daniel Slade, and he wasn't giving.

During the entire trip from Laramie, Reno had kept clear of St. John's wagon. He had, however, spent some time with Easy, and he was surprised when the bandy-legged cowboy hailed him late one afternoon with a broad smile on his face.

"Hey, Jim, the Prince of Wales sez fer you to come and eat with him tonight."

Reno hesitated and Easy said quickly, "Wants you to brang Dooley, too. The Mex is cookin' up more than aplenty, so y'all come on and greasy up your mouth!" He left before Reno could decline, and he did not tell Reno how the invitation had come about.

"I say, Jones, what sort of chap is this Reno fellow?" St. John had asked as he lazily finished off his breakfast. He was sitting with Jean at a small table that folded neatly into a specially built compartment underneath the wagon. "Seems decid-edly unfriendly."

"Good-looking, though," Jean said with a smile.

St. John gave her an indolent smile. "I didn't think you'd miss that. But he's a strange fellow, isn't he now?"

"Wal, I reckon in some ways," Easy said. He saucered his coffee, blew it, then added, "Folks would let him tote the key to the smokehouse, I reckon!"

St. John stared at the small cowboy and finally shook his head. "That eludes me, Jones. Or am I correct in assuming that your statement implies that the gentleman is so worthy of trust that his peers would do him the honor of trusting him with their prize possession?"

Easy stared into the eyes of St. John for a long moment, then said, "And here I allus thought I talked English!"

Jean laughed and leaned back in her chair. With a loose-ness in her behavior and a look of speculation in her eyes she said to Easy, "My guess is that Jim Reno has been to see the elephant."

Easy laughed at the look on St. John's face. "Thet means he's been around. Yep, I'd say so. Went through the whole war from Bull Run to Appomattox. Went a leetle wild, so I hear, and he's even been a lawman."

"A wild man *and* a lawman." St. John smiled and leaned forward. "Sounds like an oxymoron."

Easy shifted uncertainly and said, "I don't know nothing about no moron. From what I hear, Jim Reno gets down where the water hits the wheel." He paused, satisfied at the look of mystification on his employer's face. "Lots of lawmen air jest about half a step from being crooks, anyway. But I'd say Reno plows a straight furrow and goes plumb to the end of the row!"

"Like to know the bloke a little better," St. John murmured. "Go ask him to dine with us, will you Jones?"

"It might be fun." Jean Lamarr smiled with a feline stretch of her arms.

Dooley stared at Reno when he told her of the invitation.

"You're going?" she asked in surprise.

"Any reason why we shouldn't?"

She didn't mention that he'd practically broken his leg staying away from St. John's woman, and she found that she was anxious to see how Reno would act when he faced her.

They had gone over to find the Mexican cook setting a steaming meal on the table covered with a snowy tablecloth. There were real china and sterling silver forks, not to mention crystal glasses and a bottle of wine.

"A bit primitive, I'm afraid. No ice to chill the wine."

"We'll just have to suffer, I reckon," Reno remarked with a straight face, and St. John's face flickered with quick humor.

"Jean, our guests are here," he called out.

The woman stepped out of the wagon and came to greet them with her hand outstretched. "Well, we meet again. You've been neglecting us, Jim, and you, too, Dooley."

Jean was all warmth and color, her greenish eyes set off by the sparkling gown of emerald green, cut low to expose creamy shoulders. Dooley caught the scent of expensive perfume as she shook hands, and when she finally risked a glimpse at Reno, she saw that he was a little pale, but he took his chair and kept up his end of the conversation all through the meal.

They ate the spicy Mexican food, perfectly seasoned by Juan, and there was always something more. Dooley took a small morsel from a plate and asked, "What's this?"

"Escargot," St. John said with an even face. He waited

until Dooley had gingerly put it in her mouth and was chewing it before he added dryly, "That's French for *snail.*"

Dooley sat there like a stone, then turned her head and spit it out, her face contorted.

"Good for you, Dooley," St. John laughed in delight. "Some fools would have swallowed that!"

It was a fine meal, and Dooley was greatly relieved to see that Reno was at ease. The beauty of the Lamarr woman he admired, as any man would, but there was no sign of the panic that had routed him out of Captain Colter's house.

They had finished the meal, and St. John urged more wine on them, asking Reno about the frontier.

"All this about gunfighting, I must confess I find it rather strange. One hears tales in England even of some of your more deadly types. Quite legendary, I dare say."

"Some of it is," Reno said.

"No such thing as a lightning-fast draw, I suppose?"

"Most gunfighters use the old single-action Colt, which has to be cocked manually after each shot. You have to grab the handle, reaching for the trigger with your finger and thumbing the hammer at the same time. They use black powder, which pretty well makes a foggy cloud that's hard to see through. I guess most men like to be about fifteen feet away from the one they're shootin' at."

"But we hear about how *fast* they are!"

Reno leaned back and there was a grin on his lips. "Was a fellow named Turkey Creek Johnson over at Deadwood in South Dakota. He invited two men to shoot it out with him in the road alongside the town cemetery. Well, they strapped their guns on, and Johnson started toward them from one end of the cemetery fence. They came at him from the other end, and when they got about fifty feet away they started firing. By the time they'd gone ten yards, each had emptied the chambers of one gun and had shifted to a second. Johnson, walking along with one Colt, still hadn't got off a shot. At thirty feet he killed one of the men. Johnson stopped, waited until the second man came a few paces closer, allowed him two or three last shots, then fired once. The dead man's finger was still on the trigger when he fell."

Easy was lounging against the side of the wagon. He broke in, "I seed a feller, a little gambler thin as a rail over at Dodge. He got into it with a strappin' big joker, must have weighed two hundred pounds. The big one sez, 'Now wait, he's shootin' at a bigger target than me. It ain't a fair fight!' Then the gambler turned around and he sez, 'Get some chalk and draw out a man of my size on him, anything of mine that hits outside the line don't count!'"

They all laughed, but a voice took them off guard, "Well, nice little party you got goin' here!"

Carl Slade stepped out of the darkness, staring at the table, his eyes resting on the naked shoulders of the woman. "Wouldn't mind having a little of that steak myself, St. John."

"Perhaps another time," the Englishman said smoothly.

"Not good enough for you?"

St. John dabbed at his thin lips with a napkin, then got up, remarking, "I understand you're the hunter for this train, Slade. If you'd do your job like a good fellow, perhaps you'd eat a little better—and others as well."

Carl drew his lip back, saying, "Not my fault if the game ain't there. Nobody could get a deer in this country!"

"Wouldn't like to bet on that, would you, Slade?" Reno

asked idly. He was leaning back in his chair, but there was a smile on his lips.

"You sayin' you can get meat, drunk?"

"I might."

"You can't get the game if it's not there!"

"You ready to bet on it?"

"Anything you say, drunk!" Carl grinned down at Reno, adding, "You put up your gelding against my bay mare?"

"Not my horse."

Dooley said at once, "Bet if you want, Jim."

"You have to bring in enough to feed the whole train by sunset, that's the bet!"

"That's a lot of meat!" Dooley protested.

"Let Big Mouth there back off it he wants to."

"Take care of the bay, Slade. Don't use your spurs on her. I don't like my horses marked up."

Slade stared at him, then laughed and whirled to walk away, saying, "You just lost a horse, drunk!"

Jean Lamarr had her eyes fixed on Reno's dark face. She seemed to find something that pleased her, for her generous lips curved and she said softly, "Bring me a steak, will you, Jim?"

There was something sensuous in her eyes, and Dooley felt uneasy as she saw Reno slowly answer her smile. He took the hand she held out, holding it so long as they looked at each other that Dooley thought *No! He can't be fool enough to fall for a low woman like that!*

She got up and they all said good night. As they went back to the wagon, Dooley said, "I think it's a shame—St. John taking up with a saloon woman."

He said not a word, and Dooley remembered with a

shock that the woman who had died for Reno had been a
saloon woman. She could have bitten her tongue off.

The next day she was subdued, but as Reno saddled up to
go hunting she said, "Can I go, Jim?"

"Guess so." He took the Henry and led her at a trot in the
direction of the hills.

What he did that day was so simple she could not believe
it. When they were about five miles from camp, he found a
spring with deer signs everywhere. He cut a sapling, peeled it,
then, tying a white handkerchief to the small end, he drove the
other end into the ground. He watched it snap in the breeze,
then said, "Come on, Dooley," and led the way to a line of
brush where they took position.

"What's supposed to happen?" Dooley asked.

"Just watch."

In less than half an hour several deer appeared, seemingly fascinated by the white cloth flapping in the breeze. He
let them get within range and put two of them down with three
shots.

"Why do they come?" Dooley asked as they moved the
carcasses out of sight.

"Curious is all. We'll get a couple more."

They rode into camp at mid-afternoon with four deer in
two travois which he had rigged, and there was rejoicing as
the men began dressing them at once.

Carl Slade's face was murderous, but he had no choice,
for he had boasted all over camp about how he'd bested Reno
in a bet.

He brought the horse to where Reno was helping cut up
the meat, and said, "You win this time, drunk. But there'll be
another day."

Reno smiled and took the bridle of the mare, but said nothing as Slade whirled and walked away.

Easy watched him go, remarking grimly, "He's fernlin' mad, ain't he, Jim?"

"Fernlin' mad?" Dooley looked puzzled. "What's that?"

"Why that's fire-spittin', arm-wavin', dish-throwin' mad. Mad enough to send cats through cat holes, children to hidin' behind chimneys, neighbors to windows, and strong men to drink!"

Reno grinned and said, "You must be from Texas, Easy, the way you talk!"

"Nope. Hail from Bucksnort, Tennessee, thank you. But serious, James, you better keep an eye on that bird. He's mean as a yard dog!"

"I expect he is." Reno nodded. He grinned then, and it made him look young. "I'd be embarrassed to death to get killed by a low-down character like that. No class to it."

Easy moved away with a load of steaks and Dooley flinched. The thought that Reno might get killed sent a shudder through her. "Stay away from him," she urged.

Reno stared at her, then said, "Guess I been staying away from too many things, Dooley. Like gettin' the meat, for instance. I could have done that a week ago, and there were people needing it."

"Why didn't you, Jim?"

He grinned and rubbed his shock of black hair, finally saying, "Well, I guess I've been president of the Poor Me Club, Dooley. Crying in my beer and lettin' everything else slide."

"I noticed."

"You did?" He raised one black eyebrow, then nodded slowly. "Sure you did, boy. Well, I guess you got a right to know about it. I was in love with a girl named Lola, and she—she got killed about a year ago."

She swallowed and nodded. "I'm sorry, Jim. I'm sure she was a wonderful girl."

He nodded and said, "Best I ever saw." Then he looked over toward St. John's wagon and added, "I don't have a picture of her, but Jean Lamarr, she's like Lola! Matter of fact, it set me back when I saw her at Laramie!" He stared toward the wagon, saying in a voice filled with wonder, "She sure is like Lola, Jean is!"

Dooley longed to shout in his ear, "Jean Lamarr is a cheap little tramp, you fool!"

Instead she said, "Can I ride the mare, Jim?"

He brought his gaze away from St. John's wagon and said absently, "What? Oh, sure, boy, anytime." He left her suddenly, and Dooley saw that Jean Lamarr was sitting on the wagon seat smiling at Reno.

Dooley stared across the way, and Easy said, "I reckon His Highness better tend to his heifer. Looks like she's got her sights on Brother James!" Dooley glared at him and walked away rapidly, talking under her breath.

EIGHT
A Party of Sioux

Behind them lay Independence Rock and the Sweetwater. Still far in the distance, just a smudgy blur on the horizon, lay the Rocky Mountains. Imperceptibly the land lifted, and the level plain was broken abruptly by buttes of sandstone. After leaving the river, the group discovered that the water problem became acute once more.

Reno had named the mare he won from Carl "Cherry," and Dooley had asked instantly, "You must have had a girl named that, didn't you?"

Reno had looked up from where he sat on the mare and grinned at her. "You're plumb interested in my love life, Dooley. Maybe I'd like to know about some of your high-steppin' with the ladies."

"I don't really care about your old girlfriends!"

"Well, I never had a girl named Cherry. Her whole name is Cherry Pie."

The mare was a delight to ride, and Reno had abandoned his solitary ways, riding miles every day to hunt for water. Usually he brought back plenty of game for the train.

St. John accompanied him on a fine chestnut stallion, and the two, so different in many ways, took to each other. The Englishman was one of the finest riders Reno had ever seen and a dead shot with a rifle or shotgun. Once he learned the ways of the native game, he brought down almost as many antelope and gamebirds as Reno.

It was late on a Saturday afternoon when St. John asked him, "I suppose we may have difficulties getting through those mountains?"

They were waiting for the train to catch up to them, and Reno looked west toward the Rockies. "Shouldn't be too bad."

"I thought the blasted things rose up like the Alps—snow and all that."

"Guess it'd be impossible if it wasn't for South Pass. Fellow named Robert Stuart was trappin' beaver for John Jacob Astor and found it. It's a flat sort of canyon that wagons can manage. About the only one far as I know."

St. John stared at the blue line of mountains and asked, "And after that—on the other side of the Rockies?"

Reno grinned at the tall man. "Oh, not much. Got to get through Sublette's Cutoff, or else go plumb to Fort Bridger. Then we have to follow the Snake River, which is a chore, since the thing has steep banks and is crooked to beat anything you ever saw! Then when we get to Walla Walla, we either have to build rafts and float the wagons three hundred miles down the Columbia—in which case some of us will get drowned—or we can take a route through the Cascades that makes a bird dizzy. But we may be lucky and hit mountains late enough to catch a blizzard. It's like a funnel there, you see? Then we'll freeze and won't have to worry about the bad trails or the rafting!"

"Jolly well put!" St. John said with a quick smile. Then he gave his companion a closer look and said, "And what will you do when you get there, Jim?"

Reno shrugged and got to his feet. "Don't know. Look, there's the train." A thought struck him, bringing a smile to his broad lips. "You a bettin' man, St. John?"

"Certainly! I have all the major vices and none of the minor ones! What sort of wager did you contemplate?"

"Why, I've listened to you bellyache for a week about having to drink that fancy wine you're totin' without ice to chill it."

St. John stared at him, a curious light in his blue eyes. "Too right, old boy! What's your proposition?"

"Bet you any amount you like I can take care of that problem by bedtime."

"Ah? Well, I shall take you up on that, Reno. Shall we say fifty dollars?"

"Done."

They mounted up and rode to meet the train.

"Spring over there, Slade," Reno called out, and soon the campfires were being lit. Reno took a poker and beat on the steel rim of a wagon wheel, and when the clanging had drawn almost everyone in the train, he said, "Anybody favor a glass of ice water?"

"Ice water?" Easy said loudly in disbelief. "You're funning us!"

"Grab your shovels and some pots." Reno led them to a spot close to a sandstone bank. The soil was soft, and he said, "This ought to do it. Dig in."

St. John stared at the earth, then at Easy. "The bloke is pulling some sort of practical joke, isn't he?"

Reno took a shovel and plunged it into the soft ground.

Everyone watched and when he had removed about a foot of soil, his shovel rang against something hard.

"Bedrock," Buck said.

Reno cleared some of the dirt away, raised the blade of his shovel and broke off some of the hard material. Reaching down he picked up a chunk and tossed it to St. John. "That ought to cool your wine."

"Why, it's ice!" St. John said in amazement. "I owe you fifty dollars!"

"This place is called Ice Slough. We're up at seven thousand feet, and there's always ice about a foot deep, even in July."

Everyone fell to digging, and although the ice was liberally studded with gravel, they got enough chunks to furnish iced drinks for everyone. Addie Grant had plenty of sassafras roots, and St. John had several large tins of tea, so after supper there was a party of sorts.

Wood was plentiful, and two large bonfires soon lit up the night. The sweet notes of Mary Moore's dulcimer soon sounded, joined quickly by Robin's guitar and Easy's harmonica.

Some of the younger people began to dance, and Reno grinned at Jude Finney. "You figure dancin' is sinful?"

Jude looked at him quickly. He felt a little uncomfortable around Reno, but he saw that there was no malice in the dark eyes. "Why, I seem to remember that David danced before the Lord. Guess if it's good enough for David, it's good enough for me."

"Ever do a little yourself, Jude?"

"Well, . . ." A humorous streak crossed the puckered face, and Reno realized that if Jude would get some false teeth, he would be a handsome fellow. "Truth to tell, I guess I done a little of everything when I was a sinner. Hate to name it to you, Jim."

Addie was standing beside him, and she had a smile on her face. "Reckon you've forgot how to dance?"

"Why, I don't think a feller ever forgets that, Addie. Would you dance with me?"

The two moved off, and there was something in the pair that Reno tried to identify, but he failed. They were not rich, certainly not handsome or flashy in any way. Addie's face was serene as she looked at Jude, and despite the scars there was a beauty in her quiet face.

"Looks like the preacher has found himself a woman, Jim."

Reno turned to find Jean at his side and removed his hat at once. She noted his action, and it brought a strange smile to her full lips.

"Looks that way."

"I guess preachers need women just like other men." There was a richness in her voice, a throaty quality that matched the curves of her body. "Why aren't you dancing?"

"Forgot how."

"I'll bet!" Jean looked at the dancers, then turned back to him. "Dance with me, Jim."

Reno hesitated, then shook his head. "Have to beg off on that one, Jean."

She bit her lip. "All right."

He smiled and said, "I'm going to the spring to get coffee water for breakfast. Come with me."

She said at once, "Sure I will."

He picked up a bucket and led her away from the train.

The spring lay in a small ravine two hundred yards away and was circled by a clump of alders. The stars were so bright they could see clearly, and when they got there he filled the bucket and they both had a drink of the icy water.

"It's so quiet out here," she said. The music drifted softly across to them, muted and faint, and the bonfires were only a glow flickering over the rise. She walked over to an outcropping of rock and sat down, "Sit down, Jim."

He put the bucket down, and sat beside her. "We're fools for doing this."

"What are you afraid of, Jim? Me?"

He grinned at her and shook his head. "Well, to tell the truth, I guess I am a little gun-shy. But I was talkin' about Injuns. We ought to have guards out every night. Just dumb fool luck we haven't been spotted by this time."

"Daniel Slade's a fool," she remarked, but she was not interested in Indians. Looking up, she said, "What star is that, do you think?"

He looked up at the bright yellowish-red star that glittered more brightly than the rest, and said, "That's Betelgeuse."

She turned to stare at him, "How do you know that?"

"Had a friend in the army who knew all about the stars. Used to point them out when we pulled guard at night. See those other two stars with the bright one? Well, that's the belt of Orion. You're supposed to see a warrior in that group of stars."

"A warrior?" She leaned closer to him and threw her head back. "I don't see anything like that."

"Well, I don't either." He was acutely conscious of her perfume and the pressure of her arm against his. "Way it goes, according to my friend, Orion was a soldier who was killed by a lady named Diana. She was a hunter, and when she killed him she turned him into those stars. One of the old fables, I guess."

She laughed and turned to face him, her hand on his arm. "I like it! Most of the time it's the woman who gets hurt, not the man!"

He was stirred by her touch. There was a sultry power in her, and she was fully aware of it. To cover his confusion he looked up, pointed at the sky and said, "That's Polaris, due north. Found my way lots of times by that one."

She leaned close, pulling her body tight against him and sighted along his arm. "Which one, Jim?" The rich curve of her body pressed against him, and when he turned his head she was not looking toward the star. Her eyes were wide open in the moonlight, inviting him, and his blood slogged through his veins, making a steady ringing in his ears. He rose, pulled her to her feet, and as he put his arms around her, she met him eagerly. Her arms went around his neck, and her lips were soft yet firm as he kissed her. The weight of her hands increased, moving over the muscles of his back with a caressing pressure. Her lips stayed with him, and the flimsy strings that held him back began to break. The steely strength in his arms suddenly bent her like a reed.

They teetered on the razor edge of passion, and then a noise drew Reno's instant attention. It was a thumping sound, followed by a brief struggle of some kind terminated by a muffled, shrill cry.

Reno pulled himself away from Jean. Then she whispered, "What was that?" He stepped back and said, "Just an owl taking a rabbit, I reckon."

She stared at him, her breasts rising rapidly and her lips half-parted. He was, she saw, shutting himself off from her, and it made her angry. "What's the matter with you?" Accustomed to stirring men, dominating them with her beauty, she knew that he had been the one to control the situation. "What are you afraid of?"

He was a strong shape before her in the silver moonlight. He stirred restlessly, and there was a sadness in his face as he answered slowly, "Guess I'm afraid of believing good things will happen, Jean."

She thought about that, and the anger left her eyes. Finally she said, "I guess you've been unlucky in love, Jim. Is that right?"

"Well, . . ." He hesitated, then said quietly, "I was pretty lucky once. But she died."

"Oh, I'm sorry!" Jean Lamarr had wide experience with men, and she had no trouble recognizing when one of them tried to engage her sympathy. Reno was not asking for pity, but there was a strange vulnerability in the tough face that made her say gently, "It happens sometimes, Jim."

He stared off into the night, then swung to meet her gaze. "You look like her."

The simple statement shook Jean for some reason, and with all her experience she had no answer.

Finally he said, "I guess we better get back." He picked up the bucket and led her back up the slope into the circle. They stood together watching the dancers, but neither of them felt like joining in.

Their walk hadn't been unnoticed. Dooley and Lee had seen them leave the circle, and Lee had remarked, "Gosh, that lady sure does look like Miss Lola!" He watched the pair disappear into the darkness and said, "Wouldn't it be something if—"

"If *what?*" Dooley snapped, her mouth turned down.

"Oh, nothing," Lee said quickly, but he kept watching the path to the spring.

"What kind of girl was Lola?" She felt like a nosy old gossip, but Lee was eager to talk.

"Why, she was real fine, Dooley! I lost my folks and did odd jobs, you see. Well, she'd cook for me sometimes, and she was teaching me to read."

"And she was a—a saloon woman?" Dooley could find no other way of saying it, and she was afraid that Lee would be hurt.

"She'd been married and her husband had died and left her his saloon. But she wasn't going to stay there." Lee's eyes were bright and he smiled at the memory. "There was this preacher who had been an officer in the Union Army, and Jim thought lots of him. Well, he got to know Miss Lola, and she got to going to church with Jim, and she was real excited about it all, going to church, you know? So after her and Jim decided to get married . . ." He broke off suddenly and stabbed at the dirt with a stick, silent with his thoughts.

Dooley sought for a way to put it and finally said in a tentative voice, "You say this Lamarr woman *looks* like Lola, Lee . . ." She paused and tried to find a way to say what was in her mind. "Do you think she's the same in other ways?"

"Don't know, Dooley." He gave her a look that seemed to plead for assurance. "I—I know she's not married to Mr. St. John—and that's not right. But she can change, can't she? Anybody can change, can't they, Dooley?"

Dooley wanted to warn the boy not to hope, but his eyes begged so blatantly for some kind of assurance that she said weakly, "Why, sure. Sure they can, Lee."

Even as she said this, she thought, *She's no good! Why can't he see that?* But suddenly she realized that the death of Lola had been the end of the world for Lee. She had been his hope of all that he'd missed and all that he'd dreamed of having—parents, home, security. *Can't blame the poor kid! I'd do the same. But it will never work. Jean Lamarr's not Lola—not by a long shot! Is Jim too blind to see that?*

Jane Ann Burns also had noted the departure of Reno and Jean. She had sat restlessly watching the dancers, tapping her foot, and as they left she said, "Look, there goes Reno and that Lamarr woman!"

Robert had said little all evening, and now he shook his head, saying only, "Reno should know better."

"Oh, Bob, you're so *rigid!* You just can't believe people can flirt a little without making a big thing out of it!"

They had been over it so many times that he knew nothing he could say would change her mind. He roused himself and said, "Would you like to dance?"

She got up at once, her face alive with pleasure, and as they danced he thought how vulnerable she was. There was no evil in her, he knew, but she had never been able to turn loose of those days when she was the belle of every dance. She regretted marrying him; this he accepted without bitterness. His Scotch Presbyterian training told him that marriage was forever, so he prayed with a fervor that would have amazed her for her to learn to love him.

When the two paused to rest, Robert saw Beau Slade turn from Ellie Satterfield. Beau started to leave, then his eyes met those of Burns, and a smile touched his lips. He made his way across the circle and said, "Mind if I dance with Mrs. Burns, Bob?"

He was a handsome man, colorful where Burns was plain, and he was aware of the attention of practically everyone in the circle. A predatory boldness was in the man, and he nodded easily and said, "How about it? I won't run off with her!"

A laugh went up from someone at this, and Robert Burns felt the pressure of the situation. He knew that if he said no, he would look like a puling jealous husband. If he said yes, he was caving in to the fear that tinged his mind when Beau Slade entered his thoughts.

Finally he said, "It's up to her." He spoke almost harshly, but his wife said at once, "Now, that's being a gentleman, Robert!"

As Jane Ann was spun around the circle in Beau's arms, a wave of shame filled Burns, intermingled with rage. Jane thought she could play her flirtatious games with any man, but she was blindly ignorant of men such as the one who held her so tightly. He had no scruples, and given the opportunity he would use her and cast her aside without a thought. *Sooner or later I'll have to fight him!* Robert thought. And the thought turned his face grim in the flickering firelight.

Buck Henry had kept himself back in the shadows, watching the dancers but making no move to join them. Ellie was the object of his gaze, and his mother shook her head, saying to Josh, "I hate to see it."

Josh Henry was smaller than his wife. It was from her people that Buck got his size, for they were all big men. He looked over and said, "I'll have a talk with him. Been meaning to."

He ambled over to where his son stood slightly behind a wagon and said, "Not dancin', son?"

"Don't feel like it."

The brevity of the reply did not discourage Josh. He knew the feelings in the huge son he had sired ran as deep as the silence ran long. He was not a man to dodge, so he said simply, "Son, me and your mother been worried about you—about how you feel about the girl."

Buck looked down at his father and shrugged. There was a sadness in his mild blue eyes and he said, "Knew that. But you probably don't have anything to worry about. I ain't fancy enough for her."

"Maybe not, but I hate to see you grieving. Man wants his son to have a good wife, to have good children. You're all we got, your ma and me. Hate to see you hurtin'."

Buck was caught by the simple statement. They were not a demonstrative family, the Henrys. This was as close as his father would ever come to declaring his love, and Buck was moved. He stood there, a massive shape in the darkness, and then he put his hand on Josh's shoulder and said, "I—I'm proud you feel like that, Pa. And I'd be a liar if I said it was easy. You know me too well, I guess, for me to make up anything. But the way it looks now, nothing will ever come of it. I'll make out all right."

Finally the fires died down, the music was silent, and the train slept. Reno lay in his blankets, staring at the brilliant display of stars overhead for a long time. Then he closed his eyes and drifted off into a fretful sleep.

He rose before dawn, saddled, and rode west. It had been some time since he had traveled through the South Pass, and he wanted to make sure of his bearings. The trail, however, was clear, and he spotted the long line of red sandstone cliffs that clearly marked the way.

The sun was directly overhead by the time he met the

train, Carl and Daniel in the lead. "We're right on the money," he said, waving at the buttes. "South Pass is about three days if we don't have trouble."

Daniel shifted uneasily in his saddle, then bit his lower lip nervously. "We had some visitors this morning for breakfast."

Reno stared at him, and suddenly he knew what was coming. "Indians?"

"Five of 'em come bustin' into camp. One of 'em could speak a little English."

"What'd they look like?" Reno asked.

"Why, like all the rest—dirty and shiftless!" Carl spat on the ground. "Tried to hold us up. Said we had to give 'em two cows 'fore we could cross their land. *Their* land! Now ain't that something'!"

"You ran 'em off?" Reno asked.

"Well, it was like this. . . ." Daniel Slade was defensive, and he couldn't meet Reno's eyes as he went on. "We told them to git, and they kept on arguin' for a while, but finally they did. And then, well, Beau had left camp early and he come in on 'em, see? Course, he didn't know what they was up to—"

"So he let fly and got one of 'em, Reno!" Carl said savagely. "And then they run off."

"They didn't have guns?" Reno asked.

"No, but Beau come on 'em of a sudden and he didn't know that," Daniel muttered. "Anyway, they're gone now."

Reno stared at him, shook his head, and stated flatly, "I doubt it. You bury the one Beau killed?"

Carl laughed loudly and said, "Not likely, Reno. You can go take care of your Injun friends."

"He's not there now, Carl. And anyone who left the train would never get back. I'm surprised you two are still alive."

Carl snorted and said, "You're crazy, Reno! All I've heard out of you is scare talk since we left Laramie. They were just a handful of scrawny Injuns."

"If they're the party of Sioux Colter mentioned, you'll find out different soon enough. Did you put out a rear guard?"

Carl said, "You ain't in charge of this train, Reno! Just you tend your own affairs, and I'll take care of the train!"

Reno stared at the big man, then spurred Cherry to a fast gallop and rode to the wagons. He pulled up and dismounted, then went to the wagon and pulled the Henry out and loaded it.

"Jim!" Dooley came from the other side where she had been walking, and her face was strained. "Did you hear?"

"I heard!" He took her by the arm and stared into her face. "Listen, don't leave the train, you hear me? I don't care *what* you hear or see, don't get away from the wagon more than twenty feet. You got that?"

She nodded and swallowed hard. "You think there's going to be trouble?"

"Yes. Where's Lee?"

"He's over there with Easy."

"Tell him to stick close."

"Where are you going?"

He didn't pause to answer, but mounted and rode toward the rear of the train. He was hailed by Buck, and stopped long enough to say, "Buck, keep your eyes open."

"I know, Jim."

"Who's on drag?"

"Pa and Burns—" He broke off and said in alarm, "You think they could get hit?"

"No reason why not." There was an iron in Reno's voice that Buck had not heard.

Buck handed the lines to his mother and said, "I'm going with Jim!"

Reno waited until he got his horse, then the two of them rode back past the line of wagons.

The herd was spread out, but Josh and Burns were all right. They were surprised to see Buck and Reno, and Burns said, "You think we'll get raided?"

"Don't know. If there's just a few of them, they wouldn't make a full-scale attack. Indians don't do that much, anyway, even when they've got the numbers. But it would be easy for them to move in from the rear and pick off the men riding drag."

Burns turned pale and whipped his head around. "I—I haven't looked behind me all day!" he whispered.

"You've been lucky," Reno said grimly. "Me and Buck will hang back and keep a lookout."

By dusk everybody was exhausted, eyes strained from searching the landscape for Indians. They circled the wagons and Daniel Slade called them together for a meeting.

"Now, we've got to be careful not to panic," he said, his eyes sweeping the faces before him. He straightened up and stated in a firm voice, "All we have to do is keep a close guard, and we'll be all right. Those bucks are probably scooting dead away from us right now, but I believe in taking precautions, so we'll double the guard tonight." He went on for a long time, and finally Beau said impatiently, "Aw, let's eat!"

Vinson Grant had paid little attention to Daniel. Now he turned to Reno and said, "Reno, you've been around Indians. What do you think?"

"Wish it hadn't happened. If it's part of a Sioux war party, I don't mind telling you I'd as soon be someplace else."

"War party!" Beau laughed loudly. "Them scrawny savages!"

Reno shook his head. "You got some real bad ideas about Indians, Beau. The Sioux are the finest light cavalry on the face of the earth! They can run twenty miles across this desert, eat a rabbit, and run back again. They can move across broken ground in the middle of the darkest night you ever saw without making a sound and slit your throat before you can blink!"

"Aw, everybody knows Indians wait until dawn to attack!" Carl countered.

"You keep thinking that, Slade, and you'll be the most surprised corpse on the train!"

Carl began to argue, but Daniel said loudly, "Hold it, this ain't gettin' us anywhere! We got to keep calm. I ain't sayin' Reno is right, 'cause I don't think he is. But all the same, it won't hurt to be more careful. So we'll double the guard and change it every four hours." He began to assign men and times, but there was an air of discontent in the group.

Reno had early watch, along with Buck, Vinson Grant, and a man named Patterson. They kept the fires up, and Reno made sure that they didn't relax a moment.

At three o'clock they were relieved by Beau, Ty Edwards, his son Luke, and Josh Henry. Beau said, "Figured nothing would happen," and there was a look of contempt on his face.

"Don't go out there, no matter what happens." Reno said as he left. "You'll never get back alive."

He rolled up in his blankets and was sleeping fitfully when gunfire sounded. Grabbing the rifle, he made straight for the sound, and almost ran over Easy, who was pulling his coat on hurriedly. They ran together toward the sound of firing, and found Ty Edwards staring with his mouth open into the darkness.

"What happened?" Reno demanded.

"They hit the herd!" he said shakily. "Luke heard 'em moving and went out to see, and he hasn't come back yet!"

The stock was scattered, Reno saw at once as he and Easy ran toward them. "Be careful, Jim!" Easy hollered. "They may be jest waitin' fer us to come bullin' in!"

"Swing to your left. I'll take the right—and stay low!"

They swung out, and Reno ran quickly across the broken ground, his eyes sweeping the terrain in the pale light of the stars. Mules and oxen were running, almost in a stampede, and he had to dodge some of them to keep from being trampled. The cattle were moving, too, and he knew that there was no hope of stopping them now. He was also fairly certain that the Indians had moved away, but he took no chances. Half an hour later he moved back, meeting with Easy, who said in disgust, "Well, ain't this a pretty come-off! We ain't never goin' to get that stock back, Jim!"

"Let's see if we can find the rest of the guards." Reno moved toward the train, noticing the stock in every direction, just dots in the distance, some of them.

"Reno! That you?" Vinson called out nervously.

"Yes! Everybody accounted for?"

"Don't know."

"Have you seen anything of Luke Edwards?"

"No. Nobody else has, either."

They gathered in the pale light, and Daniel said, "Blast them! Look at those cattle! We'll be a week rounding them up!"

Reno looked around, and there was a sudden tension in the still morning air. "Spread out and search for Luke. And be careful!"

He need not have told them that, for by now even the Slades were wide awake and jumpy.

They found Luke twenty minutes later. His throat was slit and he had been scalped.

They stood looking down on him, and Reno said harshly, "Well, Beau, you want to tell us again how easy it's going to be?"

Beau stared at the mutilated boy, and said stubbornly, "He shouldn't have gone out by himself. I told them that!"

Vinson Grant cursed him and ended by saying, "You go tell his ma that, Beau! It'll be a real comfort to her!"

Ty Edwards had never spoken a kind word to his son in all his life. Now he came from where he had stood in the shelter of the wagons and the men parted to make way for him. He stood there silently, so skinny that he looked like a young boy in the faint light. He stooped down then, and touched the boy's face, a touch of reverence in the act that did not go with the receding chin and buck teeth, but the aura of death had done what life could not do. It had shown him how fragile a hold any human being could have on existence. Now he knelt there, his eyes fixed on his dead boy, and there was for the first time a true humility in his voice as he said, "I'll go tell his ma." He put a trembling hand on his son's still face, the first caresses he'd ever given the boy, and then he slowly rose. They saw the tears on his thin cheeks as he turned and walked toward the wagons.

NINE
Nightwalker

They buried Luke Edwards at first light. There was no time for a coffin, and as his blanket-wrapped body was lowered into the shallow grave hastily scooped out of the thin soil, the harsh yellow light tinged the faces of the mourners with a pale, sickly cast. Ty and Lulu Edwards, Luke's parents, looked frail and old as they stood beside the grave. The mother had buried so many babies that her grief had been spent years before. A tear made a track down her withered cheek, and her dull eyes and worn body signaled the total surrender to the blow she had endured. Ty Edwards clenched his fists until the knuckles were white. Grief and bitterness met in his faded eyes, and as Jude quoted a chapter of Scripture over the body, Ty gave an involuntary shake of his head as if denying the hope he spoke of. Sally Edwards held tightly to Hiram and Missy, her face ravaged with grief. She had loved Luke best, and his death had chilled her, paralyzing her mind so completely that her plain features seemed frozen.

Jude's voice was thinned by the emptiness that stretched away on every side, and the small group of wagons seemed to be an island in the middle of a trackless ocean. As he finished and the Edwardses moved away to avoid seeing the clods strike the body of Luke, the strained solemnity thrown over them by the funeral was transformed. Hasty fires sprang up, and breakfast was prepared as the men met in a ragged group drawn together to make decisions.

"We got to get the cattle quick as we can," Daniel announced. He stared at the group, and noting the haggard look on the tired faces, he raised his voice. "This ain't no time to slack off, men. If we don't get our stock right off, we won't never get 'em. They can't be too far, and I want every man out on roundup."

"What about the train?" Will Satterfield asked. "Injuns might attack while we're huntin' the stock."

"Well, we'll leave a few men here, but I want every man we can spare rounding up stock."

He was a tall shape against the morning light, and the stubbornness of the man was etched in deep lines on his cavernous cheeks. He knew no way to lead men; he could only drive using harsh words and his fists when that failed. "Mattox, Sims, and you, Preacher—you three guard the wagons."

Easy said with a wicked light in his eyes, "Shore, Slade. Them three ought to be able to stand off a whole tribe of fightin' Sioux."

"Never mind!" Slade could not abide any criticism. He shook his head, adding, "Some of us will always be in hearin' distance of the wagons. Anybody hears a shot, come runnin' back to the train. Now, eat and git started!"

Robert Burns exchanged a look with Reno and said under his breath, "Somehow I am not inspired by the man. If he didn't own most of the cattle, I wonder how anxious he'd be to gather them up?" Without waiting for an answer, he turned and walked back to his wagon. They would not have time to eat at noon, he realized, so he planned to cook a large breakfast. He was surprised to find that Jane Ann had the meal ready for him.

"Let's eat before the food gets cold, Bob." She fussed over him, filling his plate with a heap of scrambled eggs, large slices of bacon, and two old biscuits softened by warm fat. "You eat, you hear me? I declare, you're getting downright skinny!"

He took a mouthful of food, chewed thoughtfully, and gave her a glance that brought a faint glow to her cheeks. For days they had been like strangers, speaking only when necessary, and she felt guilty under his quiet gaze. "I . . . those are the last of the eggs." It was not what she had intended to say, but she could not bring herself to speak naturally. "Are we moving on today?"

"I don't think so. It'll take time to round up the cattle."

"Are you going with the others?"

"We'll all be helping, except for a small guard for the wagons."

Jane Ann put her plate down and leaned forward, fear in her eyes. "Don't go, Bob! I'm afraid to be left alone."

"Maybe you can get Beau Slade to keep you company." As soon as the bitter words left his lips, he was sorry. Noting the sudden quiver of Jane Ann's lips and the involuntary gesture she made with one hand, he shook his head. "I didn't mean that." His food was suddenly tasteless. He got up and said shortly, "You'll be safe enough," then walked toward the horse herd. He was angry with himself, feeling helpless against the bitter rage that had taken root in him. He was not a hard man, or had not been until the trouble with Beau Slade. Getting a wife such as Jane Ann had never ceased to be a wonder to him. He had, of course, seen all too quickly that she was not ready for marriage, that she desired romance and color he could not provide. Until the incident with Beau, however, he had plodded along, humoring her in small ways, believing that she would settle down and become a real wife to him. Now the scars left by Beau's insults were deep and would not be easily healed.

Reno and Easy were saddling their horses, and Burns said before he thought, "Why does a man make such a fool of himself over women?"

Easy yanked at the girth, gave Burns a wry smile, and said, "Shoot, Bob, gettin' along with women folks is kinder like puttin' a wildcat in a croker sack—it can't be did!"

Reno noted the haggard look on Burns's face, but said nothing. He had given the neat Scotsman several lessons in the use of a Colt and realized that it was hopeless. Burns would never be able to match the skill of a man like Beau Slade. When he had hinted at this, Burns had tightened his lips, shaken his head stubbornly, and said, "It won't stand, Jim. Better to be dead than a coward!"

They gathered cattle all day, staying in groups no smaller than six or seven riders. By sundown they had recovered two-thirds of the stock, and Slade argued that they ought to continue the search for another day.

"Don't agree, Daniel," Barney Moore said. "We'd have to go farther from the train to find any more stock, and I don't mind sayin' I don't fancy givin' the Injuns that kind of chance at me—not to mention leavin' the wagons at their mercy."

"We can't leave valuable stock out there," Daniel argued.

"Most of 'em belong to you, Slade," Vinson Grant remarked. "You can't ask men to do your work."

"Besides, we ran on to quite a few critters the Injuns killed." Buck shook his head, adding sadly, "Most of 'em they just tore a steak out. Just killed 'em for meanness, I reckon. But I agree with Barney. We need to move on quick as we can."

Slade argued, but in the end they agreed to move on the next morning.

Nobody slept much that night. A double guard was posted, and when Buck and Reno were relieved, they found Buck's parents at Dooley's fire. They had made biscuits in a Dutch oven, and the two men ate hungrily, washing the fresh bread down with draughts of scalding black coffee.

Mrs. Henry had brought a jar of apple butter for the biscuits, and as she fastened the lid on she said, "I'll be glad to leave this place."

"Me, too," Josh Henry said. He glanced over at Reno and asked, "Jim, you think them Injuns will hit us again?"

"Can't say, Josh," Reno murmured. "They may follow us right up to the gates of Fort Bridger, sniping away at us all the way after dark. Or they may get hungry for buffer tongue and light out tonight. Never can tell with Injuns."

"You don't seem to hate them," Alice Henry remarked. She stared across the fire at Reno, noting his indolence. "You've fought them in the past, I expect?"

"Sure have, ma'am. And I fought Yankees for four years. You wouldn't have me pull down on every Yankee I meet, would you now?"

There was a sly thread of humor in Reno's words, and Mrs. Henry bridled, saying almost angrily, "That's different!"

Reno shrugged and put both hands palm upward in a mute gesture. "Maybe that's what's wrong with me, Mrs. Henry. I don't see any difference."

"Aw, Jim, you gotta see some difference between a red-skin and a white man!" Josh protested. He was the mildest man on the train, but there was a faint stirring of anger in his mild eyes as he added, "They butchered Luke like he was a yearling!"

"And what did Beau Slade do to the Indian, Josh?" Reno asked.

Josh Henry opened his mouth, but could not find an answer. Finally he said, "Well, I guess there ain't no way I can say that was right. But, Jim, they're *savages!*"

Reno leaned forward, and there was a stirring in his still face that caught at Dooley. She did not miss the flash of anger followed by a distinct sadness that crossed Reno's face.

"I was at the Bloody Angle, Josh, at the battle of Antietam."

"Heard about that," Josh said at once. "it was pretty bad, wasn't it?"

"Worst day of the war," Reno said slowly. He poked at the fire with a stick, and when he looked up there was an expression in his eyes that made Dooley flinch. "We fought in a trench, with men falling like grain cut down by a scythe. They fell into the trench, some wounded and some dead. And we stood on them, Josh. I felt some of them squirm and cry out, but we were being overrun, and it was so hot that we were using our guns as clubs. Too close even for bayonets! The ground was running red with blood, and men were crawling around like squashed bugs, holding their guts in with their hands!"

He paused then, and there was a fierce spark of bitterness in his dark eyes as he asked harshly, "Who were the savages there, Josh? I can tell you quick—*I* was one of them!"

The violence of his voice lashed out so suddenly that the others were stricken mute. He was usually so soft-spoken that people forgot or failed to notice the raw savage streak that was in him. Dooley swallowed, realizing the danger of the man.

Then Reno glanced around the fire, smiled thinly, and said, "Guess I'm an Injun myself, Josh. At least, I spent enough time with them to understand a little bit of how they must feel when they see us taking the land they've always thought was theirs."

"But, Jim, you can't say that a few Injuns have the right to keep this land," Josh argued. "Why, the whole country is movin' this way. It takes space to farm, to raise cattle. You can't really expect the Injuns to use hundreds of miles for hunting grounds when white people need a place to live!"

Reno was silent for a long while. An owl hooted from far across the prairie, and Reno seemed to find the sound interesting, for he waited until it faded before he said gently, "Why, I guess you'd be right in that, Josh. The old days are gone for the Injuns. All I say is that I'm not sure that they can understand why we're taking it away from them. And I guess I'd have to admit if anyone pushed at me like we're doing to them, why, I guess I'd do just what they're doing."

"Don't understand that man," Josh said when Reno had disappeared.

Leah had not said a word all night, but now as she got up to clean the dishes she suddenly stood upright, a strong shape in the flicker of the firelight, and said suddenly, "Guess maybe I do." The woman spoke so seldom in front of strangers that her words held them still. "Seems to me like that man has got a powerful feelin' fo' folks who is hurtin'!"

The comment caught at Dooley, and she glanced into the darkness where Reno had gone. "Why, I guess maybe that's right, Leah. He's so hard and tough—but he's real sensitive in some ways." She was thinking of Lola as she spoke, and of how Reno had taken Lee under his protection.

"He better not be too soft on Injuns," Buck said thoughtfully. "It could get him killed."

Lee had been so quiet that Dooley had forgotten him, but after the Henrys left for their wagon, she saw him sitting in the shadows.

"Better get a little sleep, Lee," she said. "Be a long day tomorrow."

As she turned to go, a touch at her elbow gave her a shock.

"Jim!" She gulped nervously. "Don't sneak up on me like that!"

He smiled at her, his white teeth gleaming in the moonlight, the angular planes of his tough face relaxed. He looked almost boyish then, and he said, "Sorry. Habit, I reckon. Guess you noticed how quiet Lee's been. I've been trying to talk to him ever since the Prather boy was killed."

"It must have hit him hard, Jim. Harry was a good kid. I guess boys Lee's age don't think much about other kids dying." Reno stood so close to her that she could feel the touch of his arm, and as always, it made her nervous to have him close. "He's a fine boy, Jim."

"Yes." He seemed to be searching for words, and suddenly he put his arm around Dooley's shoulders, and there was a warmth in his voice as he said, "Guess he needs a friend closer to his own age than me. Say, how old *are* you, anyway? Fifteen?"

The weight of his arm on her shoulder sent strange sensations through her. It was, she knew, a friendly gesture of an older man to a boy, but it disturbed her. The hard muscles of his body pressing against her sent a shock along her nerves, and her breathing grew short as she said, "Fifteen? Oh, at least!" She pulled away from his embrace, saying quickly, "I guess I'll try to get some sleep."

He stood there, aware of her quick reaction, and cocked his head, a small grin on his wide lips. "You're a real touch-me-not, Dooley. Don't like people touching you much, do you?"

"Oh, I don't know . . ." She pulled her coat closer and thought suddenly that this might be a way to keep him at a distance. "I was always like that. Just don't like to be hugged."

"Well, can't blame you for not wanting a pug-ugly like me falling all over you. Now with that Marie girl, I guess that's different."

"She's just a kid!" Dooley said, uncomfortable as usual when he mentioned the girl's infatuation. "If you got hugging on your mind, why don't you go find that Englishman's woman. She'd be willing, wouldn't she?"

"Couldn't say, Dooley," Reno said evenly.

Some demon prompted her to say, "No? What do you two do when you go for your long walks in the woods, Jim Reno? Play checkers?"

He stared hard at her, but she ceased to care what he might think. "You fancy yourself in love with her?"

"Dooley," he said slowly, "you're gonna have to learn how to act. If you was a little older, I'd break your nose! Why, you're as gabby as a woman!"

She flinched and then said, "I'm sorry, Jim. I just think you need to be careful with that woman."

"Because of St. John?"

"No! Because she—she looks like Lola!" His face changed and she went on quickly, knowing that she was treading on dangerous ground: "Oh, I know you think I'm a busybody, Jim, but you told me about Lola, and then you start chasing around after this woman just because she *looks* like her! Can't you see that's wrong?"

He stared at her. "What's that mean?"

"Why, you can't accept the fact that Lola is dead! You won't let her be dead, Jim! Why won't you realize that Jean Lamarr is herself—a fancy woman! You're dishonoring Lola's memory when you try to find her in a woman like that!"

His face twisted and there was a sudden movement in his arms. She thought for one frightening moment he meant to hit her, but he did not. He simply stood there staring at her. Finally he forced a thin smile.

"Dooley, you got to overcome this habit you got of holding back things. You got to learn to just blurt out whatever's on your mind, no matter how rough it is!"

"I—I'm sorry, Jim. I talk too much. It's none of my business."

She started to turn, but he said, "Well, I don't agree. Looks like we've turned out to be each other's business, Dooley. Guess that's what friends are, don't you reckon?" Then he said grimly, "Anyway, if we don't have a wagonload of luck, we won't have to worry about my love life—or life at all!"

"Is it that bad?"

"It's worse than anybody knows, Dooley. Injuns are pretty poor shakes at some things, but there's one thing they do real well!"

"What's that, Jim?"

"Hating, Dooley." Reno smiled grimly staring into the night. "Don't know as I've ever seen them beat at that!"

St. John looked around at the broad grassy meadows dipping down toward a distant horizon and remarked, "I say, Reno, where are the mountains?"

The two rode point half a mile in advance of the train, with Daniel and Carl a few hundred yards to their left. Reno's eyes searched the terrain constantly. "Why, we're in Oregon now. Like I told you, the South Pass is the only way through, and the eastern border of the territory is right about here."

"Glad to hear it. This Indian business is getting serious, or so I gather."

Reno reined his horse up and stared intently at a clump of trees clinging to the lip of a small canyon to the east. He answered without turning, "We've still got a thousand miles to go and the Cascades to cross. But I'm more concerned about what's in those trees."

"Trees?"

"See that dust cloud just behind them?"

"You think that might be the savages?"

Reno gave him a sudden grin, "Well, Algy, it's not mice!"

St. John laughed and stared at the trees. "I dare say not. Shall we charge, old boy?"

"I reckon I'll pass on that," Reno said dryly.

He turned at the sound of horses approaching and waited until Carl and Daniel pulled up shortly. "What's going on?" Carl demanded.

Reno pointed toward the canyon. "Got company."

Even as he spoke, three riders appeared, riding out of the

screen of trees. They were riding small ponies and carrying rifles. They were at least half a mile away, but as they pulled their horses to a stop and stared at the white men, Reno said softly, "They're wearing paint."

"What does that signify?" St. John asked.

"Looking for a fight," Reno answered.

"Come on," Carl said eagerly. "Let's get 'em!"

He and Daniel spurred forward, but when Reno and St. John remained still, he hauled up and looked back. "Well, you comin' or not!"

"Not." Reno pointed toward the motionless Indians. "Why do you think they showed themselves, Carl? They'd like nothing better than to lead us into that canyon. And I'd bet my war pension there's a nice little party just waiting for us."

Carl shook his head and said, "You don't know that, Reno. I say we run those three down and it'll teach the rest of 'em a lesson!"

"You'll never run a Sioux down on that horse. Those stringy ponies will be going when that big chestnut is plumb out of steam. But if you did catch them, you'd be right sorry."

"I'm ordering you to come, Reno!" Carl said angrily. "We got a chance to even up the odds."

Reno shook his head, saying mildly, "If you want your ticket punched, Carl, you fly right at it."

"I'll go get some help, Pa," Carl said with contempt in his voice. "We'll get a party and attack that bunch."

Daniel bit his lip and glanced at the Indians, who had not moved. "Why are they just starin' at us?"

"Waiting for a bunch of fools to follow them into that canyon." Reno pulled his horse around and said, "Come on, St. John."

The Slades followed them back to the train, and as Carl started shouting "Indians!" the wagons pulled to a halt and a crowd soon gathered around him.

"What's going on, Carl?" Barney Moore demanded.

"We got them spotted!" Carl grinned. "All of you get mounted and we'll wipe the suckers out right now."

A silence fell on the group, followed by a hum of talk, and Satterfield asked cautiously, "How many are there, Carl?"

"Just three."

"Well . . ." Satterfield looked around uncertainly and said, "I guess we can handle it."

Vinson Grant was staring at Carl, and then he shifted his glance to Reno. "Jim, what do you think?"

"Never mind him," Carl said savagely.

"Jim?" Vinson insisted, and despite Carl's curses, the pressure fell on Reno.

"Well, Vinson, I only *saw* three, like Carl says." He had dismounted and stood motionless, slapping the reins gently against his leg.

Something in the way he answered made Buck ask, "You think something is wrong?"

Reno merely said evenly, "Only time you see a Sioux is when he wants you to see him."

"I reckon you're sayin' that church is out, ain't you, James?" Easy had mounted his horse, but now he slid to the ground and shook his head. "I mind the only time Ol' Blue Light got his tail in a crack. Got fooled by a leetle ol' bunch of Yanks."

"Who's 'Old Blue Light'?" Daniel asked.

"Stonewall Jackson," Easy said, grinning. "Well, he seen a small bunch of bluebellies in 'twixt a couple hills in the valley, and he told us to go git 'em. Well, we run over there and just as we reched out to grab 'em, a whole division of Segal's corp jumped out from behind a hill and pitched into us!"

"They give you a sufficient walloping, Easy?" Vinson said with a grin.

"Wal, I wuz ready to quit 'fore they was, Vin, no foolin'. But when Jackson come up and took a look-see, why, he just said, 'You fellers quit foolin' with that Yankee trash right off!'"

"Well, what happened?" Carl demanded impatiently when the small rider paused.

Easy stared at him and said solemnly, "Why, they kilt me, Carl!"

A laugh went up, and when it died down, Vinson said, "I reckon I'll sit this one out."

Carl stared at Reno with rage in his face. "You're yellow, Reno! If you wasn't such an old woman, we'd settle this business today!"

"Don't worry, Carl," Reno said. "You'll have all the fighting you can say grace over before we get out of this."

As Carl pulled his horse savagely around and galloped away, Easy gave Reno a nudge. "Aw, James, you done gone and hurt his feelings!"

St. John was staring after Carl. He remarked evenly but with a keen light in his blue eyes, "That chap could prove to be a liability."

"Wants to be the whole kit and caboodle." Easy nodded. "Why he's so danged bossy he wouldn't go to a funeral unless he could be the corpse!"

"I beg your pardon?" St. John asked with a puzzled look at his employee.

"Don't mention it," Easy said with a wave of his hand.

They made a dry camp, Daniel driving them hard until nearly dark. Reno was on the midnight watch, and he sat in front of a small fire, talking to Lee. Finally the boy went to sleep, and one by one the fires died out until only the one they kept going all night glowed in the darkness.

Dooley pulled her blanket around her shoulders, keeping close to the fire. She dreaded going to sleep, and for over an hour she kept the conversation going, mostly by making Reno tell stories of the war.

She grew drowsy then, and with a wide yawn she got up saying, "Well, that's about all the lies I can listen to at one time. What I want to know is, if you and the Third Arkansas did all you say, how did Grant ever whip the South?"

"Hard to understand at that," Reno said. "Why, if—"

He broke off suddenly, for a voice came floating out of the night, a strange voice, hollow and seemingly coming from nowhere.

"White man! White man!"

The cry broke the silence, and a sudden mutter of alarm arose from the wagons. By the time the voice cried out again, men were grabbing their guns and staring out into the darkness.

"White man! White man!" The voice floated across the night, then came words not in English—guttural and choppy.

"Guard! Guard!" Daniel Slade bellowed. "Who's that out there?"

They waited, and Beau Slade called, "Pa, we can't find him!"

The voice came again, this time from a different direction. Again the words were not English, and at once Beau cried, "Over there! He's over there!" But as the guards milled around in the darkness, the voice came from yet another direction. "White man, you die!"

Panic struck at women and some of the men, but Carl Slade called out, "Easy now! Calm down!" Then he turned to Reno and demanded, "You understand that lingo?"

"Some of it, not much."

"Tell them to come in and talk," Daniel said.

Reno shrugged. "An invite to tea? They won't do it, Slade. But I'll see what I can do." He lifted his voice, speaking a short sentence filled with coarse sounds and few vowels.

There was a silence, then the Indian spoke again. Reno listened carefully. "Wants to know who can speak the language of The People."

"The People?" Dooley asked.

"That's what they call themselves—just like they were the only ones," Reno answered.

"Well, talk to them!" Carl cursed and added, "Maybe we can make a deal."

Reno knew little enough Sioux, but he stretched his scanty supply enough to carry on a conversation of sorts.

"I am Reno."

"I am called Nightwalker."

Reno took a deep breath and said quietly to those who were listening, "That's a bad one!" Then he lifted his voice, saying, "Why does Nightwalker come?"

The Indian ignored the question, asking, "How does Reno know the language of The People?"

"I have hunted with Black Wolf." Reno had encountered the great chief of the Sioux once while he was trapping beaver. Fortunately, Black Wolf had been in one of his rare good moods, and after a touchy encounter he had welcomed Reno and his partners to his camp. They had stayed for a week, after which the Indians had pulled out.

"Black Wolf is a great warrior," Nightwalker said after a pause. Then the voice hardened: "We come for blood, Reno. Give us the murderer of my son, and we will let the rest of you live."

Reno struggled with the meaning, then said to the others, "It's bad. The Indian Beau killed is this man's son. This man is Nightwalker."

"Heard of that one," Easy said, and for once there was no smile on his homely face.

"He's pretty bad, is he?" Buck asked.

"Way I heared it, he's tough enough to raise hell and put a chunk under it," Easy said.

"That's putting it mild," Reno added. "He says if we'll give him the man who killed his son, he'll let the rest of us go."

"You'd like that, wouldn't you, Reno?" Carl snapped.

"Tell him I'll give them ten cows to let us through," Daniel Slade said.

Reno stared at him and asked, "Would you take ten cows for one of your sons, Slade?"

"Just tell 'im!"

Reno called out the message, and a soft laughter floated back across the night air. "We will have all the cows, Reno. You know Nightwalker?"

"Yes."

"You know I speak truth. Give us the man, and you can pass."

"Tell him *twenty* cows!" Daniel said, sensing that the offer had been refused.

"He says he'll have them all in the end."

"He's out there! Let's go get him!" Carl whispered.

Reno murmured, "Didn't you hear his name, Carl? *Nightwalker.* Indian names mean something. Let me tell you what this Indian did a year ago over in Arizona. A bunch of pony soldiers shot up his village and killed some of his people. They were three days' ride from the fort and in the three nights the troop lost eight men. They had a full guard, all of them trained soldiers, and he came in the dark and slit their throats."

"How—how'd he do that, Reno?" a small man named Potts asked.

"He's like an owl, Potts. You know how an owl has all those downy feathers? Well, they let him sail through the air without a sound. So the little mouse is mooching around, and suddenly, without a sound, he feels a set of talons sinking into his body and a beak tears his head off. And I guess those soldier boys didn't hear a thing until they felt a knife slicing into their throats." Reno gave a grim smile and jibed, "And that's the Injun you want to go charging after in the dark, Slade?"

Suddenly Nightwalker spoke up, and there was a hint of laughter in his voice. "I have a message for you, white man. Perhaps even those who cannot speak the tongue of The People will be able to understand this!"

There was a pause, then a soft thudding noise off to Reno's left broke the silence.

All the fires but one were out, and Jane Ann Burns felt something strike her foot. She said, "Oh!" then leaned over and touched the object. Someone said, "What is it?"

When she recognized what it was, she began screaming— a mindless sound that scraped across the nerves of every person in the train.

"Jane!" Burns called out, and caught her as she collapsed.

Reno stepped to the spot, bent over, and picked up the object. As he suspected, it was a human head, and he saw by the pale light of the single fire it was the head of Josh Henry.

He said at once, "Buck!" and when the young man started to move he said, "Your Pa's been killed."

Nightwalker mocked Reno as he took a few steps into the darkness and found the body of Josh Henry: "We want only one man, Reno. We want the one who killed my son. Will you let the others die for his sake?"

Reno stared at the body, then out into the darkness. *If I had my way, friend,* he thought, *I'd make you a present of the whole Slade tribe right now!*

TEN
Run of the Arrow

Josh Henry was buried on Thursday at dawn, and the train drove steadily until dusk. They made a dry camp, and that night four mules were taken. Daniel Slade raged and cursed the guards, but the next night three oxen had their throats slit, and the guards heard not a sound until the strangling, bubbling cries broke the silence. On Saturday night when a mule screamed, Leon Prather raced out into the darkness and took an arrow in the leg. Three mules were down, hamstrung, by the time help arrived.

The next morning, when Jude Finney and a small group gathered for a service as they had done every Sunday morning, Daniel Slade rushed over shouting, "Finney, we're breaking camp! We ain't got no time for preaching now!"

Jude said quietly, "Why, Daniel, I reckon that in times like these we need the Lord more than ever."

"I ain't gonna argue with you! We're pullin' out!"

"It wouldn't take but an hour," Addie Grant said gently.

Vinson Grant was set to go, but he looked at Addie and

said, "I guess an hour won't matter, Slade. Get on with your preaching, Brother Finney."

Daniel glared at him, but had to content himself with shouting, "One hour, then!"

Jude opened the worn black Bible and began running his finger over the page. Usually he quoted from memory, but now he read aloud, struggling with a contorted face. "By—faith A-Abraham when he was—was called to g-go out into a place—which—he should after receive for an—for an—inheritance, obeyed—and he went out n-not knowing whither—he went."

The effort seemed to exhaust the tall man. When he looked up there were tears in his eyes. "All my life," he said in wonder, "I wanted to read more than anything else. Books were just black squiggles. But now I can read the Word of God! It's—it's like I was blind and God gave me eyes!"

Dooley was far to Jude's right, and she had a clear view of the faces of the hearers. Addie Grant's scarred face was filled with pride, and it was beautiful in the pale morning light. Lena Prather looked about sixteen years old, and there was a mixture of sorrow and hope in her eyes. Ellie Satterfield looked bored, but most of the hearers listened carefully. They were simple people, and they needed to be told that there was hope.

"I've thought a lot about this fellow Abraham," Jude began conversationally. "He appears to be an ordinary sort of man, maybe like Barney Moore there—no great shakes, but a good man." Jude gave his toothless grin at Barney, then went on, "The only thing I can see he did that made him different was that he believed God without any guarantees. When God told him to git, why, he skedaddled! Bible says he didn't even know where he was headed. If one of his neighbors had said, 'Where you going, Abe?' 'bout all he could have said was, 'I ain't got no idee, but God knows!'

"Guess that's about our condition, folks." Jude waved his hand toward the west and said, "We ain't none of us ever seen what's over there, but we believe God's in our going. Now I want to give you one verse of Scripture to digest. Sort of swallow it, then as the wagons roll today, just bring it up and chew on it, sort of like a cow spends some time eatin' but then brings it up and chews it over and over. Well, here's what I want us to swallow this morning: 'Without faith it is impossible to please him, for he that cometh to God must believe that he is, and that he is a rewarder of them that diligently seek him.'"

As Jude went on talking about how faith was what they all needed, a movement across the circle caught Dooley's eye. She had noted Reno standing idly between two wagons, and now Jean Lamarr came up to him and touched his arm. He turned, smiled, and they began to talk.

"You don't believe any of that preaching business, do you, Jim?" Jean had asked with a contemptuous nod toward the small group.

"Sure do."

His ready answer gave her pause, then she shook her head, a bitter smile on her full lips. "I've had too many deacons and even preachers chasing after me to believe any of that church stuff!"

"Don't doubt that, Jean," Reno replied, but added with a sober look on his lean face, "but I reckon there's more to the story."

"What else is there?"

"Why, there were quite a few sorry soldiers in my outfit when I was in the army, but I didn't quit because of them. I believed in what I was doing, and no matter what somebody else did, I still believed in it." He rubbed his chin thoughtfully, then added, "Guess there's a few rotten senators in Congress, but I don't plan to quit bein' an American because of that. Why, when a member of your family does something bad, you don't disown the family, I reckon."

"That's not the same!" she insisted.

"Seems to me like it is," Reno argued gently. "I've seen lots of sorry folks inside the church, but I've seen the real article a few times, Jean."

She stared at him, then nodded reluctantly, "Well, sure, I've seen a *few* church people I guess were all right." She turned her head to study him, then asked, "Are *you* a Christian, Jim?"

He hesitated, then said, "Well, there was a time when I'd have said no to that. And there was a time when maybe I'd have said yes."

"But what about now?"

He stared out across the open space and listened to the voice of Jude Finney for so long that she thought he didn't intend to answer, but finally he turned to face her and there was a light in his dark eyes. "About all I can say about *now,* Jean, is that I'm about in the same shape as that prodigal son that preachers like to talk about. I've sort of gotten away from home, and I'm with the hogs a lot more than I'd like to admit. But I know there's more to life than a hog wallow, and I'm hoping to get back home before too long."

Jean was struck by his earnestness. Her face looked hard in the morning light, but a wave of uncertainty swept her features, softening them. She whispered, "I—I guess I'm a prodigal, too!" Then she whirled and left so quickly that it took Reno by surprise.

Dooley, who had watched all the while, jumped when

Easy leaned over from behind and whispered, "Reckon that ol' gal's done found a place to let her bucket down!"

"Shut up, Easy!" Dooley hissed. "She's St. John's woman!"

"Gal like that, she's gonna have more than one mule in the barn!"

As soon as the service was over, Daniel Slade galloped around, urging them as they broke camp. The air sweeping down off the Rockies bit at their faces, and they made good time, not stopping until nearly two in the afternoon.

Jackson built a small fire and cooked up a pot of mush made of corn dodgers. Leah made a pan of sawmill gravy, and along with biscuits soaked in fat and some bacon, they had a good meal.

St. John ambled by, looked down at the food and asked curiously, "What is that?"

"Corn dodger mush and sawmill gravy," Reno answered with a smile. "You care for a sop, Algy?"

"Ah, no, thank you, I believe not." He stared at the food, shook his head sadly, then looked down the line of wagons toward the herd. "Have you seen Jean? She went out for a ride a couple of hours ago, and that's long for her."

Reno got up and handed his tin plate to Jackson. "That was good mush." He walked over and swung aboard Cherry, saying, "Haven't seen her, but I'm riding drag. I'll find her and send her home."

As Leah and Jackson started cleaning up, Dooley and St. John talked idly about small matters. The Englishman fascinated Dooley. Despite the rigor of the trip, he dressed as if he were in London. She took in the spotless brown trousers tucked into a pair of custom-made low-topped boots, the white shirt, and the fawn-colored coat. He looked like a fop, but he had a straight-grained nerve that did not go with his diffident attitude.

He was restless, and after looking repeatedly toward the rear of the train, he said anxiously, "I shouldn't have let her go. She's a city girl. Never been on a horse in her life before this trip."

"Have you—known her long?" Dooley stumbled over the phrase, and a humorous light leaped into the Englishman's eyes.

"Not long, Dooley. She was stranded in Dodge City, and we, ah, pooled our resources, you might say."

"I see."

"Do I detect," St. John asked slyly, "a note of righteous indignation in your tone?"

"None of my business what she does!"

St. John took off his hat and ran his thin hand over his blond hair. He studied Dooley's face without seeming to, then said, "You're very severe with Jean Lamarr, Dooley. I think I know why. You are jealous of Jim Reno's obvious interest in her."

"Reno!" Dooley faltered and felt her face begin to glow. She lowered her voice and said roughly, "Jealous of Reno? That's crazy! How could a man be jealous of another man?"

"Why, he couldn't, of course," St. John said, then he reached out and pulled her face around, searching her features with his shrewd blue eyes. "But that hardly applies to you, Dooley."

Dooley felt as if she had been struck in the pit of the stomach. She couldn't get her breath, her knees trembled violently, she felt nauseous, and St. John's face began to blur in her sight.

There was no mistaking his meaning, and finally she said shakily, "When—when did you find out?"

"Why, bless you, child, about five minutes after I met you!"

"But—but I fooled everybody else!"

St. John snorted and threw his hands up helplessly. "I admire so many things about Americans, but they are so obtuse! Why, to any man of culture and observation, your masquerade was a total failure! Your walk, the way you use your hands, your speech, your shape—even hidden in a shapeless pair of pants—why, everything about you proclaims your femininity!"

"Please don't tell!" she begged.

"Why, certainly not!" he assured her. "Sooner or later you're bound to be discovered, but it will not be my doing." He stared at her again and said, "James Reno can look at a three-day-old hoofprint of a horse and tell you the weight, color, and probably the birthplace of the beast! But *you* put on a pair of overalls and he hasn't got eyes to see the lovely young woman so poorly disguised!"

"I'd like to tell you why I'm disguised like this," Dooley said, and for the next thirty minutes she gave him her history.

He said when she finished, "Well, you certainly had provocation, I must say! And if I can assist you in any way, you can count on me."

"Oh, thank you, Algy!" she said.

"Of course, you haven't said anything about my statement."

"Which statement was that?"

"Why, I said you were jealous of Jim Reno." He saw her mouth drop open. "Well, I am available for consultation, Dooley, and if you need a shoulder to cry on, feel free to call." He turned and walked toward the front of the train, leaving her weak and trembling.

Suddenly a voice almost in her ear made her jump.

"Well, he done found you out, ain't he, now?"

"Leah! You were listening to us!"

"I allus do," Leah said calmly, a humorous light in her faded eyes.

"Oh, Leah, what's the *matter* with me!" She wanted to fall onto the breast of her old nurse, as she had when hurt as a child, but it was too late for that.

"Why, there ain't nuffin' wrong wif you, chile, 'less you call growin' up and gettin' to be a woman wrong."

"But St. John said I was jealous of Jim! That can't be!"

"Don't know why not," Leah snorted. "He's 'bout the mos' man you done ever see. And he jes' doan know how good-lookin' he is! Now, it's nice to be humble, but not downright *dumb!*"

Dooley shook her head and said, "He's in love with a dead woman, Leah. And besides that, he's chasing around after that awful Jean Lamarr!" She dashed the tears from her eyes and her mouth went firm. "When we get to Oregon, I'll have lots of men after me, Leah. And they'll make that old Jim Reno look like a sick kitten!"

She whirled and raced away, leaving Leah to murmur, "You jes' keep on thinkin' that, honey—long as you kin!"

An hour later Lee and Dooley were riding on the wagon seat, tired and ready for the day to end. "Look!" Lee said, pointing over to their right. "There comes Jim."

He came quickly but directed Cherry to St. John's wagon. He had some sort of urgency, Dooley thought, for he wheeled his horse and came to her wagon with a strange, angry look in his eyes.

"What's the matter, Jim?" Lee asked as he turned Cherry and walked beside them.

"Indians got Jean." There was a spareness in his speech, but Dooley saw that the calm on his brown face concealed a wildness that flickered in his dark eyes.

"Is she—is she dead, Jim?"

"No. They picked her up when she wandered away from the train."

"That old Nightwalker has her, Jim?" Lee's face was pale and he asked, "You gonna get her back?"

He stared at the boy, then said, "I found out where she wandered off, and I guess they were waiting for something like that. They pulled her off her mare and dragged her to where their ponies were staked out. Then they made her mount up—with her hands tied, I'd guess—and they rode off to join the main party."

"What do you think will happen?" Dooley asked. She had horrible thoughts of atrocities committed by Indians, and guilt swept her as she remembered how harsh her judgment of the woman had been.

"Nightwalker's too smart to kill her," Reno said. "He'll come tonight and talk a trade."

"A trade? What kind of a trade?"

"Have to see." Reno sat there silently, thinking, then said, "I want to get some sleep, Dooley. Can I use your wagon?"

He caught them off guard, and Lee asked in surprise, "Sleep? Ain't you goin' after Miss Jean?"

Reno stared at him. "Nobody's going to find Nightwalker if he don't want to be found, especially at night! How about it, Dooley?"

"Just let me get my stuff out of the way," she said. She practically dived into the wagon and frantically stuffed anything that might give her away into a sack. She had kept only a few feminine garments, but one would be enough to tip Reno off. When she had stuffed the bag into a trunk and locked the lid, she climbed back on the wagon seat and said, "All right, Jim."

He dismounted, tied Cherry to the rear of the wagon, then swung inside. Dooley got one glimpse of him lying on his back, staring at the canvas over his head.

By the time they circled and struck camp the word had spread, and a group came to Dooley's wagon looking for Reno.

"Where's Jim, Dooley?" Vinson asked quickly.

"He's asleep," she said defensively.

"Guess the Indian lover's not going to lead a party to save anybody," Carl Slade chuckled.

"Did he say anything when he got back?" Moore asked.

"He said nobody could find Nightwalker if he didn't want to be found—and that he'd be coming to the train tonight to strike some kind of a deal."

They could make nothing of that, and when the group left, Dooley sat there with Leah, Jackson, and Lee. Once Lee said bitterly, "I didn't think Jim would let them have her without a fight!"

"Lee," Dooley said at once, "you know Jim better than anybody else. Do you think he's the kind of man who'd let a friend down?"

"No! He ain't!"

"Then I think you'd better not judge him until we see what happens."

The camp did not settle down as usual, but waited in a nervous silence for a visit from the Indian. It came about midnight.

"White man!" came the now familiar voice. "Reno! I am here!"

"Nightwalker! I hear you."

Nightwalker was standing not ten feet from Reno, and his eyes glinted in the starlight.

"I have the woman, Reno."

"Yes."

"Life for life. You give me the man, and the woman is free."

"The man is bent, Nightwalker. He will not give himself for another."

Instantly, the reply: "You are many, he is one."

"My people will not do that."

"Then the woman dies."

"It is said by many campfires and in many lodges that Nightwalker is not only bold in battle, he is bold to gamble."

There was, for the first time, a trace of humor in the voice of the Indian. "Nightwalker has been known to wager."

"Reno would make a wager—his life for the woman."

A hesitation, then Nightwalker said, "I have the woman. Soon I will have you all."

"You are afraid to gamble with me?"

"Afraid? What is that?"

"I would not like to think that the stories told by old men of Nightwalker are lies!"

There was a hesitation, then Nightwalker asked, "What game do you speak of?"

"Run of the arrow."

"Ah! That *would* be a good gamble."

Dooley was watching Reno's face, and as the Indian hesitated, she saw a tenseness in his lean jaw. Then Nightwalker said, "It is so. At dawn you will be ready. It will be the last time the sun will rise for you, Reno!"

Then there was a dead silence, but Reno had a faint smile

on his broad lips as people crowded around to hear what had happened.

"What about Jean?" St. John asked at once.

"She's alive—and we got a thin chance to get her back. A long shot, but looks like it's the only game in town."

"Spell it out, Reno!" Beau Slade insisted.

"All right—they want your head in a sack for the woman," Reno said.

Shock rippled across Beau's handsome face, and he shot an involuntary glance around the circle. He had few friends there, and his hand dropped to his Colt. Carl stepped to his brother's side, growling, "Ain't his fault the fool woman wandered off!"

"Wait a minute," Daniel Slade said, a sly look on his face. "Maybe we can trick them. Like maybe we can tell them we'll trade, then when they bring the woman, we shoot them down."

"I gave my word to Nightwalker, Slade," Reno said instantly. "Any man who violates that, I'll cut him down myself!"

"There'll be no word broken!" Algernon St. John spoke harshly, and there was a steely light in his blue eyes. "There is some honor left in this train, and I will personally destroy any man who violates a truce." He stared at Daniel Slade, then asked, "What is this thin chance, Jim?"

"Ever hear of a game called the run of the arrow? Nobody? Well, the Sioux like it. It's really a race. Way it works, a man shoots an arrow far as he can, then he gets that much of a head start. When he gets to the arrow, he takes off, and the young bucks take out after him. If he can keep from getting caught until dark, he wins."

"What if they catch him?" Dooley asked.

"Oh, they pound on him with sticks, rough him up."

"Doesn't sound too bad," Beau said. Then he caught them all off guard. "Guess I'll try it."

"Don't be a fool!" his father said.

"I guess I can run pretty fast. And I reckon I can stand a few licks if it'll get the woman back."

Reno smiled then, but shook his head. "You surprise me, Slade."

"Didn't think I had the nerve, did you?"

"Well, actually, there's more to it. What I told you was just when it's a friendly contest. When it's an enemy, everybody has a knife—except the one they're after. If he gets caught, they butcher him."

"Oh," Beau said, flinching at the thought. "Well, I guess I'm pretty fast."

"Can you run ten miles?" Reno smiled. "Some of these Sioux can run twenty at a fast clip."

"Why, it'd be suicide!" Beau said, his face pale beneath the tan.

"You're not thinking of actually going through with this, Jim?" St. John asked.

"Like I said, Algy, it's the only game in town!"

Morning came after a long night, and Dooley dreaded to see pale red light jaggedly outlining the mountains on the east.

Only the children slept—and Reno, apparently. He had gone back to the wagon to rest. First light was ordinarily a time of bustle and activity, but except for a few breakfast fires, the camp was strangely quiet. No one moved to hitch the teams, and the cold morning air was heavy with oppression as they waited for something to happen. Even the Slades were subdued, especially Beau, who sat in front of a small fire staring at the coals moodily.

Buck Henry wandered by, his face lined with worry. "Dooley, somebody ought to stop Jim. It won't help the woman to get himself killed."

"You want to try and stop him, why, just help yourself, Buck," Dooley said, glancing at the glowing light in the sky. "I tried to talk him out of it, and he just ignored me."

Easy was standing beside Lee, and he shook his head, saying soberly, "I reckon they ain't nobody gonna change his mind. But I seen some of these Injuns run, and I tell you, folks, I ain't never seen a white man who could keep ahead of a good one."

"There they come!"

Everybody in camp moved to stare at the group of riders who appeared suddenly, cresting a ridge to the west of the camp. Dooley counted seventeen of them, all mounted on small ponies, and as they pulled up a hundred feet away, she caught her breath.

The Sioux in front of her were not large, but the wilderness had sheared away every ounce of spare flesh, leaving sinews of elastic muscles defined with every movement. Beneath the black strips of paint were eyes proud as Lucifer's, and although cruelty was etched in the slanting planes of their coppery faces, it was the cruelty of the wild, not rapacious greed or mindless lust.

"Right on time," Reno commented. He had come out of the wagon, and Dooley stared at him.

He was wearing a worn pair of leather pants fringed down the sides and a pair of old moccasins—nothing more. He had no more fat than the Indians who awaited him, and every muscle was cleanly defined.

He was like a cat, Dooley thought suddenly, lazy and

casual—until aroused. Then the speed and power would explode into motion. For the first time, she had hope that he might somehow manage to survive the terrible ordeal.

"Dooley, if I don't make it back, you stick with Easy and St. John. They'll look out for you."

"Jim—" She tried to speak normally, but death was in the face of the Indians outside the circle, and she could only say, "I—I couldn't have made it if it hadn't been for you!" Then Lee came up and whispered, "Jim, do you *have* to?"

Reno looked down at the boy, put a corded hand on his head, and said gently, "Would you have me run away, Lee?"

Lee stood there, face haggard in the pale light, and finally whispered, "No, Jim."

Then Reno laughed, and said, "Don't go countin' me out now! I'm a pretty tough old bird. Leah, you have me some of your pancakes ready when I get back tonight, or I'll cut a switch to you!"

Leah nodded and said with a light in her eyes, "I sho' will Mistah Jim!" And Jackson nodded, adding, "You scoot quick, you hear me, Mis' Jim?"

Reno slapped him on the shoulder, then walked to the edge of the wagons. "Easy, you want to make a little trip?"

Easy grinned. "I didn't know I had an invite to this here rat-killin', James!"

"Want you to ride along and bring Cherry back to camp."

As Easy went to get the horses, Beau Slade came up to Reno and said nervously, "I don't get it, Reno. Why you doin' this? She ain't your woman, is she?"

St. John was standing by, and a quick anger swept his face. He brushed by Beau and said quickly, "I don't like this, Jim. It seems like my fight, and yet I know you're the only one who has a prayer at this sort of thing. Always fought my own fight, you see. Goes against the grain to just stand by."

"Got a favor to ask of you, Algy."

"Name it!"

"If I don't make it, look out for Lee and Dooley, will you? They'll need some help."

"My word on it!" St. John said, and offered his hand.

Reno gazed around at the faces, all tense and filled with fear. "I think I'll make it," he said, loud enough to be heard by all. His eyes fell on Jude Finney, and he said, "If you had a mind to say a prayer for me, Brother Jude, I wouldn't argue."

"Already doing that, Jim."

Reno nodded and walked out of the circle, motioning Easy to stay back with the horses.

A tall Indian slipped from his pony, authority in his face. "You have come." Deep-set obsidian eyes dominated his face, and the wide mouth was more mobile and expressive than in any Indian Reno had ever seen. Cruel, to be sure, but there was a turn at the corners that revealed the pleasure of this encounter, and a glint of humor in his eyes flickered as Reno said gravely, "These are your fastest runners, chief? I had hoped for better sport!"

The young Indian beside Nightwalker bristled, his countenance broke, and a string of words flew too fast for Reno to follow.

Nightwalker nodded at the Indian and said, "This is my youngest son. His name is Ocheco. You do not know the meaning of that?"

"No."

"Running Antelope." Nightwalker did smile then, and wrinkles creased his smooth face. "He says he will destroy your manhood before he cuts your throat."

Reno gave a contemptuous look at Ocheco, uttered a vile phrase he had picked up while hunting with the Sioux once, and it was enough to make the young man leap off his horse and start for Reno.

Nightwalker called out a sharp command, and said, "Enough! We will begin." He took a bow from a thong tied around his horse and added one arrow. "Can you draw a bow?"

"I remind you, chief, that the hunted has the right to choose the spot of beginning."

"You do not choose this place?"

"No. We will ride." Reno motioned to Easy, who brought up Cherry at once, and Reno mounted with a smooth motion. He knew what the mare could do, and he knew Easy's gelding was fast. Easy had been one of Moseby's cavalrymen, and he rode like a centaur. He nodded toward the Indian ponies and allowed a jeer to carry into his voice, "It is far, maybe five miles. The People have only horses fit for women. My friend and I will go slowly so that you may not be left behind."

The smile left Nightwalker's face, and he said in a hard voice, "Let Reno try and leave The People!"

Reno cut loose with a wild yell, and was joined instantly by the shrill scream of Easy.

"That's the old rebel yell!" Vinson Grant cried, and he threw his hat to the ground and joined them as the Indian ponies went out of control, set off by the wild screams.

Reno and Easy tore across the open country at a dead run, their mounts evenly matched for speed. As the scenery flew by, Easy called out, "James, I swear you're making that Injun touchous! He's done got his tail over the dashboard for sure!"

"All part of my plan!" Reno shouted back. "See that butte

over there? If things go like I plan, I'll hang this Injun's hide on a fence!"

Easy glanced back at the string of Indians racing after them, the riders low and driving the small mustangs like demons. "Yeah, *if.* But *if* a toady frog had wings, he wouldn't bump his rear!"

Reno turned, a grin slashing across his brown face. "You got any advice for a time like this, Easy?"

Easy had been through the worst of the war, and he knew Reno had, too. There was a bond between the two, and he grinned back and shouted, "I reckon the best I can tell you is, trust the Lord, write your mother, and vote the Democratic ticket!"

After a dead run, and with the horses beginning to play out, Reno pulled up at the lip of a canyon and said to Easy who came to stand beside him, "That's my plan."

Easy looked at the sheer drop at his feet—two hundred feet—then took in the swift river at the bottom. "That's a fast river, Jim." The opposite bank was apparently as steep as the one they stood on, and the short puncher turned to stare at Reno. "Lemme see if I can figure this out, James. You say you get a head start as fur as you can shoot an arrow—I'd guess you're aimin' to get a shaft to the bank over there?"

"Your mama didn't raise no dummies, Easy!" Reno flashed a quick grin at his friend, then his face sobered. "I'd have no chance in a race with these bucks! They can run down a deer! But if I can get an arrow across this canyon, they have to wait until I get there."

"All you gotta do is climb down this cliff that would cause a fly to slip and break his neck! Then you have to swim that there river—which would give some trouble to a channel cat!

Then you swarm up that cliff—which ain't gonna be possible. Is that about it, James?"

"Tells the story complete!" Reno allowed admiration to shade his tone, then turned to face the first of the Sioux who were pulling their blown horses to a halt a few feet away. "I figure I can cover my tracks in the river and stay hid out till dark."

Easy looked dubiously at the sheer walls of the canyon, shook his head at the pulsating water of the river, then said, "Well, church ain't out till they quit singing, James! But I ain't never heard that none of you Third Arkansas fellers quit on nothing, so you tree this ol' coon!"

Nightwalker arrived shortly, and his face was a mask. He stared at the canyon, nodded silently, then handed Reno the bow saying, "Reno is a fox."

Reno took the bow, notched the arrow, and turned at right angles to the edge of the canyon. He put the arrow up at a forty-five-degree angle and slowly and without effort drew the bow, then released the shaft. It sailed high in the air, and to his relief it cleared the open space by at least fifteen feet.

"A good shot," Nightwalker said. He glanced at the sheer cliffs and the swift river. "One must be a goat and a fish to get to the arrow."

Reno grinned at him and said, "Light out, Easy. I'll see you tonight."

He waited until Easy was well out of range, then took off his moccasins and tied each of them to one of the fringes on the sides of his buckskins. He stared at the wall and at the river below. Shooting a quick look at Nightwalker, he said, "I go!" and dropped over the side, falling to a ledge less than six inches wide that ran along the edge five feet below the rim.

This was not blind chance, for he had followed the rim of

this canyon three days earlier in a search for game. The high walls were less than five miles long, flattening out on both ends, so that getting to the river had not been difficult. But he had liked the wildness of this spot, and it had leaped into his mind when he had searched frantically for a way to get Jean back alive. He had no hope of outrunning the Indians, but he had put in a hard year trapping in the Jackson Hole country, and he had discovered that he had a good head for heights and was more surefooted than any he hunted with. The river was no problem, for it was as narrow as it was swift. No man could fight it, but he felt sure that he could reach a sand beach on the far side before being snatched into the jaws of white water. The one thing he didn't know was how well he might fare in climbing the far wall.

Going down cost him some skin off his palms and bruised the soles of his feet, but by sliding when there was an incline, grabbing with his fingertips at crevices, and finally shoving off in a daring leap and making a deep dive, he entered the river. He hit bottom with both hands, jarring his brain, and then the force of the water rolled him over, tumbling him head over heels. Fear grabbed at him, and he clawed wildly to find the surface. His head cleared just as he was forced to expel the last of the air in his burning lungs.

He was facing back toward his starting point, and he saw at once that he had been carried around a slight bend, out of sight of the Indians. He then put all his force into beating his way across the river. He found that he could let the water push him in that direction. The roar of white water was loud in his ears as his feet touched bottom and he scrambled up on the gravel bar. He wanted to rest, but the thought was strong that Nightwalker would be smart enough to send a scout down the canyon to spot him.

He drove himself upward, and his mind blotted out everything except the crevice, or an outcropping of shale that would hold under his grasp. Once his feet slipped, and he dangled by one hand a hundred feet in the air by the tips of his fingers. Slowly he pulled himself up, feeling desperately for a niche for his toes, finally finding it. His fingers were all bloody, and his lungs were on fire, but without a pause he inched his way up the face of the cliff until finally, with a sobbing gasp, he heaved himself over the lip, and rolled over on his back. Even then he drove himself, rolling down an incline that hid him from the far side. It was well he did, for as soon as his limbs stopped trembling and he could breathe, he cautiously risked a glance and saw almost directly across from where he lay an Indian searching the river and the cliff he was on.

He longed to rest, but he knew that Nightwalker would be sending parties in both directions along the river and that they would both find passage at a less arduous point on the fast river. By noon, if not before, they would find this spot, and they could, he knew well, track him as fast as they could travel. He had one more trick in his bag, and if that failed there was nothing else to try.

He moved south along the canyon, toward where the arrow had fallen. He kept well back, not wanting to be seen, and for the next hour he ran steadily along the ridge. He turned and found a spot he had noted as he had ridden the banks three days earlier. It was a broad, deep river here, and he plunged in and swam to the other side, but when he was almost there, he turned and let the current carry him downstream. This was the most dangerous part, he knew, for he could be seen from the bank. He was trusting that any parties sent out in this direction would already have passed. After twenty minutes, he found the spot he was searching for.

He had been standing on the lip of the canyon, which was only about thirty feet up at this point, and he had seen a grizzly, a large silver-tip, fishing in the shallows below. The bear had not spotted him, but as he moved toward the bank, he had suddenly disappeared. Reno was puzzled, but when he moved carefully toward where the bear had dropped out of sight, the large animal had suddenly come out of a hole in the sheer rock, a cave that was scarcely large enough for the enormous beast. Reno had let him wander downstream, then explored the cave. It was a layer of pure white soapstone, eaten away and leached by the action of the stream, and he had gone in to find out that it was only about ten-feet deep. There was a sharp turn, and then it narrowed down to about a four-foot ceiling, then to an abrupt dead end.

He now looked around for a weapon and saw a piece of driftwood, a clublike stick three inches in diameter, up on the bank that sloped up to the gently rising banks of the canyon. He hated to even touch the bank, knowing that a good tracker would not miss his sign, but he would be helpless against an armed Sioux, so he moved carefully, picked up the club, and moved into the rear of the cave.

As the hours passed he grew cold and sleepy, but ignored both weaknesses. He knew that any man who could find this place would be no easy victim. He sat there clutching the club, watching the oblique side of the cave, at right angles to the turn. Anyone who came would cut off the light from the outside entrance and tip him off. The sound of the river would drown out any sound of a good stalker, so he hardly dared to blink all through the long afternoon.

In the late afternoon fatigue pulled his energy down, and he caught himself nodding more than once. Angrily he snapped his head against the wall, the pain waking him up, but an hour passed, and he nodded once more.

Instinct was strong in Jim Reno. It had kept him alive during the war and in the mountains when danger lurked behind every rise. He heard nothing, saw nothing, but suddenly he knew that someone was there. Then he raised his club, but he was struck in the stomach by a plunging body!

Instantly he dropped the club, and by pure chance his left hand grabbed the wrist of the man, but not before a wild slash had sent a searing line of pain across his chest. He should have died, for the Indian was strong, fast, and had a blade, but Reno risked everything on one chance—he drew his right hand back over his left shoulder and uncoiled his arm in one tremendous blow at what he hoped was his opponent's face. If he missed he would be off balance—a fatal condition in such a desperate struggle.

He did not miss, however. The bottom edge of his palm connected with soft flesh, and instantly there was a gagging, choking sound, and he knew he had hit the throat. The terrible pain took the fight out of the Indian, and without releasing his grip, Reno reached over and took the knife out of the nerveless hand.

The Indian had not taken the blow in the front, or he would have died at once. Reno drew a length of the rawhide wrapped around the Indian's ankle and quickly whipped his hands together behind his back.

He waited until the gasping stopped, on guard for a possible companion. In ten minutes he pulled the Indian to the light and gazed into the face of Ocheco.

"Welcome to my lodge," he said with a smile.

The face of Ocheco was contorted with shame of defeat, and he said through clenched teeth: "Kill me! I am not afraid!"

Reno stared at him for a long time, shook his head finally, and said in Sioux, "No, I'll give you that, Indian. You are a chip off the old block!"

It was a long time for Reno until dark. Ocheco stared at him in the dark cave, hatred in his eyes, not saying a word.

The only time his expression changed was when dark had come, so thick that no light filtered through the entrance to the cave. Reno pulled him to his feet, then shoved him through the opening. The stars were out, and it was very bright after the darkness of the cave.

Reno held out the knife, and a flicker touched Ocheco's eyes, but there was no fear. Then Reno whirled him around and cut the rawhide off his wrists.

The two stared at each other, and Reno said, "Game's over, Ocheco."

The young man stared at him, and once he opened his lips to speak, then slowly closed them. A strange look came into his face, but he said not a word, but turned and plunged into the night.

Reno stared after him, then grinned wearily, thinking of the long walk back to the train.

"You're welcome!" he said, then laughed softly.

ELEVEN
Fort Bridger

Night had wrapped itself around the circled train by the time Reno walked back from the river, and the guards were already patrolling the herd and the camp. Reno gave Barney Moore a fright, walking up to within ten feet of him, before calling out, "Hello, Barney."

"Who's that!" Barney cried, swinging his rifle around blindly.

He thought he'd made enough noise approaching the camp for anyone to hear, and he couldn't believe how blind and deaf some of the guards were. "Don't shoot, Barney."

"Jim?" Moore lowered his rifle and peered suspiciously into the darkness. Then, grabbing at Reno, he raised his voice and yelled, "Hey! It's Reno! He's back!"

"Jim! Jim!" Dooley was the first to get to him, and Reno was amazed at the worn look of fear on the young face. "Jim! You're all right!" For a second Reno had the impression that Dooley was about to grab him in a hug of welcome, but then he saw the old habit of rejecting physical contact take over. She bit a full lower lip and her eyes widened as she saw the cut on his chest. She touched the raw wound with an unsteady hand and whispered as the others came rushing to welcome him, "I was afraid for you!"

Then they all came at him, the men pounding him on the shoulders and pulling him into the circle—Jude Finney on one arm and Buck on the other, Lee squeezing in between with relief on his pale face, Robert Burns grinning in an uncharacteristic fashion from ear to ear, both Grant brothers trying to pound on his shoulders. Then when he was beside the fire the women and children joined in the welcome.

Surprise stirred Reno's wide lips, cracking the habitual serenity he imposed upon his cheeks. His dark eyes glowed now like a hidden heat unwittingly exposed. He made a tough shape, standing there barechested in the flicker of the fire-light, but there was a pleasure in the crowd's response that stirred his customary reserve. "Well, it's good to be missed," he said with a smile that made him look younger.

The Slades had not fully joined in the enthusiastic welcome. There was more curiosity than relief in Daniel's rugged features. Carl hung back at the edge of the crowd indifferently, but there was a smile on Beau's face as he said, "Glad you made it, Reno."

Daniel looked around, and the response to Reno seemed for some reason to be a threat to his own position. "Well, he's back—but where's the girl? And whut're you guards doin' here? Get back to your posts!"

Algernon St. John arrived then, buttoning up his vest as he asked anxiously, "What about Jean? Is she with you, Jim?"

"No, but don't worry. She'll be back by morning, I'd guess." He released the pressures that had been building up in him over the last twenty-four hours by slapping the slender

Englishman on the back. Grinning broadly, he looked at Daniel and added, "Always a good idea to keep a guard, Daniel, but you won't have anymore trouble with the Sioux—not this bunch, anyhow."

Slade snapped truculently, "What proof you got?"

"I had good luck. Managed to stay away from the party—which is all I had to do to get the woman back. But I managed to take Nightwalker's son captive."

"Good! That gives us something to bargain with!" Daniel Slade smiled so rarely that the grimace he made was not much, but his pleasure was evident when he nodded and added, "Reckon we got the Injun now! We'll give him a head this time! Where you got him tied up, Reno?"

"Turned him loose."

Not only Daniel but most of the others were struck by Reno's laconic reply. "Turned him loose!" Daniel shouted, his face tense with anger. "Why, you fool! We could have used him for a hostage!"

"Not part of the game." Reno glanced at the disapproving faces and said, "It wouldn't have worked, anyway. Nightwalker can't be bluffed."

"I'll bet he can!" Carl said. "I'd have sent him a finger at a time!"

"No, you wouldn't." Reno didn't raise his voice, but there was a chill in the steady tone. "I gave my word, Carl. Maybe you need a lesson in that kind of thing."

"Come on, Jim, you must be starved." Dooley pulled his arm, and as the crowd dispersed, she led him to the fire where Leah and Jackson were waiting.

"Got yo' pancakes, Mistah Reno." Leah nodded, a glad light in her eyes. "I nevah doubted 'bout you!"

"You set right heah!" Jackson took Reno's arm and levered him into a position near the fire. Jackson kept his plate filled with tender pancakes and Leah carefully cleaned the cut on his chest and put a coating of her favorite salve on it. St. John and Easy came to listen as Lee pried the story of the chase out of him.

The ordeal over, Reno let the tension drain out, and as he sat by the fire, eating and relaxing, he embroidered the tale to please the boy. He made them laugh more than once, but when he held up his torn hands, Dooley at once insisted on smearing the cuts with Leah's remedy.

St. John saw Dooley's hand go to her breast in an intensely feminine gesture at the sight of Reno's wounds, and he said to himself: *Doesn't Reno have eyes? Why, any savage ought to see the truth!* He finally said, "You think he'll bring Jean back soon?"

"Sure of it."

"That'll be a relief," St. John said with a faint smile. "Of course, as we know, we're still in a ticklish situation."

"Aw, don't thump a free watermelon!" Easy said. "They's a whole new tomorrow that ain't even been teched yet. Why, shoot, if I had a whole day go by without any trouble, I'd look inside my hat to be shore it wuz me!"

St. John stared at him, then laughed and shook his head. "I suspect you're called 'Easy' as a result of your relaxed philosophy. How'd you develop it?"

Humor gleamed in Easy's pale eyes and he popped a portion of Leah's pancakes into his mouth and nodded. "Wal, you're right about my handle, Algy. My initials come to E.Z. But I reckon they ain't but one human in the world gonna find out whut they stand for."

"Who's that, Easy?" Lee asked.

"Why, Miz Jones on the day we tie the knot!" The diminutive cowboy laughed then, and said, "And as fer how I got my ways of jest being easy, why, it comes from bein' careful. I figure if I jes' watch what's goin' on, why, I kin take keer of it."

Reno laughed and said, "Not a bad way to live out here."

He started to say something else, but was interrupted as Nightwalker's voice floated on the night air: "Reno—Reno! I have come!"

Reno got to his feet and walked quickly to the far side of the ring. He called out, "I am here, Nightwalker. Will you come in?"

A slight hesitation, then: "I will come."

Reno swept the crowd with a hard gaze, then said, "If I see a man pull a gun, I'll kill him!"

He turned then, and Nightwalker walked out of the darkness into the light of the fire. He was accompanied by Ocheco, who held Jean Lamarr by the arm. He released her, and she gave a faint cry but ran to meet Reno. He caught her in his arms, and she was shaking so hard that if he had not held her, she would have fallen.

"Are you all right?"

"Yes!" she said and raised a haggard face to him. "They didn't hurt me. But I was so frightened!"

"Don't doubt it," Reno said. St. John was standing close, and he came forward to put his arm around her as Reno turned back to the Indians.

Nightwalker looked less ominous without war paint. He did not move, but stared at Reno, his dark eyes glinting in the firelight. Ocheco folded his arms on his chest and kept his eyes on his father.

"You are a fox." Nightwalker allowed a slight gleam of admiration to shade the statement, and he added, "You have won the woman fairly."

Reno nodded, but said nothing, and Nightwalker said, "You set my son free."

"Yes." Reno glanced at the young brave and touched the wound on his chest. "He is a worthy opponent, Nightwalker. Only by fate did he miss taking me. You have a son worthy of your name."

Ocheco turned his burning gaze on Reno, and after he had rattled off something too fast to follow, Nightwalker said, "He asks if the Fox will fight him man to man."

Reno smiled, then shook his head. "No. Perhaps one day we may fight in battle, but I have had good medicine once. To attempt more would be a bad gamble."

Nightwalker nodded slowly. "You have won the woman."

"That was the wager," Reno said at once.

Nightwalker looked slowly around the circle, staring at the white faces, all of them hostile. Finally he said, "You have won more than the woman, Fox. The People will strike no more."

Reno nodded, saying only, "You are a brave warrior. The world knows that. I now find that you are generous as well."

"My son is dead. He will not return. I have no feeling for these." He waved at the spectators, then turned his face back to Reno. "You have a brave heart for a white man. Their lives are your gift, Fox." Then he said something to his son, and the two turned and walked into the night without another word.

"What was all that, Jim?" Buck asked quickly.

"He said the war was over." Reno cocked his head and stared out into the darkness. A wry thought went through him, and he turned to face them, saying, "First war I ever won."

"You mean they won't come again?" Beau asked. His handsome face wore a puzzled frown, and he shook his head stubbornly. "I don't get it, Reno. Why's he doing it?"

"Just wants to, I guess. Indians don't use a lot of heavy logic Beau."

"How do we know he's not lying?" Ty Edwards asked, looking nervously into the dark.

"They don't have a word for lying, Ty," Reno said.

"Well, that's a relief!" Clyde Prather said. "Shape we're in, we'll be lucky to make it even without Injuns to fight!"

"What's ahead, Jim?" Buck asked.

"A fork in the road, Buck." Reno nodded toward the west. "In a day or two, we'll have to either head for Fort Bridger or take Sublette's Cutoff. I've been on the cutoff, and it's pretty bad. Fort Bridger's out of the way, but we're in bad shape for taking the cutoff."

"What's wrong with it?" Daniel Slade demanded.

"Well, it'll be fifty miles without grass, and no water except on the western side. Got to cross deep ravines and dried-up alkali lakes. Some of the stock won't make it."

They had a lively debate, then over the protests of Carl and Daniel Slade they made the decision to go the long way, stopping at Fort Bridger to replenish their stock and supplies.

Reno turned in early, and Dooley was about to climb into the wagon when Lee said, "I don't see how it can miss, do you, Dooley?"

"What's that, Lee?"

"Why, Jim saved her life! A woman would *have* to fall in love with a man after a thing like that!"

"Oh, Lee, that's a storybook thing!" Dooley jerked her arm away from the boy's grasp and pulled herself into the wagon. She stuck her head out and added angrily, "You got to quit daydreaming, Lee!"

"Why you so mad, Dooley?" Lee asked, but when the cover of the wagon was yanked tight without an answer, he muttered, "Good night! What a grouch Dooley is! He sure ain't bothered with no romance in *his* soul!"

Dooley slammed things around inside the wagon, finally flinging herself on the bedding. "Fool boy!" she gritted between clinched teeth. "No sense at all! But he's got as much as Jim Reno!"

After tossing and turning for an hour, a thought struck her. She lay quietly for a time, then got up and carefully lit a candle, putting it in a metal holder fastened to the sideboard. The wagon was packed, but she managed to yank a small chest free. Opening it, she pulled out the small store of feminine attire she'd kept. Quickly she put on the lavender-scented underclothes and then the frilly white dress with tiny blue ribbons around the low-cut bodice. She could not stand up, but taking a mirror from the trunk, she stared at the image.

The glossy brown hair was grown into a mass of ringlets which framed the oval-shaped face. She glared at the short, straight nose, examined the gray-green eyes, wide-set and shadowed by long curling lashes that she had forgotten to trim. She frowned at herself, then made a coy smile, and said in a thick accent, "Why, ah do declare, if you ain't just the *handsomest* ol' thing ah evah did see, Jim Reno!" Then she sobered, and slowly put the mirror away, along with the clothing. Concerned to keep up the masquerade, she carefully trimmed back the thick lashes. Pulling on the worn overalls, she fell into the bed facedown, her shoulders shaking and muttering fiercely, "It's not *fair!*"

They stumbled into Fort Bridger a week later, the last week of September, and the cold air flowing out of the north reminded them that they were very late for making the last leg of their journey.

Dooley was riding alongside Reno when they crossed a shallow canyon, dropped into a flat semicircular basin, and plodded down a short, muddy street.

"Is this *it?*" she asked incredulously. She had been expecting something on the scale of Fort Laramie. What she saw was a shabby collection of cabins built of poles and daubed with mud. Strictly speaking, there was no main street, for the rough buildings were scattered randomly, with no attempt to keep a straight line. The road wound in a serpentine fashion through the collection.

"Why do they call it *Fort* Bridger? It doesn't even have a wall!"

Reno shook his head. "Don't know. Never was an army post, Dooley. Just a meeting place for trappers and hunters. Usually there was a pretty tough bunch of mountain men here, so after burning it once or twice, the Injuns let it alone. Jim Bridger built the place in '43, and I reckon now that the fur trade's about played out he makes a living providing trains with fresh supplies and recruited oxen."

"What's that—recruited oxen?"

"Oxen that get here all played out. Bridger takes them in on trade and gets them in good shape with rest and good pasture. We'll have to trade ours. They'll never make the trip."

"I don't have much money, Jim."

"See what I can do. I know Bridger."

Early the next morning Reno, Dooley, and Lee found the famous mountain man in a poker game with four dark, weathered men. He was a huge man with a full salt-and-pepper beard, dressed in overalls rather than the buckskins favored by the others.

He looked up from the game, stared at them, then nodded. "Reno, ain't it?"

"Wasn't sure you'd remember me, Bridger."

"Guess mebby I wouldn't if it hadn't been fer that business with that purty leetle Shawnee gal." Bridger roared with laughter, and got up to give Reno a hard punch on the arm. "Got your tail in a crack over her, didn't you, son!"

Reno grinned at the huge man, then he rubbed his chin ruefully and said, "To tell the truth, Bridger, I'm tryin' to forget that one." He nodded toward his companions. "This is Dooley Judd and Lee Morgan. We need some good stock. Maybe we can trade a little."

"Shore can," Bridger said. "Come on down to the corral and we'll have a look."

They took two hours settling on a deal. Dooley and Lee spent some time in Bridger's store. Bridger sat in on the card games during slack time in the store, and Dooley got up courage enough to ask him, "What's this about Jim and a squaw, Mr. Bridger?"

"What's that, boy? Oh, yeah!" He threw back his massive head and laughed, then said, "Don't know why you want to fergit that leetle escapade, Reno. Way it wuz, Dooley, bunch of Shawnee bucks lifted our fur and Reno here took out after 'em, all by his lonesome. Come back with all the cache and a smart-lookin' squaw to boot! Never could figure the way of that. Guess you was sech a pistol she just had to hev you! Purty as a strawberry roan and a gone beaver over you!"

Lee's eyes were big as dinner plates, but Dooley's were

changed to little slits. "Didn't know we were runnin' with such a ladies' man!" she said stiffly.

"Whatever happened to that gal, Jim?"

"Wound up at a mission station in Oklahoma, Bridger. She wasn't Shawnee, you mind. Captured in a raid on the Pawnees."

"Well, ain't you the gentleman now!" Bridger snorted. Then he stared at Reno and said, "You remember that coon you rubbed out in Jackson Hole? Took so much of him, you did, and dast him to go for his iron and kilt him afore he cleared leather! You mind that, Reno?"

"Yes." Reno's reply was short, and Bridger's sharp eyes caught the look on his face, so he said no more. Dooley was shocked at this side of Reno.

Later in the afternoon she came across Reno beside the wagon, stretched on his stomach, dozing in the warmth of the sun. A perversity struck her, and her step was that of a mouse. Extending two brown hands with fingers spread like the claws of an eagle, she shot them out to rake his ribs with a fiendish glee.

Reno let out a yell of shock, and grabbing blindly, he caught Dooley's arm and wrestled her down on top of him.

"You fool kid! I can't stand to be tickled!" She pulled away, but had not run twenty feet before he pounced upon her. He knelt astride her and dug his steely fingers into her ribs. Even had she not been ticklish, such contact from his hands would have been hard to bear. He was yelling at her all the time, but she was so conscious of his hands she didn't understand a word he said. Finally he pulled her to her feet and boxed her ears, saying, "Now you just try that again!"

Without a word she ran away, stopping only when she

was out of breath. She looked down at her hands, which were trembling, and accused herself: *You just did that to get your hands on him!* But she had not anticipated the devastating response, the wild beating of the heart and the weakness that drained her—all brought on by his touch!

That night after supper he had noted her silence, and when they were alone he asked, "You mad?"

"No!"

"Well, I was a little rough, Dooley. Never could stand to be tickled. But I keep forgettin' you're just a kid. Why, you must be fifteen at least."

"At least!" Dooley said, and there was a mockery in her voice and a strange look in her gray-green eyes that mystified him.

"You're about the strangest boy I ever run up against, Dooley."

"Really, Jim?" She smiled straight at him and turned, leaving him to stare after her.

The three-day layover was a welcome rest, and they were able to buy enough supplies to get to Fort Hall. Most of them managed to trade with Bridger for healthy stock, though there was some muttering about prices.

There were only a handful of friendly Indians and a few hunters and trappers at Bridger, but on the second day of the stay, a wagon pulled in accompanied by two mounted men.

"That's Case Purdy," Bridger said, looking up from where he slouched in a sagging cane-bottomed chair on the front porch of the store. "They been off doin' some trappin', but they ast me to send word if a train came by."

A tall rawboned man, about thirty-five, Reno judged, leapt

off the wagon, throwing the lines to a pretty Indian woman heavy with child. He was hard-featured, but this was perhaps due to the fact that his right eye was milky, thus giving a sinister cast to his craggy face. He wore dirty buckskins, moccasins, and a trapper's hat. He gave Reno a searching inspection, then nodded to Bridger. "Much obliged, Jim."

"Sho. Get some good hides?"

"Poor pickins'."

"Jim Reno, this is Case Purdy."

Purdy nodded toward the wagon. "That's my woman—my brother, Jesse—and that's my cousin, Keno Baker."

Jesse Purdy was tall like Case, but heavier and thickly muscled. He was, Reno knew instinctively, a man who would not rest until he had tested himself against others. He wore buckskins and was about twenty-five.

Keno Baker was no more than twenty. He was a small man, almost scrawny, with a long tapering face highlighted by the lightest blue eyes Reno had ever seen. He came off his horse in one smooth movement, and he was wearing cowboy attire rather than the dress of a mountain man. Reno took in the high-heeled boots, the fancy vest, the high-crowned black hat, and the matched set of Colts in the polished leather holsters. There was a dangerous quality in Baker that Reno did not miss.

"You the man to see, Reno?" Case Purdy asked. "Like to make the trip to Oregon with you."

"Wagon master is Daniel Slade. Ought to find him over at the camp."

The tall man nodded and said, "I'll go see him. You fellers take the furs in and make Bridger give you top dollar." He went to the wagon and helped the woman down carefully. "Get what you need," he said, and she walked heavily into the store as he turned and walked toward the camp in a loose-jointed gait.

Keno Baker lounged against a post while Jesse Purdy unloaded the heavy bundles of furs and carried them effortlessly into the store.

"Ain't I seen you someplace?" he asked in a high tenor voice. He studied Reno carefully, paying close attention to the Colt at Reno's side.

"Could be," Reno said idly. He was tilted back in a chair, his low-crowned hat partly shading his eyes.

"You ever been in Texas?"

Reno stood up, shoved his hat back, and stretched. "Sure. Lots of times."

Baker stared at him and said, "What kind of outfit is this, Reno?"

"All right. Pretty worn-out, but I reckon they've got enough grit to make it to the coast."

Jesse Purdy came out and pulled another bundle of bales out of the wagon bed. "This is all. Let's get a bottle, Keno. Be a thirsty trip."

"Sure. Maybe a little poker." He was something of a dandy, but Reno had seen too many of the breed to mistake the message of those pale blue eyes. The man was a killer.

"Guess not, Baker. I'm broke."

"Yeah? Well, maybe there'll be a little money in the train." Baker moved through the door after Jesse, and an hour later Reno saw the two in a game with a couple of trappers and Beau Slade.

Later that day Case moved his wagon over to the camp, and Daniel Slade was pleased with the addition. They represented more protection, and he went out of his way to make them acquainted with members of the train.

Reno was helping Clyde Prather repair a wagon when Case brought the newcomers by, saying, "This here is the Prathers—Leon and Clyde there—you met Reno—that's Marie—and this is Lena. Want you to know the Purdys—Case and his wife, Mary, his brother, Jesse—and this is Keno Baker."

They moved on quickly, but neither Reno nor Clyde missed the way that the two single men had looked at Lena. They were almost finished when Leon limped over, saying, "You met the Purdys?"

"Yeah," Clyde said. "Real raunchy bunch."

"They's not bad. Three tough hands may come in handy."

"Didn't like the way they looked at Lena," Clyde said angrily. "The two young ones—they'll be trouble."

"Aw, you're imaginin' things, Clyde!"

"No, I ain't. Ask Jim."

Reno nodded. "Clyde may be right, Leon."

"I'll put a spoke in their wheel if they fool around with Lena!"

"Be careful," Reno said quickly. "The big one's a mauler. He'd bite your nose off and pull your eyes out."

"He ain't as big as a .44 slug! And the little one's dressed too cute to be any trouble."

"Wrong there, Clyde. He's more dangerous than the big one. He looks soft, but I'm bettin' he can pull iron quick as a wink. And he'd like it, too!"

The train pulled out of Fort Bridger at dawn and for the next seven days made the best time of the trip. The air was sharp and tangy as wine, and the fresh animals moved briskly.

The Purdys kept to themselves as a rule, but Reno had gone on a hunt with Case and found him to be an excellent companion, though on the quiet side.

Once he asked Reno, "Why you goin' to the coast?"

"Don't know, Case. Why you going?"

The answer came slowly, and it was a surprise to Reno. "Goin' because of Mary." Case shook his head, and added, "And the youngun, I guess. You know what people think of squaw men, Jim. I'm hoping it'll be different on the coast." He blinked his good eye and said, "I nearly kilt a man in Texas who made a remark about her."

"You'll find a place. She's a fine woman."

Case nodded and said with more feeling than Reno had heard from the man so far, "Your folks have been real friendly with her, Jim. 'Preciate that!"

They had said no more, but once Reno had asked about Keno Baker. "Oh, he's a cousin of mine, Jim. Was brought up pretty hard, and I reckon he ain't no bettern' he should be. He was in a range war when he was only sixteen, and I hear tell he could carve plenty of notches in them fancy guns if he was so minded."

"Figured that."

Case grinned. "I thought you might. You're kinda in that line yourself, Jim."

Reno stared at Purdy. "Didn't know it showed."

"You smelled powder somewhere, that's all I meant, Jim." Then he frowned and said, "Keno's different. He *likes* trouble. Guess that's why his pa asked me to take him on to the coast. But it won't do no good."

"No. Man can change his location, but that don't change what he is."

They had been on the trail a week, and the next day they

came to Soda Springs. The naturally carbonated water was potent enough to raise bread, and Easy thought it tasted like beer.

"How far to Fort Hall?" Clyde asked Reno the next day.

"Fifty-five miles, if I remember right."

"Be glad when we get where we're goin', Jim." The small man seemed uncomfortable.

"What's wrong, Clyde?" Reno asked.

"Jim, them two fellers, they been pesterin' Lena." A rash streak of anger crossed Clyde Prather's face, and he swore loudly. "That Baker came around yesterday when me and Leon were both gone and he put his hands on her! She never said nothin', but Marie told me. Jim, I'm gonna stomp that sucker!"

Reno shook his head. "Clyde, don't do it. I know you're mad, but you'll get yourself killed if you tie into those two."

"I ain't scared of 'em! I don't care how tough they are! They can't get away with what they been doing!" He stubbornly refused to take Reno's warning seriously.

Reno found Lena alone and said, "Baker been botherin' you, Lena?"

She looked up, startled, and Reno saw by her expression that she was afraid. "Jim, I don't know what to do!" She tucked a stray wisp of hair under her bonnet and Reno was struck with the beauty of her face. "I can handle Baker. He's a pest, but that's all. But I'm afraid of him for the twins."

Reno nodded. "I'll see what can be done."

He had no idea how to handle Baker, but finally he talked to Easy. The little rider was a sharp observer, and he said at once, "Shore, I seen this a-comin', Jim. And thet other one, Jesse, he's running around the women with his tongue hangin' out like a red necktie."

"Don't like to interfere with another man's business,"

Reno said slowly, "but the Prathers stand no chance against that pair."

"That's gospel," Easy admitted. "Jesse Purdy won't get bowlegged totin' his brains, but he's a mean one. And that Keno feller—why he's mean enough to burn bresh of a Sunday."

"He'd kill a man for a dime, Easy. Look at his eyes sometimes."

"Yeah, but what you gonna do about it, Jim?"

"Don't know. Talk to Case, maybe."

"That's a good idee. He's a purty good feller. Too bad his relatives don't take after him."

The next day, however, Keno Baker and Jesse Purdy rode out together. Reno watched them go, and moved in close enough to say to Case, "Will they be gone long?"

"Who knows about them two?"

"Keno's been giving Lena Prather some trouble, Case."

"Why you tellin' me?"

"It's got to stop. You stop it or I will." Reno liked the one-eyed man, but as he spoke there was no gentleness in his voice, nor was there any mistaking the steady light in his dark eyes. "Hate for there to be any trouble about this, Case. That's why I came to you first. Baker's going to leave the woman alone—that's all she wrote."

Case stared at the implacable face of Reno, then said, "Do what I can, Jim. But he's pretty wild." He bit his lip and said, "Be careful."

"Sure." Reno nodded, realizing that he had put Case in a tough spot and that the man was still trying to warn him.

The pair stayed gone for two days, but the night they returned, trouble broke. They had brought a plentiful supply of whiskey, and by eight o'clock a poker game was underway, and several of the men were roaring drunk. The Slades were in the circle, along with three other men from the train. Case had watched for a short time, then turned in, but Jesse and Keno kept the whiskey flowing, and the game got louder as time went on.

Reno sat with Dooley and Lee around their fire. Leah and Jackson were asleep, but the three of them often glanced at the large fire that gave light to the gamblers, and Lee said, "I wish they'd go to bed."

Less than ten minutes later a scream rang out, and instantly Reno rose and ran toward it. He was in time to see Jesse Purdy smash Clyde Prather with his fist. The force of the huge man's blow drove Clyde against the side of a wagon and he collapsed bonelessly, his face a bloody mask.

Lena Prather was kneeling by him at once, and Reno saw that her dress was ripped down the front. She held it together with one hand, and pulled Clyde's head up with the other, crying steadily.

Jesse Purdy swayed slightly, obviously drunk. He cursed loudly and wheeled, making his way back to the fire. Reno knelt beside Clyde and saw that his nose was broken and his mouth was bleeding. Leon shoved him aside and stared at his brother's face. He said nothing, but there was a fixed expression on his face as he rose and headed for the fire.

Reno caught him. "Leon, let's take care of Clyde. He's hurt bad."

They carried Clyde's limp body to the light, and Addie Grant took over, holding Clyde's head gently and cleaning the wounds.

Leon wheeled then, dipping into the jockey box of his

wagon. He pulled out a gun belt and strapped it around his slender middle, then started for the bright fire.

Reno said, "Watch yourself, Leon."

The laughter had stopped now, and Jesse Purdy stood tall and bulky against the fire, flanked by the smaller form of Baker. The others drew back, and Reno saw that both men were smiling, amused at the sight of the small figure of Leon Prather.

"Get a gun!" Leon said to Jesse Purdy.

"Naw, I do the fistfightin'. Keno there, he's the man with the gun."

Reno saw then how it would be. Leon could not draw on the unarmed Jesse, and there was something obscene in the look on Keno Baker's face. Keno licked his lips and said in his high tenor voice, "Why, you got any complaint, I'll be right glad to take it up with you, Prather."

The situation was explosive, for Leon was blind angry, crazy enough, Reno knew, to fight the gunman. He started to speak, but another voice beat him to it.

"Keno, you touch that iron and it'll be the last thing you ever touch!"

Case Purdy stepped out of the shadows, a Colt in one hand fixed steadily on Baker.

Baker froze. He said uncertainly, "Come on, Case, you can't—"

"I can put you down with one shot, boy, and I will."

Keno nodded quickly, but Case ignored him. He stepped in front of his brother and whispered, "How can you treat a decent woman like that!"

Jesse licked his lips, and then fear streaked across his face. "Wait a minute, Case, I just—"

"You just *nothing!*" Case Purdy was a fearsome sight just

then, his milky white eye glowing like a ghostly pearl. The other eye was wild as a hawk's, and although he did not have Jesse's bulky muscle, something in his lanky frame made the other man look defenseless. He was on the verge, they all realized, of killing. One word from either of the two men and he would gun them down instantly.

He stood there, a fierce shape in the firelight, then he raised his free hand and cracked Jesse across the face, rocking the big man backward. "Get out of my sight!" Case whispered fiercely. "Both of you! Get your stuff and head for Fort Hall. I don't care if the Injuns catch you and stake you out on an ant-hill."

There was a silence, then Baker and Jesse moved to collect their gear. Case holstered his gun, turning his back on them in contempt. He said to Leon, "Prather, I apologize for them. My fault. Reno warned me."

Leon relaxed and shook his head. "Not your fault, Case."

"Well, they won't trouble you no more." The tall mountain man looked around and said softly, "You folks have been mighty good to me and Mary. Wish this hadn't happened."

He moved out of the light, pausing only to be sure that the two men rode out, then disappeared.

"That Case is a feller you can go to the well with!" Easy said softly. "Too bad he's got all them trashy relatives."

"Case is all right," Reno agreed. "Hope we've seen the last of those two."

"Yeah, we need them like a tomcat needs a wedding license," Easy said, then added moodily, "but I got an idee we *ain't* seed the last of 'em!"

TWELVE
Death on the Trail

A slanted, slashing rain hit five miles out of Fort Hall, striking at the wagons with icy teeth. Vinson Grant said, "Feel that ice? Time we get to the river it'll be froze solid!"

Reno scrubbed his face with a wet sleeve, then answered Vinson, who was riding drag with him. "May be right about that." He stood high in his stirrups, adding with a wry smile, "Maybe we can put runners on the wagons and skid on the ice to Oregon."

"From what I hear that'd be a heap easier than floating the Columbia! Here it is the middle of October. We started too late." Grant was tough as boot leather, but he had been worn down by the trip. His straight back was bent, and there was, Reno noted, a tremble in his hands. Strain had drawn his lips tight, and often there was a tic in his right eye.

He's about played out, Reno thought. *Guess he's in no worse shape than most.* He said only, "Guess we'll get to Hall before dark, according to Case. And since tomorrow's Sunday, guess we'll rest up for a day."

They pulled into the fort just as the last feeble light faded, allowing them only a glimpse of the place. "Not much of a place, is it, Jim?" Dooley said as they made camp in the darkness. She was so tired her bones ached, and the cold, damp air that had soaked her to the skin burdened her spirit.

Reno glanced at the small figure, gauging the weariness in the fine planes of Dooley's face. Deciding that the boy was running on nerve, he said, "You better get out of those wet clothes, boy. It's too wet to cook, and besides, I'm tired." He caught Dooley by the arm as she started to protest and led her to the rear of the wagon. She was helpless as his iron grip pushed her up, and as she tumbled inside he added, "Must be some kind of cafe. I'll find some store-bought grub and bring it back."

Dooley got out of her wet clothes, shivering and teeth chattering. Hurriedly she pulled on some dry clothes. When she lay down just for a moment, wrapped in a warm blanket, she dropped off at once into a sound sleep.

The next thing she knew someone was pulling at her leg, and she awoke terrified, screaming, "You stay away from me! You let me alone, Jake!"

She awoke to find herself hammering at Reno's chest ineffectually. He had climbed into the wagon and as he pulled her to the opening, his teeth gleamed as his face was highlighted by the fire outside. He was laughing silently, and holding her slender wrists in one hand, he said, "I ain't Jake, but we got some hot grub waiting."

She jerked her wrists away, shaken by his closeness, and said huskily, "I—I went to sleep."

"Sleep! You must have died!" he chuckled. Then as they stepped to the campfire, he winked at Jackson and said, "Who's this Jake fellow Dooley has nightmares about?"

Jackson was speechless, and Leah said quickly, "You go to wakin' folks up out of a sound sleep, Mistah Jim, you liable to get a knife in yo' gizzard! Now, you wants this grub or not?"

A cold drizzle was still falling, so they crowded under a tarp Jackson had rigged and fell on the food Reno had brought back—a large ham, a thick round of cheese, several loaves of fresh-baked bread, a gallon jar of pickles, and a sack filled with sugar-crusted doughnuts. After the monotony of trail food, they devoured the meal, almost groaning with pleasure.

"That was *good!*" Dooley said, licking the sugar off her fingers and leaning back against a wagon wheel.

"Sure was!" Lee sighed. He stared at the last doughnut, torn between manners and greed, and finally said righteously, "I guess I'll eat this so's it won't get stale."

They sat warming at the fire, too full to move, and Easy came over and said, "Hey, looks like a picnic." He waited for an invitation, then built a monstrous sandwich. "You see them two yahoos in town, Jim?"

"Which two?"

"Case's brother and thet two-bit gunfighter."

"Didn't see 'em, Easy."

"Yeah, well, I reckon you'll see enough of that pair." He took a huge bite of his sandwich, then waved it vaguely in the direction of the fort. "They wuz in the bar where I went to lubricate my gullet."

"I've seen all I want to of those two," Dooley put in quickly.

"Yeah, well, Slade has agreed to let 'em go with the train the rest of the way to Oregon."

"What about Case?" Reno asked.

"Aw, he wasn't so keen on it, Jim, but he told Slade that it would take all the men we could get to make it over the mountains and down the river."

Reno shook his head, saying impatiently, "Slade ought to know better."

"Reckon he's got a bad case of the simples," Easy agreed. "I tried to tell him that, but he's jest plain techous!" He polished off the last of his sandwich and said as he wandered off, "Somebody better keep an eye on Leon. He ain't forgot how they treated Lena."

Dawn was a sullen light in the east when most of the men met in the bitter cold. Slade had sent Beau around to say there would be a meeting, and the first thing Reno saw was a group of men standing to one side close to Case Purdy's wagon. Beside Jesse and Keno stood two hard-faced men.

"I've agreed to let these men make the trip up the Snake with us," Daniel said pompously. He waved his hand toward them and added, "I know there's been some hard feelings, but we got a tough row to hoe, and we need all the men we can get."

Leon Prather's face was pale in the morning light. He nodded toward the group and said, "You're lettin' skunks like that join us?"

Baker moved his hand, but Case Purdy said, "You set, Keno." He faced the crowd, and his single eye glared fiercely as he said, "I'll answer for them. They won't give you no trouble. But if you don't want them, they stay here."

"Let's vote!" Daniel said quickly. "Just let me say that we've got a long way to go and the weather's going to get worse. Time we get up the Snake to the Columbia we'll need help. Got to make rafts, and the more hands we got, the quicker we'll get to Oregon City. Now how many vote yes?"

The vote was ragged, and it did not appear to Reno that a majority responded, but Slade said quickly, "All right, that's it then! Now this is the last chance to get supplies. Get what you got to have 'cause we're pullin' out first light tomorrow and we ain't stoppin' short of Oregon!"

He was a man without the power to inspire, and a sullen air of silence greeted his attempt to stir them. They broke apart, most of them headed for the general store.

Reno was approached by Jude Finney and Addie Grant. Jude said, "Jim, there's a few Indians here. We're going to have a service, and I thought maybe you might give me a hand."

"You want me to preach, Jude?" Reno smiled. Dooley was watching his face, and she marveled how young he looked at such times.

"Well, not really. I just don't know if they speak English. Could you maybe interpret for me?"

"Do what I can, Jude. But there must be somebody at the fort who can do a better job. What tribe are they?"

"Some kind I never heard of," Jude said, his brow wrinkled in perplexity. "Cahooie, or something like that."

Reno nodded, "That's Calapooia, Jude. Mary Purdy— that's her tribe. I'll go along, but you'll need her."

They stopped off at Case Purdy's wagon and found the one-eyed man working on some harnesses. He nodded when Jude explained what he needed. "Yeah, that's some of Mary's tribe. They mostly come from south of here. But my woman ain't feelin' too good today."

"Oh, well—"

"I talk the lingo pretty fair, Reverend." His good eye lit up with a sudden humor and he said innocently, "If you ain't afraid of the gospel being filtered through a sinner like me."

Jude smiled and nodded. "I'd appreciate it. Maybe some of it will stick in the interpreter, Case."

Reno tagged along, Lee and Dooley at his side, and Easy attached himself as they made their way to the small wooden building with a cross on top. Jude said, "Two fellers named Whitman and Spalding started lots of Indian churches a few years back. Some of them didn't make it, but this one has a preacher come in once a month regular."

They stepped inside and found the congregation waiting. Nine men sat in straight-backed chairs lined in front of a rough desk with a Bible on it. Several women stood around the walls, most of them having either babies or small children clinging to them.

"Let 'er fly, Reverend," Case said with a touch of laughter in his voice.

Jude stood in front of the men, opened his Bible, and stole one quick glance at Addie, who gave him an encouraging nod. "Tell them I'm glad to be here. And I have good news.

Case rolled out a long sentence, using his hands to shape the ideas. He talked as if he had a mouthful of hot mush, and when he finished, he listened as one of the Indians asked a question. Turning to Jude, he said, "Wants to know when the meal comes."

"Meal?" Jude asked, puzzled.

"Guess they're used to gettin' fed in exchange for listenin' to the preachin'," Case said with a grin. The affair amused him highly, and he added, "Guess we should've brought a lunch."

Jude stood there, his head bowed, and there was a flush on his homely face. He knew that he was a figure of fun to most men, but as he looked up, there was a sudden glint of determination in his eyes. He said firmly, "Tell them that I have come to give them bread from heaven—that if they eat it, they will never be hungry again."

Case Purdy stared at him, a skeptical cast on his dark face. Finally he translated the words. As soon as he had finished, Jude spoke again, and there was such a simple honesty on the face of the man that the Indians listened quietly, staring at his face.

He told them all men were wrongdoers, and because of this all men were unhappy. He told them that there was one God and that he was the creator of all things. Steadily, with a simplicity that Reno had seldom heard, he preached a gospel unadorned with complex doctrine.

Reno noted that Case Purdy's face had sobered. He did not look at the Indians as he spoke, but at Jude.

Finally Jude said, "There is only one who can make you good. There is only one who can feed you with bread so that your spirit will be satisfied."

One of the Indians spoke sharply after Purdy translated this, and he said, "Wants to know who this one is who does so much."

Jude said, "His name is Jesus Christ. He is the Great Spirit!"

Case hesitated slightly, then gave the translation. The sermon did not last long, and as the group left the building and headed back toward the train, Addie said, "That was very good, Jude."

He shook his head. "It's hard, Addie. Can't tell what's behind those faces!"

"It's a beginning." They made their way back to the train, deep in conversation.

Easy stared at them and said, "I feel like I been to a camp meetin' for sure."

"That feller's got something, Reno," Case said slowly. "I

ain't much of a one for preachers, and I may not believe in God—but that Jude Finney sure does!"

"You're right," Reno said. He turned to Easy and asked, "You a church member, Easy?"

"Me? Why, shoot, Jim, I wuz a feeler fer a spell!"

"A feeler?" Lee asked. "What's that, Easy?"

"Why, I was an assistant at baptizin', boy! Used to scout out streams and pond bottoms 'fore the baptizins, poking with a pole and feeling the way so no converts wouldn't step into a hole!"

Reno, Dooley noticed, seemed slightly downcast. When they got back to the wagon, she asked, "What's wrong, Jim?"

He shrugged as the ragged light of a feeble sun slanted across his cheeks, turning them irregular and remotely sad. He made a tough shape in the morning light, and there was a strange longing in his voice as he said, "Guess when I meet up with somebody like Jude, it reminds me of the bad turns I made back away."

Dooley was caught by the sadness in his face. "Why, all of us think like that, Jim."

"No." He stared at Dooley, and there was a sudden break in his face as he added, "Like to see you pay attention to Jude, Dooley. Don't make my mistakes."

She watched as he turned abruptly, and it saddened her to see the stoop of his strong shoulders, as if the load had grown unbearable. Suddenly she felt very much alone. Her throat grew thick, and she finally bit her lip, wondering how the sadness of Reno could mar her own spirit.

Following the Snake was nothing like the journey along the banks of the Platte. They were forced to creep along a narrow, bolder-strewn rim. Getting water involved clambering down a precipice into the gorge of the river, then toiling back up again. By the time a man got back to the train he needed another drink.

The air grew colder, and snow was up ahead, but the train made good time the first two days.

One morning Case Purdy, with a look of strain on his craggy face, met Reno. "Mary's took bad, Jim. I'm gonna go back to the fort. She needs a doctor."

"Want me to go with you, Case?"

"No." The knife-edged mouth softened in a rare smile, and he said, "That's handsome of you, Jim, but I can make it. Thing is, I don't rightly know what to do about that crew I brought."

"They going on?"

"Well, I dunno." Purdy bit his lip and said, "Jesse ain't never had no sense. If he wasn't my brother I'd have got rid of him a long time ago. And them others is no good. I figured I could keep them in line, but now . . ."

"You take care of Mary, Case."

Case smiled. "Thanks, Jim. Thought maybe if you and Easy could ride herd on them, it'd be okay." He seemed to take it for granted that Reno was capable of dealing with the wild bunch.

"Better get started, Case," Reno said. "You got a son to get into this world."

"Yeah." Case hesitated again and said, "Jim, if you have any trouble, don't let it bother you that Jesse's my brother. Like I said, he ain't got much sense, and them others is hard cases. But you do what you gotta do if it comes to it."

Case pulled out of line and headed back toward Boise in

less than an hour, but not before he'd had a sort of conference with the four men he'd stood for.

"Guess he must've talked to them like they wuz red-haired stepchildren," Easy reported to Reno. "I didn't hear none of it, but all four of them got the blessing. Leastways when Case got through, they all looked plumb chastised."

"You know about how long that'll last, don't you?" Reno mused.

"Yeah, 'bout as long as Pat stayed in the army—which wuz no time at all!" Easy answered.

But Case's farewell address must have been potent. For over a week there was no sign of trouble from any of the four. They stayed to themselves during the day, and every night they gambled and drank until late. Aside from the racket they made, however, there was no sign of any trouble.

"Won't last," Easy said. "I've knowed of mules that would be good for two years jest to git a chance to kick a feller once! It's jest a matter of time, I tell you, James, till one of them galoots turns his wolf loose!"

The trail got rougher, and it took all they had to struggle along the winding Snake River. Every day the temperature dropped, and once there were strips of white along the river as gusts of snow fell. Hands grew numb and faces raw with the cutting wind as they arched slowly upward toward the rising Blue Mountains.

Reno had seen little of Jean since her adventure with the Sioux. The next morning he met her on his way out of the camp as he headed on a long scout of the country. Something of strain was in her manner, almost as if she were embarrassed.

As she was walking along the brink of the canyon, she turned suddenly, and he thought she meant to avoid him.

Then she turned with a look of resolution on her face and came to where he stood. "Hello, Jim."

"Jean. Haven't seen you much lately. You all right?"

"Yes. I—I haven't really thanked you for saving my life." Her eyes lifted as she touched his arm. "You know how they say your whole life flashes before you if you're about to die? Well, it's true!"

"It was a bad time."

She shook her head and bit her lip, stirred by the memory. "I never had anything like that happen to me, Jim—never! I thought I was going to die—and it made me think."

"It can do that."

"I found out a bad thing about myself, Jim. When I thought I was going to die, all I thought about was myself."

"We're all like that."

"No, you're not. You cared enough to lay your life on the line." She shook her head sadly. "All I thought about was me. That's a bad thing to know about yourself." Then she threw her head back, and he saw tears in her eyes. "That girl I look like? The one who died for you?" She saw him flinch as she put it so badly, and she shook her head almost fiercely. "I guess something was left out of me, Jim. I'd never die for anybody else."

"Why, I don't think—"

She cut him off and said sadly, "Forget about me, Jim Reno. I'm not that girl. I won't change my life either. I made God all kinds of promises when I was in trouble, but now that I'm safe, I guess I'll just keep on the way I always have."

He tried to speak, but she put her hand on his mouth, saying with a sadness that went to the bone, "I'm doing you a big favor, Jim. It would be so easy to lead you on, but I can't. I owe you that much." She suddenly pulled his head down and kissed him hard, then said, "Good-bye, Jim!"

He watched her go, emptiness like an ache filling his chest. She had shut the door with such finality that there was no room for hope, and he said briefly in a clipped tone, "Well, that's that!" then turned and walked blindly toward the river.

Crossing the Blue Mountains took all the strength they had. It seemed to Jane Burns that every day was like every other, full of work and worry, weariness and cold. Her fine skin had roughened under the harsh sun and the rasping wind that whipped out of the north. She had always been a woman who prided herself on her physical charms, but the rigors of the trip had drained her so completely that she had no energy to spend on her appearance.

She had been protected by loving parents and had known nothing of hardship. She had not been very much in love with Robert, and her marriage had been a role which she had decided it was time to play. He had been so desperately in love with her that he had endured her frivolous ways, her kittenish behavior with other men, hoping that she would mature.

She had wept and threatened to leave him rather than make the trek to Oregon, but he had endured it all with a dour Scottish stubbornness, and she had finally agreed. She entered into the adventure, seeing herself as a pioneer woman, but it had gone flat almost at once. The physical discomforts alone were enough to deflate her, but the scene with Beau Slade and Robert's attitude since that time were worse than any physical discomfort.

From the day Beau had humiliated him in public, Robert had been so aloof and withdrawn that she felt as though she were living with a stranger. He had never been demonstrative in public. When they were alone, however, that shyness had been transformed into a vigorous passion that had at first shocked her, but that she had later welcomed with delight. No matter how badly she behaved, she was conscious that when they were alone she had the power to captivate him.

But night after night as they lay together beneath the canvas top of their wagon, he made no move to touch her. In the past he had always been quick to tell her how he loved her, but not a word like that now passed his lips, although she willed it with all her heart.

For the first time in her life, Jane Ann found herself unable to bend a man to her will. She realized that the unhappiness of her life was the harvest of the seeds she had sown. She had not been unaware that she had put her sweethearts through much unhappiness, and Robert more than any.

She was a spoiled girl, made proud by her experience with men, but as she and Robert lay together one night, she was so miserable, so lonely, that she attempted to open the door to him.

He was not asleep but lay silently beside her as he had done for weeks. Every night he said a polite but unemotional "Good night," and she had answered him in kind, certain that he would eventually come to heel. It was cold outside, and the warmth of his body drew her. Touching his arm lightly she whispered, "Robert? Are you asleep?"

His body grew even more rigid and he seemed to draw away from her touch. "No." He turned his face toward her and asked, "What's the matter?"

"Nothing." She let her hand rest on his shoulder and asked, "Are you going to be angry with me always?"

"I don't know what you mean."

His voice was sharp, defensive, and she answered quickly, "Yes, you do! Robert, I'm so lonely!"

Ordinarily this would have been enough to melt him, but he pulled away from her touch, saying, "I'm not angry with you."

"Then why are you acting like this? You haven't been yourself for weeks. You haven't . . ." She faltered, then went on with determination, "You haven't *touched* me since . . ."

He said bitterly, "Why don't you say it, Jane Ann? Since I played the coward in front of everybody!"

"I don't care about that!" she cried, and with a passion that caught him off guard, she threw her arms around him and buried her face against his chest, saying in a muffled voice, "I love you, Robert!"

He lay there, his heart pounding as she pressed her body against him, weeping as she said the words he had never heard in such unrestrained passion.

But he did not move, and when she raised her head and attempted to kiss him, he pulled away. "I think I want your love more than I want anything on this earth," he said slowly. Then he spoke with such a hard-edged finality that it froze her heart: "But I'll never be a husband to you until I become a man, Jane Ann."

"Robert, don't be foolish! Nobody expects you to face up to a gunman like Beau Slade!"

His answer, when it came, was so steady, so cold, that it seemed to freeze her heart: "I'll fight him, Jane Ann. I may get killed, but better to be dead than a coward!"

He rolled away from her abruptly, leaving her more alone than she had ever been in her life.

232

Burns rode drag the next day, along with Leon Prather, and the exhausted stock moved so slowly that all the riders needed to do was amble behind. As the trail narrowed into a long pass, they drew together, and Leon noticed that the Scotsman was even quieter than usual.

"Trip gettin' to you, Bob?" he asked.

"Not really, Leon, although I guess we'll all be glad to see the end of it. It's just . . ."

Prather liked Burns, and he was an astute young man. "That business with Beau Slade, it's botherin' you, ain't it, Bob?"

Burns was not given to sharing his personal troubles with others, but the pressure had been so great that he nodded and said, "Yes." He paused and thought about it, then added, "I'm going to have it out with him, Leon. Jim's been teaching me how to use a gun, and I can't live with a thing like that over my head."

"Know what you mean. But Beau Slade's an expert." Leon shifted uncomfortably in the saddle. "You ever pull a gun on a man, Bob?"

"Pull a gun? I never even had a fistfight!"

"Didn't think so." Leon had been brought up in a hard school, and fighting had been as much a part of his life as eating. "Well, I reckon you know what you have to do, Bob. But I'd hate to go up against Slade. Don't think anybody would have much of a chance of beatin' his draw—except Jim, of course."

"I don't care anymore, Leon." Burns shook his head, stubbornness written on his sharp-featured face. "He may beat me to the draw, but he'd better make his first shot good. I'm not so fast, but I'm pretty accurate. I can hit a sapling six inches thick at thirty paces five out of six times."

"Yeah, but a tree ain't a man, Bob," Leon said seriously. "In the first place, a tree ain't gonna shoot back. And in the second place, killin' a man is a hard thing. Lots of men just can't pull a trigger when it means killin'."

Burns said nothing, but there was a stolid look in his gray eyes that Prather recognized. Nothing, he knew, could stop Robert Burns from going up against Beau Slade, and it saddened the young puncher to think how little chance Burns had of coming out of such an encounter alive.

The conversation with Burns went deeper into Leon Prather's mind than he supposed. When the trouble came the next day, it was the sharp memory of the look on Burns's face that made him step into a quarrel not his own.

The train had stopped early beside a spring, and at supper Clyde had said, "I'll stand guard tonight, Leon." His face was puffy and the broken teeth made him miserable. Leon could not look at him without a cold rage rising inside, but he said, "I'll do it."

"No. You done enough." Clyde had picked up his rifle and gone slowly to his post.

Lena noted the look on Leon's face, and said, "He'll be all right. Don't worry." She touched his shoulder and gave him a brief smile. "We'll get him to a dentist soon as we get to Oregon City, Leon. He'll be good as new."

"Sure, Lena." He looked up at her and said with a tired grin, "You have quite a chore raising all of us, don't you, Lena?"

"Oh, you're not so bad." She paused and said, "I miss Pete."

"Yeah, I know." He got up and said, "Let me help you clean up this mess." He reached for a dirty plate, then paused. "What's that?" A small crowd was gathering across the circle and he said, "Looks like trouble. I better check it. Save these dishes for me, you hear now?" He gave her a sudden hug, which was unusual, and it brought a warm smile to her face.

He waved a hand as she called out, "You be careful, Leon," and walked quickly to the crowd. He saw at once that Robert Burns, his face white as chalk, was standing rigidly ten feet from Beau Slade, and both men were in that frozen attitude of men facing off.

The two men were the center of attention for two groups. Over to one side stood the latecomers—Jesse Purdy, Keno Baker, and two others, a rider named Cotton Kennedy and Breed Johnson, a tall half-breed with burning eyes. Across the way stood the men of the train, and the lines were clearly drawn.

Jane Ann Burns was pulling at her husband's arm, saying desperately, "Robert! Don't!" But he said in a clipped cold voice, "Get out of the way, Jane Ann. I'm going to teach this dog he can't mistreat a decent woman on this train!"

Beau Slade stood facing Burns, but there was an uncertainty on his handsome face. He bit his lip, looked around the crowd, then said, "Look, Burns, I know I was out of line once before, but not this time."

"That's right, Robert," Jane Ann said quickly. "He just asked if I needed help with this." She pointed to a large bundle of branches at her feet. "That's all it was, really."

Burns didn't even hear her. He had primed himself, and nothing was going to stop him. He took Jane Ann by the arm and pushed her toward Dooley, saying, "Get her out of here, boy!"

Dooley pulled the woman back, and as the crowd faced back, she searched desperately for Reno, but he was not there. "Somebody stop it!" she said loudly.

Burns walked back and faced Beau squarely, his face pale and determined. "You told me to get a gun, Slade. Well, I've got one. Now you can either use yours or crawl like the yellow dog you are!"

He left Slade no choice. The crowd backed further away, and then Jesse Purdy said, "What you waitin' for, Beau? Blast him!"

The sight of Jesse's brutal smile sparked a violent anger in Leon Prather. A hatred for the huge man had been in him since Jesse had ruined his twin's face. He was remembering, too, the conversation he'd had with Robert Burns the day before, and these two things triggered a reaction in him.

Stepping beside Burns he said, "You want some of this, Jesse? I say you're a yellow cur! You're wearing a gun. Let's see you use it!"

Before the slow-moving Jesse could answer, Keno Baker stepped away from the men in the shadows and came to stand beside Beau. There was a sheen in his pale eyes, and he licked his lips as he said softly, "Like I said, Prather, I do the gunfightin'. You want to try it?"

Perhaps it could have been avoided. Several men from the train were moving. Vinson Grant lifted up his voice at about the same time as Buck Henry, saying, "All right . . ."

Burns touched it off. Beau Slade, who had a harassed look on his face, said, "Now, look, there's no need for this, I tell you—"

But he never finished the sentence. Burns took the wave of Beau's hand for a draw, and the Scotsman's hand grabbed the Colt at his side.

A startled look leapt into Beau's face as Burns drew. Seeing that the smaller man was intent on killing, he drew his gun with practiced ease and got off one shot just as Burns's gun cleared leather. The slug drove Burns backward as if he had been struck by a giant fist, and his gun fell to the ground as blood welled out of a wound high on his chest.

The sight of Burns down drove Leon Prather over the edge. He reached for his gun, but Keno Baker drew both Colts and fired a slug from each before Leon could pull the trigger of his own gun. Dooley was watching with horrified eyes, and she could not believe the flickering speed with which the little gunman drew the Colts and fired. It was not a series of motions, but smooth as the striking of a snake—and more deadly, for both bullets struck Leon Prather in the heart. He fell backward and arched his body in one spasm, heels digging into the dirt, then slowly he relaxed, sagging into the earth for the last time.

"Self-defense. You all seen it." Baker did not holster his guns, and his friends edged up to stand behind him.

Only Jane Ann Burns moved. She tore herself from Dooley's nerveless grasp and ran to throw herself on the bleeding body of her husband, keening in a wild cry that split the silence of the night.

THIRTEEN
Reign of the Gun

After the explosion of violence that destroyed Leon Prather, a strange quiet fell across the train for two days. They buried Leon beneath a spreading oak, Jude Finney reading the Bible in his halting fashion. Robert Burns had survived, to the wonder of all. Beau's bullet had angled upward through his upper chest, narrowly missing the lung. Alice Henry felt the lump high on his back and removed the slug with a paring knife. Then his fever broke and he regained consciousness.

"Jane Ann?" he whispered faintly, and then he felt her tears on his face.

She took his face in her hands and kissed him gently. "Oh, darling! I've been so frightened!" She took one of his hands in both of hers, and he saw more clearly the worn expression of her face as she said intensely, "If I lost you . . . !"

He closed his eyes, which were suddenly moist, and nodded as he said in wonder, "Why, I guess it's worth getting shot to find out that you love me, isn't it?" Then he faded off into a healthy sleep, but she remained there holding his hand tenderly, marveling how narrowly she had missed finding out the depth of her love for her husband.

The train pulled out the next day, moving slowly upward through the serrated pass that sliced through the Blue Mountains. On the third day of Reno's absence, Dooley, driving the oxen with Leah beside her, scanned the horizon anxiously. "He ought to be back by now, Leah. Maybe he's had an accident."

The black woman turned on the wagon seat, giving Dooley an intent stare. She took in the worried frown, the nervous biting of the full lower lip, and the twisting of the fine hands handling the lines, and she said with an odd note in her voice, "You thinks about Mistah Jim a lot, don't you, chile?"

Dooley turned to face Leah and saw the peculiar light in the wise eyes of her old nurse. She twisted nervously on the seat and shrugged, trying to seem casual as she said, "What's that supposed to mean? You're always saying things like that to me." She touched off the ox with an expert flick of the blacksnake and added sharply, "Sure, I think about Jim. Why shouldn't I?"

Leah did not answer at once. She finally shook her head, and there was an ancient sorrow in her face as she said, "You gonna get hurt bad, Miss Julie."

It was the first time Leah had used that name since they had left Missouri, and it caught the girl up short. "Leah, why'd you use that name?"

"'Cause it's who you is, chile, and you can wear pants and cut yo' hair and talk like a man till the cows comes home, but . . ."

When Leah paused, Dooley turned to meet her gaze and whispered, "But *what,* Leah?"

"You got to face up to the fact dat to Mistah Jim, chile,

you ain't no woman." Leah put her pink-palmed hand on the girl's shoulder and added slowly, "You is jest a nice boy he's lookin' out for."

"Well, that's what I *want* him to think!" Dooley's eyes were enormous as she faced Leah angrily, but then a blush swept up her throat and touched her cheeks. She suddenly broke off, and there was a break in her voice as she whispered, "Oh, Leah, what am I going to *do!*"

"My baby!" Leah crooned, pulling the girl close and caressing her hair. Her face changed as she remembered suddenly doing the same when Julie had been a baby with a skinned knee. She held the girl tightly, saying finally, "Don't cry now, chile! I reckon it ain't never easy for a girl to have to grow up and be a woman. And you ain't got nobody 'cept old Leah and Jackson to take care of you." Then she added gently, "But I reckon the good Lawd ain't dead, is he now? He gonna watch out fo' my baby! You'll see."

Dooley said little for the rest of the day, but after a scanty supper, she was glad when Easy came over to say, "Hey, Dooley, His Highness says for you to come and eat some pie the Mex stirred up."

She followed Easy over to St. John's wagon, and the tall Englishman had a twinkle in his eye as he said jovially, "Sit down, young man!" There was, she thought, a slight emphasis on the word *man,* and she took the piece of pie Jean handed her and stuffed a huge bite into her mouth to cover her confusion. St. John's knowledge of her secret put her at his mercy, but there was in the man some quality that made her feel safe.

As they ate, Dooley watched Jean carefully. Many times she had searched the beauty of the woman's face, trying in vain to find a hardness, a coarseness that signaled the weakness that led her into an immoral life, but once again she was baffled. There was a smooth ease on Jean Lamarr's face, and Dooley finally decided that the woman was either totally amoral or else an accomplished actress, able to cover her feelings with confidence.

She came out of her concentrated study of the woman when she heard Easy ask St. John, "You hear about Waylon Simmons?"

"Simmons? No, I believe not."

"Got stomped into a mud puddle."

"Oh? Who did it?"

Easy took a huge swallow of steaming coffee, wiped his mouth with a sleeve, and frowned as he said, "Jesse Purdy. It wuz an argument over poker."

"Hate to hear it." St. John shook his head, then stared at Easy with something like anger in his bony face. "The whole crowd is a disgrace! I did hear that the half-breed and the one called Kennedy took a steer from Moore."

"You heard right. Took the critter and laughed at Barney when he asked them to pay for it."

"But they can't do that!" Dooley argued.

Easy gave her a hard look and asked at once, "Why can't they? They ain't nothin' but crooks, Dooley. Why, either one of 'em would steal a plug of tobacco out of your mouth if you yawned!"

"But why did Moore let them do it?" Jean asked, a puzzled frown on her brow.

Easy shrugged and reached for another piece of pie. "If this here piece don't hurt me, I'll eat all I want next time." Chewing noisily, he finally swallowed and said, "What could Barney do? They're both tough as nails in a coffin. They'd kill a man for the gold in his teeth!"

"But, my good fellow," St. John protested, "there is such a thing as *law!*"

"Law?" Easy waved a hand toward the east. "You left law back there somewhere. I'd say right now the only law we got in this train is what a man carries in his holster." He stared across at the wagon where the nightly poker game was going on. "And looks like that bunch ain't got no intention of startin' no temperance movement. Things is gonna get worse 'fore they get better."

"I heard that they've been bothering some of the women," Dooley said.

"Yeah, and I been meanin' to tell you, Miss Jean, don't you never get off alone. You want to go somewhere, you let me know."

"I'm able to take care of myself, Easy," she said at once.

"Sure, on your ground. But what you ain't seen yet is that there ain't nothing to stop these jokers." He stared at her intently, and added, "They can do anything they want. Who's gonna stop 'em?"

St. John immediately began to argue that the train itself was capable of dealing with the roughs, but Easy shook his head stubbornly, saying as he left, "You ain't never been without law, St. John. Them birds won't never be satisfied. No matter what they get, it ain't gonna be enough!" He bit his lip and said, "Wish Jim would get back!"

He went to his bed, and Jean left also. As soon as they were alone, St. John said, "Your little experiment is still working, is it, Dooley?"

"St. John, why did Jim leave?" she said, ignoring his remark. "Did he say anything to you?"

"No, but I suspect that it has something to do with Jean."

"Jean? What about her?"

"Why, I saw them talking together, and she came back white as a piece of paper, and he rode out as soon as he could get his things."

"Oh." Dooley gnawed her full lower lip. "I wonder . . ."

When she didn't finish, he said with a frown, "You know, I've thought he might keep on going."

"No!" The denial broke from Dooley sharply, and she flushed as St. John smiled at her with a quizzical light in his blue eyes. "He—he wouldn't do that!"

"Perhaps not." St. John shrugged his thin shoulders and said as Dooley turned to leave, "I hope you don't get hurt, Julie." He put his hand on her shoulder and added gently, "I'm very much afraid that he's in love with Jean."

"And what will you do? She's your woman!"

"No, not really."

"She's—she's not good enough for him!"

St. John shook his head, kindness in his eyes, though his words were not gentle. "And I suppose you think you are? Julie, I'm practically old enough to be your father, and though I have a great admiration for Reno, I must say he's no saint! You've built up a romantic image of the man—a knight in shining armor!" The Englishman shook his head firmly, and there was a sadness in his voice as he said, "Julie, I have wasted my own life, mostly by chasing around after things that were not the things I should have wanted. I should hate for you to do the same."

He got up and left her so abruptly that it took her off guard. She was suddenly aware that the man from across the ocean was a man of sorrows, and that the light manner he wore was a disguise as complete as her own. As she lay awake that night, she thought of the sadness in his face and agonized at the confusion in her heart about Jim Reno.

Easy had been right about the behavior of Baker and his friends. In the two days that followed they made life miserable for the train. They took what they wanted, laughing loudly at any protest, and the nightly poker game drew in two or three of the young men of the train. Worst of all was their crude behavior to the women, which got so rank that no woman was able to meet one of them without being accosted.

Buck Henry, coming back to the train after first watch, saw a dark shadow near a clump of pin oaks. Then it divided, and the bulky figure of Carl Slade went one way, and Ellie Satterfield practically ran into Buck.

"Oh!" she said with a touch of fear, then she peered at him in the moonlight and said, "It's you, Buck."

He looked down at her, and said, "Ellie, you shouldn't be meetin' Slade like this."

"Oh, Buck, you sound just like Jude Finney," she said gaily.

"Finney's got sense."

She laughed and took his huge hand in both of hers. She marveled at the power and strength in the fingers and the corded wrists, and said, "Buck, I'm young! A girl has a right to have a little fun, doesn't she?"

Buck stood there, muted by the feeling he had for this wild girl. She had the power to move him, and her presence stirred him so that he never could find the words to say what he felt.

Feeling like a pompous fool, he shook his head and said, "It's wrong, Ellie—you know it is!"

"I know people think I'm wild—that I'm too loose around

men." She bit her lower lip and searched his face, saying in a subdued voice, "I'm a good girl, Buck. Do you believe that?"

Slowly he nodded, and then he said, "You must know how I feel about you, Ellie!" Then he shook his head and added, "But you're going to get hurt if you keep on playing with a man like that!"

"I can handle a dozen like Carl," she laughed gaily. Then she cocked her head, and looking up at him pursed her lips, pulled his head down, and kissed his cheek.

"But if you ever let yourself go, Buck Henry . . ." She turned and left him standing there touching the cheek she had kissed, and he heard her voice floating on the night air, "I don't know who could handle *you!*"

He thought about that, then went wearily to bed, praying his simple prayers and wondering how to be the kind of man she wanted.

Reno rode into the camp the next morning while Dooley was eating breakfast. He came over to take the cup of coffee she held out to him, and she had to pause and fight back the wave of gladness that went through her at the sight of him. "You've been gone a long time," she forced herself to say steadily. "I was beginning to worry."

There was a heaviness in his face, not trail weariness, but something deeper. He had none of the lightness which had been a part of him for many days. He said only, "Got some fresh meat." He went back to his horse and pulled an antelope free, tossing it to the ground. "Things all right here?"

He spoke indifferently, but as she told him about the shooting, his dark eyes grew hard. He said nothing until she had finished, then glanced over at the Prather wagon. "So Leon is gone."

"Yes. It was murder, Jim! He didn't have a chance!"

"He shouldn't have gone up against Baker." He stood there, silently thinking about the friendly little man, and then he asked, "What about Burns? He gonna make it, Dooley?"

"I think so. His wife is a good nurse." She looked to the Burns's wagon and added, "She's a different woman somehow. I think she didn't know how much she loved her husband until she nearly lost him."

She sat him down and Leah fussed over him as he ate. Dooley told him about Baker and the rest and how they were making life miserable for everyone. "Easy says they're going to get worse, but I don't see how they could!"

Reno stared at her, then got up and said, "Things always get worse, Dooley." There was a bitterness in his manner that pained her, but she knew that there was nothing to say.

Going to the Prather wagon, Reno found Lena feeding her baby. Clyde was leaning against the wagon, and there was a bitterness in his battered face that shocked Reno.

"You heard about it?" Clyde asked sullenly.

"Yes." Reno moved to stand beside Lena who looked at him steadily, sorrow etched across her face. "Tough," Reno said finally. He touched her arm, and there was a gentleness in his dark face that said more than the single word.

"Jim," Lena said, "I know you'll say you want to help. There's one thing you can do."

"Name it, Lena."

"Keep Clyde from going after Baker."

"He was my brother." Clyde's battered face was bleak as winter, and the words might have been carved in stone. He was, Reno realized, part of a Southern culture that had made blood feuds into a fine science.

247

"Won't help to get yourself killed," Reno suggested. Then before Clyde could protest he added, "You got a family to look after, Clyde. After Baker polishes you off, you think he's going to take care of them?"

It hit the smaller man hard, and he finally swallowed, then said, "Jim, it ain't right for scum like that to kill good people!"

"Well, maybe something will happen to him someday."

Clyde stared at Reno, then apparently found something in that statement to satisfy him. "Yeah, I reckon."

Reno nodded, a slight smile crossing his bleak lips. "I'll be around, Lena," he said, then crossed to Slade's wagon where breakfast was being served.

"You got back." Daniel Slade took a bite of biscuit, stared at Reno, then asked, "What's up ahead?"

"One bad pass about a day from here. Have to winch the wagons up, I reckon. Ought to make it to Walla Walla in a week if that's not snow building up over there in those clouds."

Reno felt the gaze of Baker and the others, but gave no indication of their presence. Finally, when Reno had passed along a few more details of his scouting, Daniel tossed his plate down and walked away to his horse with a grunt.

"Guess you heard about the trouble, Reno."

Keno Baker moved to intercept him, and he was playing to the crowd. A broad grin was on the albino, Cotton, and the slate-colored eyes of Breed Johnson struck like flint as he stared at Reno. Jesse Purdy and Carl Slade stopped eating to watch, both of them grinning, but Beau Slade did not lift his glance, seeming to be interested in something off in the distance.

"Heard about it."

"Self-defense, of course," Baker said with a mocking tone. "Didn't think the runt had it in him."

Breed Johnson said loudly, "Friend of yours, wasn't he?"

Reno took a pipe out of his pocket, then a worn pouch. The silence built up as he packed it carefully, took a kitchen match from his shirt pocket and lit it with a thumbnail, letting the silence run on. When he did look at Johnson there was a summer-soft gentleness in his tone that did not match the steady glow in his dark eyes.

"They were both friends of mine."

The half-breed glanced at Baker, then said, "You was one of the rebels—like Prather, I heard."

"That's right."

"You fire-eatin' Southerners stand up for each other, I hear. Maybe you got an idea of taking it up."

Reno drew on the pipe, let the smoke trickle up until his eyes were half-veiled in the smoke, then said as he turned to go, "If I'd done that, Indian, some of us would already be pushing up daisies."

He walked away, hearing Baker say loudly, "I sort of had the idea you was a touch hairpin, Reno. Guess I heard wrong."

Reno, ignoring the laugh, went to St. John's wagon. He had felt a sudden flash of anger at the scene, but he had learned to wait. He knew more about his courage than they did and no longer felt impelled to answer every raw challenge that came at him.

"Hey!" Easy whooped as Reno appeared beside him. "I wish to my never if you ain't back!" He pounded Reno on the back, his ugly face almost splitting in a grin. "I swan, James, I wuz startin' to think you met up with a bunch of 'Paches and was sayin' 'Howdy' to St. Peter!"

St. John came out of the wagon, closely followed by Jean, and the Englishman's horse face, usually banked in strict reserve, was marked with a grin that almost equalled that of Easy's. "I say, old boy, it's about time you came back!"

Reno looked at the two, shook his head, and said with a smile, "I feel like the prodigal son. You got any kind of fatted calf for me?" He was smiling, but at that moment Jean came close and laid her hand on his arm.

"I'm glad you came back, Jim."

Easy and St. John did not miss the change in Reno. His grin fell away, turning his angular cheeks austere in the morning light. He nodded slowly and said, "Thanks."

Easy tried to restore the buoyancy of Reno's spirit, but the light was out of his friend's eyes. Both he and St. John thought alike, and they made their excuses about getting ready to move, leaving Jean and Reno alone.

"Jim, you've got to forget about me." It was like her to come right to the point, but it angered Reno.

"I reckon I'm supposed to just throw away what I feel for you like an old shirt."

Jean ignored his anger. Looking up with a face not free from some sort of secret grief, she shook her head. "You never had any feeling for me, Jim. You had a feeling for that girl you lost. And I think it's fine that you remember her. But you can't find her in me. You can't find her in any other woman."

"I never tried to do that!"

"Yes, you did!" She took his arm, which was knotted with the strain he imposed upon himself, and shook him saying, "Jim, what you two had—why, that was special. And I guess it always will be. But you can't live at her grave! She wouldn't want that, would she?"

Reno considered her, a stubbornness glinting in his dark eyes. His lips flattened, signaling the tenacity that lay beneath his easy ways. He settled back on his heels, saying doggedly, "You're wrong, Jean."

She gave a futile gesture with her hand as he wheeled and walked away without another word. She knew men, and it was clear to her that the kind of woman that Reno wanted would have to be totally different from what she was. The thought saddened her, but she accepted it with a streak of fatalism that had come to be part of her character.

The snow that had been stored in the low, heavy clouds began to fall two days later. It lay in long white strips across the trail, then stuck to the trees in patterns like fine lace. The sound of iron wheels on rock was soon muffled by a carpet two inches thick, and the hooves of the stock slipped on the treacherous surface, often going down in a roiling mix-up of harness and frightened animals threatening to kick the wagons to sticks.

The temperature edged down, and Jane Ann Burns piled every blanket she had on Robert to keep the dreaded pneumonia away.

On Thursday, however, there was a merciful break, and a powerful sun melted the blanket of snow, allowing the train to make good time.

Even Keno Baker and his friends had pitched in to help move the train and the stock through the snowstorm, but as soon as the warm spell cleared the trail and the journey seemed on the verge of being complete, they went back to their old ways—the poker games at night, the heavy drinking, and even more callous treatment of the women—all worse than before.

"Guess they gotta get in all the devilment they can in the next few days," Jude Finney said with tight lips. Cotton Kennedy had actually put his hands on Addie Grant, and then laughed when the preacher had rebuked him for it.

"It'll be over soon, Jude," Addie said. She had been afraid that Jude would be drawn into a fight with the hard-eyed gunman, and she drew a sigh of relief when the incident ended with no violence.

"They ain't going to stop until they hurt more people, Addie." Jude shook his head and added, "I try to be like the Lord says, loving my enemies, but it's sure enough a hard battle!"

It was later that same day that Keno Baker saw Lena Prather standing beside her wagon. Baker winked at Breed Johnson and said, "Mebby I better comfort the widow in her affliction, Breed."

Lena was deep in thought, staring off at the line of snow-capped mountains that Reno had told her were the last obstacle. She gasped as a hand closed in on her arm, and when she turned to see Baker, a lustful light in his eyes, a streak of fear shot through her. "Turn me loose!" she said quickly.

Baker held her, grinning at her futile attempts to escape his hold. "Aw, honey, you just need a little loving to cheer you up. Reckon I'll fill the bill?"

Breed Johnson was slouched against the wagon, grinning at the girl's struggle, and the sudden voice coming from behind him took him off guard as it did Keno Baker.

"Turn that woman loose!"

Baker released Lena, whirling with catlike speed. His hand dropped to his gun, then stopped as he found himself looking into the twin bores of a twelve-gauge shotgun. It was not just the gun, but the steady hatred blazing out of the eyes of Vinson Grant. Baker had seen death often enough—had even faced it—but never had he felt it so close.

"Wait a minute, Grant . . . ," he began, hopeful that Johnson would make a move to take the old man's attention.

When Johnson did make a stealthy move to get his gun free, Grant swiveled the twelve-gauge slightly and pulled the trigger. The shot kicked up dirt at the half-breed's feet and froze him in place.

"I just got one more shell," Grant said steadily. "If both of you went for me, I could only get one of you." He smiled grimly and said, "Why don't you try it?"

Nobody had made Baker take water, ever, but as the shotgun twitched between him and Breed, he knew that not even he could draw and get off a shot before the old man pulled the trigger. He had seen one man cut in two by a similar gun in Dallas, and the thought made him hold his hands very still.

When Grant saw that, he spat to one side and said, "I didn't think so. Drop them belts and git! If I see you come within fifty yards of this woman, I'll drill you like I would a snake."

Baker and Johnson, their faces white, dropped their gun belts on the ground. It was the first time Baker had been without a weapon in a long time, and he felt naked and helpless. If Grant could have seen the insane rage in the pale blue eyes of the gunman he might have pulled the trigger, for there was no way that Baker would let this thing pass.

Reno told him so when he heard about it. "Baker won't forget it, Vinson."

"He better not!" Grant snarled. "I meant what I told the snake, Jim! I'll kill him if he bothers Lena again—or any other woman!"

No one ever knew if the incident was related to what happened that night, but the poker game turned into a hard-drinking, mean affair, and it was known that when Carl Slade had prodded Keno Baker about the incident, the little gunman had snapped, "You ain't doin' so well with that Satterfield gal, Slade! She don't even need a shotgun to play you for a sucker!"

Buck Henry met Ellie the next morning, but before he could speak she ducked her head and tried to get away. He caught at her, and when he pulled her around, the raw bruise on her cheek stopped his question. More than that, the laughing eyes of Ellie were filled with a shame and self-loathing that wrenched at Henry. He asked in a harsh voice, "Who done that, Ellie?"

"Nobody! I—I tripped and fell," she lied, and there was such hurt in her voice that Buck could only stand and stare. When Ellie pulled free and ran away with a sob, Buck went at once to see her mother.

"She come in with her clothes all tore and her face bleeding," Martha Satterfield said. She was very fat, and had been a jolly woman at one time. Now tears made tracks down her round cheeks, and her lips trembled as she said, "It was that Carl Slade, Buck. I tried to tell her about him, but she was so sure she could handle him." A sob shook the shapeless bulk of her body, and she rolled her head back and forth, saying, "He hurt her, Buck!"

But that was not the end of it, for even as Buck was talking to Martha Satterfield, Baker was taking his revenge on Vinson Grant. He had not slept since the old man had faced him down, and his first impulse when he got his weapons back was to go after Grant. With the law only a few days away, he realized that the thing had to look like a fair fight. He was thinking hard on this when R.G. Grant rode by, headed for the herd. Baker had found nothing in the terribly scarred man to interest him, but now he remembered noting that Vinson Grant and the sister, Addie, took care of the tall fellow as if he were a child. A bright light flickered in Baker's eyes, and he called to Breed, saying, "See that one, Breed, the one with the eye patch?" The Indian listened intently as Baker talked in a whisper, and after awhile the two men mounted and headed for the herd at the rear of the train.

Reno had gone ahead, ostensibly to seek a safe pass for the wagons, but actually because he didn't want to talk. The encounter with Jean had soured him, and the only thing in his mind was to finish the trip and get as far away from her as possible. He realized that he was turning into a dour, vindictive man—all the love in him curdled by the loss of things held dear.

When he turned back and rode into the camp there was something wrong. Instead of the sound of cooking, washing, and kids playing, there was a silence that struck at him like the sudden buzzing of a snake's rattle. He pulled his horse up and stared across at Slade's wagon, where a tight group stood around looking tense and restless.

"Jim, come over here!"

Buck Henry appeared suddenly and motioned for Reno to follow him. There was a small open space to the right of the circle, and the anger in the faces of those gathered there shocked Reno. "What's going on?"

Vinson Grant whirled from where he was holding Addie, and he looked a hundred years old to Reno. There was a sag in the muscles of his face, and his eyes were ringed with red, as though he had been crying.

"They killed R.G.! They killed my brother!" he said in a high-pitched voice. His hands were trembling, and Reno saw that he was not the same man who had begun the journey. In his time Vinson Grant had ridden with the wildest men on the planet, the cavalry of Jeb Stuart, and the fact that he had commanded such men was evidence of his strength. But the years had drained him, and now he was only a shadow, shaken as if by palsy.

"What happened?" Reno asked, and as Grant told him, he realized that Baker had taken the sure way to get his revenge. The two men had left the train, and when they came back it was to claim that R.G. Grant had attacked Breed Johnson in an argument over the war, and that Johnson had used his knife in self-defense. When some of the men had gone to the body, they found a gun in the dead man's hand with two empty shells, which Breed claimed were fired at him. There were knife wounds on the thin body of R.G. Grant, savage, ferocious slashes that made more than one of the men turn away with heaving stomachs.

"My brother was a child," Vinson Grant said in a low voice. He was exhausted by the rage that had first hit him, and now there was a palsied shake in the hand he raised to brush away something that would not leave—the sight of his dead brother cut to ribbons by a savage.

Buck Henry slapped his thigh with a meaty hand and cursed. Reno was slightly shocked, for the big man was not known to use profanity. Now, however, he saw a wildness in the big man's eyes, like that of the men he'd seen in their first battles in the war. Buck was not the mild, plodding figure then, and as he related the story of Ellie Satterfield, Reno realized that the train was a powder keg. It would only take one spark to set off a war.

Finally Buck said in a voice wire-tight with hate, "We're going to stop them, Jim! They're nothing but killers!"

A mutter of agreement went around the circle, and when Reno said, "Think about it, Buck," he saw grimaces of disapproval.

"Think about it?" Grant said in contempt. "There ain't nothing to think about!"

"We got enough men to do the job," Buck said, looking around at the crowd.

Reno shook his head. He knew he would be misunderstood, but said anyway, "You don't have enough, Buck. Sure, there's *more* of you than there is of them. But that's not the whole story."

"What are you saying, Jim?" Buck lashed out, his face white.

"They're gunfighters," Reno said, but he saw that meant nothing to Buck or Grant. "They'll slaughter you like sheep."

Grant said, "I thought you was one of us, Reno. I thought you was a *man.* But I was wrong!"

Reno looked around the circle and saw no friend. Even in the faces of Dooley and Lee there was a sadness at his stand. The ending of the affair with Jean had drained him, and he had nothing left to give. *A desert inside,* he thought grimly. *That's what I've become.* He looked around the crowd, seeing faces that once had smiled at him now filled with anger and contempt. He wanted to argue, to shout, to make them realize that what they were going to do was insane and futile, but he did not. He turned and walked away without another word.

Feeling empty, he wandered out of camp, walking for hours, his mind a blank. The meeting was going on, and he had seen enough mobs to know that they would try to move against the gunmen—and most of them would die in the attempt.

Finally he went back and slipped into his blankets near to Lee.

"Jim?"

"You awake, Lee?"

"They're going to do something in the morning, first thing."

"Thought they might."

A long silence ensued, but Reno knew the boy well enough to realize that a terrible battle was going on inside. "You think I ought to help, don't you, Lee?"

"Gosh, Jim, they murdered that nice Mr. Grant! And they hurt Miss Ellie real bad! And Leon, they killed him!"

"And they'll kill most of the men who try to do something about it tomorrow."

"Not if we all stick together!"

Reno rolled over and touched Lee's arm. "I know you feel bad about all the bad things, son, but you have to understand that those men are experts. They fight all the time, and they've spent years honing their skills. It won't be a nice fair fight like you think. They might open up as the men go to talk to them, and you'll see ten or twelve men in the dirt bleeding their lives out. They're wolves, Lee, and they'll butcher that crowd in the morning!"

Reno realized that the bitterness and frustration in his own heart had lashed out, but he could not hope that the boy would understand. Lee lay there for so long that Reno hoped that he'd gone to sleep, but finally he spoke.

"Jim, do you believe in God?"

The question hit Reno hard, his mind going blank, then he took a deep breath and said, "Yes, I do."

"Then if that's all so, what Jude Finney says about the Bible, I don't see how you can sit around and just watch your friends try to do something that's right. Don't the Bible say you're your brother's keeper or something like that?"

Reno lay there, his breath coming a little short. He could not tell Lee that those words had been almost the last thing that his stepfather had said to him on his deathbed. "Look out for your people, son," Lige had gasped. "Be your brother's keeper, no matter what."

Reno never heard those words without a sense of remorse, for he had failed to live up to the hopes that Lige Stevens had had for him, and the shame of it now made a bitter taste in his mouth.

He had no defense, and he gave Lee no answer, but the boy said quietly after a long pause, "All right. You do what you want to, Jim. But I'm going with them!"

Reno did not sleep at all, and he left his gun belt off when he arose. Dooley looked at his side, but said nothing. He stared at her, then said, "You think I ought to help the others, don't you?"

"Yes!"

Her answer came like a shot, and though her face was pale, she wore a Colt at her side, and he lowered his head, standing before her, drained of emotion.

"You got so many friends you can throw these away, Jim?" she asked in a tightly controlled voice. "These people are the closest thing to a family you have on earth, and you're going to let them die without lifting a hand?"

He shook his head mutely. Then, unable to meet her eyes, he turned and busied himself with saddling his horse. "I'm looking out for you and Lee. That's all. I'll go along to see that you don't get yourselves killed. I'm not wearing a gun because it's the only way to get you out of it."

Dooley stared at him, and when he finally turned to meet the blazing green eyes of the youngster he had to force himself to keep from wavering. "I guess you might as well stay here, Jim—or get on your horse and light out. Get in a hole and pull it after you."

"Dooley!"

"Get out! Ride so far away to a place where they don't have mirrors! You won't be able to look yourself in the face again! To think I thought that you . . ."

She whirled and ran toward the crowd that was pulling itself together at the far side of the train, and Reno saw that Lee was already there, standing between Easy and Barney Moore. With a sigh he walked slowly toward them, noting instantly that a battle line was being drawn.

Directly in front of the larger group, Keno Baker stood in the center of a line that was spread out widely. Breed Johnson was on his left and Cotton Kennedy fifteen yards beyond. To Baker's right were Jesse Purdy and Carl Slade, also heavily armed and spaced far apart. Beau Slade and his father were behind Baker and to his right, but it was the others who were the threat. They were few, but each man wore two handguns and carried repeater rifles.

Reno wanted to call out to Buck Henry, "Spread out!" for they were all bunched together. *Like sheep for the slaughter!* Reno thought grimly as he moved to a neutral position between the two groups.

Baker spotted him at once, noting that he was not armed. "You out of this, Reno?" There was a note of relief in his pale blue eyes, for he knew full well that Reno was the most potent danger.

"I'm looking out for two boys—Dooley and Lee. If they get hurt, I'm in, Keno."

Baker said quickly, "Ain't got no quarrel with them, Reno." He looked up and called out, "That's far enough! One more step and we open up!"

Buck's face was pale, but he called out, "You men are through here. Put down your guns and we'll see you get a fair trial in Oregon City."

Baker laughed, and Reno felt an unwilling admiration for the man. He was evil, but there was nothing wrong with his nerve. He stood there facing the crowd with a smile on his face. "You make one move, farmer, and you're dead!"

Suddenly, as if at a signal, the group led by Baker lifted their rifles, and the morning sun glittered along the barrels. It chilled the ardor of the men with Buck Henry, and only Vinson Grant spoke up. "They can't get us all!"

But it was over. There was a wavering in the crowd, and Buck's face moved with anger as he said, "We didn't come here for a tea party, did we?"

If Carl Slade had kept quiet, it might have been the end, but the big man walked toward Buck, and said, "You the man that lifts a whole wagon, Henry? Well let me tell you about that little gal, Ellie. I tell you . . ."

He was caught unprepared as Buck looped a huge blow into his face, driving him back and bringing the blood to his lips.

"Hold it!" he yelled, as Breed Johnson almost blasted Henry. "I think Bucky here needs another lesson!"

Carl Slade had one ruling passion, and that was to be the best man in a roughhouse fight. He put his rifle down carefully, then stripping off his gun belt, he said, "Put that gun down, Henry. I'm gonna bust you up good this time!"

Buck stared at him. He knew that if he backed away from

this fight he was doomed, so he handed his rifle and Colt to Easy, who said softly, "Wear him out, son!"

Carl Slade laughed and, moving quickly, he caught Buck with a hard smashing blow right to the heavy jaw, but it merely rocked the big man's head back. "Slice him up, Carl!" Baker yelled.

Buck stood like a huge bear in the open space, and Carl Slade moved around, his feet making a pattern as he wove in an out. He hit Buck at will, and in two minutes, blood was pouring from the cuts on the big man's face, but there was no fear in the eyes of Buck Henry.

In and out Carl circled, and a silence gripped the spectators, for it was now apparent that despite the damage that Slade was doing, he was getting winded. The effort of the blows, the dodging and feinting, took energy, and sweat burst out on his forehead. He began to reach for air, his gasps sounding loudly in the leaden silence that had fallen on the crowd.

He caught Buck with a hard right to the stomach, then threw a long looping left to the face—only the blow never touched Buck's face, for Buck had put out one big hand and trapped the fist of Carl Slade.

Slade tried to jerk away, but he might as well have had his arm set in concrete. He yanked again, and this time gave a frantic grunt as he stared into the eyes of Buck Henry, fear shooting through him as he felt the mighty power of the hand that held him fast.

A light of battle blazed in Buck's battered face. As Carl Slade began to thrash around like a fish on a line, Buck could have smashed him with pile driver blows, but he did not. He stood there holding Slade's fist, concentrating on throwing every ounce of his strength into that right hand. Then Slade screamed, a high-pitched, womanish sound, and his left hand fluttered, uselessly plucking at Buck's shirt. He screamed again and then his face turned white as paste and he suddenly went limp, held in place by Buck Henry's grip.

Then Buck looked down as if surprised at what he held. He opened his fist and Slade slipped bonelessly to the ground. Easy, who was standing close, took one look, then shook his head, saying, "Ain't a bone in that hand that ain't busted!"

Buck seemed stunned by what he had done, and Jesse Purdy suddenly moved quickly. He stepped up close, and, raising his rifle, he struck Buck in the back of the head with the butt. The force of the blow drove Buck to his knees, and then as Purdy raised his rifle to strike again, he was suddenly hit in the middle by Lee who had raced forward to throw himself at the burly man.

Caught off guard, Purdy grabbed at the boy and stared at him. Then he gave a rough laugh and threw Lee toward Breed Johnson, saying, "Cut the liver out of this puppy!"

Breed caught Lee with one hand, dropped his rifle, plucked a long slender knife from his belt, and held it at Lee's throat, his face a cruel mask.

As the knife touched Lee's throat, a gasp went up, but then a voice shattered the air: "That's all!"

Reno had crossed the distance between himself and the half-breed in one mighty catlike jump, and now he stood not an arm's length away from where Breed held Lee.

"That's all!" Reno said in a harsh voice. "Drop that knife, Breed!"

"And if I don't?"

There was a smile on Reno's face, a cruel smile, and as Dooley saw it, she realized that this was the Jim Reno she didn't know well. This was the killer of men that she had heard of.

Reno pulled from his belt the sheath knife he always wore and hefted it in a peculiar fashion. "You can have it right in your eye, Injun—or you can turn that boy loose and we'll see how you can fight a man—not a crippled old man or a boy."

Silence then almost hurt the ears, but slowly, the hand of Breed Johnson relaxed, and Lee was free. Then the Indian said with a sharklike smile, "I will cut your heart out, dog!"

The morning sun glittered on the knives as Reno and Johnson circled each other, weaving and feinting, and Dooley felt her chest tighten as if an iron band clamped it, for she knew that in a matter of seconds one of the two men would be dead, his life spilling out on the hard ground.

FOURTEEN
*Shoot-out at
Blue Mountain*

The two men followed some sort of intricate pattern that reminded Dooley of a minuet. They moved slowly in a clockwise direction, both on their toes, knives held high in their right hands, the left arm held out from the body in a balancing motion. The slow grace of this movement was interrupted from time to time as one of them would make a lightning feint with his blade toward the body of the other. The other would parry the thrust with a movement of his own weapon and usually would attempt to make a thrust of his own. They would reverse their turn, and once Reno was almost faked out of position by a quick reverse on the part of the Indian. Only by arching his back in a twisting move did he manage to escape with no damage except a slice in his thin blue shirt.

Except for a grunt as they parried or lunged, neither man spoke, and Dooley knew if she lived to be a hundred years old she would still see the scene as clearly as a painting. The face of Breed Johnson was frozen in a fixed stare, his hooded eyes burning with hatred. A contortion pulled his lips into a thin line, accenting the high cheekbones. He was thinner than

Reno, and taller, and the whiplike movements of his limbs gave him a serpentine look. Dooley thought of the large diamond-back rattler she had once seen, and saw in the figure of the Indian the same efficient deadliness of the snake.

Reno's face was almost as bronzed as Johnson's, but there was, Dooley noted with wonder, no tension in his wedge-shaped face. The raven hair, grown long and ragged on the trail, moved in the breeze, and the black eyes that peered out from under the heavy ledge of bone under the thick, black brows were watchful and keen, but not without a trace of some strange humor. *He's enjoying it!* Dooley thought in horror, and a sudden gust of rage ran along her nerves when she thought of the agonizing fear that shook her own heart, while Reno played a game of death as if it were checkers!

Reno broke the pattern of the dance by screaming loudly and jumping straight at Johnson, stabbing right at the dark throat, and it took the Indian off guard. He took a step backward, caught his heel on a ledge of stone and went down flat on his back. Reno swooped down on him, but Johnson rolled to one side with a tremendous effort and scrambled to his feet, his eyes wide with shock.

Reno grinned at him and said lazily, "Little different from pushing a cripple around, Johnson." Reno lowered his knife with a contemptuous gesture and looked across at Baker, saying, "I've seen Pawnee squaws who could make this *keneebah* run for the woods!"

Reno turned away to entice his opponent into making a totally committed attack, for he knew that his own skill was no greater than that of the man in front of him. Unless he could draw him into a trap, his own chances were only fair.

Breed Johnson launched himself at Reno, blade drawn

SHOOT-OUT AT BLUE MOUNTAIN

back in preparing for the final blow as he came into range. He thought that Reno's attention was on Baker, but suddenly he saw, too late, that he had been trapped! Reno whirled and blocked the wild thrust of the Indian's with his left hand, and was driving his own blade straight at the body of Johnson!

Only the small round stone that Reno stepped on saved Breed Johnson, for it threw him off stride, and his blade raked a nasty gash along Johnson's arm but did no real damage.

Reno tried to recover but was falling as the other whipped his knife around in a flash. The tip of it scored the back of Reno's knife hand, then clashed against his blade. Reno felt the hot blood flush his hand, and as the knife slipped away, he gave a tremendous kick that caught Johnson in the side and drove him backward. He recovered at once, and Reno, who was poised to make a dive for his blood-stained knife that lay on the ground, saw that it would be fatal to put himself in range of the Indian's blade.

As he backed slowly away, Johnson followed, and a gusty cry went up from the onlookers. Dooley heard herself say, "No!" and Cotton Kennedy gave a shrill yelp: "Cut the sucker up, Breed!"

Reno backed slowly away, and the Indian said, "Now you get it!" and advanced, the blade in his hand flickering like a living thing.

Reno held his hands out, his elbows half-bent, knowing that his only chance would be to parry Johnson's blade even if he had to take it in the arm or shoulder. But even that was denied him, for he saw that the Indian knew that as well as he.

They had moved in their fight along a lift of gray granite that flanked the trail, but Reno knew that behind him some-where was a fault, a drop of at least ten feet, and he felt carefully with his feet, not taking his eyes off the deadly figure of Johnson.

Just as he felt the sheer edge beneath his right heel, Baker called out, "Now you got him, Breed!"

With one sweeping movement, the arm of Johnson swept back, then forward with a scything motion that would have ripped into Reno's belly had it landed—but it did not, for Reno, instead of stepping back, leaped forward, getting inside the sweep. He wrapped his arms around the slender figure of Johnson and whirled him around.

Now the back of the Indian was to the sheer fault, but he was raising the knife to drive it into Reno's unprotected back. In one swift motion, Reno arched his back, and blindly made a stab with his left hand, and somehow he caught Johnson's wrist. They tottered on the edge of the rock, the knife between them. Reno felt the strength of Johnson winning, for it was his wounded hand that had caught the wrist of the other. Their faces were inches apart, and a flare of triumph lit the dark eyes of Johnson as he felt Reno's grip giving way.

Reno did the one thing that was left to try. He shoved with both feet, and the two men suddenly went cartwheeling over the edge of the fault. Breed Johnson grunted in surprise, then yelled in a shrill cry of rage as they dropped out of sight. But the cry was cut off shortly as they struck the ground.

A silence bound the spectators, the suddenness of the action holding them in place. Lee reached over and took Dooley's arm in a tight grip, but she did not even notice. They all stood there, and then there was the sound of a rock rolling from behind the drop-off. Someone was climbing back to the level of the trail. Dooley found herself saying over and over in a whisper, *Let it be Jim!*

Then the dark face of Reno appeared, and Easy let out a whoop that startled them all: "Eh law! He done 'er!" He ran forward to grab Reno, pulling him up over the ledge, adding, "We ort to put up a stob to mark this place, James! You done the necessary!"

Reno walked over to the crowd, dripping blood from his wounded hand, and he said in a voice of wonder, "He fell on his own knife, Easy."

"Look out, Jim!"

Dooley had seen a movement to her right, and Baker had drawn both guns and trained them on Reno.

"You had all the luck comin' to you, Reno!" Baker called out. He lifted his guns a fraction, and there was a wolfish grin on his face as he added, "Your number come up this time!"

"I say, old man, would you mind pointing those revolvers another way—they might accidentally go off."

Baker started at the voice and twisted his head to see Algernon St. John, who had moved far enough clear of the crowd to maneuver his heavy rifle to his shoulder. He was bland of face, and there was something almost comical about the man—but there was nothing funny to Keno Baker about the steadiness of the large-bore rifle that focused on his heart.

"Drop that gun, St. John!" Jesse Purdy snarled, covering him with his Spencer.

"Maybe you ought to try that your ownself, Purdy." Easy Jones lifted his Colt with a motion that matched his name and laid it on Jesse with negligent ease.

"Gun 'em down!" Baker said, red-faced. "Blow 'em up!"

A movement in the ranks began to form. Buck Henry, his face still red from the beating it had absorbed, took his rifle and let it rest on Baker, then Clyde Prather and Barney Moore bracketed Cotton Kennedy, and the pale face of the albino twitched nervously. He shot a glance at Barney Moore, Ty Edwards, and Will Satterfield, all of them spreading out with guns lifted and no mercy in any face.

One by one they drew a circle around the small group of gunmen, until finally, no matter where the roughs looked, they saw guns trained steadily on them.

"Guess we finally grew up, Jim," Buck said with a grim smile.

"I say let's hang 'em now," Ty Edwards yelled, and he might have had enough support to carry out a lynching, but there was one problem.

"Hold it right there!" Baker yelled. There was a strange glint in his eyes as he surveyed the crowd. "You got the drop on us, right enough, but there's this one thing . . ." He stared at Reno, then lifted his guns toward Dooley and Lee. "You think I'm scared to die? Not likely! But let me tell you this, ain't nobody here can stop me from placin' at least two shots—and they'll be right in them two boys yonder, Reno!"

Reno moved to stand before Baker, and he saw at once that the nervy little gunman meant exactly what he said. Carefully he said, "Looks like it's your play, Keno."

"Figured you'd see it that way. What we got here," he said seriously, "is the chance of quite a few of us gettin' shot. Now, you can get us, but you ain't a fool, Reno. You know we'll get some of you—and them two boys for sure."

"Make your deal," Reno said.

Baker nodded, and a faint grin touched his lips. "Just you and me, Reno—that's the way. We'll shoot it out. You get a gun and meet me. If you put me down, why, that's what you're lookin' for, ain't it? If I get you, all of us go free."

"Not likely!" Vinson Grant snorted. "We ain't about . . ."

"He's got us, Vinson," Buck Henry said, staring at Baker. "I don't want to see anybody get killed—none of our folks, at least." He ignored the mutter that went up from the crowd, and Reno saw at once that the big man would never again have to wonder if he had sand. He had taken over the leadership of the crowd, and that was that.

"Looks like it's your say, Jim," Buck said. "What'll it be?"

Reno stood there, a flat shape in the morning light, his dark hair falling over his forehead, blood trickling from his right hand. He seemed to be staring at something far away, his dark eyes fixed on the glistening peaks of the mountains to the west, and a look of sadness crossed his face. His broad shoulders drooped, then he straightened up and nodded.

"You got it, Keno."

"I got your word?" Baker insisted, and it was odd how the gunman was willing to trust the word of the man he'd soon be trying to kill. "Get a gun and meet me over by that clearing. You birds," he said to Cotton Kennedy and Jesse Purdy, "get your plunder. We're pulling out soon as I tend to Reno."

The careless assurance of Baker sent a chill through Dooley, and she remembered the flashing speed of Baker's draw.

The crowd moved about uncertainly, the tension broken. Someone laughed shrilly.

Reno ignored everyone, walking steadily back toward the wagon. He went straight to his saddle, pulled his gun belt out, and put it on. For a long moment he stood staring at it, his bloody hand resting on the cedar handle, and despair written across his face.

"Jim!" Dooley came close then, but unable to meet his

eyes, she took his wounded hand and said, "Let me clean this for you."

"Don't reckon it matters much, Dooley," Reno said slowly.

Dooley's hands trembled, and she poured out water into a basin and gently cleaned out the gouge. He watched curiously, noting her trembling fingers as she poured antiseptic into the wound. "You'd make a good doctor, Dooley," he said with a smile. "Got a real easy touch—almost like a woman."

She had jerked at his words, and she knew that her face was burning. "Jim, don't go! Let them ride out."

"Gave my word, Dooley."

"But he's just a cheap thug!"

"That's right—but that's *his* problem. Mine is, I got to keep my word." He tried to close his fist, winced slightly, then saw that Dooley's face was pale and that she was swaying slightly. "Hey—you all right, boy? You look a little green!"

"I can't stand the thought of you—of you being killed!"

"Sure." Reno nodded. "I feel the same about you, Dooley. And if the train hadn't stirred itself to facing up to Baker, I'd be worried. But like it turned out, you'll be all right. Buck will look out for you, no matter—well, no matter what."

He reached over and picked up Lee's saddlebags, removing a Colt .45 and trying the action, his face steady in the morning light.

"Jim, I—I'll pray for you."

He nodded, and there was a curious light in his dark eyes as he said, "I need it, boy. Guess I went through this a hundred times in the army, just before we went into action. Always the same—man wishes he'd lived better."

"You will, Jim!"

He smiled and dropped his arm over her shoulder in a quick gesture of affection. "Sure. Now you get out of here!"

She left then, making her way back to where Lee was talking to Easy. While he told the little rider about Reno's ability with a gun, she stared across at the clearing where Keno Baker waited, smoking a cigarette.

"Jim may be pretty fast, Lee, but this Keno is 'bout the best there is pulling a gun." Easy stared across at Baker and shook his head. "Jim ain't a man to take water, but in a case like this, he ought to!"

Lee shook his head stubbornly. "That's what they said back in Rimrock when Jim went up against this gunfighter named Blanton. He was fast, too, but Jim outsmarted him."

"How'd he do that?"

"Well, Jim come at him from a block away, and he had this little ol' gun, a Navy Colt .36."

"Thet's a woman's gun!" Easy said in disgust.

"That's what they all said!" Lee grinned. "But the way it was, Jim had a nine-inch barrel put on it, and it was 'bout as accurate as a rifle! Anyway, he called to Blanton from about two hundred feet away, and they started shootin'! Boy!" Lee's eyes glittered at the memory and he said, "Jim turned around like they do in duels—sideways and arm straight out."

"Did this Blanton feller get off the first shot?"

"Sure, two or three, but Jim had it all figured out. He had on this special vest with leather an inch thick, and it covered his side. That's why he took that duel stance, don't you see? He knew most gunfighters ain't very accurate, so he got a long ways off with that little ol' .36 and he polished Blanton off! Just like he's going to do with Baker."

"Don't appear so," Easy said. "Here he comes, and he's packing two .45s and not wearing no armored vest."

Reno appeared, and Lee saw at once that Easy was right.

As soon as Reno got close enough Lee asked, "Jim, where's your special vest—and the .36 Navy?"

"Lost both of 'em in a poker game at Independence, Lee." He reached out and struck the boy on the shoulder lightly. "That trick wouldn't work with Baker, anyway. He'll be close when he pulls."

"But Jim, you always said that one gun was enough, and now . . ."

"Have to play it as it happens, Lee."

He turned to go and found Jude Finney standing there quietly. Reno saw the nervous look on his face and said, "Reckon you got a word about my soul, haven't you, Jude?"

Finney was pale and he swallowed nervously before saying, "Jim, I wish you and me had taken more time to talk before this."

"Sure, Jude. It's a little late now, I guess."

"Never too late to trust God, Jim!"

Reno nodded but said nothing. He looked across at Keno Baker and murmured, "Wonder which one of us will be around for supper, Jude?" Then he shrugged, and the strong streak of fatalism that ran in him surfaced, turning his face still as he moved away and walked steadily toward where Baker waited.

Reno moved to within a hundred feet of Baker then stopped, saying, "I'm here, Keno."

"Yeah, I knew you'd come." There was an odd note in Baker's voice, envy perhaps.

Reno knew that pride was what held the life of Baker in place. Take it away and he was lost. He knew this, for he had once been on the same path, but now he saw clearly the futility of such a life.

"Wish you'd ride on, Keno," he said. "I sure wish you'd ride on."

A quick anger touched Baker's face and he yelled, "I don't need no edge from nobody, Reno! Pull your iron and I'll kill . . . !"

He never finished his threat, for Reno had done a strange thing. He had pulled both the heavy guns and thrown himself backward!

Easy could not believe his eyes, and the sound of Baker's shots came so quickly that many of the spectators thought that he had drawn and shot Reno down.

Reno had known that his only chance was to take some sort of action that would take Baker off guard. The idea had come to him while he was strapping on his gun, and he saw at once that it was his only chance.

As he fell backward, he drew with practiced ease and fired a shot from his right gun before he fell flat on his back. That shot saved his life, for it brushed so close to Baker's cheek that he flinched, and the shot that would have taken Reno squarely in the heart merely tugged at his sleeve.

Reno's unexpected move rattled Keno Baker. The little gunman had had the fight pictured in his mind, and when suddenly Reno was not in front of him, but rolling in the dust sending a hail of bullets in his direction, he did what he had never done—he panicked, and the morning silence was broken by the roar of his guns!

Reno kept moving, rolling left, snapping off a shot, then right and getting off another. He had little hope of hitting his man, but he was trusting that Baker would miss as well.

As the slugs from Baker's guns came closer, however, he knew that the little gunman was getting the range, that sooner or later he would take a bullet. Lunging to his feet, he feinted left, went right, then a slug knocked his boot heel off, but just

as he sagged to his left, one of his shots rocked Baker back—
not a fatal wound, but enough to give Reno time to swing his
arm up and grasp his weak right wrist with his left in a steady-
ing position.

Time seemed to slow down, and he remembered that it
had been that way in the war. He saw with absolute clarity the
shock in Baker's face as he bounced back from the flesh
wound and found Reno's gun sweeping up to cover him. The
tiny wrinkles on Baker's pale face, the pink freckles on his
hands, even a tiny fishhook scar on the bridge of his nose—all
leaped into focus as time slogged along.

They stared at each other as their guns swung into position, and Reno pulled the trigger one split second before
Baker's finger tightened. His shot took Keno Baker squarely
in the right eye, and Reno felt a sting in his right ear lobe as
the last bullet sang by.

Baker dropped to the ground, never moving, and it was
over.

Reno walked slowly to stand over Baker, who seemed
much smaller in death, and when Jude Finney came to stand
by him, dropping a hand on his shoulder, Reno said in a dull
voice, "'Thou shalt not kill.' That's what it says, isn't it, Jude?"

Finney squeezed the thick shoulder of Reno, and said quietly, "You just did one thing, Jim. You did something for somebody else. Deep in your heart you know the only reason you
did this was to save Dooley's life, and Lee's." The gangling
preacher murmured some words that brought tears to the
eyes of Jim Reno: "You are your brother's keeper, Jim!"

Reno looked at Finney and nodded, then turned to catch
at Lee and Dooley as they fell against him.

FIFTEEN
Ride the Wild River

Down by the river's edge log rafts pitched in the smashing rollers. The canvas tops of the wagons cast a pale glow against the gray flicker of sand and rain, and weather-whipped fires burned a violent yellow, darkly dotted by crouching or moving shapes. All through the camp was the constant traffic of loose stock moving in a wall of mist.

After two thousand miles and five months of land travel the train was ready to make the last ninety miles into western Oregon by water through the gorge of the Cascades.

Reno passed by the large raft he and Jackson had built, checked the lines holding the wagon, and said to Dooley, "I don't like the idea of your riding this thing down to the white water."

Dooley's hat sagged around her face, the water running over her shoulders in a steady stream. She was physically exhausted by the task of getting the raft ready, but she straightened up and made her voice alert as she said, "No other way, Jim, that I can see. Somebody's got to be there to stop the raft, and you can't be two places at once." She noted that he was

They had gone over this perilous stage many times. Reno had explained it to the whole train very carefully when they had finally reached Walla Walla: "Only way to get the wagons to Oregon City is to build rafts and float them down. That's a lot of work, but there's only one danger."

He had pointed with a stick to a map of the territory sketched in the dust. "Down about here is a bad stretch of river—white water, and lots of it. Can't take the rafts through. We'll have to land on this side, unload the wagons, and drive about six miles on a pretty fair road. We'll send the rafts down through the white water, catch them, then load up and we're home free. Only thing, when the rafts get to the bad spot, they have to be stopped! Nobody could survive a trip along that bad stretch!"

Buck Henry came up as Dooley and Reno did one last check on the lines. His heavy eyebrows were white with fine flakes of snow, and there was a worried look on his broad face. "Wish there was some other way to do this! Ain't there a trail of any kind, Jim?"

"Nothing wagons can get across—especially in winter."

Barney Moore joined them, asking, "When we supposed to let the first wagon go, Jim? I'd sure hate to have a mix-up!"

"Won't be any," Reno said. "I'm leaving now with the stock. Soon as we get there, we'll build a small raft to use catching our big rafts. When I test it out and it looks good, I'll send a man back. I want you to be in charge Barney. Let a raft go, then exactly forty-five minutes later, another one. Keep it up till they're all gone, then you ride the last one."

"All right."

"I want just one man on a raft to work the sweeps. Everybody else goes on horseback—women, kids, and all."

"What about Burns? He can't make the ride."

Reno nodded. "Yes, I guess he better ride in the wagon."

"You leaving now?" Moore asked.

"Soon as we can. It'll be slow going in this weather."

Two hours later, Reno led a procession west along a well-worn Indian trail. The camp and its echoes faded, and the loose stock moved ahead of them toward the throat of the gorge forty miles away. The river was beside them, rolling whitely in the narrow channel. The trail, too rough for wagons, crossed an ancient field of lava and moved through a succession of sand dunes until about two hours from camp it rose in stairstep creases along the face of a hill. Around noon they followed the rim of a bluff loosely covered by pine—the river was a thousand feet below, unseen in the fog.

It took two days to make the trip, and by the time they had endured a rough night with only tarps for shelter, it was a relief to pass into a narrow strip of open land. Down below he heard the rising roar of the rapids. They camped at a beach covered with the remains of old rafts that had been scrapped at this stage.

"What now?" Easy asked.

"Make the raft."

Together they cut twelve-foot sections from a fir, then dropped another tree to make the crosspieces to bind the logs. By the time they had gotten the spikes from his pack, hauled the logs to the river, and nailed it together, they were both half-frozen, but Reno said, "I better try it out, Easy. You get dry."

He spent an hour learning how to maneuver the small raft, then gathered all the rope he'd need to snare the big rafts as they came downstream. When he got back to the camp, he said, "We'll be ready first thing in the morning. Somebody's got to go back and tell Barney to let the first raft go at exactly eight in the morning."

"I'll do it." Reno was surprised to see Beau Slade stand up and take one last swallow of hot coffee.

The offer was unexpected. Those who heard turned to look at Beau, and his cheeks flushed.

"Appreciate it, Beau," Buck said. Then he asked hesitantly, "How's Carl's hand?"

"Be all right, I guess," Beau said quietly.

Something was bothering the big man, and he said, "I'm sorry I busted it up, Beau."

Beau, his handsome face sober in the murky light, looked up at Buck. Ellie was sitting well back from where he stood, but he felt her eyes on him, and he said, "None of your choosing, Buck. Carl didn't give you a choice." Then he shook his head and there was regret in his eyes as he said, "Man can sure do a lot of fool things, can't he now?"

"Man can change though, can't he, Beau?" Buck said, then he put out his large hand suddenly and Beau, surprised, took it. He stared at Henry for a long moment, then grinned and said, "Now don't mash *my* hand up in that paw of yours, Buck!"

He smiled and rode out of camp at a fast gallop. Buck passed by where Ellie sat, and hesitated. He had not spoken to her since the fight, and there was a constraint in both of them. Her playful spirit was quenched, her eyes dead in her face. She ducked as he stood over her, but then she looked up and tried to smile. "Beau ain't a bad fellow when he's away from—from other people."

She had been about to say "Carl" Buck knew, but she couldn't get it out. He squatted down beside her and picked up a stick. He began to measure it carefully with his huge fingers. Then he threw it down and said in a steady voice, "I want to marry you, Ellie."

"What!"

"Nothing new in that," Buck said. He put his hand on her arm and there was a gentleness under his terrible strength that reached out to her. She leaned against him, as though she were totally exhausted, then shook her head. "No, I couldn't do it, Buck."

"Well, I can't say I blame you none," he said finally. "I know I ain't nothing special to make a pretty girl like you . . ."

"Oh, Buck! Buck!" she cried, turning to him, her eyes glistening. "I've been the worst fool in the world, but I—I always liked you. But now . . ."

When she couldn't go on, he said, "I know. But we're going to start from right now, Ellie. I won't rush you, but sooner or later you and me will be standing up in front of Jude Finney saying some mighty good things!"

Reno, standing far off, could not hear any of this, but he saw the timid smile that touched Ellie's face, and he saw Buck keep on talking until her eyes laughed, and he knew that it was going to be all right.

They waited impatiently for the night to pass, and in the morning Reno was in his little raft waiting long before the first large raft appeared. Finally, Easy hollered, "There she comes, James!"

Reno looked up to see the raft come through the cas-

cades, swinging end to end, sinking below the surface, rising
with all the force of the current behind it to leap from the
water like a clumsy fish.

Reno maneuvered the small raft into midstream and dug
the oars deep to hold it. A wave sucked it down, and buckshot
pellets of spray drew a sharp shout from Easy, who was riding
the prow. When they rose from the trough they discovered the
big raft dead ahead, slowly revolving in the current. Reno
brought the small raft directly in its path and waited for the col-
lision.

The big raft came on, spray breaking over its downstream
edge. Reno checked the small raft as a roller lifted it. As the
small raft struck the big one, Easy fell flat. He jumped up at
once, tied the tow rope fast, then ran back to help Jim at the
oars.

It was like pulling at a stump, for the force of the ten-mile-
an-hour current surged against the big raft's broad surface and
against them until the green wood gave. Reno used the little
raft as a kind of anchor to haul the big raft around, but it was a
quarter-hour before the little raft was upstream and the big
raft above. They were four hundred yards downstream when
Reno brought it to the beach.

"Forty-five minutes ain't enough, Jim!" Easy panted. "If
we have any trouble, we'll be in a pickle!"

"Should have allowed at least an hour and a half." Reno
nodded. "Come on, there comes Lena's raft!"

They had learned from the first experiment, and as raft
after raft came down the river, they snared them and got them
safely to shore, where the wagons were unloaded and readied
for the portage.

Dooley made the trip with no problem, and after she and

Jackson got the wagon off and ready to move, she came to
where Reno and Easy were getting ready to shove off for the
next raft. "I'll spell you, Easy," she said.

"Well . . . maybe just long enough fer me to get a bait of
St. John's snake cure." He limped off toward the camp, obviously worn out.

"I better get Buck, Dooley," Reno said. He looked at the
slight form wrapped in the heavy coat and added, "Takes lots
of beef to muscle those big rafts."

"Just one, Jim," Dooley said, and despite the cold she
smiled. "Someday we'll be telling our grandchildren about all
this. There'll be a pioneer day and we can tell lies about our
adventures."

"Won't have to lie much, I reckon. It's been a rough trip."

The five month's crossing had taken its toll in faith and
flesh. Pete Prather was dead. Harry Prather, dead. Leon
Prather, dead. R.G. Grant, dead. Josh Henry, dead. Maureen
Taylor's baby, dead. Larry Shane's elderly mother, dead. Luke
Edwards, dead. Keno Baker and Breed Johnson, not part of
the train, but just as dead as the others who had been.

Many others bore scars that didn't show. Carl Slade
would never be the same after his encounter with Buck Henry,
and Clyde was like a man who had lost his arm, so badly did
he miss his twin.

But there were those who had gotten strong. Robert
Burns and his wife would make it, their love purified in the cru-
cible of trial. Addie Grant, who never hoped to have a home or
husband—why, she'd live to see her children's children!

"We'll never be the same, will we, Jim?"

"Reckon not, Dooley." Reno swung his gaze and smiled
suddenly. "You're not the same boy that left Independence, I'd
say."

Dooley found something humorous in the words. "Guess that boy is gone for keeps, Jim." Then she looked up and exclaimed, "There comes Ty Edward's raft."

They scrambled aboard the little raft. Dooley had watched the operation several times. When they touched the large raft, she had no trouble making fast with the line, then ran back to help with the oars.

A sudden gust of the bitter cold wind combined with a large surging wave to twist the big raft out of the water. It was badly loaded, with too much weight on the rear, and when the front end reared up like a terrified horse, the line tightened, jerking the smaller raft out of the water with such force that both Reno and Dooley were thrown to the deck.

"Ty! Hang on to that sweep!" Reno yelled as he struggled to his feet. Edwards was, he saw, paralyzed with fear, his face white as a fish's belly, his eyes staring blankly.

"He's lost his mind!" Reno shouted to Dooley. "I have to get on and handle the sweep. Do the best you can with the oars!" He wished with all his heart that Buck was at the oars, but it occurred to him that he could send Edwards to help Dooley while he handled the sweep.

He left the small raft in a running dive, grabbing at the lines that held the wagon on, and was on his way to the sweep when another huge wave lifted the bow to an acute angle. He fell again, sliding toward the stern, nearly going off into the roiling river. Catching a line with one hand, he hauled himself upright, just in time to see Edwards falling headfirst with a scream over the port side!

Reno's first impulse was to go after the man, but as the stern sank, rolling with a sickening motion to starboard, he heard a snapping sound over the roar of the wind. As the nose dipped, he saw that the smaller raft had been drawn in close by the plunging of the large raft. The tip of a log caught the small raft, flipping it over like a toy, and he saw Dooley fly into the icy water like a doll!

Stopping only long enough to whip out his sheath knife and slice the tow rope, he took a running dive toward the spot where Dooley had disappeared. The large raft was right over him, and the shock of the icy water hit him like a club. He drove himself down with powerful strokes, sweeping his arms wide, and just when his lungs were beginning to ache and burn, his hand encountered a twisting body. Grabbing a handful of the heavy coat, he drove upward and to the side, praying that he would clear the large raft.

Breaking the surface, he sucked in a lungful of air, and held Dooley's head clear. The big raft was twenty feet away, so he had gone further than he had thought in his dive. Dooley was a dead weight, pulling him deeper into the depths, and they were tossed like corks by the surging waves. Despair filled him as he fought to keep their heads clear. He knew he could never make it to the bank with Dooley, but it never occurred to him to let go and try and save himself.

He found himself crying out to God in a way that he hadn't since he was a child. His boots were filled with water and so tight he couldn't get them off, and his strength was drained to the last reserve.

Dooley might be dead, but he refused to give up, and just as he was sucked down, strangling in the frothy water, something struck the back of his head. With a powerful kick of his legs and his free arm, he used his reserve to turn, and there was his raft! He had no time to wonder what had kept it from floating away, but grabbed the side with his free hand and gave a lunge with his other arm, half-hoisting the limp body of Dooley onto the logs. The power of the river had them, almost pulling the raft away from his aching grip, but he held on, and as the raft dipped, he hauled himself aboard, rolling and kicking. Then with a final burst of his feeble strength, hauled Dooley on and fell across the limp body, holding on to the oar racks.

He lay there sucking in great gulps of air. The world was cold water striking like a waterfall as the frail raft dipped and rose in the savage waves. The screaming of the wind and the roar of tons of water being forced through the narrow passage beat at his ears.

As soon as he could, he dragged Dooley to a more secure position. Placing her face down, he began to force the water out of her lungs with hard, driving stabs of his palms. He marveled at the fragile frame, the slender waist, and a thrill of fear shot through him when there was no response. It struck him hard, there in the midst of sound, fury, and the likely possibility of sudden death, how much this slim lad meant to him. Desperately he massaged the slender back, and was rewarded when Dooley gave a gagging cough and a heave rippled across the slender back.

He pulled her head free, and she coughed and gagged until finally her eyes opened. "Take it easy, boy." Reno tugged until Dooley was sitting up, and he put her hand on the oarlock. "Try to hang onto this." He sat down behind her, wedging his legs to form a barrier on each side, then reached over her, gripping the three-inch saplings.

Dooley was still dazed, but she looked at the turbulent river and then at Reno. "How'd you get me out of *that?*"

Reno said soberly, "I reckon the Lord gets the credit for

that. No man's got that much luck!" He raised his head. A deeper roar rose from up ahead, and he said, "Hold on, Dooley. Even if we go under, I think we got a good chance if we can stay on the raft."

"I thought nobody ever got through this part of the river?"

He smiled suddenly, looking very young in the misty light, and putting his lips close to her ear so that she could hear him over the steadily mounting roar, he said, "This is a pretty bad river, I guess, but if God has it on his mind, why, I guess we'll make it. Hang on!"

The raft dipped, and time ceased to exist for the two frail human beings clinging to the brittle sticks that shot down the savage river. There was nothing to be done. Even if he had had an oar, the power of the river made the thought of steering laughable. The raft spun, dipped, and careened from side to side, and they were blind from the spray and deaf to all except the roar of a million tons of white water crashing through the cleft of the rock.

Once when there was a short interval of relative quiet, Dooley reached back, pulled Reno's ear to her lips, and shouted something.

"What? I can't hear you!"

He bent forward to catch her expression, but even as she tried to say it again, there was a sickening lurch of the raft, and Reno gave his will to staying locked onto the saplings. He had long since lost feelings in his hands, and he feared that he might let go without knowing it.

The end came when they struck a submerged rock. They were thrown off at once, and Reno thought, *A strange way to end it all!* but then his feet touched a gravel bottom and he pulled Dooley into a small, flat beach left by a short meander.

It was no larger than seven or eight feet at the widest, and no more than twenty feet long at most—but it was life for the moment.

They staggered to the wall, finding that the action of the water had cut into the soft limestone, making a small cave, perhaps ten feet high and about five feet back. They fell into the shelter, and the roar of the water was filtered to some degree so that they could speak in normal tones.

"You all right?" Reno asked.

"I'm alive," Dooley answered.

Reno walked to the edge of the stone floor, looked both ways, then up. Finally he came back and sat down by Dooley.

"Can we get out?" Dooley asked.

"If we were fish, we could swim down the river. If we were birds we could fly up to the top of that bluff."

Snow was in the air, fine and grainy, mixing with the rising mist. The sun was a dull gray light at the top of the sheer cliff. Dooley stared at Reno, then said, "Can they find us here, Jim?"

"No."

The single word held their plight. No boat could get to them, and it was beyond the range of hope that they could be spotted from the rim and be rescued.

Dooley got up, walked to the edge of the river, shivering in the water-soaked coat. She walked to the end of the ledge and cried out, "Jim! Look!"

He moved to stand beside her, and followed the direction of her gaze. "There's our raft!"

Reno allowed himself a tight grin, and said, "Guess it's our day for miracles." The raft had caught in a nest of debris not twenty feet from where the ledge ended. He stared at it, then shook his head. "Don't see how we can get to it. Have to make a run, and if the current takes us, we're gone. Have to catch it the first time."

"But it's there!" Dooley said with a strong smile. She touched his arm, and there was a fine light in her gray-green eyes that held him there, wondering that anyone could take pleasure in anything under the circumstances. She asked, "How far is it, do you think—to the end of the rapids, I mean?"

"No way to tell, but it can't be too far. If we can just get out of this white water, we'll be home free."

"Let's try it!" she said.

He stared at the river, and as he gauged their chances, he was caught by an involuntary shiver, the icy water and the exposure raking his nerves. "We have to go soon, that's for sure." He glanced back into the small cave and nodded at it. "Let's rest for an hour. That trip took a lot out of both of us."

Dooley followed him back to the limestone cavern, and the wind cut through her like a knife. "We'll freeze, Jim! Let's try it now."

"No. My hands have got cramps. Got to thaw out a little!"

"Thaw out!" she stared at him, and laughed. "There's no way to build a fire here."

"One fire we got, boy." Reno grinned and with a quick move pulled Dooley down and pushed her against the rock. "Read a pocm once about a fellow who had fire in his blood." He grinned and sat down. "Guess me and you got a little of that. Lay down there and get out of this wind."

Dooley's mind spun and she opened her mouth to protest. Her nightmare had been that he would find her out by some accident, but she had time only to turn quickly as he pulled her down and lay closely against her. He threw his heavy arm over her, saying with a chuckle, "Me and Bill Spence was in a mess like this once. Lost our horses in a blizzard in the Missouri headwaters. Know what we did? Cut the inside out of a buffer, crawled in and waited twelve hours."

Dooley lay totally still, holding herself stiff as a rail, hands clutching the heavy overcoat. The voice of the river was muted, and he had been right about the wind. His body blocked it from her, and the slow tremors that had been shaking her began to pass.

"That's a little better," Reno said. He pulled her closer with his arm, and the warmth from his body began to help. "Sleep if you can," he added, then dropped his head right against the back of her neck and said, "Wish we could get dry." The warmth of his breath sent little shivers down her back as he said, "Funny thing, Dooley, how little a man needs. Most of us spend our lives looking for something over the next hill, and when we get it, why, it's not what we want, so we gallop off again. Right now all I want is to get warm. Think about how many times we've sat around a fire, and we didn't appreciate it much. Have to get cold and frozen to appreciate a fire."

She lay there, soaking up the warmth from his body, and finally she asked, "Guess you been looking over lots of hills, Jim. Ever find what you wanted?"

He stiffened, and she knew she had touched a nerve. Then he relaxed and murmured, "Thought so not long ago."

"Lola?"

"Yes." He moved his body, seeking a more comfortable position on the hard stone, then added, "Been thinking about that a lot lately."

She bit her lip, then said, "What about Jean?"

"Hard for a man to let go of a dream. I had it all planned

290

out, boy. Get married, find a little place, maybe have some kids . . ." He paused, then went on talking softly almost as if to himself. "Then she died, and it was like the sky fell in on me. I gave Lee a bad time. Went right to the dogs, Dooley, where you found me that first time. Then I saw Jean, and she looked so much like Lola, I guess I tried to make it happen, that old dream."

He stopped then, and finally she said, "You going to marry her, Jim?"

"No. That's all over. She saw it before I did." He lifted his arm from where it rested on her and brushed his hair back, saying, "Guess dreams have to die, Dooley, just like us."

"Not always! Sometimes good things happen!"

He put his arm back over her and chuckled softly. "Yeah, that's the way for you to think, Dooley. Don't listen to an old prophet of gloom like me. You got a dream or two, I guess. Find a girl—maybe like Marie Prather—and have a good life."

"It's not too late for you, Jim," she said, and then there was a fierce note as she said again, "It's not too late!"

He didn't answer at once, then he sighed and said, "We've come a long way, haven't we, Dooley? Guess I never told anyone what makes me tick like I have you. Good to have a friend. Now, try to rest a little."

Thirty minutes later he got up, opening and closing his fingers stiffly. The wound from Johnson's knife was healing, and he said, "Guess it's time."

As he walked to the point nearest the raft, she said, "Jim?" and he turned to face her. "We may not make it."

"Got to consider it, Dooley."

"Well, I—want to say something to you. And I feel foolish!"

Reno looked down at the small figure, then smiled briefly. "Guess I won't think so, Dooley. What you got on your mind?"

"Well, since we may die in a few minutes, I want to tell you how much . . ." Dooley's face flamed and there was a tremble in her full lips not caused by cold. She clasped her hands together and then said evenly, "Ever notice how hard it is to tell someone how you feel about them? I mean, we can say almost anything *else,* but it comes hard to be honest and just come right out and say . . . well, here it is. Jim Reno, I've never known a man like you! Even when you were dirty and drunk in that jail, I felt different about you. And you saved my life. So what I want to say is this." She swallowed hard, and her gray-green eyes were enormous as she said, "I love you, Jim Reno!"

She put her back to him, her eyes filled with tears and sobs shaking her frame. Then she felt his hand fall on her shoulder, and he said, "You're right, Dooley. I can think of some right good friends I let go without ever saying the thing I felt. Glad you told me. Now let me have my turn." He pulled her around and there was a gentle smile on his face as he said, "You're a strange boy, Dooley, but I gotta say this. I love you, too." He bit his lip, and laughed softly. "That wasn't too hard. Wish I'd learned how to do that a long time ago. Well, you ready?"

"Ready, Jim!"

"What we do is make a dive for the raft. The current will try to get us, but you hang on to me and I think that part will be easy. Well, here we go!"

They plunged into the icy water, and the racing stream tugged at them, but Reno caught the raft with ease and pushed Dooley up, saying, "Hang on! I'm going to shove off and then get on!"

He braced his feet against the wall of stone and gave a huge pull, and as the raft surged free, he hauled himself up.

They were in the funnel, he knew, the worst part, but somehow they missed the sharp stones that shoved up through the lacy water like ragged teeth. The raft spun until they were dizzy, and once they were thrown hard against the wall, but Reno shouted, "Hang on! I think we're about there." They plunged in wheeling, drunken lunges through the wild stretch of the river. The raft's nose dipped and lodged, and the back end rose, throwing them forward. Then it broke free, and great layers of water rushed over it. Reno tightened his grip around Dooley, braced his feet and felt the power of his straining go through him, softening his flesh. He had no clear idea of the time they had been in the water. He had only two fixed impressions—the nearness of Dooley and the increasing looseness of the logs beneath. Some of the cross-boards had worked free. He felt them slide beneath him knowing that one hard jar would tear the raft apart.

It came just as he caught a glimpse of the end of white water. He yelled, "Look! There's the end of it!"

Even as he yelled, a submerged rock dug a sharp tooth into the raft, ripping the crosspieces off, and Reno felt the logs separate. "Here we go! Stay with me!" He pulled at Dooley, and they were rolled head over heels as the current took them. He held his breath, and when they surfaced he saw that they were in smooth water. But he felt the weight of Dooley pulling at his arm. Turning quickly, he saw that something had struck her— a rock or perhaps one of the logs. Her eyes were closed and over her left eye, high up, a cut stained her forehead with scarlet blood.

He called her name, struggled until he found bottom, then carried her to the shore. He was not alone, for as he fell to the ground, he saw several wagons in a clearing and people were running toward them, calling aloud.

Dull thoughts slogged through his mind as he stared at Dooley's white face. She did not seem to be breathing, and a wild protest ran through him: *Not now! Not after all this!"*

He felt strong hands pulling him up, and looked up to see a big man with a full black beard and piercing black eyes. "You'll live forever! No need for you to wait for a resurrection—reckon you just had one!"

Reno said, "What about . . . ?"

The bearded man said, "Got a doctor on our train. Eben!" He called to a tall young man and waved at Dooley. "Take this one to Doctor Williams's wagon."

Reno watched dully as the young man picked up Dooley as if she were a child, and with the bearded man's arm locked in his, he made his way to the wagons.

"Name's Shore. These are my people." He led Reno to a big Conestoga wagon, climbed inside, and after a few minutes reappeared holding some dry clothes in his hand. "Climb in and get changed. You look bad."

"I want to see about . . ."

"Whatever it is, it'll wait!" Shore said. He was apparently a man of authority, and he shoved Reno into the wagon, saying, "Get dry and we'll see about your friend."

He pulled wool socks on his stone-cold feet, put on dry underwear, wool pants and shirt, then a heavy sheepskin jacket and a hunter's fur cap. Reno found the clothes too big, but they were warm and dry.

Jumping to the ground, he found Shore handing him a bowl of stew. "Eat it, son. Doc is looking out for your friend."

"I'm Jim Reno. Our train's late, but we did pretty well until one of the rafts broke up."

"You must be a good man, friend Reno! Or a bad one,

maybe. Always heard the Devil looks out for his own!" There was a look of wonder on the bearded man's face and he shook his heavy head. "Don't think anyone ever made that ride, Reno."

Reno told a little more of the details to the small crowd that had gathered around, but his mind was on Dooley. He was about ready to ask about her when Shore looked over at a wagon, and nodded, "Reckon Doc's finished. You better go talk to him."

Reno walked quickly to the wagon, and was greeted by a small, thin man wearing a dark coat and a string tie. "I'm Doc Williams." He had a pair of sharp black eyes, like a bird, and he moved nervously as he talked. "You all right? Didn't break nothing?"

"I'm all right, Doctor. How's Dooley?"

"Well, now, I thought it might be pretty serious—maybe fractured skull—brain damage or even worse."

"Doc!" Reno said loudly, "tell me what's wrong!"

Williams looked up at the wagon and called out, "Martha, you finished?"

"Yes, Caleb." A heavyset woman with bright blue eyes stepped out from under the canvas and jumped to the ground. "All cleaned up and dry clothes."

"Can I go in?" Reno asked.

"Don't see why not. I did administer some laudanum, so there'll be some drowsiness. Might be good if you hurry. That stuff can put a body to sleep quick."

As Reno ducked under the hoop that held the canvas, he heard the doctor say, "No need to worry, son. She's not hurt bad. Be fine in the morning."

Reno was only half-listening, but something in the words of Williams caught at him. But he shook his head and searched the dark interior. His eyes were accustomed to the outside light, and he could see nothing by the small lamp which was turned down as far as possible.

"Dooley, where are you? I can't see a thing!"

He heard a moan and swiftly reached out, took the lamp, and turned its flame up full. He turned to his left, saying, "Dooley, how bad is . . . ?"

Then he stopped, and there was a strange roaring in his ears, not altogether unlike the roaring of the Columbia. His mind stood still, and he could not put his thoughts together. Once when a shell had gone off at Cold Harbor the concussion had destroyed his sense of time and place, and it was so now.

In the bed, with a quilt neatly pulled up under her arms, lay a young girl. She was wearing a white cotton nightgown, and her eyes were closed. The slim contours of her body were outlined beneath the cover, and the slender arms and hands lying outside the coverlet were as feminine as anything Reno had ever seen.

As he stood there, his mind reeling, the girl's eyes opened, and she gave a frightened cry, her eyes wide with fear. Then she focused on the man beside her, and her soft lips relaxed. "Jim, where is this? What . . . ?"

Then Dooley's eyes dropped to see the nightgown, and her olive skin changed to a sickly pale. Her lips trembled, and she shut her eyes tightly together.

Reno got up, swaying dizzily, and lurched out of the wagon. He jumped to the ground and walked away as quickly as he could, not seeing the surprise in the eyes of the doctor and his wife, closing his ears to the sound of a voice that called out: "Jim? Don't leave me, Jim!"

SIXTEEN
Kissing Kin

Oregon City was composed of perhaps forty raw-boarded houses scattered along a street that dipped and rose to the contour of the land and had no particular order. Here and there some enterprising soul had built a fence, and at intervals a section of boardwalk made walking possible. Otherwise the street was two dirt footpaths bordering a lane churned to loose mud by wagons and rain.

Reno and Easy had cruised the muddy street, passing a church, a hotel, a blacksmith shop, a coopering place, and several saloons.

Easy looked toward the far end of the street, which contained a big warehouse and farther on some sort of mill. Out in the river the falls were a great horseshoe of ragged water overhung by mist. He pulled at Reno's arm, saying plaintively, "Come on, James, let's get outta this weather. I swear it's cold enough to butcher hogs!"

Reno allowed himself to be led into a cafe, and the two of them ordered a meal. "Always rain like this around here, honeypot?" Easy asked the skinny waitress who took their order.

"Why, we had a drought last summer." She grinned back at him. "Lasted almost two days! Want coffee with your eggs?"

They ate fried eggs, bacon, and potatoes, along with fresh biscuits smeared with honey. Easy wolfed his down with relish, then leaned back and rolled a cigarette. "Hoo boy! I'm full as a dog tick, James!" He took a long draw on his cigarette, his sharp blue eyes taking in the way Reno played with his food, and said idly, "Well, we done 'er, James. It turned out pretty good, I reckon. Too bad about Ty Edwards. He got so close not to make it."

"Bad thing."

Reno stared out the window at the leaden sky, and there was a heaviness in him that disturbed Easy. All of them were worn to a fine edge, but the end of the trip had put some excitement into most of the travelers. Reno had worked hard helping to get the train into Oregon City from the Columbia, but when the train had circled for the last time outside of town the previous night and there had been a mild celebration, Easy noted that Reno had kept back, grinning faintly when spoken to, but not really joining in.

"What about Dooley, James?" Easy asked casually. "Get any word on her?"

"Supposed to be here at the hotel." There was a bleak economy in the words, and Easy saw the frown that knotted his brow, which quickly was smoothed away.

Doctor Williams had been concerned with Dooley's injury, and Shore had insisted that she ride into Oregon City with his train.

Easy fidgeted around in his chair, biting his lip and scratching his tow-colored hair. He was curious by nature, and he had developed a deep affection for Reno on the trail. They had much in common, and now the scrappy little rider was itching to find out what was going on in Reno's head. Since the news of Dooley's secret had gotten back, the train had talked of little else. Leah and Jackson had been pumped dry, forced to tell the story of their flight over and over again, but Reno had not commented on the affair. There was an austere quality in his manner when the subject came up, and nobody had dared go beyond the bleak look in his eyes to pursue the subject.

Finally Easy's face got red and he slapped the table exclaiming: "Dang you, Jim Reno! You make me mad enough to chew nails and spit rivets!"

Reno was startled. "What's the matter with you, Easy?"

"Matter!" Easy snorted and leaned across the table to poke Reno in the chest with a rigid finger. "What's the matter?" he mocked Reno's words and then almost shouted, "Sometimes I think yore egg got shook, James! The whole train ain't talked about nothin' but Dooley, and here you are, closer to her than anybody, and you set there like a great stone face and say, 'What's the matter?'! It's enough to make a preacher cuss!"

Reno allowed a slight smile to crease his face, then shrugged his heavy shoulders. "Guess there's not much to say, Easy."

Clearly Reno wanted no more talk on the matter, but Easy ignored the rebuff and plunged ahead. "You knew about it, didn't you? I mean, about Dooley bein' a girl?"

"No."

"You *had* to know!" Easy insisted. "I mean, you was around her all the time. She could fool the rest of us easy, but, shoot, you was like a *family* sort of, wasn't you?"

Reno sat loosely in his chair, but there was a hooded reserve in his face that covered a hair-fine temper, and he let it flare out suddenly as he slapped his hands together and grated out in a hard voice, "Guess I'm just plain dumb!"

Easy was shocked at the raw gust of anger that escaped. He protested at once, "Aw, Jim, you hadn't ort to take it like that! Way Jackson tell it, there wasn't much choice for her."

"Sure," Reno said, and a wry humor made streaks across the planes of his face. "Guess I'm just feelin' like an idiot, Easy. Did you know St. John got her number right off?"

"Yeah, he told me, but he's a sharp one, James," Easy said. He toyed with the cup of coffee, and the silence ran on. Finally Easy asked quietly, "You sore at the kid, Reno?"

The answer did not come at once. Reno sat there staring at the half-healed scar on his right hand, then finally said, "I guess not. Or maybe I am. Dooley's a good kid, and I know she had to do it, but it took the wind out of my sail, Easy. Don't know why, it just did."

"Yeah, I can see that." A thought struck Easy and he asked, "You ain't stickin' around, are you?"

"Nothing to stay for." Reno got to his feet, put a coin on the table, and said, "I guess Lee and me will go prospecting. Maybe that new strike at Alder Gulch."

They left the cafe, and Easy said, "You going to see Dooley now?"

"I guess so."

"I'm going to the saloon. When you want to get drunk, come find me."

"Why would I want to get drunk?"

Easy stared up at the larger man, then pulled his hat down over his ears to shut out the cold. "Because you're feelin' mean, and you're mad, and you're gonna go to that girl and make a jackass outta yourself. Then you'll feel like a sheep-killin' dog. So after you get all that done, you'll find me at that saloon right down there."

Reno stared at the bowlegged rider, and there was a confused look in his eye as he turned and headed toward the hotel that he had spotted earlier.

He made his way slowly down the plank walk, pulling his coat up against the bitter cold, and there was a hesitancy in his movement that he noted but could not shake off. He had made many wrong decisions in his life, but even those had been arrived at with little difficulty, for he was basically a simple man, seeing most things as a fork in the road: You take one or the other—and if it turned out to be the wrong one, why, a man had to live with such things.

He had picked up some of that kind of simplistic thinking in the war, when life and death were the only real things, all else becoming vague. The hard life he had led since the war had reinforced the habit of facing decisions squarely, then forging straight ahead once the decision was made. He was by nature a fighter and a driver, but lately the direction of his life had been confused, hard to focus on.

Wish things were as simple as they used to be, he thought sourly as he crossed a muddy intersection. *Wish I was an Indian—go out and kill a deer, get a woman, pull up and move when the game gets scarce. That's the way a man ought to live!*

He shook his head angrily, realizing that even that was not so, that the Indian way was being crushed by the torrent of settlers. He was restless and edgy as he came to the entrance of the Royal Hotel, and a notion to keep on walking swept through him so strongly that he had to force himself to turn and enter.

A tall, thin clerk was at the desk against the right wall of the small lobby, busy registering two men roughly dressed. Two older women and a younger man were grouped in chairs by a glowing potbellied stove, talking loudly about the election. Reno walked to the desk, and the clerk looked over the heads of the miners. "Help you?"

"Got a Dooley Judd registered?"

"In 208. Up those stairs."

Seldom had he gone more reluctantly to meet someone, and again he had an impulse to leave. But he shook it off and made his way up the stairs. A well-dressed couple met him at the top, and he moved to the outside to make room.

"Jim?"

Reno's mind had been on the room down the hall, and when he turned to face the young woman in a dust-gray dress which held her tightly around waist and breast, he yanked his hat off, feeling like a fool—just as he had the last time he had seen her.

"Don't you know me, Jim?" The voice, a low one for a girl, was still noticeably different from the one Reno had grown accustomed to. Julie's glossy brown hair had grown just long enough over the past months to form a halo of curls that framed her oval face, and it softened her features, making the large gray-green eyes seem enormous. The lashes had grown back, long, thick and curling upward in a full sweep, resting on her cheeks when she closed her eyes for one second. The olive skin seemed lighter, finer than he thought possible, and her lips were ripe and full in a way that he would have sworn he had never seen before.

Then, aware that he was gawking at her like a bumpkin, he shook his head and said, "No, I sure didn't. You've changed a little."

The words carried a rebuke, and there was no smile on Reno's lips, Julie saw. She knew his moods too well to mistake the half-veiled isolation of his dark eyes and the hardening of his wide mouth. She'd seen him look that way when he was disgusted or angry, and now it was directed at her.

"Jim, I have to talk to you." She turned to the tall, well-built man who had been watching Reno with shrewd brown eyes, saying, "This is Mr. Laurence Shore, Jim. He's Joel Shore's brother, the man who pulled us out of the river. This is Jim Reno, Mr. Shore."

Reno took the hand Shore extended, saying, "Didn't get a real chance to thank your brother, Shore. Like to see him."

"A day too late, I'm afraid," Shore said. "He took the train out this morning headed for the Willamette Valley. You may see him there, Reno. Most of the best untaken land's in that section."

"Won't be seeing him," Reno said quietly. "Maybe you could pass my thanks along next time you write."

"Certainly." Shore glanced at Julie, who was staring at Reno, biting her lower lip, and there was a tension in the meeting that he did not understand. He shifted uncomfortably and said, "I was just taking Miss Judd for a late breakfast. Wish you'd join us."

"Like to, but I've got to meet a man."

"Well, I suppose you two have things to talk about." Shore turned to Julie, and Reno did not miss the easy gallantry as he bowed, saying, "I'll see you later, Miss Judd."

"Do you want to eat, Jim?"

"Don't have the money."

"I—I have a few dollars."

"From Mr. Laurence Shore?"

She nodded and said, "He let me borrow twenty dollars until the train got here."

"Not hungry." Reno knew he was behaving badly, but could not seem to help it. The whole thing was tinged with unreality. The well-dressed young woman in front of him had nothing to do with the dusty kid dressed in baggy clothes. There was something comical about the thing, but he could not look at her without feeling cheated somehow. From the moment his eyes had fallen on her lying in Doctor Williams's wagon, he had felt outraged, betrayed, and the barren cast of his face reflected the bitterness.

She moved nervously, then said, "Come on, Jim. We can talk in my room."

The room she led him to was plain fare, but it had two straight-backed chairs, and he waited for her to sit down before he took the other chair. A passing thought brought a small smile to his lips, which she noted and asked at once, "What are you smiling at?"

"Just laughing at myself, Dooley—or is it Miss Judd?"

"Don't talk like that, Jim. Please!" Her shoulder sagged, and her long lashes brushed her smooth cheeks as she closed her eyes.

"Sorry. I just can't get myself to thinking right about all this. I was smiling because here for five months I haven't given two whoops about which one of us sits down first. Now I catch myself acting like a fancy dude at a society affair."

"It doesn't matter which one of us sits down first, Jim."

He looked down at his square hands, clenched his fingers slowly, then looked up at her with some unfathomable thought screened in his dark eyes.

"Yeah, it does."

Julie fingered the lace of her bodice nervously, then in an attempt to ease the strain, said, "I want to get back to the wagon. I guess everybody will be leaving to find a place."

"Guess so. Going to have a sort of farewell party tonight at the camp."

"Oh, Jim, I can't miss that! It might be the last time we'll see some of them!"

"Expect that's right." There was an infinite sadness in his eyes as he said, "Seems like the thing I've done the most in my life is lose track of folks I care about."

She was caught by his expression. He was not a man to complain, but there was a vulnerable streak in him, and she sensed that the knowledge that the trip was over and done stirred up old memories. He was the strongest man she had ever met, the most self-sufficient, but there was something plaintive and lost in his manner. The desire to put her arms around him and comfort him swept through her so strongly that she got up suddenly and took a few steps toward the window. Crossing her arms over her breasts, she stared down at the muddy street, not really seeing it, for her mind was fluttering like a bird in a cage. She had been long aware that his physical presence somehow swayed her, but it was much worse now that she was out of her grubby, shapeless men's clothes. Changing back into her own character brought out some sort of physical response in Reno that was unexpressed but powerful enough to make just being in the same room with him traumatic.

"What will you do now, Dooley?"

She turned back, and he got up to face her. "I don't know, Jim. Leah told you why I had to get away from my home?"

"Yes. Can't fault you for running away. But what's next?"

"Find work, I guess."

"Not much in that way for women out here, is there?"

"I don't need much. I'll find something." She dropped her hands and asked, "What about you, Jim? Are you going to stay on?"

"Don't think so." Reno got to his feet. The room seemed too small, and he said, "I've got some chores." He nodded briefly, then would have turned, but she stepped forward and took his arm.

"Jim, don't be angry with me!"

"I'm not."

"You *are!*" she flashed out and took his other arm, shaking him as she said. "You think I don't know when you're mad?" Then she said directly, "I should have told you, Jim. I wanted to, but I was afraid."

He was stirred by her direct honesty, and yet there was a perverse stubbornness that lay deep inside that made him say, "Guess you had to have your fun."

"Fun! You think it was *fun?*" She shook him harder and shook her head fiercely. "I hated it, Jim! If you just knew how much I—" She broke off abruptly, then colored and dropped her head beneath his gaze.

"How much you what?" he asked.

"Oh, nothing," she stammered. "I just wish I'd told you. I did once."

"Oh?"

"In the cave, when we were about to break up. I told you, but you didn't hear me, did you?"

He remembered it and then said, "No, I didn't hear you."

"But you heard what I said just before we got on the raft for the last time?"

I love you Jim Reno!

He looked down into her face and lied, "I don't remember."

She flinched as if he had struck her. Her lips trembled, and she turned without a word and walked to the window, her back stiff and unyielding.

He could not stand the room any longer, but he paused with his hand on the knob and turned to stare at her. "I'll see you later, Dooley."

"All right." There was no life in her voice, and she did not change position.

Still he hesitated, and finally said, "You—you look fine, Dooley."

"Thank you very much, Jim."

He yanked the door open and swept out of the hotel headed straight for the saloon, a bleakness on his face.

Easy glanced up, and after a swift look at Reno's face, he said with a lopsided grin, "See you handled it real well, James."

"Shut up, Easy!"

The little rider took a drink out of his glass, smacked his lips, and said in a slurred voice, "Good ol' James! I guess you really let the kid have it, didn't you? Guess you showed her that no pint-sized female can mess around with you!" He took another swig and winked drunkenly. "Knew I could count on you to push that uppity kid around! So what if she's an orphant with no folks, what'ta you care, Reno? Treat 'em rough."

"Easy," Reno said with his face contorted, "if you don't shut your face, I'm gonna split your wishbone! I mean it!"

"Fly right at it, James," Easy roared, slamming the glass on the table and staring up at Reno. "I ain't but half your size, but I allus knowed one day you'd have to push me around to show what a tough man you are. Well, go on! Beat me up!" The little cowboy stood up and shoved his face pugnaciously at Reno's chest. He was making no attempt to be quiet. He shouted, "Well, what you waitin' for, Reno? You done give it to the little orphant, now you can knock your best buddy around! And I seen a little kitten out on the walk when I come in. You can go stomp on it."

He swung wildly at Reno, who pulled his head back and stood there with a pale cast spreading under his copper tan. Easy stepped back and stared at his friend, then dropped his hands and said, "You must be about ready to get drunk, James, 'fore you skedaddle."

"Skedaddle?"

"We had a colonel who seen a passel of Yanks comin' and he looked around at us and said, 'I propose that we begin a pre-cipitous departure from the fray.' Well, we just stared at him, and he yelled out, 'That means *skedaddle,* you fools!' I figure you're gonna light out, James."

Reno reached up and pulled his hat down firmly, then nod-ded. "You got it, Easy. Me and Lee will be pullin' out soon as I can get a few supplies." He held his hand out and tried to grin. "You're a pretty smart fellow, Easy. I'll miss you."

"Where you headed?"

Reno gave an involuntary glance in the direction of the hotel and said, "Away from here. So long, Easy."

Easy stared after Reno, then shook his head sadly and slumped down in his chair.

"Poor James," he muttered as he downed the remains of the dark liquid in his glass. "He's shore in the low cotton. He can run from that leetle gal as long as geese go barefooted, but it ain't gonna do no good! Poor feller's a gone coon!"

Lee had said little when Reno told him they were leaving right away. He had looked at Reno and asked, "What about Dooley?"

"Mining camp is no place for a girl."

Reno had borrowed some money from St. John, and the Englishman had given him a shrewd look as he handed him the cash. "Got over Jean, did you?"

Reno was embarrassed. He had said good-bye to Jean, and it had shocked him a little to see how wrong he had been in his feelings toward her. She had merely smiled and said, "You take care of yourself, hear?" and he had seen what St. John had observed all along: that his attraction for the woman was shallow and based on a wrongheaded idea.

"Guess I was pretty much of a fool there, Algy," Reno said ruefully. "I'll send this back soon as I make my first million in gold."

St. John waved his hand, saying only, "You know, Jim, when a man makes a mistake in one direction, the most common thing is for him to make another, trying to compensate."

Reno stared at him, baffled. "Say it plainer than that."

St. John shook his head, then asked carelessly, "I suppose you'll be taking Julie with you?"

"Julie?" Reno asked. "Oh, Dooley!"

"No—Julie!" St. John insisted.

"Well, no, I'm not. What would I do with a kid like her in a gold camp?"

"Yes, that's a good question." St. John stared at Reno and repeated it, "What could you do with a—'kid' you said?—with a kid like her?"

"You're not making any sense, Algy," Reno protested. "I did what she wanted—got her all the way out here. Now you're suggesting I ought to take her *back?*"

"Don't be so confounded obtuse!" St. John snapped. He stared at Reno intently, then shook his head sadly. "You Americans are so *dense!*"

Reno bought two pack animals and loaded them with supplies, and by noon he and Lee were on their way out of Oregon City, headed for the pass.

"We're in trouble if we get caught in a snowstorm," he said to Lee, staring at the low-lying clouds rolling in from the west.

"Guess so." Lee was depressed, but Reno supposed it was the result of leaving his friends from the train. *Just have to live with it,* he thought grimly, *like the rest of us!*

They made an early camp at a spring, and Reno was chopping wood for a fire when he looked up to see a rider pounding leather. He straightened up and Lee called out, "That's Easy!"

"Yeah, something must be wrong!"

They saw as Easy piled off his horse that it was serious. His face was tense and he said at once, "Dooley's in jail!"

"What?" Reno and Lee said together.

"It's a real mess!" Easy shook his head and asked, "You got any water?"

He took a long drink from Reno's canteen, and said, "You know about that skunk that tried to take advantage of Dooley back in Arkansas?"

"Her stepfather?" Reno asked. "Name was Jake something, wasn't it?"

"Jake Skinner, that's it. Well, he ain't quit trying to get her back, James. The sheriff came out to the camp and he had a warrant signed by the judge. He arrested her and put her in the pokey!"

"On what charge?"

"Grand larceny!"

"What?"

"Aw, it's a frame-up, James!" Easy spat and his face was red as he added, "The skunk claims she run off with a bag of gold—which was hers by right, Leah says."

"Why does this Skinner want her back, Easy?"

Easy stared at Reno as if he had said something particularly stupid, then shook his head. "Well, in the first place, Dooley's name is on the deed for the plantation, and he's goin' to marry her to get it. In the second place, he ain't blind."

Reno stared at him blankly, then it struck him. "Oh, yeah."

"Oh, yeah!" Easy mocked him. He looked at Lee, and said, "You explain all this to him sometime will you, Lee, about how men take out after good-lookin' gals?"

"All right, you've made your point," Reno said soberly. "I don't think he can make her go back."

"She'll be on the boat day after tomorrow, that's how wrong you are."

Reno pulled his hat off, and stared at it. Both Lee and Easy watched him, and when the boy searched Easy's face for a sign, he got a quick wink from the puncher that made him lift his eyes to Reno.

"Well, . . ." Reno lifted his head and pulled his hat on and there was a fire glowing in his eyes as he said in an aggravated voice, "Why don't you two get the animals loaded! We can't bust her out of the pokey standing here, can we?"

Easy threw his hat in the air and gave a rebel yell that set the mules to kicking and braying, and Lee exclaimed, "Golly, Jim, I ain't never busted no lady out of jail before!"

Reno stood there, his dark hair falling in his eyes, and there was a new freedom in him that lifted Lee's spirits. He reached over and knocked Lee's hat off his head, then struck him a hard rap on the shoulder.

"Well, it's time you did, boy. And stop sayin' *ain't!*"

"Yeah, you gotta learn to talk good like me, boy," Easy said, picking up his hat. "Now then, James, you got any idea how we're gonna prize this filly outta the hoosegow?"

"I figure either I'll dazzle the sheriff with my wit and charm—or we'll blow the jail up!"

Easy looked at Reno carefully and said with a shake of his head, "After having seen you at close quarters fer quite a spell, I guess we better blow the sucker open!"

The change in Reno was obvious—except to the dark-haired man himself. He hurried them back to Oregon City, rousted Jackson and Leah out of bed, and by daylight the next day was in town doing business. He sold Julie's wagon and bought five pack animals, the best available. They worked most of the morning sorting out what had to go and sold the rest.

It was nearly dark when Easy said, "Want me to go buy some black powder—to blow the jail, I mean."

Reno shook his head. "No, I got a simpler way." He explained his plan to Easy and Lee, and they both grinned with pleasure.

"That'll answer!" Easy explained.

"Can you give us a hand, Easy?" Reno asked. "We'll need a little help getting away, then you can come back. Don't think there's much chance of getting in trouble over a little thing like busting somebody out of a pokey little jail like this one."

"Can't do it, James," Easy said. He lit a cigarette, then as Reno was saying, "Know it's a lot to ask," Easy said, "I don't cotton to this country. Too wet. Makes me feel like a bullfrog in the bottom of a well. Guess I'll tag along to the gulch."

"Hey, that's great!" Lee said.

"Sure about that, Easy?" Reno asked. "Might be rough."

"Aw, shut up and let's get this did!" Easy said with a grin.

"All right, you think you can get in to visit her?"

"I'll dazzle the jailer with my wit and charm—or knock his brains out—if he's got any, which I doubt!"

"Well, don't make any trouble. Just get the word to Dooley to be ready to move at midnight—right on the nose!"

Reno was busy getting Jackson and Leah ready, for he knew that they would be in big trouble after the jailbreak. "You'll have to go over the mountains with us," he told them both. "Either that or I can maybe get you hid out somewhere and come back for you."

"We ain't lettin' Miss Julie go off to no gold camp by herself!" Leah said promptly. "Jes you get us something to ride, and we be all right!"

"All right. Let's go."

At eleven-thirty they were in an alley down the street from the jail. The town was quiet, and only a few dim lanterns flickered through the falling snow.

Reno said, "This snow will make things rough later on, but it'll make it harder to get up a posse to come after us. You all got this thing straight?"

"Can't I help hook up the mules, Jim?" Lee begged.

"No, because I need a steady hand with the horses. If they get away, we're gone coons. I'm trusting you, son."

"Sure, Jim! Don't you worry. I'll have them all ready."

They waited until five minutes until twelve, then Reno said, "Let's go!"

They moved the mules, all eight of them, out of the alley and led them down the street. The blanket of snow muffled the sound of hooves, and Reno ran on ahead, moving awkwardly.

He was carrying a heavy logging chain wrapped in sacking. He rounded the corner and went directly to the back of the jail. There were two windows about ten feet off the ground, and he put the chain down and went into the alley. He saw the ladder he'd put there earlier with a sense of relief. If someone had moved it, the plan would've been useless.

Leaning the ladder against the side of the building, he removed the chain and found the end with the large hook, then started up toward the windows. As he got to the top he looked down to see Jackson and Easy leading the mules into the alley. As they got the team in line, he raised his head slowly over the ledge and whispered, "Dooley?"

"Here! I'm here!" It was very dark, but two small hands came out of the window and he held them in one of his for a moment. They seemed very small, and he gave a confident squeeze, then whispered, "Anybody else in there with you?"

"No! What are you planning?"

"We're going to pull this window out. Help me get the chain around the bars."

The chain seemed to make a great deal of noise, and once Reno stopped, thinking he heard someone, but there was nothing. Finally he got the bars looped and fastened the hook. "Now listen—when the window goes, it's going to wake the whole town! You'll have to jump, and I mean quick."

"It's so dark!"

He reached through the bars with one hand and she gripped it so hard he marveled at her strength. "You have to jump, Dooley. I'll be right down there to catch you. You won't be able to see me, but I'll be there." He heard the sound of the harness chains ring below as the mules shifted, and he knew they had to act fast.

"Will you trust me, Dooley?"

He felt a soft touch on his hand. "I'd trust you with myself always, Jim Reno!"

He paused, then said, "I'll be there, Julie."

He slipped down the ladder, moved it to one side, and whispered, "You got the chain hooked up?"

"Ready to go!" Easy said cheerfully.

"All right, let's go! Hup! Whoo-up!" Reno shouted, and the hooves of the mules dug into the snow-packed earth. The logging chain was fifty feet long, which Reno figured was enough to allow the mules to be running full speed by the time they hit the end of it. Jackson was sitting on one lead mule and Easy on the other, and they were screaming like Comanches.

The chain rattled as it played out, then the team hit the end and it popped up, snapping into a quivering line of steel! At first Reno thought with a sinking heart that it had not worked, for although there was a terrible crash, the team was pulled to a dead stop. Then by the dim light he saw that the window had not moved—but the whole back of the jail was falling outward!

He jumped back just in time to miss being buried in a hail of mortar and bricks, and there was a terrible roar in his ears, and dust rose up to choke him.

Springing forward, he scrambled wildly to get beneath the spot where the window had been, and looking up he thought he saw Julie.

"Jump!" he bellowed as loud as he could, and the shadow separated from the building as he opened his arms to catch the falling girl. He didn't exactly catch her, but she fell right onto his chest. He fell backward, wrapping his arms around her slim body to protect her as they rolled down the mass of rubble.

He was stunned by the impact and lay there holding her tight until his head stopped spinning, and to his amazement she laughed.

"All right, Reno, I've found you out!"

"What . . . ?"

She lay in his arms and her giggle was clear in the sudden silence. "You did all this just to get to hug me, didn't you now? Oh, I know what men like you are like!"

She was laughing, her face pushed against his chest, and suddenly he was laughing too. Great gusts of laughter ran through him, and though he knew they were in danger, he couldn't stop.

Finally Easy came back to bend over and peer at them. He saw Reno lying on his back, Julie hanging onto him, and both of them laughing like crazy.

"My, my!" he said loudly, "Time do go by when you're having a good time, don't it now?"

Reno, still laughing, got to his feet, and pulled Julie to her feet. "Let's get out of here! Easy, you got the mules off the chain?"

"Sure. We wuz jest waitin' on you two to finish up your party."

They ran to where Jackson was holding the team, and Reno took Julie by the waist and tossed her up on a mule, then mounted the one next to her. Easy and Jackson got mounted and Reno called out, "Hay-up!" and they sailed out of the alley onto the main street of Oregon City. Lights were going on all up and down the street, especially upstairs, where many shopkeepers had their quarters. The front of the jail lit up suddenly, and many voices were heard calling as Reno and company galloped the team at a tearing run out of town.

A shotgun let go, and Reno thought he felt the hiss of a pellet close to his ear. Then a handgun went off, and as they raced down the street the world seemed to be exploding.

As they cleared the first intersection, Easy turned and yelled, "This is gettin' pretty warm, ain't it, James?"

"We'll make it!"

"Yeah, but like the romantic possum said to the accommodatin' lady skunk, 'I've enjoyed about as much of this as I can stand!'"

They left the lights and the gunfire behind and found Lee waiting with the horses at the edge of town. Quickly they piled off the mules and got on the horses. Reno said, "Let's go," and headed back toward town.

"We can't go back there, Jim!" Lee protested.

"When they come after us, Lee, which way will they come?"

"Why, *this* way, but—"

"So we'll ooze back, real quietlike, and leave town the *other* way. In an hour this snow will have our tracks covered and there's no way they can follow."

"By gum, James," Easy said in admiration, "that sounds horse-high, bull-strong, pig-tight, and goose-proof! Let's get it did!"

"This is the crest," Reno said. "It's all downhill from here on."

They had pulled the horses up at the crest of the last of a series of hog-backed ranges, and looking back they saw little but the tops of the clouds that lay beneath them in rolling shapes.

The group had ridden three rough days. The constant snow had made footing uncertain, but it had also prevented anyone from following them.

"Look!" Lee said, pointing at the trail ahead. "The sun's out!"

The valley that lay before them was covered with snow, and the rays of the sun made it look like diamonds.

"Shore is pretty, ain't it now?" Easy said.

"Guess we might as well camp over by those trees." Reno looked at the group with fondness and said, "You all did fine. Real fine." He slid off his horse and pulled an ax from one of the pack animals. "I'll cut some firewood while you set up camp."

They staked the animals out, put up tarps for shelter, and started a fire with small sticks while Reno cut some large limbs from a fallen tree.

Supper was deer steaks from a doe that Reno had dropped with a snap shot early that morning. They ate until they were full, then weariness hit them like a sledge.

"Guess I'll check the animals one more time," Reno said yawning, as the others rolled into their blankets. He came back ten minutes later and stopped to pour the last of the coffee into his cup.

"Jim?" Julie stepped close to his side, and said, "I hate to go to bed. Might miss something."

"Me too. Always been that way."

She was wearing a pair of jeans and a wool shirt, and when Reno looked at her he shook his head, saying, "It won't do!"

She looked up at him in surprise, her eyes large in the firelight. "What won't do, Jim?"

"Why, I thought if you'd take off that dress and put on men's clothes, it'd be just like it was on the train."

"You mean I'd be just a kid again?" she said in a deceptive tone.

"Well, yes. It was a lot simpler that way."

"Why does it bother you so much that I'm a woman, Jim?"

He moved uncomfortably, and there was a puzzled light in his eyes. "Well, I thought I had things all figured out. The one thing I wanted to do was make a place for Lee. Then when Lola died I got sidetracked."

"And you almost got sidetracked with that Lamarr woman."

"Yeah, that was a mistake. But what I had on my mind was raising you two kids, see, and then . . ."

"Jim Reno!" Julie said loudly, and she took his arm and shook it fiercely. "I'm a *woman!* Can you understand that? Not a kid!"

He grinned at her and said, "I'm old enough to be your daddy."

"You'll be twenty-eight years old on May 24," she said coldly.

He stared at her. "How'd you know that?"

"Never mind!"

"Well, how old are you? About fifteen?"

"I am seventeen, which is practically an old maid where I come from!"

He smiled, and there was a wolfish look about him at that moment. He had not shaved on the trip, and his teeth gleamed whitely in the firelight.

"Well, I *feel* old enough to be your dad," he said.

"I don't care what you feel like, Jim Reno!" she said tersely. "You are not old enough to be my father. You are old enough to be lots of things, but not that!"

"What am I old enough to be, then?"

She shrugged and said, "My uncle, my brother, my—my

lover." She stumbled at that, and even more on the next: "Maybe my husband. . . ."

He leaned forward and said, "Why, Julie, that's crazy!"

She didn't answer him, but then she smiled slightly as a thought passed through her mind. She put her hands on his elbows and stepped close to him. "I know what I want us to be, Jim!"

"What?"

"Why, we're kin—just a little bit—isn't that so?"

"Well, sure, in a way . . ."

"Why, then we can be kissing kin!"

He stared at her, and asked in a baffled tone, "Kissing kin? What in the world is *that?*"

"Don't you know?" she asked with a smile. "It's when a man and a woman are second cousins—or something far off like that. So they're sort of kin, but they can—they can—they can kiss each other." She leaned against him and her eyes were enormous pools in the firelight.

Suddenly she was a shape and a substance before him, and a fragrance and a melody all around him, so that the loneliness that had possessed him grew insupportable. The wall he held up against the world went down. He was suddenly deaf to the night sounds and blind to everything except her face, and he wished only to hold her, to make her safe. Her warmth was as great as his own. The softness of her body came against him, and he kissed her.

There was never any completion to that kiss. There was a moment of firm pressure, a fragrance, and then he lifted his head, and a thought ran through him: *There's never been anything like this!*

Then she pulled back, her eyes damp.

He said, "Julie, this is crazy!"

"Is it?"

"You know it is!" He shook his head. "I'll look out for you, and I'll find a fine young fellow more your age."

Julie stretched like a cat, and she looked up at him with a secret smile on her lips. "Will you, Jim? Well, we'll have lots of time to talk about it, won't we?" She walked to her blankets, pausing to whisper before she lay down, "Do you remember what I said to you on the river—just before we got on the raft the last time?"

He nodded slowly. "I remember."

She tilted her head and asked even more softly, "Do you remember what you said to me?"

"Yes, but—"

"Then we know where we stand, don't we, Jim? Good night. Go to bed and get some sleep."

He did the first easily enough, but sleep eluded him. He tossed and turned for a long time, thinking about the next day, about Lee, and about how they'd make it at Alder Gulch.

But when he finally went to sleep, he dreamed of nothing but a pair of enormous gray-green eyes and a pair of lips whispering softly, *I love you, Jim Reno!*

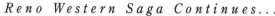

BOOMTOWN

One
Virginia City

Leaving the Hellgate River, Jim Reno traced his way through great dark gorges. The fierce blizzard that had torn the land like an angry beast had left huge drifts in the hollows, and he carefully skirted the crevasses. Peaks showed high above him in the early spring's sun, and creeks roared and tumbled white in the rocky beds. Everything seemed new and alive after the frozen silence of winter. As he paused on the crest of a jagged promontory and looked over a snug little valley, emerald green and rich with red and yellow flowers, he leaned back in the saddle and rested his eyes on the scene.

Riding had trimmed him, and there was a hollowness in his wedge-shaped face. His hair lay thick and black and ragged against his temples, and his eyes were sleepy under jet brows. A youthful look was countered by lines slanting out from his eyes across his tanned skin. Except for a slight break on the bridge of his straight nose and a small scar over his right temple, his face was unmarked. He wore a heavy dark wool coat, a fawn-colored shirt with bone buttons, and faded butternut breeches with a faint stripe down the side of the legs. A gray, low-crowned hat anchored by a leather lanyard was shoved back on his head, and a narrow black belt supported the gun at his side.

He looked at the scene before him, said, "Pretty," then urged his horse down the slope. All day he rode hard, then camped on the Beaverhead beside a stream. At dawn he was on the trail again. At noon he reached the Stinkingwater at the mouth of Alder Gulch. He followed the road upgrade, noting along the edges the potholes of prospectors. Camps clung to the edge of the Gulch, but he pushed his tired horse steadily along until he rode into Virginia City as the shadows were growing long.

Four thousand prospectors were scattered along Alder Creek with their sluices and pans and Long Toms gutting the hillside where once a river's channel had dropped its gold treasure. Virginia City, its streets and cross streets marked out by tents and brush wickiups and a few board houses, was beginning to wake up as Reno made his way down the muddy street. Like all boom camps, this one had been hurriedly thrown together with cheap lumber, canvas, and logs. Fully three-quarters of the camp was made up of saloons and dance halls. The rest of it consisted of stores, miners' supply houses, livery barns, and restaurants.

Reno was hungry, but, ignoring the pangs, he pulled up in front of a stable. A man with a steel hook instead of a left hand stepped out to meet him. "Help you?"

Reno handed him the reins and nodded. "Grain her good."

The one-armed man gave the horse a sharp look, then turned a pair of steady hazel eyes on Reno, and commented, "Pretty well used up, ain't she? You just come in?"

Reno nodded and pulled a pipe out of his pocket. As he packed it with tobacco from a worn leather pouch, he was aware of the stable man's interest. "Yes. From the Bitterroots."

"Pass's been closed for months. Must be clear now if you got through." He led the horse inside, removed the saddle and bridle expertly with his one hand, and said, "You want to leave the animal here for a spell?"

"Pulling out tomorrow morning," Reno said. "I need a couple of horses—or mules, if you know of any."

"Mules? None in camp. But I got a team you might look at." He dumped a bucket of feed in the box, turned, and put out his hand. "Sam Bible's my name."

"Jim Reno." The stable man had a hard, calloused hand with a grip like a vise. "Don't think I've ever met anybody with your name," Reno said.

"That's likely," Bible said with a grin. He had one tooth missing, and there was humorous expression on his moon face as he added, "Give me a pile of trouble, that name. Everybody expects a man with a name like mine to be a saint. Crimped my style considerable when I was chasin' the gals. But it has its advantages, Reno. Far as I can remember nobody ever forgot my name, like it was Smith or Jones. You wanna see that team?"

He led Reno to a corral, and after a quick examination, Reno said, "They'll do. How much?"

"You better sit down afore I set the price," Bible said. "I got to get six hundred for the team." Reno's eyebrows shot up, and Sam Bible hurriedly added, "I know, I know—they ain't worth it. But things is different here at Virginia City. Gold's the cheapest thing there is! Why, I paid five dollars for a little apple this morning. Everything has to be freighted in, you see?"

"I'll take the team," Reno said. He pulled a black leather wallet from his coat pocket, removed a sheaf of bank notes, and counted out the money. Handing it to Bible, he said, "Like to rent a horse for a few days."

"That's a good bay," Bible murmured, motioning with his steel hook toward a rangy animal in the corral. He was holding the notes in his hand and there was an odd look in his hazel eyes. "Guess this is more bank money than I've seen in a spell." He lifted his eyes, then stuck the money in his shirt pocket and said, "I ain't much of a hand to meddle in other folks' business, Reno, but was I you, I'd keep that wad of bills tucked out of sight. This is a tough camp."

"Sure." Reno nodded, then he gave a smile and added, "I've been in the backwoods so long guess I've forgotten how to be careful." He added as he turned to leave, "I'll be around early to pick up the horses. You got a pack you can put on one of the team?"

"Sure." Bible almost asked a question as to the purpose, but he cut it off and added, "Creighton's is the best place for supplies, if you need any, Reno."

Leaving the stable, Reno made his way along the muddy street, which was already beginning to fill up with men coming in from their claims. Creighton's General Store was on the main street, a large unpainted board building between a blacksmith shop and a saloon. The interior was dimly lit by three lanterns, which cast their feeble glow over a jumble of wares. The floor was crowded with barrels, saddles, harnesses, boxes, crates, while along the walls canned goods, clothing, cooking utensils, and a hundred other items filled the rough shelves.

Several miners were inside, sitting around a potbellied stove, and two women with highly colored cheeks were handling bolts of material in the rear. A muscular blond man with sharp, good-looking features was looking at a repeating rifle at one end of the counter. He lifted a pair of pale blue eyes to Reno, bracketed him, then went back to working the lever on the rifle.

"Something for you?" A tall, stately man with white hair and a Vandyke beard moved away from the customer to stand before Reno.

"Need some supplies—bacon, beans, canned tomatoes . . ." As Reno named off the items, the tall man moved efficiently, pulling the food from the shelves.

"Creighton, you want to sell this gun or not?"

The blond man had moved up, rifle in his hand, and there was a steady arrogance in his pale eyes as he stared at Reno.

"Didn't know you were ready to take it, Lyons," the merchant said. "It's seventy-five."

"Take it out of this dust." The blond man reached into his pocket and tossed a bag on the counter, but did not take his eyes from Reno as Creighton moved to a pair of scales to weigh the dust. "Don't know you, do I?"

"Just came in," Reno said softly.

"From where?" The question came out sharply, and when Reno didn't answer at once, he said, "I'm Haze Lyons, deputy sheriff. What's your business in Virginia City?"

Reno turned to face him, aware of the silence that had spread out over the store. Lyons was a dandy in dress, but the foppish attire did not conceal the straight-grained nerve of the man. He would never rest, Reno realized, until he had tested his strength against a man.

"Just came in from the Bitterroots, Deputy. Left Oregon a spell back and got snowed in. Name's Jim Reno."

Lyons relaxed with a thin smile and said, "Yeah, it's been a bad winter. You stakin' a claim?"

"Thought I might try my luck."

"Here's your dust, Lyons," Creighton said. He handed the bag back to the deputy and said to Reno, "That all adds up to forty-three dollars."

The others in the store had turned away from the scene, but Lyons stood watching, and Reno had no other choice but to take his wallet out and pull a few notes out to pay the bill. He did not miss the look on Lyons's face, and he saw a frown on the face of Creighton at the sight of the thick wallet.

"Take this with you now?" the merchant asked.

"Like to leave it here until after I eat, if you've got room."

"I'll put it under the counter."

Haze Lyons nodded, said, "See you around, Reno," and left carrying the rifle.

"Appreciate your business," the tall merchant said, straightening up. "I'm John Creighton." He glanced toward the door the deputy had gone through, started to say something, but glanced at the men sitting around the stove and changed his mind. "Stop in any time."

Reno nodded. "Sure. Where's the hotel?"

"Two blocks down—the Royal. Food is pretty good, too."

The mention of food started Reno's juices flowing, and he made his way down the street to the hotel. A fat man with a beefy red face took his money and said, "Take number six."

The room could not have been much more primitive. A bed with a worn, dingy purple spread and a sagging mattress took up three-fourths of the space. The only other furniture was a table with a cracked pitcher and a washbowl. Reno dashed his face with water, dried on the thin towel, then went downstairs at once. The fat man motioned toward the door leading off to the left. "Get your eats in there."

The restaurant was a narrow room with two windows and a door on the wall facing the street. The place was half-filled, but men were coming in steadily, so Reno took a table, placing his back to the wall. There was a sign on the wall that read, "If you don't like our grub, don't eat here."

Most of the customers were roughly dressed miners who put their heads down and ate with the same intensity as they ripped the earth for the golden dust. At the back sat a couple, an older man with gold-rimmed glasses and a young woman in a dark dress. A waiter wearing a dirty apron came to stand before Reno. "We got steaks or stew, potatoes and onions."

Reno grinned at the simplicity of the menu, but he had been in mining camps before and was not surprised. "Bring me some of that steak—a double helping. And about a quart of hot coffee."

He ate his meal slowly. The steak was tough, but the vegetables were well-cooked and seasoned, and the coffee was strong and black. He had learned to take the good moments and savor them. The waiter brought him a huge slice of apple pie, and he ate it slowly, washing it down with sips of black coffee.

Three men came in and went to a table in the rear near the couple Reno had noticed. One of them was Haze Lyons. He spotted Reno at once, and as the trio sat down, he leaned forward and said something to a tall, broad-shouldered man wearing two guns and a star on his shirt. The man turned a pair of dark eyes on Reno and nodded, then turned his back.

Reno got up, put on his hat, and caught the waiter near the door. He paid him, and as he turned to go, he collided with the couple.

"Sorry," he said with a smile. "Guess I'm getting clumsy in my old age."

"Well, it's pretty crowded in here," the man said. "I'm William Merritt. Don't believe we've met."

"Name's Reno. Just came in today."

Merritt was a slight man with hair going gray. He had light blue eyes behind the thick lenses and a gentlemanly air that seemed strange in a mining camp. "This is my daughter, Mrs. Warren."

The woman was fair with smooth skin and a round face. Her hair was honey-colored, and her eyes were so blue they seemed violet in the flickering lamplight. She nodded but did not speak when Reno said, "Glad to meet you."

There was a moment's silence and then Merritt said, "We're having a service tonight at our church, if you'd like to come."

Reno looked at him with interest. Ministry was the last profession to come to many mining camps. "Thanks for the invitation, Reverend. Probably not tonight, but I'll take you up later."

"Fine, fine!" Merritt's face lit up, and Reno suspected his invitations did not always find a welcome with the roughs in the camp. "Come along anytime. The church is at the north end of town." He looked at the young woman, but she said nothing, and there was a faint look of skepticism in her dark eyes that puzzled Reno. As they left the restaurant, Reno wondered about her husband. Women were scarce in any mining camp, and one as attractive as Merritt's daughter would be the center of hungry attention from the men of the camp.

For an hour he walked the streets, which were crowded with miners who had come in from their claims. They hit Virginia City like a wave, roaming the muddy streets in groups or individually, and the night air was loud with music from the hurdy-gurdy houses, accompanied by the shouts of customers and the calculated laughter of the dance hall girls.

Trail weariness was heavy on him, and he started back to the hotel to get a good night's sleep. Passing by a row of saloons, he heard someone call "Reno" and turned to see Sam Bible crossing the street. The steel hook glinted in the light of a lantern as he gestured toward the end of the street. "I was in Creighton's and he told me you bought some supplies. I figured you wanted them on that horse, so I had my hired man take 'em down with the stuff I bought and load on the pack. That all right?"

Reno grinned. "Thanks, Bible."

"Come on, let's have a drink." Bible pulled at Reno, drawing him to a saloon called the El Dorado. The bar was crowded two deep, and the two men had trouble making their way across the floor. Half of the room was filled with gambling tables, and two roulette wheels clinked as they spun. The middle of the saloon was cleared for dancing, and half a dozen highly painted saloon girls were spun around violently by heavy-booted miners. A mahogany bar ran half the length of the room, and in the back were several tables where men sat drinking and talking.

Bible shoved his way through the crowd to the back of the room and pulled up before a table. "Well, Reno, if you ain't too careful about the company you keep, guess this table will do as well as any." He grinned down at a short, bulky man wearing a heavy black overcoat and said, "Make a little room, X. This here is Jim Reno just come in from the Bitterroots. Reno, this is X. Beidler—Ringo Jukes—Nick Tbolt—Link McKeever. You already met Creighton."

Beidler peered up at Reno with sharp black eyes. "Passes clear at last, are they? We'll have two thousand more men in a month. Sit down."

"And most of 'em will leave here with less than they brought in." Ringo Jukes was a thick-shouldered fellow with dark eyes and black hair. He had the long arms and scarred knuckles of a brawler, and there was an angry light in his brown eyes as he added, "Fools expect gold to pop out of the ground like daisies!"

Link McKeever was the youngest man in the game, not over twenty. He lifted a pair of wide eyes and smiled at Jukes. "Well, Ringo, I came here pretty much the same way." He stared down at the palms of his calloused hands and murmured, "The stuff sure don't come easy, does it?"

"The only ones who get it easy are the crooks who take it from us." X. Beidler looked like a bulldog as he glowered around the room. "Did you hear about Jake Randall? A rough held him up in broad daylight yesterday. Jake didn't have much on him, and the scum said, 'Next time I brace you, have more money or I'll kill you!'"

"Looks like the law could do somethin'." Nick Tbolt was a young Dutchman with blue eyes and fair hair. "Seems like with four deputies they ought to be able to put a cap on this robbin'."

Ringo Jukes snorted and took a drink out of his glass, cursed and snapped, "Them yahoos? Why, they ain't no better'n the crooks they're supposed to be catchin'!"

"Be careful, Ringo." John Creighton spoke softly, but Reno noticed that the rest of them listened. "We all have our suspicions, but best keep them quiet for awhile."

Bible said at once, "That's good advice, John. Reno, what'll you have?"

Reno hated the taste of liquor, but said, "Well, I'd fancy a glass of wine if it's to be had."

"Most saloons serve only some sort of rotgut made the day before yesterday, but Saul Logan keeps a good stock," Creighton said. "Get us some of that French stuff, will you, X?"

Beidler got up and made his way to the bar, and Reno was looking at Creighton carefully. The talk ran around the table until the stocky Beidler got back and poured each man a glass of wine, then Reno said, "I've seen you before, Mr. Creighton. Can't place you, though."

"You're from the South?"

"Yes."

"I was a colonel under Longstreet."

Reno snapped his fingers. "I remember—at Gettysburg!"

Creighton's eyes suddenly burned, and he asked quietly, "You were at the Round Top?"

"Third Arkansas, Colonel."

"I know the regiment. Not many left at the end, were there, Reno?"

"Not many." Reno took a sip of the wine and the moment came back—the long lines sweeping up the hill, falling like grain hit by a scythe as the Union fire cut them down. "I remember you now. You were on the right flank. I remember because it was the only time I ever saw General Longstreet. You were both mounted and talking. He was shaking his head and seemed to be mad about something."

Creighton's face grew sad, and he shook his head. "Dutch didn't want to charge the hill, but Lee insisted." He took a small sip of the wine and said softly, "For once General Lee was wrong. We had no chance at all that day. That was the day the Confederacy died, I think."

"It was a hard war," Reno remarked gently.

Ringo Jukes shifted rebelliously and declared, "Well, I tell you, I don't feel no safer here than I did in the army. At least I knew who was shootin' at me and who to shoot at." He rolled his heavy shoulders and stated harshly, "Look out there." He waved toward the crowded room. "Any one of them jaspers could be one of the Innocents!"

"Innocents?" Reno frowned. "What's that?"

"That's the name for the outlaws who've got a stranglehold on this camp, Reno," Sam Bible explained. He gouged a track in the scarred table with his steel hook, and there was a smoldering fire in his hazel eyes as he looked over the room. "Ringo is right, though. Anybody here could be one of them."

Reno sat in his chair loosely, hating to leave the warmth of the saloon for the cold hotel room. The talk was mostly of mining—new claims, new methods, old camps that had played out and new ones cropping up. Creighton and Bible were, he noted, watching him carefully, but he could not fathom why. He joined in a penny-ante poker game, lost ten dollars, and grew familiar with the men at the table. He had known men, good and bad, and it was his quick judgment that these men, especially John Creighton and X. Beidler, were leaders of some sort in the camp. Ringo Jukes was a bruiser and probably could influence the rough miners, but the two older men had a steadiness Reno had seen in good officers during the war.

Finally he sighed and forced himself to stand. "Guess I'll turn in. Enjoyed the game."

He left and made his way along the crowded room, and Nick Tbolt said, "How come he couldn't be one of the Innocents, Sam? You don't know nothing about him."

"Why, I just *know*, Nick!" Bible said, tapping the table with his hook.

"I've seen his kind before," Creighton said. "He's the sort who always got killed off quick in the war because he was always quick to run to the guns. But he's got cunning as well as courage."

"He ain't very big, though," Jukes said doubtfully. "Can't be no more'n one-sixty."

"You big ox!" Bible glared at Jukes and spat. "If muscles was the test of a man, a mule's hind leg would be the best man in the world."

"Hey, look at that!" Link McKeever said, and as they all turned to look toward the door, he said, "Haze Lyons is bracin' him!"

Reno had been threading his way through the crowd when a hand gripped his arm and pulled him around. He turned quickly to face Haze Lyons, seeing at once that the man had been drinking heavily.

"Well, my old friend Reno!" Lyons said loudly. He kept his grip on Reno's arm and winked at the other deputy Reno had seen at the restaurant. "Hey, Jack, this is Jim Reno. Jack Gallagher. Have a drink with us, Reno!"

Lyons's eyes were gleaming, and his grip was harder than it should have been. He was not as drunk as he appeared, and Reno knew at once that Lyons was on the prowl for a brawl.

Reno said evenly, "Glad to meet you, Gallagher. Don't guess I'll have another drink, Lyons. Some other time."

He tried to pull away, but Lyons tightened his grip, and there was a wicked smile on his full lips as he said loudly, "Why, blast your eyes, Reno! You're not gonna insult a man are you?"

The sounds of the room washed away, and Haze Lyons looked around, satisfied that he had everyone's attention. He picked up a glass of liquor with his free hand and shoved it toward Reno, saying, "Now, you just drink that down and it'll be all right."

Time flowed over him, and Reno thought, *Nothing ever changes. Always something like this.* He thought of the many times he'd stood before some man and had to decide whether to stand or fold. And he knew that if he were to survive in Virginia City, he had to meet the challenge.

A smile touched his broad lips, and he spoke so gently that at first Lyons failed to catch the words. "Haze, if you don't take your hand off me, I'm going to tear your face off."

A quick thrill ran around the room, and men started shifting to get out of the line of fire.

Lyons was a dandy, but he was three inches taller and twenty pounds heavier than Reno, and he was solid muscle. He stared at Reno, and his fair skin flushed with pleasure at the prospect of a fight.

With a sigh he looked around and said, "Well, you all heard it. A man can't listen to talk like that, can he now?" He unpinned his badge and laid it on the bar, then carefully lifted his .44 and laid it beside the badge. "Just put your gun right there, Reno, and we'll have our fun."

"There's no fun in fighting, Haze," Reno remarked, pulling his gun free and placing it beside that of Lyons.

"Not for you, maybe," Lyons said with a smirk. "Back up there, let's have a little room! Give this joker room enough to fall down."

Gallagher said, "You ought not to fight this man, being as you're a lawman, Haze."

"I'm a lawman, but that don't give this—" Lyons glanced toward Gallagher, but it was a ruse to catch Reno off guard. He threw a powerful right at Reno, which would have ended the fight if it had landed. But it missed, as Reno, expecting something tricky, pulled back. The force of the effort caused Lyons to fall against Reno.

Quick as a cat, Reno grabbed Lyons by the shoulders and sent him crashing into a table, overturning chairs. He did not attempt to follow up, but stood there, a tough shape in the light, as Lyons kicked at the chairs and came to his feet, face blazing with anger. "You'll be dead meat, you sucker!"

The long left of Lyons flicked out, but Reno moved aside. In a lightning motion, he slashed Lyons's mouth with a blow that did not travel more than six inches. It stopped the advance of the large man as if he'd run into a railroad tie.

Lyons was driven back by the force of that single blow, and it was obvious to every man that he was stunned. They expected to see Reno charge in and beat him to the floor, but Reno dropped his hands and said quietly, "I told you there was no fun in it, Lyons."

For one instant Reno hoped that Lyons would call it off, but as the man's eyes cleared and he reached up to touch the blood running down his chin, several of his supporters said, "Get him, Lyons!" and he drove at Reno with a yell of rage.

The force of the charge drove Reno back against the bar, and he caught a wild blow on the temple. Lyons felt him going down, and Reno twisted just in time to parry the knee that would have crippled him. He held on as Lyons battered at his head and tried to shake free.

With a surge of power, Reno wrested loose, and his head cleared as Lyons came at him with both hands pounding. Reno backed away, catching most of the blows on his arms and shoulders. They had a numbing force, but he had learned to endure an enemy's attack. *Let him wear himself out, then one good blow will take him out. That had been Old Blue Light's way. Put everything you have in one blow that will destroy the enemy's confidence.* So he backed away, dodging and parrying, and finally Lyons's blows grew weaker and his breathing began to rasp in the smoke-filled air. Suddenly Lyons stepped back and yelled, "Fight, you louse!"

It was what Reno had been waiting for. He planted his feet and drove a right into the face of his opponent with every ounce of his weight. The blow exploded like a mortar in the face of Haze Lyons, smashing his nose and flattening his lips against his teeth. He was driven backward, and there was a looseness as he collapsed. Every man knew he was out.

Reno stood there for one instant, then whirled to get his gun and get out, but a fist caught him in the neck and he fell to his knees hearing a coarse voice yelling, "You ain't goin' to get away with it, sucker! I'll bust you up myself!"

Reno came to his feet to find a huge man glaring at him. Another man, smaller but broad and muscular, moved in, saying, "Yeah, Boone, let's put him down."

"Brunton, you and Helm ain't gonna do nothin' to nobody!"

Ringo Jukes burst out of the crowd and stood there, as big a man as the hulking Boone, and added, "If you want a little action, Boone, why, you just let me call the tune!"

"Back off, Jukes!" Jack Gallagher drew his gun and waved it toward Jukes, adding, "This ain't your fight."

"It's not theirs either, Gallagher." Sam Bible advanced, his face flushed, as he said, "You can't let these two loose on the man!"

"Why can't I?" Gallagher said with a smile. He turned to the two men and said, "You fellers fight fair, you hear me?"

Boone Helm was a hulk of a man with blunt features and pale eyes. "I'll bust you to pieces!" he hissed, advancing on Reno.

Sam Brunton was shorter, but broad and thick through the shoulders. He had the face of a heavy drinker, and there was a light of pleasure in his eyes as he came at Reno from the left.

As they closed in, Reno knew that two of them would get him down and kick him to pieces if he didn't stop them. They had him wedged in, and there would be no help, not with Gallagher holding a gun on the crowd.

A thought struck him, and he remembered what a sergeant had said just before they had made the attack at Franklin. "We got to hit 'em where they don't think we will in a way they won't never think we'll do."

In that moment, Reno knew that Helm would expect him to go for the smaller man, so he did just the opposite—but not with his fists as the huge man expected. He made a pass with his right, which drew the big man's hands up, then he pivoted and swung his right boot forward in a tremendous kick that caught Helm on the left kneecap.

There was a loud thudding sound as his sharp pointed boot struck the knee, driving the leg from under Helm, who dropped suddenly with a shrill cry of pain.

Without pausing, Reno swept up a half-filled bottle of whiskey and in one smooth motion brought it down on the unprotected head of Sam Brunton. The force of the blow split the scalp and drove the man to the floor, where he lay with one leg kicking the floor in a reflex action.

The wild eruption of violence had taken only a few seconds, and the miners, accustomed to fights that went on for much longer, were hushed, staring at the two men on the floor.

Then Jukes let out a yelp. "Well, you son-of-a-gun!" But as a swarm of men rushed over to pound his shoulder, Reno heard Gallagher say, "Stand back! You hear me!" He cursed and waved his gun at the crowd. "This man is under arrest!"

"Under arrest?" Bible cried. "For what?"

"For disturbing the peace!"

A yell of laughter swept the room. Every night there were fights and Gallagher had never arrested anyone. But the laughter angered him, and he looked down at Haze Lyons, who was getting to his feet slowly, his mouth a ruin. "Haze, you all right? Let's get this man to the jail."

Reno took one look at the raging anger in the two men and knew that he would not live through a night in their jail, but there was no hope of making a getaway.

They were moving toward the door, Gallagher pulling Reno and covering the crowd. The irate miners were yelling, but they did not dare to do more.

Then a voice cut across the air: "What's going on, Jack?"

Reno turned quickly to meet the eyes of a tall, thin man with a star on his vest. He was about forty, and there was a smile on his lips as he looked across the room and said, "Hello, Jim. Still in a jam, I see."

"Hello, Jay." Reno remembered the last time he'd seen Jay Dillingham, the man who'd been his lieutenant for most of the war. He'd seen him last just outside of Appomattox. Reno's squad, or what was left of it, had been pinned down by Yankee artillery, and Jay had said, "See can you hold 'em, Jim, while I go for help."

He had not seen Dillingham from that time until now, but he remembered suddenly how many times the tall man had helped him in those days.

"What's going on, Jack?" Dillingham asked again.

"This bird is under arrest!"

"On what charge?"

Gallagher turned red as he said, "Disturbin' the peace."

A shout went up and someone said, "He sure disturbed Haze Lyons's peace!"

"Who started this brawl?" Dillingham asked, looking curiously at the ruined mouth of Lyons and the two men on the floor.

"Lyons!" a dozen voices called out. Then John Creighton stepped forward and said, "I'll testify to that in court if necessary, Dillingham."

"No arrest, Jack," Dillingham said.

The room grew still, and Reno saw the two men locked in a struggle. Though they both wore the star there was enmity between them, and for one brief moment, Reno thought that Gallagher would push the issue.

Then with a forced smile, Gallagher said, "All right. Come on, Haze."

The two men walked out of the room, followed by several others, and there was a shout from Jukes as he said, "Done!"

Reno felt a dozen hands pounding his shoulders. He made his way to Jay Dillingham and said, "You still got that habit of pulling me out of trouble, Lieutenant!"

Jay Dillingham settled back on his heels, and there was a mock severity in his gray eyes. "Jim, are you ever gonna grow up and stop fighting wars?"

Reno shook his head. "I'm trying to quit, Jay. But every time we get a good war started, peace keeps breaking out, don't it now?"

Dillingham stared at Reno, then smiled and said, "It's good to see you, Jim. I've thought about you many times." Then he looked at the men who were crowded around.

"If I'd been here when those three tried to tree this coon, I'd have told them that the whole Union army had a heap of trouble doing that little chore. Come on, Jim, we've got some catching up to do!"

Books in the Reno Western Saga

From Gilbert Morris, the author of the Reno Western Saga and the House of Winslow series, comes a new Civil War series. . . .

The Appomattox Saga

Gilbert Morris is the author of many best-selling books, including the popular House of Winslow series and the Reno Western Saga.

He spent ten years as a pastor before becoming professor of English at Ouachita Baptist University in Arkansas and earning a Ph.D. at the University of Arkansas. Morris has had more than twenty-five scholarly articles and two hundred poems published. Currently, he is writing full-time.

His family includes three grown children, and he and his wife live in Baton Rouge, Louisiana.